THE FRENCH THING

The French Thing

by Chris Keil

ISBN: 0-86381-768-8

Cover illustration: Kathy deWitt
Cover design: Sian Parri

First published in 2002 by
Gwasg Carreg Gwalch, 12 Iard yr Orsaf, Llanrwst, Wales LL26 0EH
✆ 01492 642031 🖷 01492 641502
🖱 books@carreg-gwalch.co.uk   Website: www.carreg-gwalch.co.uk

For Ruth and Thomas and Elin

Chapter 1

An hour or two passed in daydreams, the yard outside the window turning faint and misty, the daylight drizzling into grey. A sheaf of old faxes in a bulldog clip lay on the window-sill, the thermal paper curling and turning sepia brown. The top sheet was stained with a half-moon smudge of coffee, the text blurred and faded.

Backing the Scania into the loading bay sometimes took a quarter of an hour; the semi-trailer would slide on the wet concrete, the tractor skidding on lumps of silage, the cab bucking on its air suspension, the brakes sighing and snorting. At Graig Goch it was always raining, especially if they were loading at night. The wind seemed to blow round corners between the buildings. The gutter above the alley where the sheep were huddled was broken or blocked, and the leaking rainwater blew into squalls.

When Huw had gone to get the sheep in, he found that a dozen or so had managed to get across the river. It took three of them and the dog to get them back, so they were soaking wet before they began. They didn't want to come out of the field and into the lane, and the boys were yelling, and chucking sticks, and Alwyn tripped over the dog and fell in the mud, but eventually they started to go, the lambs leaping high in the air as they came through the gateway, until finally all four hundred were on the road, stretched out in a long column between the hedges, their fleeces silvery in the failing light. Huw and Alwyn trudged behind them, the dog loping and darting between them, their coats and leggings flapping. When the lambs at the front stopped to graze the verges, the whole column would thicken and clot in a sort of ripple that ran back down the lane. The boys whooped and lobbed tumps of turf – *Get on boys! Get on!* – the lambs moved on again. Tom thought of all the sheep that had moved down these roads in endless droves through the years.

The next day, as they tooled down the autoroute, the cab's suspension producing swooping and soaring sensations, breasting the little hills and surging down the inclines, Tom had a strong sense of the sheep, ranked in the decks behind their heads. He pictured them turning their faces into the slipstream that poured through the ventilation panels, their eyes slitting in the wind. He imagined, from imperceptible hummed beginnings, a growing chorus of song filling the container and streaming out the back of the wagon: the Slaves' Chorus from Nabucco, perhaps, or Happy Days Are Here Again. As they bucketed braking through little villages, he imagined that the people at the tin table outside the cafe, one of whom at that moment turned in his chair and laughed or spoke through the doorway to someone unseen inside, were suddenly washed and ruffled by this great warm breath of motion and destination and wool and blood and song.

Tom thought about the glory days of livestock farming, when Britain seemed set to be drovers to the whole of Europe, when the long two and three deckers rumbled and rolled off the ferries and fanned out with a continent in front of them; north and east to Belgium and Holland and Germany, south to the Loire and beyond, rolling finally all the way down to Spain. In the beginning the enterprise was all movement and adventure, a campaign of maps and humour and French lager. Now, looking back, he saw its bleak concrete flanks cutting across the past like a wall, rigid, unalterable, streaked with regret.

You start with an idea, he thought, a scrap of conversation, perhaps no more than a fragment of dream half-remembered in the morning, lingering merely as a faint sense of elation or dread. Down a long avenue of biography this puff of smoke, this ghost, is pushed, patted, shaped. What kind of substance acts as connective tissue here? It is netted in strings of consequence, hooked and wired in. Sequences of phone calls solidify into faxes, letters on hard paper. A kind of exoskeleton forms, animated by the idea. This silvery creature can talk, move its limbs. One day carelessly it knocks a book off the corner of a desk, and a Frenchman goes bankrupt in Poitiers.

*   *   *

Tom met Beti Evans for the first time while he was buying store lambs. Beti had bid against him on one or two lots, and Tom spoke to her after the sale and arranged to call round at her house that evening. Beti was forty-something, shortish, with a powerful, well fed look; not fat, but as though her flesh was somehow denser than other people's. From within this solidity, though, she crackled with energy. Her father had been a substantial dealer himself, and you'd still hear the old boys talk about him in the marts, but Beti had gone way beyond what she'd inherited from him, becoming the biggest livestock dealer in the county, and the most easily recognised and talked-about figure in the business There was a Mercedes in the yard, and the house, or what Tom saw of it, was absolutely newly done out, every surface shiny with plastic, ceramic, formica, brass. As Riquet said months later when he first saw the place: '*Mais c'est tout nouveau quoi!*' his expression perfectly poised between admiration and contempt.

Beti liked the sound of live exports. She poured drinks, and the two of them clinked glasses and shook hands. So Tom had a partner, and some real money behind the business. The arrangement, with a woman who was famous for never making alliances, made him feel both flattered and apprehensive. They started to send regular shipments of lambs to M. Bonnet. Tom hired Phil Jones, who lived a couple of miles away, in the next valley, as a sort of foreman. Phil had his own place, Greenhill, but seemed to have plenty of time on his hands and obviously could do with a bit of extra money. A nice boy, good looking, in his late twenties or early thirties, hard working and good humoured. His wife was a cook in the school; they had a little boy, six, seven years old.

Chapter 2

The second time Phil got a letter from the finance company about his arrears on the new tractor, he simply crumpled it and, from where he was sitting, lobbed it at the bin. He missed. The first letter, he'd responded to by drawing up an action plan: *Find another milking contract. See if Tom Wood has got more work.* But in the end they'd caught up by raiding Liz's Building Society account. Now, all of a sudden, he abandoned his plans to start on the new fence this afternoon. It was a beautiful day; it was a Saturday. He'd take the terrier out and see if he could get a rabbit.

He got the gun out from under the bed. There were a half dozen shells in the pocket of his overalls, and he transferred these to his jacket pocket. He went out to the yard to let Patch out of his cage. As always, the sight of the little Jack Russell, his quivering, pneumatic vitality, cheered Phil up.

He parked in the quarry at Myrtle Grove. Patch jumped over him and out of the van as soon as he opened the door. He rummaged about in the back of the van for the gun and a cartridge belt, and then whistled up the dog. Straightening up, he saw him on the lip of the quarry, forty or fifty feet up, and as he watched, the terrier launched himself off the edge. It wasn't quite vertical; there was a steep incline of scree and tumbled rocks, down which he skidded and rolled, yelping, to land nearly at Phil's feet.

'Mad bugger. Come on then'

He worked his way along the edge of the forest for nearly two hours without so much as seeing a rabbit. In the end, out of a sort of irritation, he shot a squirrel that skittered across his path. Maybe it was time to go home. There was no sign of the terrier. He yelled for Patch at intervals as he trudged back towards the van. He felt tired and on edge. At one point he fired a shot in the air, in case the dog was too far to hear his shouts, but without result. He wasn't waiting by the van either. Phil cursed, and started slowly back the way he'd just come, calling more frequently. After a couple of miles, he thought he heard a faint, faint yapping, coming from somewhere on his right, from within the dark ranks of spruce. Shouting and listening, he worked his way into the trees till he found the hole. Putting his ear to the ground, he could clearly hear the terrier's muffled yelps.

By the time he'd dug Patch out of the rabbit hole the afternoon had gone. As he passed the Lock and Key, he remembered that Liz was collecting Eddy from Nellian's this evening. A couple of pints wouldn't hurt. He pulled into the car-park. Starting his second pint, he remembered an odd story that Tom Wood had told him, about how, in the main bar of one of the ferries the lorries used, there was a photograph of this pub, in a frame, hanging on the wall, definitely this pub, there was a caption: *The Lock and Key, Llanfrychan*. He started to tell Bob about this.

'Tell you the oddest thing about that story', the landlord interrupted him. 'Is how many people have told me about it. How many people that come to this pub have been on that boat? Makes you think, doesn't it. Pint?'

Later on, a further thought struck him.

'Bob! Yes, same again. Listen, what you ought to do is have a photograph of that boat in the pub here.'

Bob gave him a professional sort of smile.

'Wish I had a pound for all the people that have said that to me.'

Phil wandered over to the jukebox. He put in a coin and punched out his selection, squinting at the labels. Tammy Wynette's voice roared out at the volume of a bulling heifer, *Stand by your Man!* before Bob turned it down from behind the bar. There was a group of students from the town sitting at the round table in the corner; two or three boys, and a girl, very pretty, very short dark hair. She pulled a face when Phil's record came on, but gave him a quick grin when he caught her eye. He was dazzled.

When the record finished, he stayed leaning against the juke-box, listening to scraps of the students' conversation. He thought the girl smiled at him a couple of times, but maybe she was smiling at something her friends were saying. He wasn't sure.

'Swansea Airport. No way they'll get away with that. D'you see how that went?'

Phil moved a little closer to the group, trying to figure out what they were talking about.

'Or Dover, for that matter. Could fly to Spain, of course.'

'Too expensive; what about the van?'

In a flash of inspiration, Phil felt sure they were talking about live exports, and at the same moment realised he was being presented with a perfect opportunity: he *knew* about live exports, he could really explain everything to these people. He went over to their table.

'I was listening to what you were saying, and you're wrong, you know'.

The four faces that turned up towards him were filled with blank shock; Phil gripped the edge of their table to steady himself. The boy on the right of the group recovered himself.

'Excuse me, we're having a private conversation here.'

Phil made an effort to collect his thoughts.

'It's not private if it's putting people out of a job. Anyway, it's just not cruel. People always going on, but I work for a couple of exporters, and I know. It's just not cruel. It's not cruel at all.'

'Look, do you mind? Don't know what you're talking about. Just go and bother somebody else, will you.'

Phil felt a sort of muddled rage erupt in him, a silent explosion behind his eyes that seemed to expand and fill his head.

'You bloody students, what do you know about it? All the same to you whether people have a job or not. I expect you're anti-fucking hunting too, aren't you?'

He jabbed his finger at the boy on the right, leaning over the table. Whether he slipped and lost his balance, or whether the other boy had kicked out at him under the table, tripping him off his feet, he found himself suddenly on the floor. He had banged the side of his head on the table as he went down. The room revolved, the light splintered in dazzling fragments. Phil didn't bother to get up as Bob came round from behind the bar. The landlord squatted down and poked a finger at Phil's face.

'You, out! And don't let me see you in here again. You're barred.'

Chapter 3

They were tagging lambs for Ovipom, the farming co-op at Tours. They were a lovely group of lambs, and it was nice to be able to picture where they were going, to those big fields Tom had seen by the orchards. Meirion from the vet group was finishing his inspection of the lambs. Stuart's lorry was backed up into the loading bay. On his last trip, Stuart had taken orders to fill at the Cherbourg superstore, and his cab was like an off-licence, filled with crates of lager, bottles of brandy and Pernod, cartons of cigarettes. The bunk was piled high with the stuff; he'd had to sleep in the seat. Phil passed bottles of beer around, as everyone finished their work and squatted down companionably. Meirion shut his briefcase with a snap.

'See about B & F then?' he said. 'Say they're going to pack it in in October.'

'Did they? They won't do that, surely'.

'Pack what in?'

'The livestock, man. Taking the sheep on the boats. Take an interest man, you could be out of a job here, Phil.'

'It's the tunnel, it is.' Alwyn said. 'They're afraid of the competition.'

'I can't see them doing it though, can you?' Phil said. 'The trade must be worth a lot of money to them.'

'And their fucking boats tip over' Alwyn said. 'If we had any sense we wouldn't trust them with our lambs anyway.'

'I don't think they'll do it.' Phil said. 'Anyway, they're not the only ferry company.'

'I dunno.' Stuart sauntered over. 'You should see it down at Dover' he said. 'They've got a little stall right by the dock there. They're there every day, getting people to sign their petitions; they reckon they've got thousands of signatures.'

'What's the problem though?' Phil asked him. 'What are they worried about?'

'Beats me' Stuart said. 'It's the folk in the caravans, they don't like to see the livestock lorries, don't ask me why.'

Tom had the sense of something on the edge of sight, an area of darkness, moving closer, like a cloud.

A couple of days later Marek van Leymans rang up. He and his partner had come over before for lambs, big ones, for Holland. He turned up the next day, with Piet. Their lorry had Belgian plates, and was borrowed; there was some unspecified problem with Marek's wagons. Physically, the two of them were hard to tell apart, both compact and blonde, though where Marek was twitchy with energy, fizzing with jokes, Piet was forever frowning and grumpy. You had the feeling that it was a double-act that they had perfected over a long period of time.

'Tom, how's it going?' Marek said. 'You got plenty problems over here right? What's the matter wit those people? What's their problem?' His breezy contempt cheered Tom up.

'Some of those bastards threw a brick at the truck' Piet said. 'At Portsmouth, just coming from the dock there.'

'Who? What bastards?'

'Just bastards' Marek said. 'You know, those bastards wit the rats' tails in the hair.'

'Also, we was followed down here, you know?' Piet sounded gloomier than ever; Tom felt a slight stir of dread. Marek wagged a thick finger at Piet.

'You imagining things now boy. You need to look after yourself better!'

'There was this damn van, all the way down the motorway; it was there at the services also. We wasn't doing more than 100kph. Why didn't he overtake? He was there in the mirror all the way down. I not fucken imagining nothing.'

'You're a poor boy Piet. You need a holiday.'

'We was followed alright' Piet said. 'All the way to what's that town? Ten kilometers back.'

He jerked his thumb over his shoulder in a reverse hitch-hiker's gesture, staring at Tom.

'They was following us, Tom, all the way here. You better watch out for them. Big van you know, what you call them? Mini-bus. Ford, I dunno. Light blue.' They went to look at the lambs.

It was nearly midnight when Piet and Marek finally pulled out of the yard with a raucous honk on the air horn and a cloud of black smoke. Marek was driving, grinning, a stump of cigar clenched in his teeth; Piet was hunched morosely in his seat; he raised his hand in a gloomy gesture.

Beti and Tom were having a drink in her kitchen when the sensors switched the yard lights on, the dogs started barking, and almost at the same moment there was a tapping on the back door. Beti got up with a frown.

'I'm sorry to bother you so late; I've run out of petrol. You couldn't spare me some could you?'

The girl was strikingly attractive, dark hair cut very short, skinny leggings and a leather jacket. Beti stared at her, filling the doorway.

'There'll be some chainsaw fuel in the shed' she said. 'Have you got a can? Never mind, we'll find you one. Where's your car?'

She bustled off, humming. The girl and Tom exchanged a smile, but she didn't say anything. She looked like a Victorian painting, one of those fairies or nymphs, slim and translucent among water and rushes. He must have been staring at her; when he caught her eye she looked away quickly. Beti reappeared.

'There you are my dear' she said. 'One gallon of fuel. Where did you say your car was? Have you got a torch?'

The girl shook her head. 'It's just down the road here. I'll be fine really. I'll leave your can by your gate. Thank you very much. Can I give you some money?'

'Not at all' Beti told her. 'Not at all.'

Graig Goch was half a mile off the main road, on its own track, which didn't go anywhere else. When the girl had gone, Tom raised an eyebrow at Beti.

'What was she up to, do you think?'

'What you say?'

'Do you think she was looking the place over or something? What was she doing out here in the middle of the night?'

'Don't you start man' she said. 'No harm in the girl.'

Jan was still up when Tom got home. The ferry timetables meant that he was out late at least twice a week, sometimes more. She got nervous at night. She wouldn't readily admit to it though, and the tension made her bad-tempered. He was just getting into bed when the phone rang. He hopped downstairs, cursing, thinking it must be important at this time of night, but as soon as he picked up the receiver, it rang off. Jan was leaning up on one elbow.

'Who was that?'

'Rang off.'

'It's doing that a lot' she said. 'Nearly every time you're out.'

That night Tom was woken by the buzz and stutter of the fax machine and was instantly panic-stricken, picturing obscene threats disgorging from the lip of the machine like devilish tongues. He must have been dreaming though; when he ran downstairs to the office, the machine was silent, the tray empty.

He saw the girl again a couple of days later. He was posting a letter in the village when she drove past in a dark green van, a Ford he thought. Tom didn't think she'd seen him; at least she didn't appear to recognise him.

Chapter 4

Phil and Eddy drove into Llanfrychan, and parked in the High Street. It had been market day, and the town was busy with people and vehicles, LandRovers and trailers parked any old how in the street, two wheels up on the pavement. The sky was deep blue, although the shadows were beginning to lengthen; the light was low, dazzling reflections in the shop windows. There was a long queue at the supermarket check-out. In front of them was an enormously fat woman in a bobble-hat, tattered wax jacket and wellingtons, then a couple more farming types, then a group of travellers, hippies, New Age whatever you call them, from the more or less permanent encampment up the Black Valley; tough looking buggers, their hair part cropped to the skull, part twisted into dreadlocks, studs through their noses, the kids had them too, and *dirty*, as though they'd gone out and rolled and roiled and grovelled in dirt, picked it up in handfuls and rubbed it into themselves.

On to the little market town of barely ten thousand people, with its two churches and eight chapels, its little rows of hunch-backed houses and its fifteen pubs, from the Castle Hotel, through the King's Arms and the Red Lion, the Drovers, the Ram, the Black Ox, the Station Hotel – names which still had a faint resonance of the days when the town was the rail-head for the vast droves of livestock that arrived here from all the outlying country, all the rainswept farms on the white moorlands emptying into the stockyards round the station in an uproar of bleating and lowing, onto this busy and intensely self-absorbed community had been grafted, first, the grey bulk of the Victorian Theological College, then, over the last twenty years, a ragged tide-mark of hippies washed up on these unlikely shores and now indigenous, locally evolved and adapted and well into a second generation; and finally the transformation of the old college into Llanfrychan Campus, University of Wales.

These absolutely disparate tribes, separated by language and by dialects within language, by codes of dress and behaviour, by sexual mores, by religion and cuisine and music, by attitudes to leisure and work, technology and children, partaking of cultures that were often explicitly hostile to each other, still somehow managed to survive together. Anywhere in town, you'd find posters advertising concerts, festivals, events, lectures. Groups of students sat on the steps of the war memorial, or hurried down the High Street with armfuls of books. They all seemed to be coming the other way as Phil and Eddy lumbered along the pavement with bulging carrier bags.

Halfway up the High Street, by the Black Lion, there was a big, arched alleyway, built for coaches; leading into the main Square of the old range of College buildings and out the other side, it was a more or less public short cut to Water Street, and Water Street, according to Ed, was the only place you could get the particular football magazine he wanted. Coming out of the alley, the light was very bright in College Square. The pigeons were ringing like mobile phones, printing italic footsteps on the flagstones; the birds minced and pouted, fluttering a few feet into the air as Phil and Eddy scattered them, crossing the quadrangle. On the other side of the square, in the mouth of the arch that led into Water Street, there were a couple of students at a trestle table. Some kind of a notice-board was leaned up against the wall, and they seemed to be handing out leaflets to the passers-by. From half-way across the square, Phil recognised the girl who'd been in the Lock and Key the night he'd got barred.

He found himself starting to hunch up, drawing himself down into the collar of his jacket. The archway was narrow, and he was going to have to pass within a few feet. He watched the toes of his work-boots for a few steps. Eddy was saying something to him, tugging at his hand. He straightened up; he didn't have anything to be ashamed of. There was another girl at the table with her, neither of the boys from that other night, thank god. Holding hands with his son he stopped, looking for a moment at the photographs on the board behind her. She had a leather jacket on, too big for her. She was handing Eddy a leaflet. When she smiled, there was a tiny crease at the corner of her mouth. She was wearing black leggings, very tight, and she was leaning forward a little against the table, pressing against the edge of the trestle. Phil had the sensation for a moment of tipping forward, overbalancing. Eddy was pulling at his sleeve, whispering fiercely: 'Tell 'em Dad.'

He recognised one of the photographs behind her; Tom Wood had shown him a copy in a newspaper. It was the inside of a cattle truck, but it was a fake, it wasn't an export box, there'd been an injunction on it, they weren't supposed to use that picture. He opened his mouth.

'Do you want to sign the petition?'

She had an English accent. When she handed him a leaflet, her fingers brushed his for a second. He looked up and met her eyes. She didn't seem to have recognised him from that night in the pub.

'Will you help us?'

He stared down at the leaflet in his hands. He looked up. The girl grinned at him.

'Well? Will you?'

'Will I what?' They both started laughing. The clock on the College tower started to chime, a cracked sound like a bucket. Eddy had lost patience. 'Dad, the shop's going to shut. You promised.'

'Will you sign the petition?'

'You promised Dad.'

Phil sighed. 'It's a bit of a long story. Are you going to be here for a while?'

'Maybe.'

'Maybe I'll see you when we come back.'

'Why didn't you explain to them, Dad? They're silly, aren't they? You could of told them it's not cruel Dad, couldn't you?'

'I dunno, Ed, it's difficult to explain. Maybe we'll talk to them on the way back. Come on, let's get a move on.'

The first news agent didn't have the magazine Eddy wanted. Phil wanted to get back, but he relented and they went on, down nearly the whole length of Water Street till they found what the boy wanted. Now they hurried back the way they had come, Eddy flicking through the magazine as he trotted, half-running to keep up with Phil. They turned into the archway at a run, laughing, headlong, but it was empty. The trestle table was folded up, leant against the wall; the girl, the noticeboard, the leaflets and the friend were gone.

*   *   *

Liz went to work early on Monday morning. After he'd dropped Eddy off at the school gate, Phil thought he'd go into Llanfrychan; he could do with a drum of tractor oil, and it was much cheaper in the farmers' co-op there. After he'd hefted the can into the back of the van, he went off to get a newspaper. There was no one about in College Square, no students, anyway; two young mothers with pushchairs were wheeling their way slowly up one side of the quadrangle, turning together at the corner and slowly back down again, like swimmers in training, doggedly doing lengths in the pool. One of the toddlers reminded him strongly of Eddy at that age, and he smiled at the child as their paths crossed.

He ducked through the empty archway, his boots ringing on the flags. On the second page of the newspaper, there was an article on live exports and Phil sighed, folding the paper into a manageable shape, skimming through the text as he walked. Most of it was an interview with someone from FarmConcern, the usual stuff; he'd show it to Tom Wood next time he saw him. It was an education listening to that bugger sometimes, especially on this subject. And of course, he was right. You never did see a farmer or a haulier being interviewed. It was as though there was only one side to the argument.

He found he was passing the Star, and came to a stop. There was a jumble of thoughts in his head which he didn't quite feel like sorting out, but which resolved themselves into a very clear image of the girl he'd seen on Saturday, the girl from the Lock and Key. The Star these days was very much a student pub, and the only public place he could think of where he might run into her. He had no idea how the University itself was organised, or whether anyone could wander in there looking for someone. For that matter, she might not even be a student. Also, he didn't really know what he was planning to say to her if he did find her. It would be better to just bump into her, like. It would be nice to see her, though. He stood there for a moment or two, then pushed at the big brass handle. The bar was dim and cool, the floor shiny and damp from a recent washing, the chairs stacked legs-up on the tables. He looked at his watch: it wasn't quite ten o'clock, for god's sake.

He thought about the girl as he drove home. For all the TV reports and newspaper articles about live exports, he'd never actually talked to anyone who was directly involved in the protests. And he'd take a bet that the girl and her friends had never met an exporter, probably hadn't met many *farmers*. There were two worlds here, running along beside each other, but as though they were separated by a high wall. You thought you knew what they were up to on the other side, but it was guesswork, really. It would be a hell of a thing to really explain the farmers' point of view to her, make her understand the care they took. They were all sheep-farmers and they really cared about lambs, they wouldn't be doing it if it was cruel; Tom Wood had told him that a lot of the places they went to in France were nearer than sending them up to Scotland for instance. He said you needed to see the lambs come leaping off the lorry at the other end to see they hadn't come to any harm.

He felt intensely aware of the girl, as arguments wheeled and swooped in his mind. He imagined her sitting in the passenger seat next to him, her legs stretched out. Probably she was resisting what he was saying, but she kept giving him quick glances, half smiles, as he organised his thoughts, driving with one hand on the wheel and the other waving and gesturing as the van rattled and bucked down the lane to the farm. He wished he knew her name.

After lunch he put the thistlecutter on the tractor and spent a couple of hours cutting rushes in the meadow that ran down to the stream. In a couple of acres they'd gone really thick, and the tractor lumbered roaring through them in low ratio, the PTO whining, the heavy rotors of the machine thrumming and thrashing, streams of shattered vegetation shooting out from under the flaps. He had the radio on full blast, but he could only hear the music in fragments and snatches. The overall uproar of sound seemed to scour his head, clearing his thoughts.

At quarter to four he saw the top of the schoolbus above the hedge on the top road. He'd forgotten when Liz had said she'd be back, so he drove back up to the yard. They were both in the kitchen, Eddy with a piece of bread and jam, Liz cleaning vegetables at the sink.

'Hope you're hungry, some really nice meat left over today.'

'You're cheerful.'

'They've given us some help in the canteen; can you believe it? Nice girl too. Difference it makes having another pair of hands.'

'I'm starving Mum.'

'You know they got protestors in Llanfrychan?' Phil said. 'Animal rights, handing out leaflets.'

'Yes Mum, we saw them didn't we Dad?'

'Students, you know. I was thinking we ought to talk to them, explain a bit.'

Liz gave him an odd look.

'You're not going to change their minds.'

'You never know. Probably some of them are nice people, you know. They just don't understand.'

As he spoke, Phil realised that he was as strongly aware of the girl, in his mind's eye, as he was of Liz, sitting across the table from him. It was an odd feeling.

That evening, Tom Wood rang.

'Load on Friday, Phil. Can you make that? Tell you what I was thinking: they're going down to Gavray, not a long trip, back on Monday. Do you want to go with the lorry? You know you were saying?'

Over the next couple of days, as he got himself organised, Phil felt a mounting excitement. He still had a passport from the international in Paris that he'd never managed to get to; he took some money out of the bank, although Tom had said he wouldn't need much, sleep in the cab, just a few beers really. The prospect of the trip, the excitement, was somehow mixed up with the thought of the girl in Llanfrychan. He realised that the lorry was rescuing him in some way. Now that he was definitely going away for a few days he could admit to himself that the pull towards the Star pub one roaring evening where they would sit together in a pool of light – she had her chin in one hand and she was looking into his eyes as he talked, intensely, a pillar of cigarette smoke standing up between them – the pull towards all that would otherwise be overwhelming, irresistible. But the lorry was taking him away; he was riding away south on sixteen wheels.

It was just getting dark when they left Graig Goch, the last purples and greens flaring out in the west. On Phil's right, James Border sprawled behind the wheel, completely at ease. Constellations of glimmering read-outs glittered and blinked in front of him on the dashboard. The cab's suspension sighed and shushed, the air-sprung seats rose and fell like waves on the beach in the evening.

'Have one of these.'

James rattled a packet of cigarettes at Phil. He was Graham Border's nephew, one of the network of brothers, uncles, sons, cousins who between them ran three haulage firms out of Herefordshire, confident, humorous types, a little condescending, a little amused by the goblins and gnomes who hired them from across the Welsh border. His tone of voice as he shook loose a cigarette for Phil was exactly the one you might use at the end of a long, difficult discussion about life, love, death; a tone that was philosophical, tolerant, resigned; that recognised pain and loss, but also strength, resilience, humour: 'Have one of these.'

'Ta.'

'Where was Beti tonight then? Thought she'd want to see the lambs off. She's a case, isn't she? What a woman! First time I came here, you know? I'd done a couple of loads for Tom Wood before that, French thing, like this, but the first time I came here to Beti's place, nobody told me about her, we loaded up the lambs, and she comes over to wish us a good trip, and I was nearly asking her *Where's the boss?* and she says 'Here driver' and she gives me a pound coin, a bleeding quid. Can you believe it? You look at her place, and there's her Mercedes parked in the yard and a hundred thousand quid's worth of cattle in the shed, and she gives me a pound! Isn't she something! I can't understand a word she says most of the time, can you? Wouldn't want to mess with her though, got to hand it to her. Course, you're a bit that way yourself, aren't you,

Welsh, I mean. You always lived here?'

'Born here. Farm's been in the family since, my grandfather had it, anyway.'

'Good for you. Run it yourself then, do you?'

'My dad died two years ago. But he hadn't done much about the place for a good few years; not since I came back from college, really.'

Phil had been thinking about his father a lot, recently. He had taken it for granted at the time, the four years he'd spent at agricultural college in England. It had seemed a perfectly normal progression from having done fairly well at school, just something you did, really, even if neither Hwyel, nor Lyn, nor any of his friends that were growing up on farms, went away. And it made a difference, not just that he had met Liz there, much more than that. God knows where Hwyel was these days, but if he thought about Lyn, for instance, there was something awful about the way he seemed to be kind of sinking back. Phil had an image of something rising up out of the earth, rising and stretching and standing, and then, slowly, bowing, humping over, sinking down, sinking back, another generation drawn back into the soil of the farm. When he thought about it, there was no reason on earth why his Dad should have decided that he should leave the farm and get further education, go out into the world and take something for himself.

Moreover, he knew now what he didn't know then, that the old man, when he took that decision, made those sacrifices of loneliness and extra work, had already been diagnosed, sentence pronounced. Maybe that's why he did it. Maybe it was precisely because he could feel the farm drawing him back into itself, that he made the frantic struggle, the last of his life really, to push Phil up and out. Of course, here he was, back on the farm again and, aside from a certain general dissatisfaction, a certain feeling of distance between himself and his surroundings, much as though he had never left it. When he looked at Eddy though, he knew that he was going to make the same sort of efforts for his son, and it occurred to him that this was really what families were for, that something precious, personal to just that set of people – humour, restlessness, ambition, patience, should be handed like a parcel, from parents to children, like one of those party games, a gift of individuality which conferred a precious difference on everyone, so that we are not just clods of mud from the farm or scraps of litter from the city street, that we are nourished by a culture that belongs only to us. He pressed the button that lowered the big window at his elbow and flicked his cigarette out onto the night, the sparks whipped momentarily into stripes by the

23

slipstream.

'Died two years ago last May' he said. 'Cancer.'

They got into Portsmouth around midnight. Phil had dozed off during the last hour or so, and he had a blurred impression of roundabouts, traffic lights and neon signs as they skirted the town.

'Where are we?'

'Just coming to the lairage now. Unload the lambs, then we can get some proper kip.'

The lorry was crunching across a big, ashy yard, backing up to double doors in the side of the shed. There was a halogen lamp above the doorway that came blindingly to life as the lorry crossed the sensor. They settled the lambs in the pens, checking the bedding and the water-troughs and filling the hay-racks, then moved the lorry over to the other side of the yard, sliding in beside the dark bulk of another rig. In the cab, James organised the second bunk. Crouched in the lower bunk in a jumble of arms, legs, zips and jumpers, he emerged moments later in pyjamas, toothbrush and mug in hand. Phil clambered into the upper berth, realising a little shamefacedly he didn't even have a change of clothes with him. He worried about his socks as he struggled out of his work-boots in the confined space.

They got an early breakfast at the cafe across the road. Back at the lairage, Phil felt increasingly useless, as James dealt with a succession of Ministry vets, Trading Standards people, an inspector from the Ministry of Transport, a police officer and one of the shipping agents. The sheaf of paperwork got increasingly thumbed and dog-eared as he shuffled through the folder after one document or another, cracking jokes, competent, relaxed. Phil was glad when it was finally time to load the lambs again, and he could make himself useful.

'How do you stand it?'

'This is nothing; we're not even at the dock yet.'

He felt a little grip of nervousness.

'Are there going to be a lot of protestors here?'

'Shouldn't think so. Usually alright here. It's Dover you get the fun and games.'

They joined the convoy for the police escort, and headed down to the docks. There were only half a dozen lorries; they were second in the queue. At the dock gates, as they passed a line of police in yellow reflective jackets, Phil found himself swallowing dry spit. James passed him his cigarettes.

'Keep the window shut.'

They stopped behind the first lorry, its tailgate blocking out the view in front; to the side, the line of police by the Port Authority building. It was windy down here. Above the rooftops Phil saw a gull snatched past on stiff wings. He could hear raised voices, some kind of chanting. He glanced at James, who was drumming his fingers on the wheel, humming. The lorry in front moved on and they followed it for a few yards. There was a little group of people, ten or twelve of them, mingling with the police line, a couple of banners. James grinned at him.

'Not exactly a riot, see.'

There was some sort of argument going on between the demonstrators and the police. One of the banners dipped, then rose again. There were three or four teenage girls, and some middle-aged women; three of these, in anoraks and woolly hats, had linked arms and were chanting, the voices filtering raggedly through the wind and the engine sounds:

'Murdering scum! Murdering scum! Murdering scum!'

There was a little skinny fellow there, about sixty, in a combat jacket, with long hair tied back in a pony-tail. Phil caught his eye as the lorry inched forward. As though some signal had passed between them, this fellow now ducked down between the police, ran over to the lorry and climbed the steps. Phil swayed back involuntarily as the man's face appeared against the window an inch away from his. He was aware of stubble, yellow teeth and spittle. The man was making a hoarse, roaring sound in which no words were distinguishable. He pursed his lips in a grotesque kissing gesture, then hawked a gobbet of yellowish sputum onto the glass, where it dribbled viscously down the pane. A moment later, one of the police officers had caught him round the legs and pulled him away. Phil leaned close to the window, looking down, fascinated. The man was struggling with the policeman, pushing his face at him, spitting; his jacket had ridden up round his ears. A fat teenage girl was looking up at Phil, tears streaming down her face. A bulky woman in a padded jacket, headscarf framing a beefy face, pushed herself forward.

'Murderer! Murderer! Murdering scum!'

He looked down at her, appalled. He couldn't take his eyes off her. Her face seemed to be going black with hate and rage.

'Murderer! Murderer!'

The lorry moved on again, through the dock gates into the restricted area, clanking and rattling as the wheels mounted the steel plates of the gangway. There was a sharp crack from behind their heads, coming from the trailer.

'Bastards!'

'What was that?'

'Firecracker, probably. They throw them in through the vents; frightens the shit out of the lambs.'

'Why? Why they do that?'

'Fucked if I know; once we're on, we'll have to check the trailer for broken glass. They like to throw that in as well.'

When they jumped down from the cab, the steel deck was already thrumming under their feet. James checked the lambs, clambering along the outside of the container, peering through the vents into the pens, and occasionally reaching in to get one to its feet. On deck the wind was cold, coming off the sea, whipping ragged peaks off the tops of the choppy little waves. The greasy water of the dock churned white at the stern as the engine vibrations increased, and the boat began to move. As they drew away from the dockside, Phil looked back at the shore. He could see a police van parked on the quay, but the line of police had dispersed, and there was no sign of the demonstrators. The wind was blowing more strongly, a salty taste, intensely clean. Leaning on the rail, he watched the slate-coloured water, streaked with foam, slipping along the ship's side. Soon, the line of the shore had begun to grow hazy, a fringe of stubble along the horizon of the sea; Phil had a sudden vertiginous sense of the depth of the ocean below them, as though they were suspended over a void, balanced on a great column of water like a test-tube in a laboratory, in which, at various levels, fish and sea-weed, wreckage and bones, drifted or surged.

'You coming to the canteen? They do a good breakfast, or you can get a beer.'

James spent most of the rest of the crossing in the saloon, a couple of times going to the vehicle deck to check the lambs. Phil had a beer and chatted with the other drivers. They made a fuss of him, treating him like some kind of weird pet, when he explained that he wasn't a driver but a farmer, along for the ride, like some kind of little dog, he thought. Most of the boys were from farming backgrounds themselves, it turned out, but it was the fellowship of driving the big rigs that counted, that bound them into a culture that was both ironic and exclusive; from where they sat, high above the road, looking over the tops of the hedges, or down on the bug-like, foreshortened cars and vans that hunted about below them, you drove a Scania, or you were merely a punter.

After a while he went back up on deck, driven out by the cigarette smoke and the ribaldry. One of the drivers had told him he should be able to see the Normandy coast by now, but whichever way he looked, the horizon was featureless, sweeps of steel-gray that at some almost imperceptible point changed from sky to sea. The wind had dropped, and the boat seemed to hang, muffled, in swathes of pale and gray light, only the drumming of the deck under his feet, and a smudge of exhaust from the smokestack, giving any sensation of movement. Out of this enormous pale emptiness, a ship materialised, crossing from right to left, a long way ahead of them, some kind of freighter, a big boat. James had come up the ladder from the vehicle deck.

'Vauxhalls', he said. 'Coming from Cadiz. You should see them getting off the other end – hundreds of them, like little beetles.'

Another hour, and he could see the coast of France. At Cherbourg, he had supposed there would be customs, and passport control and god knows what, but nothing held them up at all. They were waved down the ramp and off the ship, and followed the first lorry along the quay-side, left between two enormous warehouses and a little further on, flagged through by a couple of French policemen, out of the dock gates and into the town. The lorry had that frowsty familiarity that your vehicle gets on a long journey, that rumpled comfort, like a sick-bed, crumbs in the sheets. He lit a cigarette and gazed out of the window, fascinated by everything.

'Never get used to how easy it is these days' James was saying. 'In the old days you could be half a day at Cherbourg. Customs agents going through all the paperwork; guys from the veterinary service poking their heads in the trailer, checking tag numbers against the list. Sometimes they'd make you unload into a shed, check every lamb. Then when you were loaded again and ready to roll, some other bastard would want to know why the seals on the box had been broken. We had some laughs, I can tell you.'

'Why's it so easy now then?' Phil was only half listening, watching a van in front of them that looked to him like it was made out of corrugated zinc.

'Single market. We're in the single market now, mate.'

'Tell that to those buggers with the placards at Portsmouth.'

He twisted round in his seat, his eyes following a couple of girls who'd crossed the road at a traffic signal in front of them. One of them caught his eye and flashed a rude gesture at him, putting an arm round her friend's shoulders and doubling over with laughter. James gave them a quick honk on the air horn as he shuffled through the gears, pushing the big truck through the outskirts of town and on into the country beyond.

A little way out of town, at Martinvast, they left the main road, plunging down a steep incline between hedges of bramble and thorn. They were entering a country of narrow sunken roads, small fields, a little sour and windswept, that lay in the shelter of stone walls and ragged hedgerows, thin trees combed over by the wind. It was reminding Phil of Wales, although the little towns they passed through – Briquebec, St. Sauveur – were more substantial than anything you'd find at home. Steeply-pitched roofs and tall chimney stacks, red brick, grey and gold stone glowing in the afternoon light, the villages and farms had a permanent look, a feeling of old established prosperity in the apple orchards and stone barns, that was very different from the tin and breeze-blocks of Wales.

Rattling through the little towns with the windows down, the cab suspension bucking on the polished cobbles, smells of steaks and cigarettes sucked momentarily in, an old fellow at a cafe table, pressing the stub of a cigarette at his lips with flat fingers, a tiny round glass of red wine winking like a warning signal at his elbow, made a beaming thumbs-up gesture at James as they passed, the truck filling the narrow street in a great wash of warm air pushed aside. James grinned.

'Stopped here last time on the way back. Bought me a beer, rattled on and on, couldn't speak a word of English. Fuck knows what he was on about.'

He poked a finger at the map in the tray between them.

'Coming into Coutances in a minute, here; see? Another half an hour and we'll be there.'

In the Cathedral square, scattering clouds of pigeons, they crossed the crazily elongated shadows of the twin spires, laid flat like black carpet. The streets were busy, offices emptying out, neon tubes flickering on in the bright interiors of cafes.

M. Laurent met them at his gate, the high square bulk of the farmhouse rising across the yard behind him. He was a short fellow, very solid, thick grey hair standing up like a yard brush, and a tremendous, beetling moustache. He was pointing and gesturing at them. A moment later he climbed the steps and appeared in James' window.

'Non, c'est pas ici, c'est par la, on les met dans une pâture, OK?'

James and Phil exchanged blank looks.

'Doesn't speak a word of English either.'

'No English, no English. Attendez.'

He dropped down, and reappeared on Phil's side of the cab, climbing up and opening the door. Puffing and fumbling he climbed into the cab, scrambling across Phil's legs and finally arranging himself on the bench between the seats.

'*Bon mais OK, allez, allez*' – pointing a finger ahead through the windscreen.

'*On les décharge la-bas. Allez, voom voom!*'

They rattled down the track for a kilometre or so, until Laurent stopped them by a galvanised gate into a holding yard, a stone building forming one side of it. There was still just about enough light to see by. Laurent was climbing across Phil's legs again.

'*On est bien ici; on les décharge ici, je fais le compte et apres.*'

'Whatever you say, sunshine. Hope there's room to turn round here.'

Laurent jumped out; they went on a little past the yard, and then backed up, James skewing the trailer round as much as he could in the limited space. The Frenchman was struggling with the gate. They lowered the tailgate. Laurent got out a notebook and pencil.

'*On est pret. Allez-y.*'

Clattering and leaping down the ramp, the lambs seemed to glow in the silvery fading light, as though lit from within. Pen by pen they rattled into the yard, bleating, calling to each other as they trotted across the concrete. Laurent was holding the notebook up to his moustache, muttering calculations. The lambs were running about the yard in little bunches, groups forming and reforming, as though urgent messages were passing between them. James stumbled down the ramp behind the last pen, brushing sawdust off his clothes. He paused at the bottom, looking across the milling backs.

'Look at those lambs. I wish those bastards at Portsmouth could see this. Just look at them; look like they just this minute come in off the field, don't they? Like to know where you'd see better looking lambs than this. What's that old son?'

He looked up as Laurent came over, jabbing a finger into his notebook.

'*Trois cents quatrevingt six, n'est-ce pas? Vous avez quel total? Combien d'agneaux?* How much sheep?'

The three of them put their heads together over the notebook, but it was too dark to see. They took it over to where the open door of the cab let out a wash of light.

'*Tu vois. Trois cents.*'

'Three hundred and eighty six! Spot on! Well done!'

They beamed at each other, Laurent shaking them both by the hand.

Then he pushed his way across the yard and opened a gate into the field. The lambs streamed out, like water emptying from a basin, calling to each other as the last faint luminosity of their fleeces was swallowed up in the dark.

The Frenchman directed them further down the track to where they could turn round, then back to his farm. In his kitchen, they sorted through the paperwork, James getting signatures on various documents. A teenage boy put his head round the door, scowling. Laurent was writing the details of the transaction in a ledger.

'*Ou est ta mère? On bois du Calva.*'

He fetched little thick glasses from a shelf, setting them down on the table in a line, then filling the three of them from a bottle with no label, dark brown, almost black, filling the glasses to the quivering brim, turning the bottle with a flourish as though twisting off a spigot.

'*Allez. C'est bon. C'est fait dans la maison.*' He lifted his own glass and poured it into his moustache. Phil sniffed and drank. 'Bloody hell, what is it?'

'No bloody; is good. *Le vrai Calvados, fait à la ferme.*' He refilled the glasses. Phil found himself staring, as he sipped, at a drop of brandy that hung, trembling, from Laurent's moustache. He waited for it to fall, but it never did. It seemed to get reabsorbed. Capillary action maybe.

'I'm starving. Where can we get something to eat.' James mimed at the Frenchman.

Laurent went to the door, bellowing up the stairs:

'*Pierre! Ou est ta mère? Mais non, merde!*'

James and Phil looked at each other.

'Don't think he understood.'

But Laurent came back into the room pulling on a jacket, and gesturing them to their feet.

'*Allez, on sort. We go eat. Mein frau no here. Non, c'est pas frau; ca c'est allemand quoi. I show you eat.*'

They bucketed off in Laurent's Renault, the Frenchman swinging the car from side to side of the road, banging through pot-holes, the front wheels thudding viciously, at the limits of the shock absorbers, the impacts kicking back through the steering wheel as he wrenched the car round the bends. He was sitting hunched forward over the wheel, his moustache poked forward at the windscreen. When he wanted to say something to Phil, who was sitting in the front, he turned fully sideways to face him, paying no further attention to the road. After a couple of uncomprehending grunts, Phil would cough and roll his eyes, do a hurried steering wheel mime, and point at the road ahead in a panic, grinning back at James. Laurent calmly finished what he was saying, his words punctuated by the shattering percussion of the road surface through the car's battered suspension, before turning to face forwards again.

They stopped outside the village cafe. Laurent led them through the bar to a room at the back, where there were half a dozen tables, laid for dinner, but empty. Surprisingly quickly, two plates of steak and chips appeared. The steak was thin and brown, tough looking, like it had been hammered flat, but delicious. Horse, James said. When they'd finished eating, Laurent reappeared from the bar with a bottle of Calvados and three glasses. He pulled over a chair with a shriek of metal on the tiled floor and sat down.

'*C'est bien? Parfait. Ca c'est a moi, vous comprenez. C'est moi qui paie.*'

'Thank you very much.'

'*Donc, qu'est-ce qu'ils vont faire, les cours chez vous? Ils montent, ou quoi?*'

Laurent nodded or shook his moustache, the great drooping thing giving his face a mournful look.

'I don't think he understood.'

'You try and explain then.'

As the level in the bottle fell, Phil had the increasingly bizarre sensation that Laurent's moustache was leading a life quite separate from the man himself. At certain points in the conversation, he became convinced that, while Laurent had managed to understand what he was saying, his moustache had failed to do so; it drooped there sadly, nodding in a pretence of agreement, knowing it had utterly lost the thread.

He had a dreamless night in the cab, with no recollection whatsoever of how he had got there. Laurent had directed them to a yard behind a garage in town where they could wash the lorry out, and Phil was now standing in the cinders, still feeling queasy, as James sluiced and squeegeed the decks and ramps, tumps of soiled sawdust tumbling down the treadplate in streams of foaming waste and water the colour of calvados. James was whistling as he directed the hose, the water drumming on the aluminium. When Phil moved, he sensed, out of the corner of his eye, just beyond the field of vision, multitudes of little creatures that scuttled out of his way beneath his feet. He felt he ought to be helping, but when he stooped his way up the ramp to call to James and ducked under the upper deck, he banged his head on a protruding bolt, somehow releasing a trickle of filthy water from above, down the back of his neck.

They took a different route back to Cherbourg, along the coast, the road running at times between high sand-dunes, in sight of the sea, bristles of marram-grass stiffening in the wind.

'Have one of these; you look as though you need it.' James lobbed a cigarette. Phil could feel the start of a tremendous excitement bubbling inside him, quite unexpected, at the thought of getting back. He supposed he must be missing Eddy and Liz more than he would have expected.

'Are we going to get a chance to do some shopping somewhere? I want to get my little boy something.'

James looked at his watch.

'There's a super-store on this road, a couple of kilometres before Cherbourg. We should have plenty of time. They've got everything there. You could probably buy a *car* there if you wanted to.'

The road stretched on ahead of them through the silvery light, running along a sort of causeway through the dunes. Phil's eyes drooped shut. He was having the most tremendous trouble with his boot-laces; he'd got rid of the old leather laces, and was using these new chain jobs, but they were the devil to get through the eyelets – you had to sort of squeeze the chain through, a link at a time. Someone squatted down in front of him, helping him, with slim, sun-tanned hands. The girl from the Lock and Key, the girl with the leaflets, was crouched down in front of him. He was looking down at the top of her head and then, as she raised her face to smile at him, down the front of her T-shirt. His chin snapped forward on to his chest as he woke up, and for a moment he thought he couldn't breathe. James was working the wheel round, his arms sweeping in sharp arcs, as they turned off the road into the car-park of the super-store.

They had an aisle of toys in the shop. Phil was finding it hard to concentrate. He wanted to get Eddy a toy livestock lorry, but all he could see were dolls and teddy-bears. In the end, James found him a model Scania, a semi-trailer, a curtain-sider rather than a cattle-box, but near enough. He had no idea what to get Liz. He picked up some cheese, and a six-pack of wine in the sort of cartons that orange juice comes in. He liked that; it was so casual, packing wine like that.

It had been raining while he was asleep, and it was still drizzling now. The dock was almost empty, a great expanse of shining tarmac running down to the quay, water standing in wide puddles. As they crossed this apron, heading for the ship, there was a curious lurching sensation, like you get in a lift as it accelerates up or down, and the lorry started sliding sideways, the trailer, in balletic slow-motion, jack-knifing round to Phil's side of the cab. It seemed to him that the leading corner of the trailer was about to come in at his door and he winced away as the whole rig careened sideways on silently sliding tyres towards the dock and the grey water. James was putting on opposite lock, smiling slightly, talking softly to himself, or to the lorry: 'Woah Doris! Don't get so excited now.'

As James got the lorry under control, Phil felt a rush of relief, a sour wash of reaction to his panic of a moment ago. The hollow that this emotion opened up in him filled, in a quick surge of depression. He was feeling ill again.

It rained throughout the journey back, a dispiriting drizzle that left him flattened and deflated. James dropped him at Reading, where he had just missed a train, and had an hour and half to wait for the next one, drinking polystyrene beakers of scalding insipid coffee. The ticket cost a fortune, wiping out the last two loads he'd tagged for Tom and Beti. Groaning to himself, he realised he should have come to some sort of arrangement with Tom about expenses before he left. He'd have to talk to him, but it was bloody awkward.

His first evening back, he sat up late with Liz. They had to abandon the cheese: 'Like old socks.'

'No, like a dead cat wrapped in old socks.'

The wine was black, thin and sour, but they tried to persevere. He wanted to tell Liz all about the trip; it had been a big adventure for him, and he really wanted to share it with her. Meanwhile, she'd been having a bad time at work. The new girl had turned out to be lazy, a real bitch who seemed intent on getting Liz fired and taking her job; it was a nightmare. Phil felt utterly at cross purposes with her. He was the one with the story to tell. He didn't see how she could have found out all that about the new girl in just a couple of days. As he drank more wine, he felt more and more strongly that he needed to explain everything about the trip to Liz, that there was something really exciting that he hadn't managed to communicate. It finally dawned on him that this sense of excitement, this feeling that he had a precious treasure to uncover and reveal to her, was in fact the thought of the girl with dark red hair. Stupid. Stupid. By this time they'd had a stupid row about something he'd said, he couldn't even remember what, and Liz had gone to bed. He sat in the kitchen by himself, drinking more wine.

When, a couple of nights later, he had another dream about the girl, inchoate this time, leaving nothing in the morning but a flickering rag of memory that was still unmistakably her, he knew he was being given a sign.

Chapter 5

That second summer, Beti and Tom seemed finally to be arriving at some sort of critical plateau with the business. They had a weight of customers behind them that was pushing them on a little further every month. From time to time a buyer would fall away: die, go out of business, find a better deal, but they had a nucleus of contracts that kept them going every week; in the meantime, Tom was always on the look-out for new deals and, more and more, buyers in France and more recently in Spain, would ring up unsolicited, word of mouth.

It was a year in which Tom could really feel his life changing. Most days he would get up in clean clothes, since he knew he would be spending most of his time in the office, on the phone. The busier they got, the less time he had to spend with the sheep, either in the market, or up at Graig Goch with the lambs that were going away. He probably saw just about every load go off, since Beti had only the vaguest notion of what was involved in the paperwork, but it was very seldom that he tagged a load of lambs. Phil from Greenhill had settled into that side of the work, and after a while didn't need much overseeing.

It was a happy time for Tom. He had embarked upon his forties in a state of controlled self-pity; his life seemed to have run into the sand. He wasn't facing disaster, but there seemed nowhere further to go. He felt he was looking at a long decline towards an old age he wasn't in any way ready for, a slow dissolve to grey, no generation coming after him. Now, he felt active, fully engaged, with that slight vertiginous edge, the sense of having perhaps taken on too much, of over-reaching yourself, a feeling he hadn't really had since he and Jan first left London and got the family place back. There was now a fax machine on his desk as well as a phone. Taking notes of a conversation, with the telephone in the crook of his shoulder, while he flipped through the pages of a road atlas or picked at the keys of a calculator, he had the dizzy feeling of working at a sort of supernatural process, the magical compression of time and distance.

Sometimes it was like being inside a strange physical construction, a sort of spidery web, like scaffolding, though he pictured the bars and connections as infinitely light, silvery, mercurial. Spar by spar, nexus to nexus, the armature would take shape; a limb might extend in one direction and then hang unconnected, forced to withdraw and find another node. Finally, all the internal logic of the system would be in place, matched up and functioning. Money and currencies, times and prices, weights and distances, would all switch on together, connected. Another deal done. Yes!

With the different time zones, the cicada chirrup of the fax machine would often start at six o'clock in the morning, and text would stutter out in loops and curls of paper for the rest of the day, and into the evening. Especially when the weather here was hot, the thermal paper of the fax, warm from just being read by the machine, carrying ornate enquiries in business Spanish, seemed to bring with it a white glare of heat, the faintest odour of pine resin, the dust of southern roads.

Once or twice they over-reached themselves. Tom found a customer in southern Spain, way down in Murcia, a place of orange groves and fortifications so exotic and far-away that it might still have been ruled by the Moors. It was a big company, mostly dealing in citrus fruits, trading in and out of North Africa and the Middle East. They fixed a price, and Tom spent a long time planning the journey with Steve, setting up a chain of lairages all the way down through the South of France and northern Spain. The trip should have been feasible, but somehow it was too much for the lambs, and of the six hundred they sent, fifteen died on the way. That wasn't good business or good stockmanship, and after that the furthest they went was to Burgos in northern Spain, to Felix del Rio.

Best of all, the real emblem of Tom's new life, his talisman, the object of his reverence and desire, was his mobile phone. Simply the weight in his pocket of this little oblong of plastic and circuitry, the touch of its black leather case, made him feel singled out, connected, that the world was here, all around, reaching out towards him, channelled through this magical object. He used to keep it switched on for as long as the batteries would stand it, at times when there was really no chance of anyone wanting to call him, simply for the feeling of it being alive, alert, scanning the airways of the world. Jan hated it; she felt invaded whenever its high-pitched peeping startled her, from the glove compartment or a coat pocket. When Tom tried to explain his feelings about it, she said that there were people who kept ferrets down their trousers, why don't you try that?

From time to time they would hear the reverberations of the protests up at the ports, the drivers coming back with stories from the front. Mostly it was just a question of demonstrations and banners, but once a lorry, not one of theirs, had a breeze-block through the windscreen. There was a picture in the paper, the driver sitting there in the blinded cab, a look of empty eye-sockets, with a diamond shower of glass fragments in his lap, and the padded interior of the cab exposed, out in the open, shocking somehow. It seemed like about twice a week there'd be a documentary on TV about the iniquities of live exports. It was sad and unfair, an urban perspective, ignorant and sentimental. Why couldn't they see the romance of it all, the excitement? The trade wasn't shocking or upsetting like their black propaganda made it out to be; the reality would have been just as good TV, the big rigs from Britain fanning out all over Europe. Mostly though, the protests seemed like dull thunder, far away, like the distant thuds and booms from the artillery range on the Eppynt, where the orange parachute flares would rise in silent arcs into the night and you would think to yourself: what are that lot up to?

Phil rang Tom one evening; he had some story about students in Llanfrychan handing out leaflets about live exports. Tom thought of the girl who had turned up at Graig Goch late one night. He couldn't remember whether Phil had still been in the yard. It was after the lorry had gone; she said she had run out of petrol, but Graig Goch was a funny place to come looking for it. He wondered whether Phil had seen her, and began describing her to him, but it then turned out what Phil was really ringing about was getting money for the train trip from Reading after he'd come back with the lorry. Tom said he'd think about it. He felt a bit pissed off, really, a bit exploited. He had tried to do Phil a favour, letting him go with the lorry to France. It should have been fun for him. He could have hitch-hiked home.

*   *   *

Their favourite customers were Societe Prevost. They had come to seem almost like friends. When Beti and Tom went through the accounts, there was Prevost's load of lambs, every week, regular as clockwork.

'Why can't they all be like them Tom, eh? Tell me that.'

They were in Brittany, a family firm; the old man, who was still nominally in charge, and his son. They were both Francois, and Tom would get put through to one or the other of them indiscriminately. The old man wasn't allowed to take executive decisions any more, but he was a nice old buffer. Tom didn't like his son at all, nasal, sneering, nothing was ever right, but that didn't matter because mostly they dealt with the manager, Valentin. He was a nice man, witty, courteous. Every week he and Tom would engage in extended and elaborate bargaining over the price of the next shipment, and Tom came to positively enjoy these sessions. The dickering would go on for two or three days sometimes, but they always reached agreement in the end, they were always satisfied with the lambs and the price, and they always paid.

Tom had a call from Valentin one morning at half past eight. *'Valentin! Ca va? Qu'est-ce qu'ils font, les cours la? Tu va bien gagner avec ces derniers agneaux, non?'*

Jan put her head round the door. 'Call him back in five minutes would you; I need the phone.'

Tom felt a pang of irritation, which he suppressed. The fact was Jan had always made more money at her work than he had done in any of his careers. Five years ago she'd gone freelance; it had seemed a big risk, but it had turned out well, and life was now a lot easier for her. She had branched out from farm accounts into more general consultancy work, filling in subsidy forms and grant applications. Her client base had built up to the point that she was thinking of opening an office in Llanfrychan.

'I need the phone, Tom, call him back.'

'OK, cinq minutes, salut.'

The other night, a week or so ago, Tom had had a strange experience, waking from a dream, or rather, realising that he was awake but still dreaming. He was in his room at home, off school with some illness that had left him weak and dizzy. Through the top half of the bedroom window he could see blue sky; somewhere, a single-engine aeroplane was murmuring its way between flat-bottomed clouds like barges. He could hear children's voices from the playground, high and indistinct, and from downstairs, the rumble and whine of the vacuum cleaner. His mother had said she would come up in a minute and keep him company. The experience was absolutely real, as though he had travelled in time and was eleven years old again. But it was like balancing on a wire; he couldn't maintain it, the bright surface shivered into blackness and he was left, lying in his bed, middle-aged and childless, in the middle of the night. Since then he had turned this memory over and over, peering at it, handling it until it had worn smooth and cloudy, like a piece of glass found on a beach. It had felt significant and mysterious, like a message in a bottle. He felt he was being told something, that his childhood self had risen up out of the grave of the past with a message, or a warning. He had a premonition, faint, ambiguous, speaking through memories.

He had said he would call Valentin straight back. He dialled the number, and as he sat waiting for a reply, began to feel again that he was on the brink of a revelation.

'*Oui, j'ecoute?*'

They talked about a load of lambs for next week. Valentin wanted to stay with the same price as before, but the market here was rising, and Tom said he would have to pass on the increase. The conversation was stately, formal, very familiar to both of them: *Yes, it was important to work. Yes, we wanted to do our best for our customers. No, at that price we would be losing money. Yes we can work for very little, but not for a loss. We are taking a risk, even at that price. No, not possible. I can show you the figures, you can see for yourself. Yes we can guarantee the quality. Better than last week. But it must be eleven francs fifty. No, not possible. Yes, Tuesday or Wednesday. Yes OK. Good. Yes OK.*

'*Salut Tom.*'

'*Salut Valentin.*'

Tom was a little surprised that they had reached agreement so quickly; these negotiations would sometimes go on for several days, faxes and phone-calls, offers and counter offers batting back and forth like a tennis match. Something was not quite right; there was a detail out of place somewhere. He could feel it rubbing, like a piece of grit. He went into the kitchen and had a coffee with Jan.

When Beti and Tom first started working with them, Societe Prevost had taken out a letter of credit in their favour, to the value of half a million French francs. This meant that if something went wrong with their payments, if they defaulted, dropped dead or went bankrupt, their bank would still pay what they owed. This arrangement suited everybody. Beti and Tom were secure, and Prevost, who in any case had three weeks credit on each individual deal, could hold on to their money until the value of the transactions reached the total value of the letter of credit. So they could buy three lorry-loads, up to twelve hundred lambs, before they had to pay anything at all.

There were four other lorries going out that week, all to different customers, and Tom realised he was in danger of losing track of things. He got out Prevost's file. They had had three lorries since their last payment. The load Tom had just negotiated would have been a fourth. They were up to their limit. He rang Valentin.

'OK Tom, no problem. *Je m'en occupe. Tu auras le virement demain matin.*'

They started getting the lambs together. Tom checked with the bank twice the next day, but they hadn't received any payments. He rang Valentin again.

'Ah non? Rien? Mais, je comprends pas. Je fais des enquetes aupres de la banque. Ne t'inquiete pas.'

There was a tone in his voice Tom couldn't quite interpret, slightly regretful, dulled. He sounded neither worried nor surprised, and the usual elasticity, the snap in his voice, was missing. Tom didn't take his advice. He began to worry. Every time he got Beti on the phone, she was busy with something else.

'Leave it all to you Tom. You decide what's best. Just tell me when you want the lambs. Prevost are good boys; they'll be alright.'

He rang Valentin again. The Frenchman told him not to worry, that he would sort it out, but there was the same flat quality to his voice, a lifelessness, like grief.

By the next day, they had reached the point where they would either have to go ahead and send the lambs, or call off the lorry. It seemed to Tom that Beti wasn't quite engaging with the problem.

'Go on Tom, let's gamble them; they've been good so far haven't they?'

Tom wanted to explain to her that, up till now they had been covered by the letter of credit; moreover, Societe Prevost would have known that they were covered. They would have known that if they had withheld the payment, the bank could simply have called it in. Equally, they must know that the cover was about to come to an end. It seemed to Tom that he had no guide here to their future conduct. Beti was worried that they would end up losing Prevost as customers if they so obviously failed to trust them. In the end, it came down to how you felt about risking twenty grand. Tom decided to go up to Graig Goch and straighten things out.

Huw was moving sheep down the lane when he got to the farm, the collie criss-crossing behind his heels. He stopped the car and switched the motor off as the mob, filling the lane, squeezed past on either side, scrambling up the bank below the hedgerow. Huw gave him a gappy smile as he passed, pushing his cap back and scratching his head.

'Warm, eh Tom? Sheep going today?'

'Not sure Huw. Beti about?'

She was at the kitchen table, hunched closely over a bowl of what looked like porridge, which she was spooning rapidly into her mouth. There was a fellow sitting at the table opposite her, looked like a farmer; nobody Tom knew.

'Help yourself to coffee Tom. Won't be a minute.'

The farmer gave a shy smile as Tom crossed the room to the sink and put the kettle on. Beti finished her food with a final scrape and rattle of the spoon, wiping her mouth with a napkin that was tucked into her shirt collar. She turned in her chair, handing her bowl to her mother, who at that moment had come into the room, shuffling across the tiled floor on slapping flattened slippers.

'Here.'

She called her back to give her the napkin, then turned to the farmer.

'Now then Davies, what seems to be the trouble?'

There was a copy of Farmers Weekly on the dresser, and Tom flipped through it while they talked. As far as he could make out, half listening, the farmer had already bought fertilizer off Beti, and now wanted to extend his credit and have some more. He wasn't going to be able to pay for either lot until the premium had been paid.

'Sorry Davies, can't do it. Treat everybody the same, you know that. You settle your bill and then we'll see. *Hoffwn eich helpu ond alla'i ddim.*'

Her voice was sharp with irritation. Davies adjusted his cap on his head and left the room without catching Tom's eye. Beti was noting something down in a ledger.

'They must think I'm soft. Have another coffee, I won't be long now.'

She left the room, and Tom could hear her in the yard, shouting something at Huw. Their voices trailed away and he was left leafing through magazines, while the old lady washed up at the sink. He tried to talk to her once or twice, but she didn't respond. She was fairly deaf, and in any case never seemed to be able to understand him, as though she found his accent impenetrable. She stacked the dripping dishes in the rack, then moved over to the big new microwave on the sideboard, pushing buttons and clicking bevelled gauges with an eerie mastery of the technology.

Beti's son Barry came into the kitchen. Tom had been working with Beti for over a year before he ever realised who Barry was, assuming he was just someone who worked at Graig Goch. He wasn't at all like Beti in looks. He was a good bit taller than Tom, and towered over his mother, even though you never saw him straightened up, but always stooping over, hunched. His hair was cut very short, almost shaved. It wasn't the physical dissimilarity between them though, but the utter lack of connectedness that was disturbing. There was none of the horse-play that Beti went in for with Huw or the other boys, the back-slapping, the jokes, still less any kind of tenderness.

Barry was in his early twenties, and as far as Tom could see did much of the day-to-day running of the farm, leaving Beti free to concentrate on the dealing side of the business. There must have been a lot of work to this, a lot of responsibility and decision making, but it didn't seem to gain him any respect from his mother. Now he made himself a cup of tea and sat down at the kitchen table.

'I see the Frank is much the same then?'

Tom was trying to think of a Frank they might have in common, when Barry went on:

'The franc, the French money. It says in the paper that it's staying much the same.'

His voice trailed away. This remark was so out of character that Tom just gaped. He had no idea how to take it. He glanced at him, wondering if he was trying to take the piss. He had a strange look, furtive, but somehow pleading. It occurred to Tom that what Barry wanted was to be taken seriously, to have a grown-up conversation, not to be ignored, discounted, left out. He tried to collect his thoughts.

'It's not so much the franc is strong as that the pound is weak.'

'So when one goes up, the other goes down like?'

The back door slammed, and Beti came banging back into the room. She shook her head irritably as she saw Barry, who was leaning back in his chair, legs splayed out in front of him.

'Have you got those bullocks down yet? I didn't see them in the yard.'

Barry seemed to twitch and shrink instantly, pulling back into himself, withdrawing as if stung or prodded.

'Just having this tea.'

'We were just discussing exchange rates.'

Barry gave Tom a hurt look. It had sounded as though he was being made fun of. Tom was trying to deflect Beti's irritation, but he had merely sounded timid and indecisive.

'So what's the story, Tom?' Beti said. 'When are we sending the lambs?'

'I think we should hold them over till we've had the payment' Tom told her.

Barry's stomach gave a loud digestive rumble, a series of bass bubbling notes followed by a trill of clicks and squeaks. He leaned forward in his chair, patting his chest, and perhaps trying to cover up the racket by joining in the conversation.

'There isn't much keep about. Where would you put them?'

'*Peidiwch â becso am hwnna.* These'll go to Kent. We'll get another lot for the Frenchies.'

Beti snapped these words out, her face working with a sort of distaste. Turning to Tom, her expression smoothed itself into a smile.

'Look at it this way Tom. They've taken a lorry a week from us for what, six months? That's: three hundred and eighty five thousand pounds.'

She had frowned only momentarily as she made the calculation. Tom remembered Alwyn, who'd been at school with her, telling him she'd been bottom of the class in everything except arithmetic. Barry whistled through his teeth, then ducked nervously into his mug of tea as Beti pointed a finger at him:

'That's not to go telling everybody about down the Ram, see?'

Barry responded with a noise like water running out of a sink. He leaned forward in his chair, punching at his stomach and producing an unconvincing cough. His mother shook her head.

'You see what I'm telling you, Tom. They've paid all that money with never a problem.'

As she turned back, the bitter glance she'd directed at Barry effaced itself again, and Tom had the impression of masks being put on and removed; white, theatrical, faces on sticks, a repertoire of passions to be assumed and discarded, beneath which brooded the real face, calculating, enigmatic, occluded.

Tom looked over at Barry, slouched in his chair, bulky, pallid, examining his hands, turning them over thoughtfully one in the other, his gaze turned down and inward. He was almost good looking, but there was a thickness, a sort of blurred quality to his features, a kind of soapy texture, the product of grief and the withholding of love. Tom thought: I could have done a better job of parenthood if I'd ever been given the chance.

'It's a lot of money though, fair play,' Barry said, interrupting another arpeggio of peristaltic peeps and burps, giving Tom a hopeful look. Probably he knew quite well that he was getting on Beti's nerves, that his mother didn't want him taking part in the conversation. Perhaps he was digging his heels in, using the presence of other people to make some sort of stubborn, inarticulate protest against the terms of his life.

Tom looked at the two of them, searching for any common feature, physical or psychological; they seemed entirely compounded of opposites. He tried to imagine what Barry's childhood might have been like, whether there had ever been any tenderness or intimacy between them. He knew Beti's husband had run off or disappeared twenty or so years ago. People said she'd got rid of him – *chased him out of the house, he ran all the way to the railway station* – though this was just the kind of story that would attach itself to Beti. Fantastic elements would naturally take

43

shape around a personality like hers, accretions like the growth of coral on a wreck, additions to her glamour, the power she had over people.

In the end, Beti and Tom found a compromise: they wouldn't send the lambs, but they would tell Prevost they had a problem with the lorry, or the boat, or the weather. These problems would in fact persist until the payment came through; in the meantime they would have the lambs lined up and ready to go, so hopefully they would be able to avoid the risk while not appearing to doubt Prevost's honesty.

Tom got up, stretching, relieved that they'd settled something. Barry got up at the same time, leaning across the table, offering a hand-shake.

'Good then. I'm glad you've sorted it out.' He was nodding and smiling, as though he had been chairing a meeting, and was now dismissing the participants. His manner was awkward, inappropriate but determined, and Tom wondered again whether he was trying to make fun of him, or his mother. He gave an embarrassed smile as Beti snapped at him:

'You finished your tea? I need those bullocks down here now. Where's Huw anyway?'

Barry left the room, ducking his head through the doorway. Tom went through some paperwork with Beti, then drove up to the big shed, where the shearers were finishing a load of lambs for Felix del Rio. He was thinking about Beti and her mother, and Barry, about their strange household, the three of them in that big place, all done out new, everything gleaming in stainless steel and formica, brass and composite marble, the fitted carpets crackling with static electricity.

Their mealtimes were shared with Huw and Alwyn and maybe a couple more of the boys; from nine to five there was a housekeeper to help the old lady, and all day and long into the evening a stream of reps and salesmen, neighbours and supplicants, drank tea and smoked, talking in quiet voices, not finding an ashtray and furtively tapping cigarette ash into their trouser turn-ups or the tops of their boots. All day and into the evening the phones rang and the fax chattered and stuttered, cars and LandRovers, lorries and vans pulled in to the yard. The dogs barked and scurried, sheep and cattle jostled bellowing through the pens.

But at last, late in the night, it would be just the three of them, Huw pissing in a corner of the yard on his way to the caravan, just the three of them in the house. Tom wondered if they chatted a little, unwinding, or read bits out of the newspaper to one another, or pecked each other on the cheek, saying their goodnights. Did they sit stiffly in front of the huge TV in the front room? He found the image that was eluding him: that of

Barry and his grandmother asleep at last, large, pale figures lying flat as planks in their chapel beds, cold hands folded on their chests; the white beak of the nose like a cuttlefish bone in the chill bedroom air. Beti of course didn't fit into this mortuary scene, this sense of coldness and solidity, an atmosphere of damp and statuary. It was hard to picture her asleep at all; or, if asleep, then still restless, thrashing and shouting her way through blind alleys of the night.

There was something about the household at Graig Goch that went beyond the ordinary strangeness of other people's lives. When he thought of the place, Tom had a sense of gaps and interstices within which things moved, seen only in ambiguous glimpses. The ferocious and demonic nature of Beti's personality produced a dazzling effect, a glare that was both hypnotic and obscuring, so that when you turned away from this you were blinded as though coming in from bright sunshine into a darkened room full of shadowy objects that might be furniture or human figures, or neither of these, where colour and meaning had been bleached out. Tom had intercepted, for a glancing moment, the look of rage and contempt in Beti's eyes as she watched her son leave the room and it had left him feeling both repelled and fascinated, a glimpse of something powerful and shaming, a secret rich in mysterious biography.

Prevost didn't send any money, and they didn't send any lambs. Tom let the rest of the week go by, and on Monday morning rang Valentin. He was out of the office for the day, and so were both Prevosts, père et fils. Same on Tuesday. He had a curious sense of everything being muffled in cotton-wool, like going deaf or losing the soundtrack, so that all of a sudden everything was reduced to movements and gestures, indecipherable.

The normal period of credit had expired on the first of the three lorry-loads they owed, had over-run by ten days in fact, so whatever happened next, Prevost needed to pay some money straightaway. The following day, Tom got hold of Valentin, explained that the payment was overdue, and asked him to speed things up. He said he would see to it. He didn't order any more lambs, and wasn't even very interested in discussing prices or possibilities. He said demand had gone very slack. After Tom put the phone down, it occurred to him that, given the spacing of deliveries, the credit limit had by now expired on two lorries, not one. He rang back to ask him to arrange two payments at once, but Valentin had gone out of the office. Tom sent him a fax, and got his copy of the letter of credit out of the file.

It was a fax copy of a telex, the lettering dense and bunched, dark and a little smudged. The language was technical, but by now familiar. He skimmed through the stock phrases of the text like filleting a fish, wary of sharp bones. The validity was good, running to the end of the year. The value was just about alright; with a calculator he established that they had over-run by about four thousand francs. They'd manage that if necessary. In another week, payment would be due on all three lorries, so there would certainly be no point in invoking the letter of credit any sooner than that. In any case, he was reasonably sure that they'd have a payment from Prevost any day now, perhaps this afternoon. As Beti had said, they'd done so much business with them that there must be some explanation for the delay. When he spoke to the bank the next morning there was still no payment. He rang Valentin, intending to be direct this time; it was time to find out what was going on.

'Tu sais Tom, j'ai donne la commande qu'on fasse ton virement; mais maintenant c'est avec Francois, je veux dire le fils. Il dit qu'il veut verifier touts les.'

Tom told him there was nothing to verify. They had sent the lambs, and now the payment was due. Valentin's tone, regretful but detached, had suddenly got on his nerves: we are not trying to conduct diplomacy here, we want our money.

'Il faut que tu comprends Tom que c'est pas moi qui commande ici. En effet, c'est hors de ma controle.'

Tom gathered together the documents they would need in order to use the letter of credit to force payment from Prevost. They needed copies of invoices from each load, a signed attestation from Beti stating that she had not been paid, the original telex setting out the letter of credit, and three CMRs – one for each load. A CMR is a standard form accompanying all international consignments of goods and freight. It's divided up into a grid of little boxes containing Beti's name, Prevost's name and address, the haulage firm, place of loading, place designated for delivery, whether freight was pre-paid or not, and various further sets of initials and acronyms whose meaning he'd never quite figured out. It's printed out in three languages, and comes ready-carboned to produce four copies. The whole thing travels with the shipment; then one copy stays with the haulier, one goes to the customer, one goes to the French veterinary service, and one copy eventually comes back to Graig Goch.

Tom typed out the attestation of non-payment, and took it over to Graig Goch for Beti to sign. The original of the letter of credit was in the files, and he collected that at the same time. He went through all the box-files in the office that related to the export business. Having done that, there was really nowhere else to look; of the three CMRs they needed, two were missing.

Beti was irritable and distracted.

'What is this anyway, Tom? Abistention? Attistention? What the hell is that?'

Tom decided that he wouldn't tell her about the CMRs just yet. It had to be worth ringing the bank in Bristol first. Sitting in the spare chair at Beti's office desk, the surface in front of him littered with files, papers, telephones, staplers, ledgers, diaries, stacks of invoices, he had one of those hot, faint, hunted moments he remembered from maths exams at school, a sensation of being trapped in mud, stifled, terrorised, the baying of some nameless pursuit in your ears, as you open the exam paper and realise you can't answer a single question, not one, and you feel as though you are physically twisting, this way and that, *there must be some way out of this*, but there isn't.

The whole point about a letter of credit, its coldness, elegance and simplicity, is that it touches in no way whatsoever on questions of justice, or pity or right, on mitigation, special pleading or extenuation, no matter how desperate. If all the conditions are fulfilled, the document will work, the money will be paid. If any element is missing or incomplete or incorrect, the whole thing becomes worthless; the claim will fail, and you will not get paid. The bank had explained all this to him over and over again. He knew that he was crouched down in the bulrushes, up to his waist in mud, the river in front of him and the hounds at his back. They were about to drop a bollock to the tune of forty thousand pounds, of which he was liable for half.

'Attestation, Beti. It's just a statement that you haven't been paid.'

'Course I haven't been paid. They can look at my statements if they want; the bank'll give them copies.'

'It's just the way the bank works, with the letter of credit.'

Beti signed her name in a thicket of loops and flourishes.

'It will work, then? This lettery credit thing?'

'You bet.'

Perhaps she picked up some tremor of hesitation in Tom's voice, because she looked up sharply.

'It had better work Tom. Want me to talk to the bank?'

'No don't do that; I'll talk to them. No problem.'

Tom rifled his own office all over again as soon as he got home. He had a number of over-lapping systems, from a proper filing cabinet with drawers that slid in and out with a smooth rumble, to box files, to cardboard boxes under the desk, to wads of faxes and invoices bulldog-clipped together. He had been through everything before going over to see Beti, and he knew really that the CMRs weren't there, but he started again all the same, riffling, shuffling, stacking and restacking, walking panicky fingers through the hanging files in the cabinet, driven, sweating, to rummage in the cobwebby recesses behind the desk, leafing, flicking through sheaves of paper like some nightmare cashier, the rustle of paper like a dry cough, nagging and unproductive. Deep in the drowning, dizzy feeling where the lost documents represented everything chaotic and malign in life, he felt choked and throttled, not just by financial catastrophe, but by a sudden, stunning loss of certainty, a stumble into the howling abyss. You don't need severed heads and hearts of darkness, he thought; the horror is here, now, stepping off the kerb into the road, where a car is coming over the brow much faster than you thought, ugly foreshortened shape rushing at you; in a section of suburban woodland among the scruffy silver birches the brambles are littered with some horrible detritus, scraps of clothing, traces of death.

He called Steve at the haulage firm. Steve told him that the CMRs would have gone in the post to Beti as usual; as soon as the drivers got back, he would bung them in with the invoices. It was routine. Tom told him which ones were missing, and asked him to double-check; they could have been left in the cab after the trip, tucked behind a sun visor or slipped between the seats. Steve didn't think so.

Jan came home. She put her head round the office door.

'What's up? Problems?'

'Could be.'

He'd been putting off ringing the bank in Bristol, but as Jan said, they had to follow up every possibility. Perhaps Steve would turn up the CMRs; perhaps the bank would find a way to make the credit work without them. He didn't have much confidence, but it was quarter to five, so if he didn't ring now, he'd have a night of not knowing. He was put through to Documentary Credits and got Melanie, who he had always pictured as cute, but lightweight.

'Hi Tom! What can we do for you?'

He explained.

'Well Tom, the LC won't work if there's elements missing. Have you asked them for the payment?'

Her tone was bright, conversational. Tom told her that they'd asked for the payment several times; that was why they wanted to see if they could use the letter of credit.

'It doesn't sound like you can, does it? I'll just get your file though. Hang on a minute.'

While he was waiting, he got out his copy of the credit. Melanie came back on the line.

'Let's see now, Credit Agricole hereby undertake . . . de-dah de-dah . . . Societe Prevost . . . this is the one isn't it? Let's see: copy of commercial invoice, copy of transport document, signed attestation . . . I don't see what you can do really. If you haven't got the right documents, the credit won't work. We explained that, didn't we? You say you've got one CMR, though. You should get paid for that load anyway.'

An idea was forming in Tom's mind.

'You see where it says Transport Document? It doesn't actually say CMR, does it?'

He could hear a note of impatience in Melanie's voice:

'But a CMR *is* a transport document Tom'.

He was contemplating a personal loss of twenty thousand pounds, and Melanie was sounding impatient.

'A CMR is a transport document, but maybe a transport document isn't necessarily a CMR. I tell you what, Melanie, let me have a word with your head of department will you?'

'He's left the office, I'm afraid.'

He told her he'd call again in the morning.

When he put the phone down he was humming with frustration; He had a feeling that there might after all be a way to make the letter of credit work, but he would certainly need to by-pass that prat of a Melanie with her whining receptionist's voice, fuck her. At supper, he had an edgy conversation with Jan. She couldn't see the point of speculating until he'd talked to the manager in the morning. Either there was a way round the problem, or there wasn't. He knew she was right, but somehow he couldn't leave the subject alone. He was filled with a blind and murderous irritation, a physical tension that felt like chicken-wire under the skin and kept him awake half the night.

The next morning his eyes felt like they were full of grit. He shut himself in the office with a mug of coffee.

'Hi Tom. How are you today?'

Melanie's voice was languid, social, a little condescending, and he felt a familiar stab of irritation.

'He's not come into the office yet. He'll only say the same as I've already told you Tom. Why don't you try talking to your customers again?'

Tom recognised, in his feelings of frustration, a sexual component. The ease with which he could picture Melanie's long white body lounging in a swivel chair, the phone cupped in the crook of her shoulder, was all bound up with feelings of helpless rage, the need to dominate the situation through her; the germ of rape.

'They may pay you anyway. But there's nothing we can do without the right documents.' She was breezy, dismissive.

'Anyway, I'll get him to call you when he comes in.'

Geoff Ward, when he finally got him, was a North Walian; he had a stutter, and that funny vocal characteristic of the backward 'r', that gave his words a throaty gargle, but as they talked, Tom felt the gradual dawning of a vast relief.

'As far as I can see, Mr Wood, 'Copy of Transport Document' could mean just about anything we want it to mean. You get your haulier to produce a nice official form, all headed up nicely *Transport Document* do you see, all the details, dates, port of shipment, all that sort of thing, I think they'll have to accept that, don't you? Generally with these credits, you just have to produce exactly what they say, no more no less.'

Tom had an impulse to ask to speak to Melanie; if he'd taken her advice, the letter of credit would eventually have expired and she would have cost him twenty thousand pounds. But he could afford to feel generous. Let her keep perfecting her fragrant indifference undisturbed by complaints from customers. He didn't need her any more. Geoff Ward was still talking.

'So get all those documents in to us. Make sure your transport company uses their headed paper. We'll send it all to the French bank by courier, and Bob's your uncle. It may take a couple of weeks, but you'll get your money. I should think your customers will pay anyway, once they get some pressure from their bank, but even if they don't, the bank will have to pay. That's the beauty of documentary credits.'

These last two words produced such a rattle of gutturals that Tom pictured a rainbow of spittle, like a halo round his head. He felt like kissing him.

Two days later he was coming out of the Post Office in Llanfrychan, where he'd just sent the documents off to Bristol by registered post, a thick plank of brown envelope bound up with tape and plastered with labels, when he heard someone calling his name from across the street. A cattle lorry rattled past, like drawing aside a curtain of grimy clattering aluminium, revealing a figure waving at him from the opposite pavement, and he squinted through the slanting sunlight to see who it was.

Chapter 6

The evening before, Phil had sorted out the lambs he wanted to take to market, so this morning it was only a question of running them into the shed from the paddock, hitching up the tractor and the sheep trailer, and backing up to the shed door. With the tractor, it might take forty minutes to get into Llanfrychan, so he needed an early start if he was to get a good pen for the lambs.

Now, just after nine o'clock, he was picking his way down the High Street between double-parked cars, the tractor engine bubbling softly, lounging high in the cab in the armchair seat, the long red bonnet with the black enamel smokestack nosing its way through the traffic. He came to a halt behind a cattle truck which formed the tail-end of a short queue of farm vehicles waiting to turn off the High Street down the alley that led to the mart buildings. He reached up to the control panel above his head and switched on the radio. In the trailer behind him he had twenty four good lambs, Texel crosses, should be thirty six, maybe thirty eight kilos; if prices were holding up this week he would have a good morning's work in front of him. He was sitting in a powerful, expensive machine. The sunlight was very warm through the glass of the cab, music flowed softly out of the speakers. Two little girls in one of those side-by-side push-chairs waved frantically at him as they passed by with their mother, and he waved back, grinning.

The line of vehicles started to move again and Phil put the tractor into gear and followed, swinging round off the main road. The trailer mounted the pavement as he took the corner; glancing in the mirror, his feet jumped to the clutch and brake, jerking the machine to a halt. He had narrowly missed knocking down a farmer in a long brown stock-coat and a thumb-stick, who had pressed himself up against the wall and now waved Phil on with a nervous smile.

He worked the tractor through the ranks of parked trucks and trailers, then swung round in an arc and backed up to one of the unloading bays. There was a little maze of iron-work pens and alleys along the side wall of the mart building. Stock could be held here and sorted, before being driven through the big sliding doors into the building itself. The mart was built of old brick, stained and pocked, the mortar crumbling between the courses. The original slate roof had been mostly replaced with asbestos sheeting; over the years this material in turn had grown clumps of moss and lichen, fertilized by pigeon droppings, its outlines growing rounded and blurred. The walls were plastered with notices and posters advertising farm sales and horse fairs, one on top of another, tattered and peeling, like archeological layers of excavation. To one side of the building was an enormous tump of old straw and manure, bedding from the livestock pens, bubbling with little black mushrooms.

Phil lowered the ramp and opened the loading gates, walking round and banging with the flat of his hand on the trailer sides to hustle the lambs out. He shut them into an empty pen, then got back into the tractor and drove right round the mart buildings and parked in the next side street down that led on to the High Street; that way he could be sure of not getting blocked in after the sale.

Walking back, he waved to Bernard, who was pulling out of the market yard in his LandRover, the old machine rattling and coughing, puffing out clouds of black smoke.

'Sut mae Phil? Lot of lambs here today.'

'Hope there's plenty of buyers.'

He picked up an old fertilizer bag that was lying on the floor and flicked it, crackling, at his lambs, driving them out of the pen and down the main alleyway that ran along the middle of the old market building between ranks of massive cattle pens. The scale of the steel gates and holding pens, built for bulls and milking cows and 500kg steers, dwarfed his lambs as they hustled down the alley, jinking and flinching in the unfamiliar surroundings, the echoing space booming with clanging reverberations, crashes of noise and disembodied shouting.

At the far end of the alley, the building opened out in to a big covered yard where the sheep pens were. The gateway into this yard was formed by the weigh-scales; up ahead, a drover halted Phil's lambs while another lot were weighed. The scales were like a little metal room, like a lift cage oddly removed from the shaft. Above it an enormous dial, as big as a station clock, marked out the weight with a quivering needle. The metal gates clanged open and Phil drove his lambs forward onto the trembling slatted floor of the scales. Above him the needle swung wildly, then steadied. In a little cubby hole to the side of the scales, Mike from the auctioneers office nodded at Phil, picking at the keys of a calculator, dividing the total weight by the number of lambs.

'Thirty eight and a half. Alright Phil?'

The grader rummaged through his lambs, checking conformation and fat cover. He too nodded at Phil and Mike.

'These are fine. Let them go boys.'

The drovers ran the lambs out of the scales and into a sheep pen in the covered yard. Phil walked round the side of the scales and followed them. He felt a surge of well-being; the lambs had weighed better than he'd expected, and they'd all graded. He noted down their pen-number, leaning on the gate as the lambs stared up at him, nostrils working, a limpid recognition in their eyes.

The sheep pens were about two-thirds filled with lambs, perhaps fifteen hundred head, in lots of tens and twelves and twenties. Groups of farmers stood about, leaning on the hurdles, chatting, scratching, tapping their sticks on the concrete floor or tinkling them musically along the railings. Phil couldn't see many buyers about yet. A smell of fried onions drifted over from the catering van on the other side of the yard, mingling with the smell of urine and cigarette smoke. He'd only had a cup of tea before leaving the house, so he wandered over to the van and asked for a bacon roll. Bernard and his pal Iori were stood at the counter of the van, stirring at plastic cups of tea that were too hot to pick up.

'What you got here Phil, ewes?'

'Fat lambs, back up there, Texels. You?'

'Old ewes. This pen yer.'

Bernard jerked his thumb over his shoulder at a pen of half a dozen old sheep who stared at Phil, cudding bulging cheeks, grey muzzled.

'Them old dears; won't get through another winter, not on my place anyways.'

They moved aside as a couple of bulky figures pushed through to the van counter; they were buyers, dealers, big florid men in bright blue stock-coats, elastic sided boots, mobile phones poking out of bulging pockets. Phil knew one of them slightly and nodded, smiling, as he scooped up his bacon roll and moved out of their way. He wondered who the other buyer was, hadn't seen him before, bushy side-burns and glasses with tinted lenses, a swaggering style to all his movements, conscious of his power as a trader, of his ability to set the price of their produce; an aristocrat of the market place. Bernard hadn't seen him before, either. Out of ear-shot, his lip curled:

'Thinks the world of himself, don't he?'

Phil recognised the feeling, the mixture of admiration and contempt, the emotions of economic vassalage. This man and his colleagues could stroll into the market and rake their claws across the price of Bernard's sheep without a second thought, or just as casually, in some butting contest for dominance amongst themselves, pay far over the odds, twice what the old sheep were worth, and send Bernard chuckling and scratching his head into the pub at the end of the sale.

In the booming acoustics of the covered yard, the noise had been gradually increasing; clash of gates, shouts of laughter, the whoops and whistles of the drovers. Now this crashing dis-harmony was itself shattered as the head auctioneer, Frank Williams, strode down the central aisle swinging a big brass handbell with a shimmering high peal, imposing in a purple stock-coat, Mike trotting behind him with a clipboard. The two men swung themselves up onto the narrow gangway of aluminium treadplate that ran along the pens above the heads of the sheep. Immediately the crowd formed itself around the pen at the auctioneers feet, owners of sheep in the adjoining pens, and a couple of dozen farmers, onlooking, but moving deferentially aside as the dealers, seven or eight of them by now, swarmed into the pen, poking and prodding at the lambs, scrambling up onto the walkway with Frank and Mike, guffawing with each other, muttering into phones.

Phil hung back a little, not wanting to get in the buyers' way, straining to hear the bidding in the general roar of sound. The auctioneer's voice, high and clear, was easy to distinguish but his sing-song gabble was incomprehensible, only the final figure sometimes coming into audible focus:

'Are you all done then? *thirty nine pound*' and the crack of his swagger stick on the railing.

Gradually they worked down the line of pens. It would take about half an hour for them to reach Phil's sheep. The better lambs seemed to be doing a bit over a pound a kilo, the very best going up to one-ten. Phil worked out what the bottom line ought to be for his own lambs, experiencing a little stab of anxiety and excitement as he did so. He could be looking at a thousand pounds today.

As the crowd jostled its way down the aisle towards Phil's lambs, he moved on ahead and climbed into the pen with them. A couple were lying down, and he got them onto their feet, brushing bits of straw and droppings off their backs. He pushed the lambs around a little, seeing if he could get the best ones to the front of the pen, but really they were all pretty good. Nevertheless he felt nervous as the uproar moved down the line towards him.

A fore-runner of the crowd, a buyer, Meirion Price, Phil knew him, climbed into the pen and prodded at the lambs. He wrote something on a card and then heaved himself into the next pen without having caught Phil's eye. Then the onslaught arrived, like a wave breaking over him, buyers climbing into the pen, pushing him aside as though he wasn't there, a wall of bodies pressing up against the pen, above his head Frank rapping with his stick to get their attention. As the bidding started there was a great wash of laughter that gusted from the crowd as Meirion Price and the new buyer broke into a joke boxing match, dancing heavily round Phil's pen, jabbing fists at each other. The bidding faltered as everyone's attention was distracted; Phil could hear the auctioneer's voice above him, stuck on the same figure: *thirty four pounds . . . thirty four pounds.* He craned round, tapping at Frank Williams' ankle: 'I'm not selling them for that. I should be getting forty anyway.'

There was a further commotion in the crowd, and Phil turned back to see Beti, shoving to the front, everyone, including other dealers, falling back to give her room. She winked at Phil, surging into the bidding like a swimmer wading into the surf. *Thirty eight . . . forty . . . forty two . . . forty three . . . forty three fifty . . .*

Frank Williams leaned down to Phil: 'Alright?' The stick cracked again on the handrail. From then on, Beti's presence dominated the sale. She bought more lambs, cracked more jokes and simply seemed to move faster than anyone else. Phil followed on, watching the selling for a while, noting how the whole circus now seemed to move at the pace that Beti set them. There was a subtle but unmistakable deflation, a sort of dimming, among the other buyers, as though they now stood in the same relation to Beti as the farmers stood in to them, dwarfed, diminished, dependent; admiring and resentful.

As the sale came to an end, farmers pressed awkwardly around her, waiting to catch her eye, wanting a favour or advice. She nodded to some of them, offering her hand to shake with a quick, careless gesture, tilting her head to listen to the murmured requests. After one of these exchanges she tapped the man on the shoulder, gesturing towards a neighbour the other side of the alley.

'Davies there, over there, see him?' she said. 'Fetch him over will you? Tell him I want a quick word.'

A little later she caught sight of Phil and motioned him over.

'Happy?'

'You bet.'

Beti nodded, and then a look of irritation, almost distaste, came over her face. Barry pushed his way through the crowd and touched his mother on the shoulder. Beti only half turned her head, as though she had been able to sense who it was behind her.

'You took your time. Right. Get them to bring both lorries round to the front. Start loading from the far end.'

Barry started to move away, and Beti turned fully round, raising her voice in a sort of furious yelp, shoving a card filled with scribbled numbers at her son.

'You want the pen numbers don't you?'

Barry's voice sank to a mumble, and he seemed to sag.

'I was going to get them from Mike anyway.'

Phil watched his stooped, retreating back move away through the crowd, then on an impulse, pushed his way through to follow him.

'Barry! Do you want a hand? I'll give you a hand with the loading if you like.'

Barry was peering at the card that Beti had given him; on it was the list of pen numbers for the lambs that Beti had bought, but he was staring at it blankly, as though it was illegible, or meant nothing. Phil took the card. He was feeling generous, decisive, capable, as though something of Beti's spirit had rubbed off on to him.

'Where shall we start? One forty eight. Is that the first? If we put a hurdle across here we can run all the lambs down to the far end. What do you think?'

Barry seemed to come to life as they worked. He had an easy expertise with animals, calm and effective. Lot by lot the lambs trotted down the aisle; they penned them up at the far end while Huw and Alwyn backed up the lorries. Phil wondered if Beti was always that nasty with Barry, and why. He watched the bulky, stooping figure as he shooshed on the lambs, opening and shutting gates, and felt for a moment an intense sympathy. What a life. Never seen him with a girl-friend. How old is he anyway? Huw was always nice to Barry though, showing him a kind of beaming, physical affection that expressed itself in clumsy shoves and pats, the kind of gestures you might use round a favourite horse. Phil shook his head; what a pair. And yet love was love, no matter how awkward and odd, and by the time the lorries were loaded up and gone, Barry seemed to have straightened up, there was colour in his face and his eyes were sparkling. Looking at him, Phil realised the boy was younger than he'd thought. He was just a lad, and really he deserved a better parent than the one he'd got, for all Beti's power and intensity. He glanced at his watch as a thought struck him.

'Barry, come and have a pint.'

They turned out of Market Lane into the High Street, Barry walking a couple of paces behind, like a bodyguard. Phil was feeling an extraordinary sense of lightness and power, a clear-headed euphoria, a mixture of compassion and laughter. Across the street he saw a familiar figure, a harassed, hot-looking character, scratching his head. He felt like laughing out loud.

'Look, it's Tom Wood. Tom! Come and have a drink!'

He could see that Tom had heard them, saw him cock his head to one side, squinting across the street in their direction. In a gap in the traffic he tugged at Barry's sleeve, as one would do to a child, and the two of them crossed the road.

'Come and have a drink with us. We're just going for a quick one.'

Tom Wood was looking at his watch, patting his pockets; he took a pen from inside his jacket. In his clumsy, muddled way he was obviously about to refuse.

'Come on. You've got to. I'm buying'.

Phil took his elbow, turning him to face down the street, and the three of them set off, Tom giving him a lop-sided grin and muttering something about needing to make a phone-call. Phil had a vague sense that it wouldn't do him any harm to be buying drinks for these two; Tom Wood and Barry's mother could between them put a lot of work his way. But, much more than that, he felt filled with good humour and energy, the pleasure of making things happen.

They ducked through the side door of the Black Ox on the High Street, into the cool of the saloon. It was very dark after the brightness of the street, and there was a strong smell of spilt beer and stale tobacco. There were a dozen or so customers in the place, a group of farmers just out of the mart disputing something at the bar. Phil looked round for Bernard, but couldn't see him. Above the bar a TV was showing racing from somewhere in England, the sound turned off. He propelled Tom and Barry over to a corner table and went to the bar to order the pints. Glancing back, he could see the two of them sitting rather stiffly, uncomfortably close to each other on the high-backed bench, not speaking. He scooped the three beers together into a triangle between his hands and carried them over to the table.

'You had a good sale then?'

Tom had been writing something in a notebook which he now snapped shut and replaced in his pocket. Phil nodded, pursing foamy lips.

'Very good. Thanks to Beti, isn't it Barry?' He nudged the boy, but Barry hunched his shoulders, sitting a little lower into his seat. There was an awkward silence, Phil and Tom glancing at each other across Barry's closed profile, his bleak, inward gaze. A chill, a sort of dull anxiety, communicated itself to Phil for a moment, oppressing him. He shook his head sharply.

'Any more trips to Spain?'

'Different type of sheep-dip?'

Phil and Tom had both started to speak at the same moment. Tom went on: 'All this about organo-phosphates? Are you going to stop using the dip? I heard the Ministry are bringing in a test; you'll have to take a written exam, show you're competent to use the stuff. Ridiculous to me. It's either safe or it isn't.'

Phil mimed brain damage, screwing shut one eye, lolling his head, his mouth hanging open as he gargled the words: 'What's wrong with the stuff then? Never did me any harm'.

Barry smiled thinly, as though listening to a conversation in a foreign language.

'It does them good,' he said. 'I'd never use it if it was hurting them, but you can see them all the better for it.'

Phil glanced at Tom, who stooped his head down into his beer, avoiding catching his eye. The door from the street slammed shut on its spring as someone came into the bar. Phil looked round, and his chest seemed to clutch tight, as though he'd breathed in a blast of smoke. The dark-haired girl, the student, walked over and leaned against the bar, one foot up on the rail.

Tom Wood was saying something which Phil didn't catch as he scraped his chair half round away from the table to face back into the bar. At the noise, the girl glanced in their direction momentarily, then turned back to the bar. She was wearing a sort of waistcoat, bright yellow, and jeans. The two didn't quite meet, and there was a silky swell of biscuit-coloured skin between them. Phil felt his heart turn over.

'Load to Burgos next week. I hope that turns into a regular job. There's a real market in Spain for the little Welsh lambs.'

The girl pushed coins across the counter as the barman reached down a packet of cigarettes. Barry was speaking: 'They say they like the lambs smaller the better in Spain, is it? Mam says.' His voice faltered and stopped. Phil turned towards him; then, out of the corner of his eye he saw the girl wriggle the cigarettes into the pocket of her jeans and walk out of the pub. The door slammed again behind her.

'What they'd really like is an 18 kilo lamb.' Tom was explaining to Barry, gesturing with both hands. 'But they're starting to take

25, 26 kilos.'

Phil stood up, tipping back the last of his beer, wiping the back of his hand across his lips.

'Got to go. I'll see you next time boys.' He was aware of their startled expressions following him out of the bar as he stood for a moment in the High Street, blinking in the sunlight. A moment later he set off up the street at a sort of skipping run, half trot, half walk.

'Hello, excuse me! Hello!'

She stopped and turned towards him, her face for a moment blank with fright. He made a kind of 'I surrender' gesture, hands up, palms towards her, and the startled look faded as she reached for a canvas bag that was slung over her shoulder. Had she forgotten something in the pub? She saw a young man, beaming at her. He was nice-looking, sort of warm and clean, not at all threatening.

'I saw you a couple of weeks ago, by the old college building, you had some leaflets, I was getting a magazine for my little boy.' He was gabbling, he knew it, but he pressed on. 'Wanted to ask you about the protests, about the live exports and all that. Are you busy? Where are you going? Can I come with you?'

Close to, her hair was full of colours, the spiky tips reddish, beneath which it was dense and dark. It looked brilliant. She obviously didn't remember him at all.

'Hang on!' She spoke sharply, but she was smiling.

They were passing the little street where he'd parked the tractor, the end of the road filled by the bare, grey front of Bethesda chapel, as gaunt and empty as an engine shed.

'Have you got far to go? Is that bag heavy? Do you want a lift?'

'No. I'm going to the library. There's no problem.'

'But that's miles! I can give you a lift. Look, it's right here!'

When she saw the tractor, she laughed out loud.

'Is this yours? You're joking! Are you a farmer? Are you really?'

She shook her head, grinning, looking from Phil to the tractor, and back again.

'You're kidding, aren't you?'

Phil was laughing.

'No, really, jump in, it's really comfortable, it's not dirty or anything.'

He opened the cab door and made an extravagant gesture with a sweep of his arm.

'Please.'

She looked at the tractor; the cab was almost entirely glass, windscreen, doors; only the roof was solid, and even there a hatch in the padded ceiling stood open, letting the light stream in. You could see right through it. It was completely open and full of light. She never would have got into a car or a van, dark, enclosed, potentially dangerous, but this was different somehow; and he looked like a nice boy, innocent, like someone's brother. She threw her bag up into the cab and climbed up the steps into the jockey seat. She slammed the glass door, then opened it again, just to check.

'This is a personal first, I can tell you that much. You're really a *farmer*, are you?' In her London accent, with its drawling inflection, the word sounded both exotic and ludicrous.

In the Black Ox, Tom gave Barry an uneasy look. He couldn't think of anything to say. He hadn't wanted to come for a drink in the first place. What on earth was Phil doing, getting them in here, then buggering off like that? He finished his beer, dribbling some down his chin. He felt it trickle beneath his shirt collar. He got to his feet, thoroughly irritable.

'Better be off. Good to see you Barry.'

They shook hands, Barry half rising. As the other man left the bar, he sank back into his seat. The lorries would have got back to Graig Goch by now. Huw and Alwyn wouldn't know where the lambs were to go. They'd go to the house to ask. Mam would . . .

He sighed deeply, squeezing his eyes shut.

The tractor had been parked in the shade and the cab wasn't hot, but Phil turned the blowers on anyway, and cool air rushed at them from ducts above the windscreen, ruffling the girl's hair. He pushed a cassette into the slot, and the sugary whine of a steel guitar formed silvery layers within the moving air.

'Very cool.'

He glanced quickly at her as he worked the tractor out into the High Street. There was a drawn-out, nasal quality to her voice that could have been contempt, but her smile was friendly, teasing, and he smiled back, his heart giving a sort of flip, like a fish.

'You're at college here?'

She nodded, watching him as he drove. He was wearing a faded denim work-shirt, the sleeves rolled up, cords of muscle moving in his fore-arms. There was a downy line of sweat on his upper lip. As usual, the High Street was half-choked with parked cars, and he had to concentrate as he picked his way between them. Up ahead, a cattle-lorry flashed its lights, waiting for him to come on, and he speeded up, double-shuffling into top with a sharp roar of throttle, working the gear-shift stiffly between his thighs.

'You like it here?'

'College is alright. Funny town, though. What does everybody *do* with themselves?'

He looked at her, again expecting to see disdain in her face, finding merely an amusement that seemed almost affectionate. She was sitting awkwardly on the edge of the jockey seat, steadying herself with an arm raised to the grab-handle above her, swaying a little as the tractor swung through the traffic. Their eyes met, their glances locking for a moment, then disengaging. They felt intensely aware of each other for a long moment, which she broke by wiggling and shuffling a packet of cigarettes out of her jeans.

'Want one of these? I'm Nicky, by the way'.

She produced a cigarette lighter, hooking it out of her back pocket, lifting herself off the seat with a movement that made Phil blink. He had a chilly, lucid moment, his attention jumping back to the traffic, as he avoided a LandRover. Her fingers brushed against his as she handed him the lighter. After the roundabout the High Street widened into Paxton Hill, a long gentle slope, tree-lined, the War Memorial at the top. The university library was halfway up on the left, a grey modern building, set back from a row of big old Victorian town houses, now mostly divided up into student flats.

'You could drop me here. I got to take these books back.'

She looked at him as she spoke, nodding her head, her lips pursed, amused.

'And thanks a lot. That was good fun as it happens.'

'Couldn't we, what about, have you got time for a drink or something?'

'Not really'.

He looked so stricken, so instantly bereft, that she relented almost without hesitating.

'Tell you what, come and have a coffee. My flat's just up here. Park up there, past the yellow lines. I'll drop these books off.'

She had the odd sense that she was dealing with a child, or comforting some lost dog, some big soft thing, warm and sad.

He followed her to her front door, up a short flight of cracked and weedy brick steps as she fiddled with the key in the lock. She led him down a dim corridor, past closed brown doors, into a kitchen at the back of the house. Everything was a sort of beige colour, the walls blotched with damp. The sink was full of washing up, and there was a fellow there, crouched down, peering into the cupboard under the draining board. He turned towards them, straightening up, and Phil recognised the guy who'd hit him in the pub that time. He was big, bony, a sort of raw look about him like something hanging in a butchers shop, long red hair twisted into stringy dreadlocks.

'I don't know where the fucking thing is.'

He gave Phil a long stare out of very pale blue eyes, red-rimmed, then pushed past them and left the room. An open door led out into a garden, quite big, rather overgrown, a copper beech at the far end. Shafts of sunlight lay across a shaggy lawn. Nicky gave him a push towards the door.

'Go on out there. It's better than this pigsty.'

She brought out cups of coffee and sat beside him on a rusting cast-iron bench.

'So. You got cows, or what?'

He nodded.

'Mostly sheep, but we got some sucklers as well.'

'What? What are sucklers then? Oh I know; pigs, aren't they?'

'No, they're beef cows. We sell the weaned calves.'

'Well blimey.' She shook her head, laughing at him. 'I'm none the wiser. You sure sucklers aren't pigs?'

She was making fun of him, but it felt good, intimate; her laughter seemed to penetrate him, rushing through his body like a river running over a stony bed.

He shifted on the bench, turning sideways to face her. She grinned at him, very close for a moment, then turned away, staring into the middle distance of the garden. The size of the bench meant that they were sitting tight together, almost touching at the hip. The sunlight magnified and illuminated every detail. He could see the down on her cheek and a faint moisture of coffee on her lower lip. He felt an immense tension, an explosive awareness that was like falling. He took a gulp of coffee. It was much hotter than he'd expected, and he burnt his tongue. He crammed a fist to his mouth, spluttering with pain, and spilling more of the damn stuff on to his leg.

'Are you alright?'

He nodded, his eyes streaming. The kitchen door opened, and the red-headed bloke leaned out into the garden, then took a step or two onto the lawn.

'Oy Nick, are you coming?'

His voice had a blocked-up sound, adenoidal. Phil couldn't place his accent, some sort of London, he supposed, maybe Birmingham. He was full of jittery movement, drumming his hand on the side of his jeans, his leg jigging from the knee in a stiff and rapid twitch.

'I'll catch you up. You go on.'

The boy squeezed his face into a sneering frown, turned and left.

A kind of panic rushed at Phil. He wanted to have her *now*. Well, anyway, he wanted to make her laugh. He wanted to see her again. She seemed to be waiting for him to say something; at any rate she wasn't getting up and going.

'Do you go, do you go?' he was *stuttering*, for christs sake!

'Do you often go to the Black Ox?' She looked blankly at him, and he went on:

'The pub you went in for cigarettes; just now, that's where I saw you.'

Her lips turned down in exaggerated distaste:

'God no! Far too many farmers.'

'Do you mind!'

'You know what I mean. They're all old in there. It's dark, and it smells. There's no music. It's a horrible place! You'd have to *be* a farmer to want to go in there.' She poked a finger at his chest as she said this and he leaned back on the angular old bench, immediately comforted.

'So where do you go then, or don't you go to pubs?'

'Course I do.' She looked at him, seeming to hesitate. 'The Star most often, I suppose. Do you know it?'

He nodded, meeting her look. He had a feeling that a sign had been exchanged between them, then almost immediately doubted it. Nicky got up.

'Listen I've got to go. I'm late already as it happens.' She turned back, smiling, as though anticipating what he was about to say.

'And I don't need a lift, it's just around the corner. I'll walk this time.'

They were standing on the pavement, about to go in opposite directions, and Phil was furiously framing questions in his head.

'Can I see you again?'

Bugger! He hadn't meant to say that; he sounded like a maniac! He plunged on, piling words on top of each other, feeling like a conjuror who's trick has gone wrong, rabbits everywhere.

'What I mean, I mean could we have a drink, I could buy you a drink sometime, we could meet in the Star like, if you like, we could have a drink. What about Saturday night?' At last, a question without the word drink in it. He must sound like an alcoholic.

'What *about* Saturday night?'

He was about to start all over again, but she cut him short. She had given him a look, appraising, tilting her head and looking at him slightly sideways. She started to move away, then turned back:

'Saturday night. I'll meet you in the Star. Nine o'clock. Alright?'

He watched her swing down the street for a moment, light and pliant, but the next time he turned, she'd disappeared; she must have gone down a side-street. The long sweep of Paxton Hill stretched away emptily below him. He walked back to the tractor.

Tom Wood rang him that evening, wanting to know if he could tag lambs the next day for a load that was going late at night. They wouldn't need to start till tea-time. He agreed, realising as he put the phone down, that he hadn't checked with Liz. He didn't know what shift she was working tomorrow, or whether she'd be back in time to collect Eddy from school. He wandered into the kitchen, where he had a bad-tempered conversation with Liz. She was having a hard time at work; they kept wanting her to work extra shifts. In fact, it was her day off tomorrow; she was offended that Phil didn't know that, and annoyed that he had made an arrangement without talking to her first. He watched some rugby on TV; when he came up to bed, Liz was already asleep.

At Graig Goch the next day, Tom Wood was in a bad mood. Phil had turned up half an hour earlier than he'd been asked to, but when they met in the yard, Tom glared at him, glancing at his watch as though he'd been kept waiting.

'I don't suppose you know where the lambs are?'

Phil shook his head.

'Beti's gone off somewhere. I assume she's got the lambs gathered, but she never told me where. No one about. Where the hell is Huw anyway? It'll be dark soon.'

He was leaning on his car, drumming his fingers on the roof. The car was filthy, and when he straightened up, he saw that he'd streaked the front of his shirt with grime. He wiped his fist down it, smearing the dirt further, looking at Phil as though it was his fault. Eventually they found Huw. He'd been sleeping on a pile of silage bales, and when he finally heard them calling, looked down at them from the top of the stack, raising a head so crumpled with sleep, so puffy and rumpled, bleary and dribbling like an old, old dog, that they both found themselves snorting with embarrassed laughter.

Huw wanted his tea before starting work; the old lady served him and Beti's son Barry with plates of stew from a pot on the back of the stove.

Barry looked awful, pale and sweating. He didn't say a word to them as he ate his supper, and left the room as soon as he'd finished, the old lady sighing and muttering as she collected the plates. It was dark by the time they set off to fetch the lambs. Tom Wood stayed in the house, trying to reach Beti on the phone. They had a long way to bring the lambs, but there were high hedges all the way, and the dogs knew what they were doing. There was a faint luminescence, a silvery sheen on things by which they could find their way about, and the shed itself was brilliantly lit by neon tubes. Tom came back when they'd sorted through about half the lambs, and they took a break.

'These aren't going to the regular boys then, what are they called?'

'Prevost? No. We've had some problems with them. They owe us a lot of money. Think the bank will pay us, but it's been two weeks. Haven't paid us yet.'

His voice faded to a kind of inward mumble, and Phil couldn't tell whether he was being talked to or not. Huw gave a huge yawn, flapping flecks of spit from his lips as he shook his head. Phil looked at his watch.

'What time's the lorry coming for these lambs then?'

Tom was still muttering to himself about banks and money, but now he turned his attention to Phil:

'About half ten, eleven o'clock?' He looked at his watch. 'See, the Dover boat goes at six tomorrow evening. So, if they leave here at midnight, get up to the lairage for seven in the morning, they got nine, ten hours rest before they have to move again.'

He got up, stretching, shaking the circulation back into his legs.

'Could turn into a regular thing. How would you be fixed for working in the night like this?'

Phil nodded, pursing his lips.

'Could be.'

'Good. There should be a load Friday or Saturday night. I'll let you know'.

It was after midnight when he got home. He didn't have his key with him, and Liz had locked the house. When he finally woke her, flicking pieces of gravel up at the bedroom window, she let him in without a word, white, as though sleep-walking.

At breakfast the next morning she was still angry; he explained about the timing of the Dover boat. He told her that Tom Wood was desperate to have him work nights from time to time and, with a vertiginous sense of deceit as he passed into outright untruth, that they would be discussing a much better rate of pay. He said they couldn't afford for him not to do it. As he was saying this he caught Eddy's eye. The little boy was staring at him, a spoonful of cereal halfway to his lips.

'Look out Ed, you're going to spill that. See, what did I tell you!'

He spent the next two days fencing a section of the boundary, down by the river. The fence there must have been at least thirty years old, done by his dad, before he was born; the wire had oxidised to a rusty, fragile web, and the posts had rotted to mossy stumps and fragments. The work needed doing, but maybe not in the bitter hurry with which he attacked it, the sledge-hammer swinging in whistling arcs that ended in a juddering shock, driving the post into the gravelly soil and running back like electricity through his body. He tore his clothes and his hands on barbed wire, cutting back the undergrowth, the chainsaw roaring through thorns and brambles. On the surface of his mind he was pacing out distances, calculating angles and quantities; a little deeper down, he was conducting an argument, a sort of court-room scene. At a much lower level, in wordless recesses at which he scarcely glanced, he knew that this debate was in bad faith, the outcome certain, the course already laid. He intended to see her on Saturday, and whatever happened next, he didn't think he'd be telling Liz about it. When Tom asked him to work on Saturday night, he agreed at once. He couldn't stay late though; he'd have to leave by half past eight.

Between eleven and eleven thirty on Saturday night, every erotic fantasy that Phil had ever had was erased, burned out of him, flaring up in a series of incandescent flashes like magnesium in a flame. He felt that his senses had been scorched, that images had been fired permanently onto the glaze of his eyes. Now the light had dimmed and softened; it was amber-coloured, like sand dunes, silky drifts and billows as she lay beside him, floating. He was flat on his back, in her bed, with a head full of peaches. Somewhere inside him was a person who wanted to punch into the air, raising a stiff, right-angled fist in the gesture of the sports field – *Yes!* – but he resisted.

He had got to the Star a little after nine, not really late at all, although flickers of anxiety and desire were licking at him. It had not been easy to get away from Graig Goch. By half past eight they were barely half way though the lambs, and in the end he'd had to promise Alwyn a tenner if he'd stay on with Huw and finish the work in his place.

He hadn't been in the Star for ten years at least. It had been a teenager's pub in his day; now it was brighter and noisier than ever, the huge space fragmented into shards and angles by music and mirrors. He stood in the doorway for a moment or two, his senses adjusting to the tumult. The double-sided bar, pillared and roofed, lit much more brightly than the rest of the room, spotlights glaring down from the panelled canopy above, encrusted with glasses and bottles, winking and gleaming like some cave in a tropical ocean, like an aquarium, formed a sort of corridor through the middle of the room, dividing it into three. As you came off the street you were confronted with the leading edge of the bar, and there was an area of stools and little tables here. Then on either side, the two main wings of the room receded in smoky dimness towards the back wall of the pub. The whole place was packed and roaring. There were three people working the bar, two girls and a boy, moving about in the intensely lit space like fish behind glass.

He got to the bar and ordered a pint, leaning on the counter, one foot on the rail. He'd worn overalls at Graig Goch, which he'd left in the van, but he realised his clothes weren't very clean even so, and looking down he saw that the tread on his work-boots had dropped lozenges of sheep-shit, like sections of chocolate bar, onto the carpet. He couldn't see anyone he recognised. The part of the pub he was in, at the front of the bar by the double doors that led onto the street, was not particularly crowded; six or eight students, a couple ordering drinks, three of them crouched intently round a tiny iron table, heads almost touching. A dull roar of sound swelled, filtered, from the depths of the room beyond. Across the brightness of the bar, through on the other side, he could sense dim masses of people, a solid crowd which constantly pushed elbows and shoulders out of the shadows into the vivid slot of light at the counter.

He felt a vast reluctance at the thought of entering these areas of the pub, and decided to finish his pint and start another one before making a move. Eventually, holding his beer protectively against his chest, he shuffled sideways along the bar between customers until he was looking down the length of the left side of the room. It wasn't quite as crowded as it had seemed. There was a darts board at the far end with a little group of players around it; halfway along the wall a big CD juke-box jutted out into the room, music bulging and thumping out of it. There were eight or ten people leaning on the bar, and about the same number sitting at three or four small tables. Everybody there seemed to be a student. Half a dozen faces turned towards him as his glance skimmed uneasily round the room, but none of them was Nicky's. He retreated.

On the other side of the bar, two doors in the back wall led to the toilets and there was a constant circulation in and out of these. The rest of the room was mostly taken up by an enormous table, a huge polished thing that could have sat thirty people round it. There were about a dozen students, most of them men, only a couple of girls, sitting in a sort of semi-circle, a loose group, half together, half separate, at the further end. At the head of the table, leaning back in a big armchair that didn't look like it belonged in a pub at all, was the red-headed boy that Phil had last seen at Nicky's flat.

The music reduced everything to mime and gesture, but watching them, it seemed to Phil that the red-head was doing most of the talking, the rest of them forming a sort of audience. As he looked across, he felt an increasing sense of power, presence, a crude but intense concentration as the boy leaned forward, pointing, jabbing a finger, throwing himself back in the chair eyes shut, grinning; heaving forward again, chin jutting, his fists white on the arms of the chair.

The music stopped, and their voices bloomed outward in a rabble of sound that expanded into the room like fireworks.

'No bloody good at all!'

'Easy to say. What about them?'

'Bollocks!'

Phil could hear the red-headed bloke's voice cutting clearly through the others: 'There's no economic necessity for it. It's as simple as that'. He looked round the group at the table with a kind of triumphant sneer, shaking his head with an air of ironic superiority. A fellow standing at the bar was calling out:

'Harris, hey Harris! Do you want a drink?'

He looked up, nodding, not breaking off from the conversation.

'It's between what people have to do, and what they *choose* to do' he said, with the same tone of contemptuous finality.

Funny name, Phil was thinking. *Harris,* what is that, a surname? He was wearing a T-shirt with an unreadable slogan across the chest, and over it a great wool or tweed overcoat, dark blue, like something you'd find in a skip. His hair was twisted into a short pony-tail so tightly that it seemed to be tugging at the corners of eyes that were red-rimmed, the lashes so pale that you could hardly see them. He was repulsive and fascinating. Phil must have been staring, because at that moment Harris looked up as though becoming aware of being watched, and their eyes locked. A record came on, the music separating the two of them in a blizzard of sound, but it had been Phil who'd looked away first. He had nodded his head in an ambivalent gesture, not sure whether Harris's look was one of recognition or challenge, then turned and asked for another pint.

Once, though, he was sure they were talking about him, Harris glancing sharply at him, then leaning forward and saying something to a couple of the boys nearest him, the three of them putting their heads together, forming a sort of nest out of which he distinctly saw Harris's pale eyes peering at him. A wave of heat passed through Phil, rising up through his body and out at the top of his head. That bastard wouldn't catch him a second time; it's easy enough to knock someone down if they're not ready for it. He glared hard at the students for a moment, then swivelled away on the barstool. He caught sight of himself, flushed and angry, in the mirror behind the bar and took a couple of deep breaths, and a long swallow of beer, his teeth clicking on the glass. Someone tapped him on the shoulder, fingers brushing against the side of his neck, and he jerked himself round on the stool, hunching up, his fists clenching. When he saw it was Nicky, he was flooded with delight. He had spun off the stool to his feet almost on top of her, pressed up against her for a moment till she took a step back laughing.

She had wanted to sit at the table, joining the group around Harris. He had caught her by the elbow, turning her towards him; he wanted to be alone with her, not sure how to manage it. He brought their drinks to the far end of the table, away from the students. She hesitated, seeming to glance between Harris and him, and then sat down beside him. There was a speaker from the juke-box on the wall above them and the music roared around them like waves on the beach, the surf racing up the sand then dragging the shingle back through your toes as though the ground was falling away below you, a sensation of being isolated and enclosed together, their heads almost touching as they tried to make themselves heard in the howling eye of sound, his lips brushing against her ear as he bellowed at her. He succeeded in making her laugh, and she leaned her forehead on his shoulder for a moment in a gesture that was both intimate and casual. Whenever the music stopped a kind of buzzing silence, crackling with electric possibilities, seemed to descend on them like a bell-jar. It seemed to Phil that a spotlight shone down on the two of them, illuminating and exclusive, a circle of brightness ringed by incoherent shadows.

'So what do you think?' She lit a cigarette and blew a stream of smoke above his head.

'What do I think? I better not tell you.'

'About this place I mean. Better than your old farmers pub ain't it?'

He grinned back at her: 'Too many students. Us farmers have got to stick together.'

'*Stick* together is right; mucky old buggers. Not you though.' She looked at him. 'Anyway, you're too pretty to be a farmer.' Then, laughing at him, poking her finger at him: '*And* farmers don't blush!'

'I'm not blushing.'

'Yes you are. Anyway, you're not old. That's something.'

'Too old to be a Young Farmer'.

'Too young to be an old one.'

'Nicky! Here a minute!' Harris was calling to her from the other end of the table, and she got up and went over. A record came on and the music descended into the room, obliterating speech. Phil watched the two of them, Harris lounging in his chair, Nicky standing at the table in the leather jacket that was too big for her, hands deep in her pockets. Harris leaned forward to say something, and Phil saw the girl stiffen and sway back, her body tensing instantly, pulling her hand out of her pocket and making a short and violent gesture, a raised finger at his face. She came back to Phil, shaking her head in anger and disbelief.

'That bastard! He's unbelievable sometimes.'

'What was that about? What did he say to you? Do you want me to?' She shook her head, lighting another cigarette with clumsy fingers. She blew out smoke in a short, irritated exhalation, half cough, half laugh.

'No, nothing. He doesn't think I should be doing this.'

'Doing what?'

'Exactly.'

She looked back at Harris, her features drawn fine with anger, the light running over smooth planes and hollows of forehead, cheekbone, the line of her jaw. Her eyes were glistening, though whether with emotion or cigarette smoke, Phil wasn't sure. Looking down the length of the table, it was obvious that Harris and his friends were talking about them. The orientation of the group had changed, and though they remained a kind of audience, their focus of attention had turned towards Phil and Nicky. Somewhat behind them, partly obscured, and hooded in cigarette smoke, Harris seemed to be urging them silently on, a malign presence orchestrating their emotions. Nicky had exchanged another hot and bitter look with Harris, shaking her head and stubbing out her cigarette.

'Stupid bastard.'

She reached over and took his wrist.

'Listen. Let's get out of here. Let's go somewhere.'

Now he was lying on his back, beached on the shore line, drowsy ripples lapping at him, a memory of undulation. She lay on her side against him, pressed close, so that he was sleepily aware of the moist touch of her breast, her ribs like the corrugations of sand under the water, the subtle rise of stomach dipping to where she pushed a faint scratchiness against his skin, a bump of hipbone, the sandy length of her legs down to where her toes stirred like little crabs. She leaned up on one elbow, tracing lines on his chest with her fingertip in a precise and dreamy pattern like the plan of an operation, frowning with a sort of distracted concentration.

'So how come you've got a little boy then?'

'Well, you know. These things happen.'

'I mean, you married, or what?'

'Well, not exactly.'

She jabbed a fingernail sharply at him:

'What exactly does *not exactly* mean?'

'It means – '

He rolled towards her, burying his face into the hollow of her shoulder, his chin bumping over her collar bone.

'That scratches! You need a shave!'

In his muffled and amorous state he couldn't at first identify the fusillade of confused noise that suddenly racketed into the room from the corridor outside, a barrage of thumps and crashes pierced by sharp cries and baffled shouting. It was only when Nicky sat convulsively up in bed, reaching out and rummaging her head into a T-shirt, the folds of white cotton slipping down deliriously over winking glimpses of nipples, that the sounds formed themselves into meaning and he was instantly engulfed in terror, waves of disorientation breaking over him. Someone was banging on the front door, and calling out his name. Something dreadful had happened. Had someone followed him here? What time was it? His heart was kicking at his ribs as he rolled off the edge of the bed with a sob, falling forever into the blackness of his betrayal and despair. On his hands and knees, he looked up.

'Bugger! Bugger!'

Nicky was hopping across the room on one leg, cursing, as she squirmed into her jeans. She turned back to him, the corners of her mouth pulled down in humorous regret.

'Sorry. That was about to be fun, wasn't it? *Hang on!*' She left the room, tugging on her zip, and Phil could hear her in the corridor, calling out again:

'Hang on will you! Is that you Harris? What the fuck?'

Phil heard her rattling the lock of the front door as he stumbled into his clothes, mopping up shirt, socks, jeans from the floor, erasing the map of his frantic earlier journey into her bed. His head was clearing, and the banging of his heart had eased to a dull thudding. He heard Nicky and Harris walk down the corridor to the kitchen.

'What you going on for? Forgot my key, that's all. Were you asleep?'

Shoving the tail of his shirt into his jeans with stiff fingers, Phil followed them down the corridor. Harris was at the sink, filling a kettle from the tap. His eyes travelled with elaborate slowness up Phil's body as he stood in the doorway, from his socks up to his ruffled hair. Then he turned back to the sink, screwing off the flow of water.

'I see,' he said.

Nicky came over and took Phil's elbow, leading him further into the room, parking him by the table as you might a blind man. She sat on the edge of the table, leaning slightly towards him, her body's vocabulary so warm and kind that he felt a flush of gratitude. Harris had made himself a coffee, which he was now stirring with a fidgeting rattle of the spoon. He shrugged his shoulders out of the overcoat, letting it fall to the floor at his feet, then stooping to throw it on to a chair the other side of the room, its dusty folds flapping past Phil, who had to lean back to avoid it.

'So, mister I don't know what your name is, how's it going? How many animals have you exploited this week?'

Phil stared at him. Harris's build was peculiar; both very big, and very thin. His reddish skin seemed stretched over a skeleton that was massive enough without the padding of any fat or musculature. He looked leathery and immensely strong; he looked like wherever you hit him you'd skin your knuckles. Nicky slid off the table and took a couple of steps towards him, stiff, snapping with anger.

'What the fuck's the matter with you Harris? What are you fucking *on*?'

She was on the balls of her feet, bristling, and he took a step back, fetching up against the sink.

'Nothing the matter with me Nicky, it's *you*. What's *your* problem? What are you *doing* with this animal exploiter?'

'What are you *talking* about?'

Phil opened his mouth, then shut it again as Harris went on:

'This guy does live exports; he packs lambs into lorries and sends them god knows where.'

Nicky turned to stare at Phil as Harris spoke, his voice rising in irritation and scorn:

'You don't even remember, do you? In that pub out of town, what's it

73

called? He came up and tried to start a fight.'

'It wasn't me started a fight.'

Nicky was laughing in a sort of horrified way.

'Oh Gawd! Was that really you? I was pretty stoned.'

Phil dragged a hand through his hair:

'This is ridiculous. For a start I just been doing some work for somebody; it's just a job, you know? Anyway, you lot have got it all wrong.'

Harris slopped the dregs from his mug into the sink with a slap that fired beads of coffee across the draining board. He crossed the room to the door, pausing to push his face at Phil:

'Don't bother trying to convert me, mate. Save your breath for *her*.'

Phil and Nicky looked at each other across the empty room. He didn't know what he was doing here. The clock on the wall said one o'clock, but it couldn't be that, surely to god? What could he say to Liz? He must smell of beer. He'd have to say he'd gone for a pint with the boys after they'd finished the lambs. Liz had never met Huw or Alwyn, and there was no reason why she should in the near future; he could say he'd gone with them. His mind flicked through the possibilities, the calculus of deceit.

'You alright? You look awful.'

'I better go. Think my boots are in your room.' So long as he didn't get breathalysed.

'Do you have to? Don't worry about Harris; he's not, you know, there's nothing.'

She looked at him thoughtfully:

'Do you really work for an exporter? Don't you worry about it sometimes?'

His watch was in his pocket; he must have put it there when they were tagging the lambs. It really was one o'clock. One fifteen, in fact. Oh Jesus!

'I've got to go. I don't do anything cruel you know. I've been around sheep all my life. The newspapers and the TV, they get hold of something. If you ever came up to Graig Goch, you'd see.'

'Graig Goch?'

'Beti's place; where the lambs go from.'

At the front door, she got hold of his shirt collar with both hands, pulling him down towards her.

'Listen, don't disappear. What's your phone number anyway?'

He gaped at her for a moment, shaking his head, trying to clear it.

'I'll give you mine' she said. 'Have you got a pen?'

She walked with him to the van, where she wrote down her number on the back of an envelope.

'Don't disappear now,' she told him again. 'And don't look so *worried!* We're going to be pals, you know. Something tells me.'

Chapter 7

Tom often wondered how he and Beti managed to work together effectively when their interests and concerns, their personalities and their approach to things seemed hardly ever to coincide. What gave Beti her vigour and drive was a kind of flamboyant carelessness, an optimism that was both ruthless and impulsive. She had a way of saying: 'It's *got* to be!' that Tom had come to know meant both that she would bludgeon events into the shape she wanted them to take, but also that she had made her move, the critical point had been passed, and she would now shut her eyes to any further consequences. She felt that *details* were simply not her problem, that they were little more than distractions from the overall shape of the decision, not, as they were to Tom, a kind of uncontrollable insect-life that would swarm over a project until nothing was left but a collapsed tatter of rags and bones.

The business of the French francs was a good example of this. It had started some time before, on Black Wednesday to be precise. Up to that point Beti had probably never thought about exchange rates. That was on Tom's side of the business. From the beginning, their customers had always paid in their own currencies, so it was crucial when fixing a price to know the exact relationship of the pound at that moment to the franc or the peseta or the D-mark. Then, when the deal was agreed, Tom would sell forward the appropriate amount of foreign currency. When they got the payment three weeks later he would buy back out of the contract and they would get the amount of money that they were expecting, no matter what the exchange rate had done in the meantime. For a long time the rate never changed much anyway. When Britain went into the Exchange Rate Mechanism, Tom *knew* that they had gone in much too high, with a grossly over-valued pound. He was actually trying to work with the damn thing, where the politicians were just theorising about it, driven by nostalgic and sentimental imperatives.

When the process began which proceeded to shake the country out of ERM, a process which Tom visualised as being like that famous piece of film of the suspension bridge in America, a classic example of bad engineering: the wind gets under the bridge somehow and it starts to sway, then to flap and twist and flex, the oscillations becoming more and more violent, feeding on themselves in the bizarre logic of Chaos Theory until the whole thing flies to bits, this process presided over by that buffoonish Chancellor with his seedy grin, his dingy, embarrassed air of a conjuror fallen on hard times and forced to do children's parties (the man who, for a few hours that Wednesday, put interest rates up to *thirty something per cent!* And this shady poseur, Tom thought, *is still in politics!*). When this process unfolded, it simply reinforced Tom's feeling of being governed by full-time, professional idiots. But on Beti it had quite a different effect. It opened her eyes to the magical glamour of the money markets.

She rang Tom up one morning, full of her new idea. They should choose a moment when the pound was low against the franc, and then sell a good chunk of foreign currency. They could then operate within a stable exchange rate while their competitors had to sail up and down the waves of fluctuation in the real world.

'Three or four million francs Tom. That should keep us going for a bit!'

Tom tried to explain to her: how would you know when the pound was low? What were the parameters? Was it at the bottom of the cycle and about to come up, or slipping off the shelf and preparing for a nose-dive into new lows? The principles involved in this sort of thing were the opposite of selling forward for a particular lorry-load of lambs, even though the operations looked so similar. On a single deal, the idea was to take the uncertainty out: they might not gain, but they couldn't lose. It brought another variable in under their control. But this plan of Beti's was the exact opposite; it was just roulette. There was no means of predicting the outcome, or of influencing it.

'If you shift half a million quid when the pound's at 8.5 and it goes straight to 7.0, we're going to feel like real idiots Beti.'

'Ah but Tom!' He could picture Beti's sly look on the other end of the line.

'That's just it Tom! We *wait* till it's 7.0, then we make our move! Simple!'

'If the pound goes to seven against the franc' Tom said, 'for all we know that means it's about to go to *six!*'

They had argued about it ever since, but Beti got her way in the end, and a few months before, on the understanding that Tom was just acting as her advisor, without financial involvement in the deal, they had taken a forward contract for half a million pounds worth of French francs. If nothing else, it was a revelation to Tom to see how easily Beti's bank had agreed to make the money available.

Since then, the pound hadn't moved more than a couple of tenths of a point either way, but for Tom it was another source of worry, low-grade but insistent. It also meant that Beti rang him up every day to see what the exchange rate was doing. She didn't seem able to see that, at least so far, they hadn't gained any advantage at all. When they talked about it she would twinkle and chuckle at Tom, rubbing the side of her nose or clapping her hands together, delighted with herself, filled with a dizzy sense of cunning.

'You see, Tom? Now do you see? You'll have to get up pretty early in the morning to catch *me!*'

In the end, it took the bank three and a half weeks to get the money out of Prevost. No doubt the people at Bristol simply sent the documents out to the French bank and forgot all about it. Tom didn't forget about it for a moment, and it wasn't a happy time for him. He told Beti that everything was in hand, that it was simply a technical matter that would take a couple of weeks to work through. Beti never gave it another thought, but Tom rang the bank in Bristol nearly every day. He had convinced himself, usually late at night, that there were technical loop-holes in the documentation that would allow the French bank and Prevost to slip out of their grasp, clutching the forty thousand pounds, which he could more and more visualize as an object in the real world, usually a leather suitcase, a bit old and scratched, but very solidly stitched, and bulging significantly.

Geoff Ward, the manager at Bristol who had proposed the solution to the problem of the CMRs, was on holiday for most of this period, and Tom was left having to talk to Melanie and her chums.

'The French bank have got the documents' she told him. 'They confirmed that by telex. They'll be looking through them, that's all'.

Her tone was both reassuring and dismissive, as you swat away an importunate child.

'But they've had them for two weeks; they must be up to something?'
'It's all perfectly normal, Tom'.

Melanie was always able to broadcast her sub-text with maximum clarity; he felt he could see the words, winking along at the bottom of the screen like a foreign movie: *You are failing to engage my interest Tom. I really couldn't give a stuff about all this. Why don't you take a flying fuck?*

They didn't seem to have a proper switchboard or system of extensions at Bristol. Tom would get transferred to International Section, but after that, it might be anyone who picked up the phone. He would announce himself, and then hear that sea-shell hissing as someone half-muffled the phone in a cupped hand:

'Melly! It's Tom Wood, for you-hoo!' the words dragged archly out in camp vaudevillean accents, and he would feel sure he had heard a groan before she came on the line. More than once the first voice would come breezing back:

'Melanie seems to have popped out of the office for a minute. Can I help?'

And once, memorably, when he'd finally got her on the line:

'I'm afraid I can't talk now Tom. There's been a bomb scare; they're clearing the building'.

When the money finally did come through, Tom felt no sense of triumph. He felt relief, of course, but it was a bleak, isolated feeling, sour and lonely. He had looked over the edge, where the blackness whistled. He had seen something moving down there that nobody else had seen. Beti never knew how close they'd come to losing the money; in any case the difference between them, which Tom was never able to lose sight of again, was that Beti would have survived the loss of the money, where Tom would have been overwhelmed by the catastrophe, swept away. Once they'd sent the documents in, he didn't discuss it any further with Jan either; but he was sleeping badly, and they had an argument about something nearly every day.

He had a final conversation with Valentin. Neither of them felt like being direct, so they didn't allude to the fact that his company had tried to rip them off for forty grand, and that only the banking system had forced their jaws open in the end. This empty space left a hollow feeling between them. They talked about business, where prices would go this winter, whether the protest movement would get any worse. Next time Tom was in Brittany he must be sure to look him up.

'Salut Valentin.'

'Salut Tom. A la prochaine.'

Tom didn't think there would be a next time. He heard later that Prevost had sacked him soon after.

They lost their most regular contract when they lost Prevost, and somehow Tom never again had as much fun doing business as he had had with Valentin. Also, he never lost the sense that one day it would happen again, and that this time they would not get out of it so easily. He used to wake up quite often from a nightmare, convinced that they had been ripped off again and that he owed Beti twenty grand with no possibility of paying her, and that he was ruined.

Still, in terms of numbers, they were very quickly able to close the gap, and the whole affair moved into the past with surprising speed and finality. Tom had new customers to deal with, and still newer ones to look for. In addition, the protest movement took a sudden step closer. When B & F finally banned all livestock from their cross-channel boats, it was as though, fiddling with a powerful telescope, you suddenly correct the focus and something highly detailed, complicated but obscure, stands revealed.

In some ways it was a development that was easy to shrug off. The move was not really unexpected; B & F had been threatening a ban all summer. They were chiefly famous for the disaster across the Channel where they had lost a boat, an event which had made the inevitable progression from tragedy to farce, so that even Alwyn could joke about not trusting the lambs to their boats, or suggest they load the lambs in upside down. Their spokesmen were PR disasters: rat-faced characters who dressed like race-course spivs. Their welfare credentials were plainly bogus: they were terrified at the prospect of competition from the Tunnel, anxious to appease the peevish queues of caravans and holidaymakers, and had also allowed themselves to be intimidated by threats from the more violent side of the protest movement. Above all, there were plenty of other ferry companies.

Nevertheless, it was a turning point of sorts. For one thing, it was *news*; it was a genuine event, which the wretched TV journalists could use to justify their incessant banging of the drum, their endless reiteration of the same polemic, illustrated with the same loop of wrongly attributed film. As a result, the whole subject moved inevitably out of the field of minority interest into the great mindless arena of public debate where the tabloid papers roamed like fabulous beasts at a Roman circus.

It became something that people wanted to talk about. This was rather odd; Tom had come to think of the business primarily as a means of making a living, a technical matter, and now everyone he met wanted to discuss basic principles, the morality, the romance, the political pressures. He developed a little talk, for use in pubs and shops, on the equity and simplicity of the arrangements; how the lambs didn't suffer; how both British and French interests benefited from the trade. Related issues emerged naturally: the importance of the EC, especially to Wales with its vast hinterland of livestock; the essentially urban, *English* nature of the protest movement; the notion – inspiring, poetic – of a Europe of the Regions. Of course, these discussions were local, with people he knew, with people from an agricultural background of one sort or another. Further afield you could sense a movement, a faint restless swell, an attitude that, however ignorant and misinformed, was above all hostile.

In Llanfrychan High Street one market day, he counted six posters advertising a meeting to protest against live exports. There was a photo, dark and badly reproduced, of a miserable looking lamb that no European buyer would have given a penny for, and a block of text below it. He had stopped and was stooping to read this, when somebody bumped into him. The person apologised, and Tom looked round to see that it was Phil Jones.

'Seen these? Who's been putting these up?'

Perhaps his tone of voice was rather sharp and irritable; Phil looked startled, as though he'd been accused him something. He leaned down to look more closely at the poster.

'Doesn't say, does it?'

'Students, I suppose. Yes, of course it is, look the meeting's being held in College Square.'

Phil was still looking uneasy: 'Doesn't have to be students.'

'Well it wasn't me and Beti for christs sake!'

This came out sounding much ruder than Tom had intended. Phil was a nice boy and a good worker, and he hadn't meant to offend him. They started to walk along the High Street.

'Where you going Phil? Got time for a drink? You OK for the load on Friday?'

He didn't want a drink, but he said he could manage Friday, and they walked along in silence while Tom tried to think of something friendly to say, both of them looking at the pavement.

'Phil! Phil!'

They both looked up. An old green Escort van had pulled up to the kerb. The door opened and a girl got out, calling again to Phil. She was very attractive, and Tom had a feeling he had seen her before. In his dreams, no doubt. Phil had hurried over to her, and they were standing talking, their faces very close, both of them lit with that glistening, ecstatic, unmistakable grin. Tom felt a stab of envy so sharp and real that he drew in his breath: *The bastard's sleeping with her!*

'I'll see you later Phil'. He patted him awkwardly on the shoulder, and the other man nodded with a grunt, not even looking round. The girl's eyes flickered blindly across Tom's face for a second. He walked on down the High Street in the grip of a rising irritation, stamping along in the rhythm of a bad mood, his heels digging into the pavement.

It was infuriating to think that right here in Llanfrychan, in the middle of a market town whose whole economy was dependent on farming, these bloody students, half of them English and the rest so corrupted by urban English values that they'd lost all sense of their own culture's needs and realities, felt free to plaster their propaganda all over the place. It was an insult to tolerance. And he felt let down by Phil; he was paying him twenty pounds for every load of lambs he tagged, so the French business had increased his income by sixty or eighty quid a week. And yet he could hardly be bothered to glance at the poster; from the way he was looking at that girl, he was a lot more interested in cheating on his wife. Just another cowboy, really, living in a world of shotguns and chainsaws, diesel, country music and cheap emotion; seedy, threatening, going nowhere.

By the time Tom got to the car, he had calmed down a little. He had been feeling more irritable with Phil than with whoever had put up the posters. And the reason was simple enough; for a moment, seeing him with the girl was like being given a violent shove, a flat-handed jolt in the chest that knocks you back in your tracks, a thump from the terminals of jealousy and dissatisfaction. *What a fox! It's not fair! What's he got that I haven't?* He ticked the points off on his fingers as he sat in the traffic in the High Street: better looking; healthier; getting on for twenty years younger. How old was Phil? Twenty seven, twenty eight? A good-looking boy. He hoped he wasn't messing up his family life, but that was his look-out, nobody else's.

Walking down the street with him, Tom had felt like his contemporary, and he realised once again that keeping in mind the passage of time is like doing mental arithmetic; you have to stay alert and remember constantly where you are and where you've been. The slightest lapse, and a decade will slide out of the calculation, it's loss contaminating all the values around it. It isn't a failure of memory. He could account for all the stages of his life, from the years in London, and the struggles with his father about his career, through the moment when his grandfather's will left him the place and raised the giddy possibility of chucking it all up and going back to Wales; then getting this business started with Beti, that strand weaving in and out of his life with Jan, the childlessness that they no longer talked about.

All the elements of the calculation are there, and yet the answer feels wrong. Ten years have been lost, somehow. Not all from one place; a little here and a little there, the wheels slipping slightly, a loss of purchase from time to time. You add up the figures, and the answer is clear: you are getting middle-aged, and ugly, and your health is going to pieces. Soon your brains will turn to sand and run out of your ears like some old mummy, unravelled at last. But inside, you feel cheated; a decade has slipped away with nothing to show for it. And that's when you are doing the sums, concentrating. Worse when you are not thinking about it, when you are simply swinging down the street and you see a beautiful girl smiling beatifically, though not at you.

He remembered where he had seen her before, a couple of months ago, late one night at Graig Goch. They had finished loading lambs, the others had gone home, it was just Beti and Tom; she came to the door, she had run out of petrol. He was sure it was the same girl.

* * *

Felix del Rio started to take lambs more regularly, so that quite often the lorry would come straight back from Burgos to pick up another load without going back to Steve's yard at all. All the drivers wanted to do this run; it was a nice distance, down through France, and then just a couple of hundred kilometres into Spain. In Burgos, Felix looked after them really well, laying on splendid meals and a place to sleep if they wanted a break from the cab. More often than not, Tom gave the job to Colin. He was from Aberdeen, in his early twenties, tall, elegant, dry and fastidious. He combined an air of sleepy relaxation with a sense of unused energies that could be uncoiled at high speed in a crisis.

He'd already got them out of trouble once; at a lairage they no longer used, in the foot-hills south east of Bayonne, they'd unloaded the lambs into a dry upland pasture, thorny scrub standing up like cacti in a Western. It had been mid-afternoon and the sky had had the colourless glare of heated steel. Colin had walked right round the edge of the five hectare enclosure till, out of sight in a fold of rocky landscape, he'd found a great gap in the boundary. He and the farmer fixed it up, but Tom often thought that most drivers wouldn't have bothered to check, and for some time after that he had visions of their six hundred and fifty little Welsh lambs spreading out into the Pyrennees.

So whenever possible it was Colin who would do the run to Burgos. This also meant that they could give him money on the way out and a list of orders to fill at the hypermarket outside Cherbourg on the way back. Sometimes he'd have commissions from Beti and Tom, and from Phil and Huw and Alwyn, so his cab would end up looking like an off-licence, the spare bunk piled high with cases of French lager, bottles of Spanish brandy and cartons upon cartons of cigarettes.

If the next load was held over for a day or so, Colin would leave the lorry parked at Graig Goch and get a room at the Greyhound in Llangarn, which was less than a mile from the farm. They liked him there; for one thing he could bring them duty-free cigarettes, which they shamelessly sold over the bar. Tom went to look for him there once and found him perched on a stool in the back bar, long hands gesturing, wreathed in cigarette smoke, involved in some long story about foreign policemen, beautiful girls and narrow escapes. There were three or four farmers in the bar, shaking their heads in shy admiration, leaning on their thumbsticks, gaping at him. It was like *The Boyhood of Raleigh.*

* * *

Tom loaded his three cases of lager into the back of the car: seventy two bottles of beer for just over fifteen quid. Richard from the vets had been through the lambs, pulling out four of them; Colin's lorry was backed into the loading bay, and Phil and Alwyn were about to start running the lambs on. He had finished the paperwork and they could manage without him, so he walked back to the house, intending to have a word with Beti. He found her in the kitchen; she was pulling on her coat, about to go out.

'*Sut mae Tom?* What you think of the lambs? Nice bunch? Got to keep them happy. Paperwork done? Sit down. Have a drink. Barry'll get you one. *Barry! Mae eisiau diod ar Tom.*'

She went to the foot of the stairs and called up. Tom heard her say something to her son in the hallway, then the back door slammed, and a moment later Barry came into the kitchen. He got a bottle of whisky from the cupboard and brought it over to the table with a tumbler and a jug of water. He didn't catch Tom's eye or say anything; he seemed to be concentrating on what he was doing as he filled the glass half full with whisky, adding a dash of water from the jug. He pushed the drink across the table, finally looking up with a shy smile.

'Sending a lot of lambs these days'

Tom nodded and took a big drink.

'Mam enjoys it, you know, this French thing' Barry said.

Tom nodded at him over the rim of the tumbler, waiting for him to go on.

'What I don't understand is this, though.' There was a long pause;

Barry had a strange, deliberate way of speaking, spacing his words out with a heavy emphasis on every syllable, as though what he was saying was so densely packed with significance that his thoughts had to be delivered with absolute precision. Tom often found that he had time to think briefly about something completely different in the ponderous rhythms of his phrasing.

'These protestors now; what sort of places do they come from?'

Tom looked across the table at him. His face was paler than ever, the strange inertness of his features, like putty, filmed with sweat which, on his forehead and nose, stood in minute, separate beads. It occurred to Tom that perhaps most of the time he was translating laboriously out of Welsh for his benefit, and that this was what gave his speech its odd, off-key lethargy.

Tom started to explain to him what he understood of the protest movement, its essentially suburban nature; the bizarre, sentimental and above all *leisured* alliance between students, pensioners and the unemployed, but Barry interrupted him impatiently, as though he had been altogether misunderstood.

'I mean. They damage the lorries. They could hurt the sheep, couldn't they?'

He seemed quite agitated. Tom had finished his drink, and Barry refilled the glass, slopping drops of whisky onto the table in his hurry. It was late at night, it was an odd conversation, and a certain hilarity was creeping over him.

'Thing is Barry, your mother and I have run up against one of the most dangerous things in Britain: a *Rainbow Alliance*. When one of them gets on your tail, you're in trouble boy, let me tell you.'

'But why do they do it?' There was a note of real anguish in his voice. Tom took another big drink.

'Who knows, Barry? They've got us in their sights, that's all. Most of them got nothing better to do. We either got to fight back, or, find another line of work. What about a nice job with the Plastic Bathtub Manufacturers Association?'

Barry gaped at him. 'They pay well?'

'The PBMA? They certainly do. Or there's, let me see, the Rowena Institute of Hair Technology. Always wanted to work for them.'

This produced a look of such confused unhappiness that Tom immediately felt awful. He wondered whether it was something in Barry that brought out a cruelty in others, a desire to taunt and bait, that in Beti seemed to take the form of outright rage and dislike.

'Only joking Barry. Got to stand up for ourselves, that's all.'

Just then they heard the sound of the lorry starting to pull out of the yard, and Tom went to the window, glad of the interruption. He could just see the top of the wagon above the roof of the little stone building that stood in the yard between the house and the range of big new sheds. As he watched, he heard a sound that he couldn't identify, a very loud, muffled clap, a bit like the air-brakes going on, or the relief-valve on the air-tank, except that he had heard it right across the yard and through a closed window. He knew immediately that they had a problem, and a moment later he saw the truck lurch to a stop, the top of the cab rocking on its suspension. He and Barry went out into the yard. Phil and Alwyn were crossing from the other side, and the four of them bunched into a little spectating group as Colin jumped lightly down from the cab and walked round the front of the lorry.

'Fucking puncture. Now what's done that?'

There was a big halogen lamp on the side of the building, and in the white light and black shadows it was easy to see the flattened front tyre with a piece of broken plank, about a foot long, fixed immovably to the tread. Colin got a wrecking bar and levered it off. It was a short length of solid planking, three quarters of an inch thick, sawn straight at one end, and broken into splinters at the other. There were two six inch nails driven through it near the clean end; one had been bent over flat, the other had slipped between the deep grooves of the tread and blown the tyre.

'Well fuck me.'

'How did that get there?'

'What is it, broken pallet or something?'

'Too solid; big old packing case or something.'

'Well fuck me.'

In the container, the lambs coughed and stamped.

Colin started to get his equipment out of a locker behind the cab; heavy duty jack and sections of tyre iron which he slotted together.

'I'll be a wee while at this. How pushed for time are we?'

Tom had a look at the journey plan and made a few calculations.

'Should be alright. What'll you be, an hour?'

He was aware of some sort of argument going on behind him, Phil's voice rising in a yelp. He looked round and saw Barry, pushing past him and Alwyn, his shoulders rounded defensively, his head down. He must have gone back to the house, because he had a shotgun in his hands, a big Russian double-barrel, and was pushing shells into the open breech.

He trotted out into the road, snapping the gun shut, and calling back:

'Come on! Maybe still about! We can still get them!'

Colin straightened up and gave him a long look; then he shrugged and turned back to his wheel. Phil and Tom exchanged glares of horrified embarrassment. Alwyn started over towards him.

'Barry? Good boy, what's the trouble?'

Tom had always thought of Alwyn as a crude bastard, lewd, sexist and foul-minded, but his voice now was soothing, warm, vibrating with kindness.

'What is it *bachgen?*' He walked out into the road and stood by Barry, the two of them staring out into the darkness.

'What you seen boy? *Ara' deg nawr. Beth sy'n bod?*'

Barry's voice was high with anxiety.

'It's them Rainbow people done this. Tom knows, you ask him.'

Everyone looked at Tom. He swallowed, gritty dry saliva; he was regretting the whisky.

'We were talking about the protest movements, you know, animal rights and that.'

He turned back and picked up the piece of wood from where Colin had tossed it, turning it over in his hands. Now that Barry had raised the possibility, it did perhaps have a look of malevolent intent about it. But who had put it in the drive? And when? As an act of sabotage it was just so chancey. The lorry might have missed it, or flattened the nails. A tractor or a car could have gone over it. As he stared at it, the thing reverted to its look of innocent functionality, part of a broken crate or something; in a yard like this there was always stuff lying about. But perhaps they should get the police to look at it tomorrow. He passed it to Phil, but he didn't want it; he shook his head with an odd look, chewing his lip.

Headlights lit up a section of sky away to the left, turning off the main road onto the Graig Goch lane. Alwyn was still speaking to Barry. Now he put an arm round the boy's shoulders, taking the shotgun from him with his other hand.

'Come on lovely boy. Here's Mam coming home again. Don't want her to find us all stood around like this.'

Chapter 8

Phil had never known anyone who wore as much jewelry as Nicky did; strings of beads that he would encounter high up around her neck or in loose coils under her shirt, bangles and clanking bracelets cold against the warmth of her skin; above all rings, sometimes a ring on every finger, so that his touch was constantly ambushed by sudden changes of texture, the smoothness of her sharp brown knuckles among knots and edges of twisted silver; globules of turquoise and polished lozenges of tiger's eye, as he followed his searching tongue into salty recesses. Being with her, he had the sensation of rushing through sudden changes, like driving fast down hill as different surfaces fired up at him through his senses, ripping through gravel and stones, hissing on tarmac or bucking through potholes, the riveting burst of crossing a cattle-grid, the sudden amazement of coming.

He parked the van in the street opposite the school gate, pulling on the handbrake with a stiff creak, leaning back in the seat and closing his eyes. He was ten minutes early. Across the street a group of mothers waited by the gate, smoking and chatting, jigging pushchairs back and forth in short strokes over the pavement. A toddler ran stiff-legged into the road and one of the mothers detached herself from the group and caught up with him, crouching down to slap the back of the child's legs, her cigarette clamped in her teeth, her eyes slitted and watering in the curling smoke. Phil was leaning his head against the van's window, the glass cool against the side of his head. The woman had grasped the toddler's arm and straightened up, so that the child was lifted into a kind of diagonal, one arm and leg off the ground, like a doll; she jerked sharply at it, as you might on a dog's lead. Phil looked away, twisting round and peering into the back of the van.

He had spent the afternoon parked on a forestry road, on a high ridge to the west of Llanfrychan, from where you could see right across the flood plain, the river winking between gravel-beds and rushy water-meadows, a smoky haze of scrub-oak in the distance. He hadn't seen Nicky for days, and he had rung her with a sudden urgency, hoping he wouldn't get Harris on the phone. She said she was busy, the flat was full of people. He had been on the point of asking if he could come round, but instead he told her he had something to show her, a special place, important to him. He had joked and pleaded, and she had come along, a little unconvinced but willing to be amused.

In the catching pen the other day, the sheep stamping and pushing around his legs as he worked his way through them with the dosing gun, Molly yapping on the other side of the gate, he had found himself groaning out loud, grinding the heel of his hand into a gritty eye-socket. He had met Nicky for a quick drink in the Star at lunchtime; she had a lecture at two, her van was still off the road, and he had given her a lift back to college. In the High Street he stopped at the zebra crossing to let some people go by. There were a couple of school kids, and a tall, chaotic figure in a long brown raincoat, tufts of grey hair flying: his neighbour Bernard. As they crossed, Bernard gave a sort of salute and then, recognising Phil's van, stooped down to peer in through the windscreen, walking folded over and twisted sideways at the waist, grinning and winking at Phil. He nodded back casually. Nicky was talking to him:

'So where does he live mostly then? With his mum? Your little boy; don't know his name.'

'Eddy' he said. 'He's called Eddy.' He smiled, seeing him.

'Where do I turn? Here?'

So this afternoon he had felt more than ever oppressed by deceit, struggling stifled through layer upon layer of cobwebby stuff as he sat beside her in the van and pointed out the distant peaks of the Beacons, cracked triangular flags, slabs of shadow and sunlight split and scored by watercourses. He shifted hot legs in the cramped van and wished he was in her bed. He had started on a ridiculous story, at once regretting it but too late to turn back, inventing an imaginary childhood experience in which he had been lost in the mist on the high hills, when she had suddenly taken mercy on him, her hand snaking down, a ring snagging on his belt as she tugged at his jeans, crouching over him in a tangle of steering wheel and gear stick and metal edges. Not long after that he remembered that it was Thursday, that he was collecting Eddy from school and taking him into Llanfrychan to buy a new pair of shoes.

'Thanks for showing me your special place,' she told him when he had parked by the archway leading into College Square; she was leaning in through the van window and grinning at him: 'It was excellent. Outstanding!'

The Green was crowded with students, people just like her; he had a sense of how much she belonged here, and how little with him. He could feel her happiness at being back in this environment; he watched her disappear into the beautiful, enveloping anonymity, like releasing a fish into water.

At the school gate, the runaway toddler was still howling when the children were let out. Phil wanted to buy a pair of little Doc Martens, tiny, perfect, but they were much too expensive, and anyway Eddy had decided straightaway that he wanted trainers, the white and red pair in the window. Now the little boy sat with him in the kitchen, eating toast and jam, his new shoes looking very big and white as he swung his legs under the table. His teacher had given him homework for the very first time, and he was filled with a giddy sense of dignity and responsibility.

They heard the Metro crunching gravel in the yard and the tinny shock of the car door slamming. A few moments later the back door opened, pushing aside Molly, who'd been asleep against it and who now got up with a yelp, and Liz came into the kitchen. She had an armful of shopping. She looked pale, and she had done her hair differently.

'You been to the hair-dressers.'

'What do you think? Like it?'

'Looks good.'

'Looks brilliant Mum! Seen my shoes?'

Liz ran her fingers through her hair, and blew a puffing, upward breath, ruffling the fringe. Her dark hair was cut short in a boyish style, flopping over her forehead, trimmed close to the contours of her head at the back. It suited her. She put the carrier bags on the kitchen table and squatted down to admire Eddy's shoes.

'These are great!'

'I know. And look, I got all these sums to do! Mrs Jones says!'

Liz was wearing a familiar blue sweatshirt, floppy from innumerable washes, and a pair of leggings that Phil hadn't seen before. They were grey and absolutely skin tight so that they gave an impression of nakedness, though in a slightly strange way, massive, sculptural. He felt a flicker of tenderness and desire. He gave her a hug, pulling her tight against him. She felt solid and warm, heavy and soft.

'Get off Phil! What's got into you then!'

She struggled out of his arms, but she was laughing. She started putting the shopping away, tins of beans and soup slotted with sharp clicks onto the shelves, clinking bottles and rustling packets of cereal, a series of soft thumps as she tossed packs of sliced bread into the freezer. She hooked a lock of hair behind her ear, and glanced over at him, smiling.

'What you do today? Did you get the lambs in?'

'There wasn't time really. Do you want a cup of tea?'

He turned away to fill the kettle at the sink. He had forgotten about the lambs. He glanced at his watch; there wasn't enough time to get them in this evening, and there wouldn't be enough daylight in the morning to sort through them before the sale, so he had missed the Friday market altogether. Bugger! Liz looked at him, waiting for him to go on, but he shrugged, pulling a face.

'I'll go Tuesday; or Wednesday in Henllys.'

She finished putting the shopping away and sat down beside Eddy at the table. Phil brought her a cup of tea. He set it down, and stroked her hair. She leaned against him, taking his hand.

'Have you thought about Saturday yet? Did you get your suit from the cleaners?' she asked. There was a moment of stillness before she went on:

'Debbie's party; you said you'd come.'

'I got to be at Graig Goch on Saturday, load of lambs. I said I'd do it.'

He'd also told Nicky he'd meet her in the Star afterwards. He had a sudden vision of a crowd of people all trying to get through a doorway at the same time, bumping, exasperated, jammed up against each other. Liz got up, scraping her chair back on the bare floor.

'I told you about Debbie ages ago, you could of missed one load couldn't you?'

She went over to the sink, turning her back on him. When he didn't say anything, she swung round, her face working with anger and hurt.

'You don't remember anything about it do you? I told you all about it. You said you wanted to come too. Well, I'm going anyway. She's my best friend. Not that you care. When did we last go to a party together?'

Feeling muddled and dismayed, his arms hanging uselessly, he took a step towards her, but she gave him a glare of unhappiness or dislike '*Just don't.*'

She pushed past him and left the room, flinging the door half shut with a soft concussion as it banged into Molly. The dog yelped and hobbled under the table. Eddy looked up, then turned back to his school book, putting his head in his hands, muttering to himself as he worked at his sums.

Sounds drifted down from upstairs; the creak and bump of springs as Liz sat heavily on the bed, muffled thumps as she kicked off her shoes. He could picture her as she leaned over to rub at her ankles, massaging away the shocks and weariness of the day. He went out in the last of the daylight to check the sheep and chain Molly up in the shed. When he came back in, Eddy was having his bath. Phil could hear the slap and gurgle of the water and the echoing harmonics of their voices broadcasting through the water pipes.

' . . . so the camel went to the Casualty Department and they told him to go in a cubicle, but he wouldn't fit because of his hump, so *he* said . . . '

'I think he should have a flashing light on top, like the tractor.'

'That's what the camel said, but the doctor said *This isn't a garage.*'

Eddy's laughter seemed drawn up from such deep wells of delight that it emerged as a kind of groan, prolonged and helpless.

On Saturday evening, Phil's Auntie Nellian came over to look after Eddy, so that he could go up to Graig Goch while Liz went to her party. The little boy was uneasy with his great-aunt; he'd once told Phil that the old lady was 'always talking about dead people'. Nellian had never married, and there had only been the two of them in that generation, so now she felt broken off and isolated, drifting away towards extinction. With the death of Phil's father, she seemed to see her family line winking out in front of her eyes, and would stare mournfully at Eddy, contemplating the last of the brood as oblivion rose over the horizon like thunderclouds.

The symbol of this decline, waved defiantly and insultingly in her face like a personal affront, was the fact that Liz had never learned Welsh, with the shameful consequence that her nephew's household was largely English-speaking. Her pale blue eyes watered when she looked at Liz, filling up with an expression of distress and reproach. This, Liz claimed, masked a bitter and abiding dislike; '*The old dear can't stand me, you know*' but she had long ago decided to meet this head-on with a brittle and elaborate affection, tinkling displays of chirpy good humour that left the old lady shaking her head in bafflement and frustration, like an old sheep.

Now Liz clattered into the room on high heels, trailing scarves of perfume, her lips dark red, her eyes hugely black and startling.

'Mum you look fantastic! Doesn't she Dad! Look Dad doesn't she look brilliant!'

Nellian was sunk deep in the big armchair. She'd been holding both Eddy's hands in hers as the boy stood in front of her, solemn in his dressing gown; now he pulled away and turned towards Liz, beaming. She ruffled his hair and crossed the room to the armchair in the corner.

'Auntie Nellian! You're looking well!'

Liz crouched down and pecked a quick kiss, ignoring the old lady's defensive gesture, the raised shoulder, chin tucked in. She left a livid spot of lipstick on Nellian's papery old cheek, and dabbed carelessly at it with her finger.

'Oh dear, look what I've done now'.

She looked back over her shoulder at Eddy, rolling her eyes in pantomime dismay. Nellian said something to Phil, a sentence in Welsh in which Liz could hear sharp notes of disapproval or complaint.

'Edrychwch ar y sgert! Odi hi'n mynd mâs yn honna?

'I didn't catch that Auntie' Liz said. 'What was that?'

Liz turned back to Nellian, but the old lady sank back into her chair, lowering her chin into folds and wattles, subsiding. Eddy's eyes were flicking from one grown-up to another.

'Translation?' Liz asked brightly, but Phil shook his head, shrugging with a kind of don't-worry-about-it gesture.

'It's the fashion' he said.

Nellian shook her head. *'Ffasiwn ife!'* she said.

Looking at the three of them and seeing suddenly in Phil and Nellian the same line of the jaw, rounded and stubborn, a family template into which perhaps Eddy too was bound to grow, Liz felt a bleak moment of isolation. Then she clicked quickly across the floor and and put her arm round Eddy's shoulder, drawing the little boy into the curve of her body so that the two of them stared together across the altered pattern of the room.

'You be good while I'm gone, alright?'

'Yes mum.' He pushed his face into her skirt for a moment, rubbing his nose into the material.

'You smell lovely mum; you smell, delicious!'

*   *   *

The day before, Phil had taken twenty of his smallest fat lambs round to Graig Goch. He had missed the market, and it occurred to him that his little lambs would do very well for the load that was going to Spain the next day. Up at the farm, Beti had bundled her way through the pen, grabbing a lamb here and there.

'These'll do well *bach*; run em up to the new shed with the others. Shearers are coming tonight.' She noted the transaction on a piece of card from her breast pocket.

Now, as he and Alwyn tagged the lambs, he looked out for his little group among the milling mass of upturned faces. The lambs were mostly

Welsh Mountain and Cheviot cross, with a sprinkling of Speckle-face among them. Without their fleeces they were unrecognisable, the little skimpy tip-toed bodies following their big heads, skittering anxiously around the pens as Phil and Alwyn pushed through the crush, through the clicking of the little hooves on concrete, the sharp clack of the ear-tag pliers. Once or twice he thought he saw one of his own lambs, a glance of recognition or betrayal flashing between them.

'They won't miss their wool when they get to the hot countries, eh?'

Alwyn grunted, not responding, bent over the lambs. He was pale and sweaty; he looked to Phil like he'd had a session the night before.

They heard the lorry backing up to the loading bay as they were finishing, the hiss and clap of the air brakes, then Colin the driver's face appearing above the gate of the alley. Alwyn straightened up, pushing his knuckles into the small of his back.

'Scotchy boy! You brought my lagers then or what?'

Colin's long, fastidious features took on a look of humorous distaste.

'Finish your work first Taff. There's more to life than beer you know.'

Tom Wood turned up with Richard the vet. Phil helped them go through the lambs, pulling out half a dozen rejects while they checked the tag numbers and filled in the paperwork. Alwyn had gone round to the cab, where Colin was reaching down cases of French lager, cartons of cigarettes and bottles of brandy. He could hear the two of them joking together, Colin's precise, clipped tones:

'When will you Welsh boys learn to speak English properly? You've had a few hundred years to practice, haven't you?'

Phil was reminded of a joke with which his father-in-law had hounded him, years ago, when he and Liz were first married. Liz's parents had finally come to visit them on the farm. Her mother, small and pale, grey-blonde hair, had seemed shy to the point of fear throughout the visit, flinching whenever Phil or his Dad spoke to her. Liz's father had been a butcher. He called himself retired, although in fact his business had gone bust, there'd been some scandal, but he'd come out of the wreck with enough to live quietly on. In the dense tones of his flesh you could sense a ghostly image of Liz as a plump little girl. Phil had known immediately that her father didn't like him; he could feel the distaste, just below the booming and jovial surface. He had a running joke about not being able to understand Phil, his accent was too strong. Phil hadn't found it funny the first time; with variations, her father had used it dozens of times. *Where's the dictionary; I almost understood that.* Now, on the visit to the farm, he transferred this joke to Phil's Dad.

'Would you like some more potatoes?' Phil's dad gave the bowl an anxious little push an inch or two across the table. Nellian had come in to do the meal, lamb chops cooked until they were almost black. Liz's father looked blankly at him, pushing the flap of his ear forward with two thick fingers:

'I'll have to learn this Welsh, you know. Can't go on like this. Lizzy, you give me a little translation, love. You must be getting used to it by now.'

'Potatoes? Or another chop? Nellian, there's chops still isn't there? How about you, Mrs Hinton?' Phil didn't think his Dad even knew he was being laughed at. Liz's father slapped the table.

'Now that really *was* Welsh, wasn't it? Nearly fooled me then.'

A couple of years ago, as his dad had started down his last, steep slope, Phil had come to recognise a new look in his eyes, a look that was anxious and somehow pleading. Afterwards, he had come to feel that his dad had been trying to ask him something, or rather, that he'd been willing Phil to ask the questions. They never had talked properly, and he was left with the memory of that expression that seemed to say: *Ask me, bachgen. I can't tell you if you won't ask.* That look had come much later, as the disease whispered its final instructions in his father's ear, but in Phil's memory he saw it as they sat round the kitchen table with his parents-in-law, Nellian standing behind her chair with her oven gloves, his dad's eyes widening, that baffled look he had.

They started running the lambs onto the lorry. Tom Wood went off to the house. Alwyn was hanging back, nursing his hang-over, and Phil found himself doing most of the work, penning the lambs in groups and running them clattering up the tailgate. Often a couple too many would run up the tread-plate and he would have to grapple them back, his fingers slipping over the squirmy shorn bodies, gripping tight on a greasy tail while the lamb ran frantically on the spot, hooves sliding on the aluminium. He was hot and out of breath by the time that he and Colin lifted the tailgate and bolted it shut.

'Stop by the house Col. I think Tom's got the paperwork there. Got time for a coffee? Good God Alwyn, you bought the brewery this time, did you?'

'Give us a hand man. Want one?' Alwyn had hefted his purchases into the back of his car, and was tugging at the stiff cardboard flap of one of the cases of beer when they both looked round, startled.

'What was that?'

The lorry had come to a stop, halfway along the concrete road between the new buildings and the house. Alwyn slid a bottle of lager out of the case and pressed the cool glass against his forehead, eyes closed. Phil looked down the road, waiting for the lorry to get moving again.

'Looks like he's got a problem, come on. What the hell was that noise anyway?'

As they reached the cab, Tom Wood appeared from the house, and behind him a tall figure, still in the shadows. This person stepped into the harsh pool of overhead light which carved and gouged their features into pits and hollows, massive brows overhanging deep shadowed sockets and cheekbones, and Phil recognised Beti's son, Barry. Colin was stooping and peering round the front of the lorry.

*　*　*

Phil parked his van in the yard through the archway at the back of the Star. It was eleven o'clock. With Aunt Nellian baby-sitting, there was no way he could stay out much later tonight. He looked at his watch again; really, there was only time for a quick drink with Nicky. His body responded instantly to the thought, an electric tingle at the base of his stomach, an automatic flicker of desire and excitement

The pub was full, a surge of noise and light, cigarette smoke and laughter blowing out into the street as Phil pushed through the double doors. He wondered again how these damn students could afford to be in the pub every night. Probably they made a couple of cans of Two Dogs last all night, talk for hours on that; talk, talk, talk. The noise seemed to increase in leaping increments as he pushed through to the bar. He felt overwhelmed by a barrier of teeth, long hair, make-up, a raucous, undifferentiated mass of rings and studs and noses, bangles, bags, books, eyelashes, cigarettes, tongues, boots and lipstick, mouths flapping at him so that he drew back into himself with a sort of physical repulsion. At the same time, he knew how seamlessly Nicky fitted into all this. These were her friends, she was one of these people, and yet he wanted to fuck her *right now*. He puffed his cheeks out in a long sigh of baffled discontent as he tried to catch the barman's eye.

'She's not here.'

A couple of people to Phil's right moved away from the bar, revealing Harris, leaning up against the counter a few feet away.

'Nicky. She's not here tonight. She's got better things to do. Assume you were looking for her. Or did you just happen to be passing?'

Harris turned and grinned at the bloke he was with, a short, dark-haired guy. Phil had seen him in the pub a couple of times, and once, he thought, crossing the road with Nicky by the library. Harris was jigging his right knee up and down and drumming his fingers on the bar. He bared his teeth at Phil. He looked immensely pleased with himself. Phil shrugged. He took a long drink from his glass and glanced at his watch, realising as he did so that the gesture looked not so much busy and nonchalant as sad and stood-up. He felt himself flushing.

'Keeping busy?'

Harris was speaking to him again. He whispered something to the boy he was with who nodded, staring at Phil.

'Lots of work down on the farm?'

Beneath the apparent small-talk, Harris's voice had a piercing note of derision. The other boy said nothing. He was watching as though through the bars of a cage.

'How many lambs have you killed today?'

Phil stared at him. 'What *is* your problem?' he asked.

'It's not *my* problem' Harris said. 'I'm not the one that packs lambs into trucks so that half of them get there dead or dying.'

'Where do you get this stuff from?' Phil shook his head in disgust. 'Who do you think would pay for dead lambs? Anyway, they sent fifty thousand lambs last year, and they lost thirty five of them. Tom Wood told me.' He stared at Harris, challenging him: 'Thirty five!'

The barman had come over to listen to the conversation, and Phil nodded at him emphatically: 'Thirty five!'

Harris grinned at Phil, the same curling back of the lips. It was as though he was burning up from inside with some internal fire of anger or evil that shot its hot and empty glare out of his eyes.

'You sound like you're proud of it.'

Phil sighed, exasperated.

'Thirty five out of fifty thousand', he said. 'They die quicker than that back home on the farm.'

'Expect me to believe that? Anyway, that's still thirty five too many. And who's this Tom Wood, ducky?'

Phil stared at him, stupefied for a moment by the aggression that streamed out at him like light from a suddenly opened door.

'*Beth yw dy broblem di?*' he said. 'What's your problem, *Sais anwybodus?*'

The barman caught his eye and frowned with a quick shake of his head.

'I don't want any trouble here' he told him. *'Smo i moyn gofid yma.'*

'Nor do I' Phil said. *'Na finne chwaith.'*

Harris's glance flickered uneasily between the two of them; he looked suddenly unfocused as he searched for meaning and reference in a language that was closed to him, turning his head from side to side as though blindfolded, the questing snout muzzled and speechless. When Phil turned and spoke directly to him, Harris stared back, curling his lip.

'I don't speak Welsh.'

He was aware that this had come out sounding like an apology, and ground his teeth with frustration. He gave a snort, which was intended to signal a detached contempt, but which Phil recognised without difficulty as a gesture of defeat. Throwing his head back, he tipped the rest of his drink down his throat, his teeth clattering for a moment on the lip of the bottle. He poked an elbow at the other student, who slid obediently off his stool, and the two of them walked to the door. Harris turned back.

'You think you can do whatever you like, don't you? You think that everything's been put here just for you. You think it all belongs to you, don't you?'

The door swung shut behind them. The barman retrieved the empties as the uproar of sound, voices, laughter, the shimmering clink of glasses, the thump of the jukebox, seemed to flow back into the empty space, filling it quickly to the brim like liquid in a jug.

'What was that all about?' he asked Phil, raising his voice above the racket.

*   *   *

On her third tequila, Liz decided that it wouldn't be a good idea to drive home. She could leave the Metro here with Debbie, and later on get a lift with Rhian. In the meantime she could have a proper night out. There was food laid out in the back bar. The long table had been pushed up against the wall and covered with a white cloth. Ranks of tall glasses shivered tinkling together as Liz crossed the room. There were tumblers of bread-sticks, bowls of dip and crisps, dishes of lettuce piled up with prawns, fleshy and moist, warm damp quiches, slabs of salmon and dimpled mounds of mayonnaise.

'I think I've gone to heaven!'

Rhian came up beside Liz and returned her empty plate to the table. She turned up a couple of glasses and splashed them full of white wine.

'Cheers, Liz love, have one of these.'

'Pub's done well.'

'It was Deb's mum done the food.'

'Course it was. Still, the room looks nice don't it.'

The wine was cold and delicious; they clinked glasses and drank again. Rhian had a smear of food at the side of her mouth, and Liz pecked it off with the tip of a napkin, the two of them leaning against each other giggling.

'Where's your lovely fellow then?'

'Phil?' Liz pulled a face. 'Working. Typical isn't it. He's known about tonight for ages. Last minute says he's got to work, can't get out of it.'

'Ah love him! Gorgeous he is. Don't you never leave the two of us alone together mind!'

Rhian's expression changed, her eyes clouding, distant:

'Course, you know where Dave is, don't you. In the bloody Rugby Club.' She shook her head disgustedly. 'Couldn't even think of a good reason not to come.'

Liz had caught sight of herself in a long mirror on the other side of the room; she had stared at her reflection for a moment or two before she recognised herself. A shiver of physical pleasure ran right through her, her body tensing and relaxing as the tremor ran up and down it like ripples, all over, but mainly *right there*. Damn she was looking good! In the mirror her dark and glistening lips pouted back at her. Rhian was saying something to her.

'Tuesday. Wednesday was darts. Thursday he was at a meeting: at the Rugby Club of course. What happened Friday? Anyway, here we are Saturday and he's at the bloody Rugby Club again.'

Liz ate an olive, blowing the pit into her fist through puckered lips.

'Listen Rhian, stuff them, that's what I say. Let's go and have a dance.'

* * *

Nellian was asleep in the armchair when Phil got back to Greenhill, the television murmuring bad-temperedly in the corner of the room. He went up to Eddy's bedroom; the little boy was fast asleep. He looked hot, and was breathing noisily. Phil rearranged the bedclothes, stroking the hair off his forehead. There was a lump under the covers at Eddy's feet; he pulled the blanket back: Patch. The terrier wriggled his muscly little body deeper into the mattress, curling up tighter, trying to make himself invisible. Without lifting his head he cocked one eye open and gave a deep groan of pleading reluctance that subsided into a series of grunts and grumbles as Phil picked him up by the scruff and carried him downstairs.

'Go to your kennel Patch. Don't you be going off to the woods now.' Hanging his head, the little dog minced across the yard.

In the front room his aunt was waking up, her jaws working, chewing her way out of sleep. He watched her as her head nodded into consciousness, her misty eyes opening, unfocused, a look as blue and empty as the sky. He felt a mixture of irritation and pity, the nagging and familiar emotions he'd had towards her since he'd been a teenager. She really was getting too old to be driving home at night. It was only a couple of miles, but look at her, somebody ought to be looking after her. Then again, the bloody house could have burned down around her ears for all she would have noticed, fast asleep with the child upstairs. He sighed.

'Had a nice rest Auntie? Would you like a cup of tea before you go?'

'*Dim diolch, Phil. Faint o'r gloch yw hi? Ble mae Liz*, not still out is she? *Duw duw*, is she going to be out all night?'

Eventually she was ready to leave, though she came back into the house a second time, couldn't find her gloves but perhaps she hadn't brought them. The old Escort was ten, eleven years old, the engine popping and missing; through the cloud of exhaust fumes that settled heavily in the still air as she drove out of the yard, Phil saw that one of her rear lights was broken. He would drop round next week and fix it for her.

Walking back to the house, he wondered if the lorry was away already. It was after midnight; Colin would have the wheel changed by now, they'd be halfway to the motorway. He thought of his own little lambs aboard the lorry, packed in the darkness as the night air whistled in through the vents, leaning together like sailors on a sloping deck as the wagon took the curves.

That Barry was weird, no doubt about that. The big, clumsy figure, jogging down the road with the shotgun. Phil shivered. And what was all that about Rainbow People? *It's them Rainbow People. You ask Tom, he knows all about it.* What did Barry mean by that? What had Tom Wood been saying to him? For some reason, Phil found himself remembering an afternoon a few weeks ago; he'd bumped into Tom in Llanfrychan. The other man had wanted to show him some poster, he'd been going on about students, and animal rights and protests. He could remember all this very clearly because a moment later he had seen Nicky's old green van coming down the High Street towards them. She had stopped right there in the street, holding up the traffic, smiling at him with such pleasure that he felt dazzled. She was wearing a T-shirt with a great sunburst of colour on it, multi-coloured rays of reds and blues and purples firing out in every direction. On the shadowy edge of this intense circle of light, he recollected the morose figure of Tom Wood, dark, stooping, excluded.

The front door had clicked shut. He walked round the side of the house to the kitchen door. Passing Molly's kennel he heard the rattle of her chain, and the soft flip flop of her tail as the old bitch recognised his footsteps. He left the back door on the latch in case Liz didn't have her key with her. Patch tried to sneak in at his feet, but he pushed him back out into the yard. He thought about making a cup of tea, but really he was too tired. The TV was still on, and he leaned over and punched quickly at the buttons, flicking irritably through the channels: a music video, an Italian western. He backed away from the screen and started to watch the film, stooped, on his feet, too weary to sit down and get comfortable. They were in a saloon; stubbled chins, shot-glasses, nervous bartender. Everybody looked round as a guy came in through the swing doors. He had on a poncho and what looked like a lot of eye make-up. When he took off his hat he had coppery red hair that immediately reminded Phil of Harris.

So what was *that* about? Phil could see Harris's venomous expression; he had been almost spitting at him as he left the pub. Could he have put the piece of wood with the nails through it in Beti's yard? What was the word? Sabotage. Phil pushed the off button and the television shut down with a little squeak. Harris certainly seemed to hate him. Perhaps he was jealous. He started up the stairs, taking them one at a time, watching his boots, bone-tired. If Harris wanted to move beyond protest towards direct action, would he know where the lorries were going from? Yes. Almost anyone in Llanfrychan could tell him; Beti was famous, a local legend. Or Nicky could have told him. She had never been to Graig Goch, but he'd told her about it often enough, although his attempts to convince her that she and Harris were wrong about live exports, that they were judging something they didn't understand, had generally not been successful. Her basic point of view, her deep sense of what lambs *were*, was just too different from his. She would stare at him, chewing her lip, her eyes huge and troubled, while his arguments faltered, fragmenting into irritation and desire. As he got undressed, the cool air of the bedroom flowing over his skin was like the light touch of her fingers, the cool silky swells of her body against his.

* * *

When Debbie's brother Idris poked an exploratory finger into her cleavage, the thick digit wiggling stiffly for a moment between her tits, Liz realised she'd lost a button off the front of her shirt.

'Get off man, what you playing at!' She pushed at him and he swayed back grinning, tapping the side of his nose as though sharing a secret with her. Liz looked down at herself. The shirt was brand new, silk; now there was a dribble of prawn cocktail over her collarbone, and she was just *bursting* out of the gap left by the missing button. She felt hot, and somehow swollen; not the feeling you get from overeating, but brimming, tumescent, flushed and juicy.

In the middle bar where the disco was set up, there were still a few people dancing, couples moving slowly round the dim room, foreheads pressed together. There were a lot more women than men, and nobody that Liz fancied dancing with. Idris had followed her onto the dance floor and now appeared in front of her, gaping, leering. He pushed his stomach at her, rubbing his crotch and rotating his hips. His shirt was hanging out of his trousers and his eyes seemed to be looking in different directions. Liz put her face close to his.

'You got something stuck up your arse, or what?' She went to look for Rhian.

'Shall we go soon? What you think?'

Rhian turned towards her; she had been peering into the big mirror, squinting, her face very close to the glass, probing the corner of her eye with a long, lacquered fingernail.

'Oh my God look at me!' She grimaced glumly at Liz. Her face looked puffy, her eyes smudged. She looked like she'd been crying. A couple walked by, heads together, talking quietly and intensely in Welsh. They were young, very smartly dressed, a sort of European elegance about them, suave and sleek; someone had said they were lecturers at the college. They glanced at Rhian, at the tight dress riding up her thighs, the blotched make-up. The girl said something to the man, taking his arm and drawing him past them. *Snob*, Liz thought. *Hard-faced bitch.*

'You alright Rhian?'

She reached a hand towards her but the other girl drew back, sniffing. She smiled lop-sidedly. 'Think you're right, time to go.'

In the car-park Rhian turned her ankle, going over on her heel, and tottered, hopping the last few paces to her car. Liz wondered whether she would be better driving herself, but Rhian found her keys at last and opened the doors. Liz shrugged and sank back into the seat. She felt warm and heavy, sleepy and soft and aroused. She wondered if Phil would still be awake.

'What time is it?'

'Two, two fifteen.'

'Did you say goodbye to Deb? I never saw her after.'

'Nor me. See her dancing with Carwyn though? Hul-lo, I thought.'

'She finished with Rod then?'

'Rod!' Rhian snorted with laughter and the car jinked and weaved for a moment in response. 'Rod!'

'What? What about him?'

'You don't have to worry about Rod, that's all!'

'Rhian Davies! You tell me this minute!'

'Rod's been spinning her a line, that's what! Our little Rod is not quite what he might seem!'

'Spinning her a line! And did she swallow it?'

The two of them gurgled with laughter, dark lights dancing in their eyes in the dim interior of the car.

Liz squirmed across the bed and pushed herself against Phil's back, wriggling her body, moulding it moistly against his. He was wearing pyjamas, and she slid her hand under the cotton jacket, drawing her fingernails down his chest. He felt hot and solid, and she pressed closer against him, lifting a leg over his inert bulk, her toenails clawing at him. She picked at the drawstring of his pyjamas. It was tightly knotted, but the trousers were loose, and she reached her hand down under the waistband. Phil groaned, and a shudder ran through his body, a taut shiver that Liz could feel right inside herself, like touching an electric fence.

As the inchoate elements of the dream melted and swam, swirling iridescently like diesel in a puddle, then suddenly shivering into solidity, Phil realised that the bundled figure in the road, its head shrouded in some sort of a scarf or bandage so that he seemed to be looking at the blind, eroded features of a mummy, couldn't possibly be his mother, never had been. His frantic pursuit of this receding figure had left his nine-year-old heart pumping dumbly. He groaned aloud. The elements rearranged themselves as he found himself passing down an avenue of metal tubes like gun barrels, tyres stacked up in towers, tubes of steel and steel nails, nine-inch nails, detailed and obtrusive. He could feel the edge of a revelation in the punning symmetry of these nines, noting with some lucid corner of his mind that his mother had died when he was nine years old; if you looked closely enough you could see that the absolute point of the nail was not a point at all but a little tiny square as though sawn off. Nails were driven in though, hammered through splintering resistance with the same pumping force, spasmodic and irresistible.

'Please, leave me alone. Don't.'

He had the odd sensation of hearing his own voice, listening to it from the outside as he came fully awake. Liz had flung herself away across the bed, turning her back to him. He lay for a moment trying to collect his thoughts, lumps of dream material still swirling past him in the stream, bumping against his legs.

'Liz?' He felt exposed, guilty and unmasked. Had he been talking in his sleep? He cleared his throat. 'Liz?'

'Fuck off Phil. If that's how you feel just fuck off.'

Chapter 9

When the wind was in the south, the sound of the guns on the artillery range high up on the Eppynt would cross the intervening valleys quite clearly, sudden thuds like something being dropped upstairs, the rumble of furniture moved about in an attic. Tom used to picture the gunners on the high moorland on blowy days, firing their mortars up into the sunshine, measuring, calibrating, watching the little puffs of smoke and waiting for the boom to come rolling back; intent on detail, absorbed and carefree. Their job lacked the demonic exuberance of the Tornado pilots ripping those huge tail-fins through the valleys below the line of the hills, or high up where you would see the F-16's barrel-rolling across the sky, leaving a silent strip of con-trail as bright and sudden as a shooting star, but he envied the gunners their skills, their innocent craftsmanship, their lack of self-doubt.

It had always seemed to him that he and Beti were engaged in the same sort of business, intricate and specialised, the projection of great masses of stuff across huge distances, magical parabolas across Europe. Deploy a set of skills, initiate a sequence, roll forward: it is Thursday afternoon, so Stuart's lorry is rumbling through the outskirts of Strasbourg while Colin is in a line of trucks on the Spanish border.

When B & F stopped taking livestock on their boats, you could feel the tension ratchet up, the sound of the pursuit suddenly nearer. The protest movement seemed to know that there was blood in the water; there was a noticeable increase in the media coverage, and you could find an interview with Farm Concern or the Animal Protection League in the tabloids or on TV just about every day. They seemed to have an endless supply of spokesmen ready to face the camera or the microphone. No one ever challenged them or asked them to justify their views or produce evidence; they were simply allowed to bang on, using words like 'cruel' and 'immoral', one crackpot after another, ignorant, sentimental and aggressive. This was when they sent the parcel-bomb to Graham Border.

Tom waited to see what the other companies were going to do. SeaFarers seemed to be carrying on as usual. Normandy Shipping issued a statement saying they were reviewing the situation. A couple of weeks later they came out with what they called a protocol: they would continue to carry livestock, but, after a period of transition, they would only ship those animals whose final destination lay in Northern France. Tom took this to be some sort of joke, a contemptuous gesture towards the protest movement. How was a shipping company going to control what happened to a lorry-load of sheep once it had arrived in Normandy or Brittany? Later, he came to think that there must have been people within the company who really thought that they would be able to bring about a massive change in agricultural terms of trade, on a level which would alter the economy of a whole region; who really pictured millions upon millions of British sheep accumulating in the north west of France, from where they would eventually be resold and distributed all over Europe.

That came later. In the meantime, he didn't think it would affect them much. They would use the SeaFarers crossing whenever possible. When they used Normandy Shipping they would have to do the paperwork differently, and he drove up to Graig Goch late one afternoon to explain the changes to Beti. It was overcast, just a long strip of bright, greenish light along the horizon where it was clearing from the west. At Pont Sais he passed the Norman ruins by the bridge, the stump of a castle like a broken tooth. The river was slow and fat, with an oily look to it; ellipses of smooth movement bulging up to the surface. Downstream, on the edge of the bank, a digger had been dredging out gravel, the long boom stretched out like the neck of a wading bird. Tom was thinking that it is possible to do good work in a climate of hostility, although something is lost. The resources of innocence and enthusiasm get depleted, leaking away into cynicism. You draw closer to the people you work with, and develop an insider's humour, an ironic lens through which outsiders goggle and mime.

There was a red kite above Graig Goch, hanging as still as if it had been tethered. As Tom approached the farm, it slipped suddenly sideways down the fading sky, trailing its thin mewing cry behind it. He turned into the yard, and nearly collided with Beti's mother. The old lady was driving the LandRover; through the narrow frown of the windscreen he could see her gripping the wheel, sleeves rolled up as she worked the heavy vehicle through the gateway. He realised she was going to keep coming and grated his car into reverse to get out of her way. As she passed alongside she slid the perspex window back and shrieked something at him. The noise of the engine obliterated her voice. Clouds of black diesel smoke boiled up around her. Her hair had come loose, white and ragged, and she didn't have her teeth in. She was a vision from Hell, but probably she was just telling him that she was off to the shops.

Beti was in her office. She and Barry were sitting opposite each other at the huge desk which as always was covered from end to end; sheaves of invoices, box files, telephone directories, diaries, address books, telephones, two fax machines, clocks, calculators and calendars, note-pads, card-indexes and piles of unopened mail. At Beti's feet there was an enormous glossy cardboard box, half as big as a fridge, ripped open, revealing a computer that was supposed to replace the one that stood half-buried on a corner of the desk, which Beti had never got working since she'd had it installed a month before.

'*Sut mae Tom.* Pull up a chair. Won't be long with this. Want a coffee? What do you know then?'

Beti's fingers were clattering over the keys of an adding machine as Barry read through a market invoice from the auctioneers, a long list of pen numbers, weights and prices. For a minute Tom thought he had come in on a moment of closeness between them, but as Beti turned back to the work, her face tightened into an expression of irritation and distaste.

'*Nage, nage, diawl! Dim byd!*' She snapped off a sentence in Welsh which Tom didn't understand, although he could hear anger ringing in it.

'He's reading off the wrong list, what can you do?'

Tom looked away in embarrassment as Barry ducked his head, shuffling through the papers in front of him. He went into the kitchen to make himself a coffee.

When he came back into the office they were finishing off, Beti writing in a ledger, Barry arranging the sheaf of invoices, tapping them into shape. Tom gave the big cardboard box a push with the toe of his boot.

'You're not all computerised yet then Beti?'

'Damn thing! They any use, you think, imputers? Seem like a lot of fuss to me. Supposed to take the other one away but they never came for it. What you know then Tom?'

Tom showed her the fax he'd had from Normandy Shipping. He told her he didn't think it would cause many problems. Barry interrupted him:

'Why they doing it Tom? What they got against us? We treat the sheep well, they should know that!'

'It's the newspapers and the TV, they whip it up all the time; I don't know why.'

He made an impatient gesture. 'But we're not doing anything wrong.'

'It's not just us, Barry. They're trying to make it difficult for everybody.'

'No no, they got it in for us. Look what they did to the lorry!'

'What lorry?' Tom looked over at Beti but she just shrugged. Barry was drumming his fingers on the edge of the desk and there were spots of blotchy colour in his face.

'You know! Colin's lorry! That time when I wanted to go after them.'

To Tom's amazement Barry gave him a look of real dislike. 'You should of let me! I might of got the bastards!'

Tom looked over at Beti again, expecting to hear some violent rebuke from her, but she gave him an odd look.

'There *was* something funny there Tom. Should of gone to the police no doubt.'

Barry was nodding vigorously. There was a kind of smirk on his face, a silly grin, excited, frightened, vindicated, *I told you so!* His voice hurried on.

'You said yourself Tom, Rainbow students, that's what you said! Tell you what, I've seen some of them too, in town, you know?' His look darted from Beti to Tom and back again, nervous but full of a sort of sly triumph. As he rushed on it was as though he was amazed that no one was telling him to shut up.

'Course I've always seen them there, in town I mean, but I never thought, see? Students. Then that night when you said, well after that I kept seeing them. That pub the Star, you know? They go in there.' He gave a deep sigh, leaning back in the chair.

Tom stared at him.

'Think you're jumping the gun a bit, Barry.'

He waited for Beti to say something that would clear the air; there was an atmosphere in the room that was like a smell. But Beti put her head on one side and gave Tom a twinkling look, that cunning-peasant expression she used when she was giving advice, people said she looked just like her old man when she did that: 'They're not all like you Tom. There's some nasty people about.'

Without turning his head, Tom could feel Barry staring at him, his eyes glistening.

*   *   *

He remembered this conversation a few days later, when Barry rang him up. Tom had spent the morning in the office organising lorries for the following week. As it stood, they had four loads lined up, and he had just spoken to Marek van Leymans, who hadn't been over for a while. His partner Piet had been away for a month or so; nothing illegal, Marek said, just domestic, but now the two of them were planning to come for a load of lambs, which would mean sending off five lorries in a week; over three thousand lambs, a record.

The phone rang again.

'You busy Tom? C' you come into town? Need to show you something'.

Tom didn't recognise the voice at first.

'Ringing from the vets, you should come and see this, it's what we were talking about, there's lots of them here.'

The words ran on for a moment or two, as though they had come loose from their meanings, scattering like beads across the floor.

'They got notices, what d'you call, posters, they stopping cars.'

Barry and his Rainbow People.

Tom parked in Priory Lane and walked up the High Street towards the vets' surgery. Barry was right; it was worth seeing. At this end of the High Street, where it met New Road, there was a stone fountain with a decorative column above it, and a drinking trough, forming an island in the traffic. Now there was a big banner draped across the steps of the fountain – BAN LIVE EXPORTS. At a glance, there were thirty or forty people there, maybe more. He could see three or four placards raised swaying above the heads of the crowd – STOP THE CRUELTY – JUST SAY NO. The traffic was almost at a standstill, and there were a number of protestors skipping about among the cars, handing leaflets to the drivers or clipping them under the wind-screen wipers. People were standing about in little groups in shop doorways, as though expecting to be entertained; there was a strange and theatrical stillness, as though everyone had been given their positions and were now waiting for the action to begin.

Opposite the Vet Group surgery there was a Panda car, parked two wheels up on the pavement; the window was wound down and Tom could hear the radio mumbling nasally. Barry and Meirion the vet were standing in the open doorway of the surgery, one on either side of the door-frame, leaning out into the street like people sheltering from sniper fire. Meirion nodded hello to Tom.

'There's a lot of them here; they can't all be from the college, can they?'

He settled his glasses further up his nose with a gesture of nervous distaste.

'I'd say there's a few here just come for a day out.'

Tom remembered the coach he'd seen parked where he had left the car. He'd caught the driver's eye as he walked past, although he hadn't responded in any way. The fellow was sitting in the driving seat, waiting, as though switched off, not smoking, not reading a newspaper, just sitting there, *waiting*, like a horse in the shafts.

Jane came out of the surgery and pushed past them into the street. She was carrying a bucket of soapy water and a brush.

'Disgusting it is. They got no right!'

A big poster had been plastered up on the glass shop-front of the surgery, and she set to work at it, slopping and scrubbing, scraping it off in strips. Barry stepped out into the street. He was holding himself tight, a muscle twitching in his cheek.

'Where the hell's Dai Plod then?'

He nodded at the police car: 'They ought be doing something shouldn't they?' He set off down the High Street, and Tom took a couple of skipping steps to catch up with him. They found Dai in the doorway of the ironmongers, chatting to Tony. He turned to Barry and Tom with that air of amused contempt that was part of his vast solidity, his glossy, ruminant bulk, his sleek, dumb assurance.

'This makes a change then, lads.'

Tom thought that it had to be a conscious technique, the ease with which he sliced down his self-esteem, that *lads*. Barry was leaning over him, talking urgently; Tom caught bits of the Welsh: *not right, you ought to do something, stop all this. Ddylem ni ddim caniatáu.'*

The policeman took a step back, opening a gap between them. He turned to Tom, switching into English:

'All perfectly legal. Asked permission in advance.' Then to Barry: 'Tell Mam I'll be coming up to see him one of these evenings. Little problem to sort out.'

He had wanted Tom to understand that too. He nodded at the two of them, his smile secretive and condescending, and walked ponderously back towards the patrol car.

Tom and Barry were standing right across the street from the drinking fountain. There were ten or twelve students sitting on the stone steps, some of them with placards lolling between their knees, smoking cigarettes, waving at passers-by. There was a little ragged chanting, rather self-conscious, good-humoured: *NO! NO! KEEP 'EM HOME!* A

110

girl got up and stretched, then leaned against the smooth stone column, putting her arm round it in a gesture of careless grace that was startling, beautiful. Without thinking, Tom nudged Barry:

'Look, there's Phil's girlfriend.'

Barry looked at him a little blankly, as though he hadn't understood. Tom could have left it there but he didn't, perhaps because, as he watched, she turned slowly, sliding round the stone pillar, her gaze slipping along the street, half smiling, as though looking for a friend. As her eyes met his, they didn't focus; she looked straight through him, as though he wasn't there, just a middle-aged man, invisible and empty. Tom felt as though he had disappeared, winking out of existence there and then. She made him feel as though the wind, which at that moment picked up a litter of dead leaves and sweet-wrappers and skipped them in a little twisting flurry along the pavement, was blowing straight through him, the dust and detritus whistling through the hole in his guts. He felt humiliated and vengeful, so when Barry looked blankly around, he gestured at the girl, a cold and empty feeling in his stomach.

'Up there, pretty girl with the short hair, see? Phil Jones' been going out with her. Seen them about together. The old dog!'

Barry stared at her, nodding his head. He had the look of someone calculating, working towards a conclusion. He turned towards Tom, and was opening his mouth to speak when they were interrupted by some sort of commotion further up the street behind them, people pushing past to see what was happening. They turned and followed the flow along the pavement as though caught in the tow of a current, a little snag of energy twisting in the stream.

A van from the TV station had arrived, the rainbow *TVC* logo winking brightly among the drab colours of the street, the crew piling out and getting themselves organised. There was a plump girl in a fake fur jacket, like rabbit skin but bright pink, a cameraman, and a third guy with one of those microphones on a long handle that was wrapped up in the same stuff as the reporter's jacket. Both the men had very short hair, sunglasses, leather jackets and jeans, an urban look, unshaven, foppish and slightly sinister. A little crowd was forming around them, fascinated and shy. All of a sudden it was the television crew who seemed to be the real celebrities, as though they were draining the colours out of the street behind them; the demonstrators continued to posture and chant, but they had the look of extras, dispirited and unconvincing. Barry pulled at Tom's sleeve.

'Go and talk to them Tom. You can tell them what's really going on.'

He was hanging on to Tom's coat and starting to pull him along the street towards the TV people. The crew had crossed the road and were talking to a student, a young man wearing a long coat who at that moment opened it in an expansive gesture to display the slogan on his T shirt. The reporter was laughing, gesturing at her cameraman, turning the student towards him, making sure they got him on film.

They moved on up the street. Tom saw the reporter stop an old fellow in a wax coat, somebody he had seen about in the mart. She was talking earnestly to him. The old boy shook his head irritably and stepped to the side, trying to get on past. Barry was tapping his feet with impatience.

'Now's your chance Tom, you can explain it all to them, tell them about these Rainbow people.'

He gave Tom a shove into the street but he stepped back onto the pavement and pulled his arm free. He really didn't want to find himself on TV, and he'd only confuse the issue. The girl and her crew would want a simple picture of Welsh exporters versus English protestors, rural versus urban; they wouldn't know what to make of him. But Barry wasn't going to let the opportunity go by altogether. Tom was sure he thought that the news crew had some magical ability to sort everything out, that he had found himself suddenly in front of a tribunal that could assess, apportion blame, reward and chastise.

'We got to, Tom. You said yourself, we got to fight back.'

'You talk to them, Barry. They'd rather hear from you, you're local. They'll just assume I'm English, you know?'

Without hesitating, Barry started to cross the street. The crew were moving up the opposite pavement, the man with the camera walking backwards. Tom had the odd impression that they drew the life out of everything they passed; that for a moment contact with them produced a galvanic quiver of animation, a rush of vigour and activity like a stick drawn through an ant-hill, which subsided as soon as they moved on. Barry caught up with the reporter as she stopped to talk to a young woman with a push-chair. Tom was too far away to hear what they were saying, but he could see his awkward figure stooped in front of her, gesturing with large, inept movements of his arms, pointing, waving.

They were nearly opposite the fountain. The girl was still up there, draped around the column. As Tom watched, the cameraman noticed her, tapping the reporter on the shoulder and pointing. They waved a brief and dismissive gesture at Barry, and the three of them trotted to the foot of the steps. The cameraman crouched down, shrugging the equipment on his shoulder into position and focusing at the girl on the monument, the man with the mike raising the boom high into the air. The reporter was on tip-toes, holding herself up as high as she could. From the top of the steps the girl squinted down at them, carefree, charmed. Tom could see Barry watching from across the street, his shoulders humped up round his ears, dejected, ungainly and angular.

The crew moved further up the street and then, shortly afterwards, packed up, switching off their equipment, and with it their attention and their interest, with extraordinary suddenness and completeness. A moment before, they had been full of humour and enthusiasm, snapping out jokes and bright questions, open and engaged. Now they hurried back down the street towards their van, dodging impatiently through the traffic, the reporter irritably brushing past a student who was trying to hand her a leaflet. Tom looked at his watch. He wanted to call by Graig Goch on the way home to check the lambs that were going off this evening. They'd been tagged the day before, so if the shearers were finished, he could get Meirion or Richard to pop over and vet them right away. He could leave the paperwork with Beti, and there'd be no need to come back later in the night when the lorry arrived.

The traffic was starting to move again as people drifted away from the demonstration. The group of students round the fountain had gone. It was as though the television crew had pulled the plug as they left and now the energy of the enterprise was deflating in wheezy gasps, like one of those bouncy castles at a fairground. Tom called in at the surgery to make sure Meirion would be free in an hour or two to come over to Graig Goch to vet the lambs. He found him in the waiting room, staring out into the street through the glass front as a group of students walked by, pausing for a moment to peer back in at him. Meirion pushed his glasses further up his nose and turned away from the window.

'You boys ought to be fighting back Tom. Shouldn't let the protestors get all the attention. Why don't you get the Union or the Young Farmers to put on a little do?'

Tom told him he didn't think it would do any good. It seemed to him that the media were only interested in one story: the horror that live exports apparently aroused in ordinary people. Exporters were the villains, and there was no point raising their heads. Their best bet was to hope that they would eventually lose interest, that the great wet muzzle of the press would snuffle on to some new smell further along the gutter.

As Tom walked back to the car he heard his name called, and looked round to see Barry crossing the street after him.

'Give me a lift home?'

'Hop in, going there anyway.'

Barry explained that his Nana had driven him in; she'd come in to do the shopping.

'Won't she be looking for you? Is she still in town?'

'She won't mind.'

They took the back road out of town, past the Health Centre and the White Swan, turning right towards the main road again by Protheroe's forlorn and half-finished bungalow, abandoned since the foundations had been condemned, the windows poked in, the neat stacks of roofing tiles gradually broken or scattered by local kids, the heap of building sand washing away in rivulets into the mud. From there the road ran for a mile or so under the steep side of the Bwlch, where the impenetrable bracken was dying back in vast russet sheaves.

Tom was aware of Barry staring at him. When he glanced at him, the boy looked quickly to the front again. Tom felt a little unnerved.

'Alright?'

'Know what you said about Phil?'

'Take no notice Barry, I was only fooling around.'

'No, I heard you say, you know, what you said . . . '

Tom looked at him; once again his gaze flicked to the front. Barry licked his lips.

'Phil's got a little boy ain't he? Brought him to the farm, I seen him. What I mean, he's *married.*'

For some reason, Tom was suddenly sure that Barry was a virgin, that he was peering over deep and vertiginous edges where mysterious liquids boiled in the darkness. He was like a great bull-calf that had been fattening all these years, white, naked, muscular and innocent, and now suddenly was being prodded and goaded down unwilling alleys, the broad bulk of his head lowered in fear and confusion.

'Not just what he's *doing* with her.'

He shook his head sharply, stung by the prick of some illicit image.

'Not just that', he went on, 'but don't you see, she'll find out things. She's against us and he'll tell her things. Bound to.'

They had come out into open country, skirting the dark sweeps of forestry that lay in folds over the slopes behind them. There were meadows on either side of the road, low and watery green, a sense that the river was not far away. Graig Goch was just out of sight over the next rise.

'Let me out here please. Want to walk back over the top, check the Texels.'

Tom watched him start across the field, a bunch of bullocks raising anxious heads out of the wet grass at him as he passed. He rolled down the window and called out after him:

'Barry! You worry too much! You leave all this to your mum and me, alright!'

He didn't look back.

Tom turned on to the farm road. The buildings began about a quarter of a mile further on, first an old stone barn beside the road, then the new sheds on either side of a wide concrete yard. The house and the original outbuildings lay a few hundred yards beyond that.

There was a big fire in the far corner of the yard, black smoke rolling bulbously over the concrete, flakes of ash driven up by the heat. He could see a couple of figures dancing in and out of the smoke, poking into the flames with pitchforks. Something big and black lay bulging in the middle of the fire. There was a steady crackle from the flames, a bubbling hissing that was broken by sharp pops and smacks, the whooping shouts of raised voices. He stopped the car as a thick and indescribable smell came rolling in through the window. As he got out, Huw and Alwyn came over, gleaming grins on their smudged and blackened faces. They were both carrying pitchforks and there were rags and scraps of burnt material stuck to their boots and oily wisps of smoke curling and clinging around them.

A gust blew the black smoke off the fire for a moment, rolling it thickly back. On a huge heap of rubbish, wood, straw, broken pallets, the melting remains of fertilizer and feed bags, lay the upturned carcase of a cow, a great blackened thing, strips of white and yellow fat bubbling where the hide had scorched off, burnt lips curling back from the long brown teeth; at the other end, the boiling bag of the udder, hind legs splayed up into the smoke, split and splintered shards of bone.

'What's all this then boys?'

Alwyn streaked smut across his forehead with the back of his hand and shook the smoke out of his hair.

'Bugger died last night. Huw found her this morning. BSE', he said. 'That's what it says on the vet paper anyhow. If it's BSE they give you twenty five quid to burn her up. And a half a ton of coal to do the job.'

Tom looked at the fertilizer bags on the pyre:

'Course you can burn your rubbish up at the same time no doubt.'

Alwyn grinned and wiped his nose.

'Coal comes in handy for the winter don't it? Beti's good like that, isn't it Huw? So it's all official see, BSE on the vet paper and a few bags of coal for Huw and me. She was a thin old bugger though, wasn't she Huw?'

There was a sort of muddy plop from the fire, and a spurt of flame rose sizzling from the cow's collapsed abdomen. Tom got back in the car. 'Where are the shearers? Up in the old building?'

As he drove off, he could see the two of them prancing up to the flames, their pitchforks shaking showers of sparks into the air as they stirred at the fire, before the black smoke rolled back and covered them over again.

The shearers were finishing off the last pen of lambs, two of the boys still working, bent over at right-angles, the machines buzzing hypnotically. As Tom came into the shed the third shearer had straightened up with a deep groan, reaching up to tug at the string that switched off his machine. There were four of them in the gang, all of them short, puffy about the eyes, teeth missing, as though they'd been beaten up, as though the conditions of life were so hard that they physically knocked you about, fingers stamped on and swollen, lumps of muscle overstrained and prolapsed, their knobby, disgruntled faces scowling under mats of filthy hair. They wore ragged sheepskin slippers, black with lanolin, and their clothes were torn, plastered with dirt and grease from the fleeces, and tied together with baler twine. Half of the shed was now filled with a great pile of bulging wool-sacks, and the fourth member of the gang, who Tom saw was a girl, though you had to be close-up to be sure, was stamping about on top of them, stuffing the last few rolled-up fleeces into the sacks.

They must have come to Graig Goch twenty or thirty times by now, shearing the little lambs that went to Spain, but Tom had never had any kind of a conversation with them, and even Huw and Alwyn seemed to treat them like a different species, as though they had come out of a cave from under the mountain. Beti had some method of summoning them up, and they would arrive with their LandRover and trailer, set up their machines, cables trailing across the floor, the wool-sacks laid out ready for filling. They never seemed to talk to each other while they were working. They never came into the house for a cup of tea or something to eat. You never saw them take a break, though there was always a litter of pop-bottles and sweet wrappers left behind after they had gone. They took the lambs' wool as payment, so at the end of the day they would load the sacks onto the trailer, sheet it down and drive off, the four of them wedged tightly onto the bench-seat of the truck, shoulders turned in, all of them looking straight ahead.

The last shearer finished his lamb and reached up to switch off his machine. The incessant buzzing of the electric motor and the soft chatter of the clippers, drowsy, mesmerizing, seemed to linger on as the silence flowed back, just the nervous shuffling of the shorn lambs at the other end of the shed, the occasional tentative bleat. A couple of lambs had hidden themselves behind the wool-sacks and the girl now chased them out, their hooves clicking on the concrete as they skittered down the shed to join the others.

They started packing up their equipment, looping the extension leads into loose coils, unstringing the shearing machines from the overhead fittings, twisting off the cutting heads and carefully wrapping them in greasy cloths. The girl was sewing up the last wool sack, punching string on a thick steel needle through the woven plastic. Tom leaned on the gate and tried to chat to them; *Yes, lambs alright, not bad. No, they hadn't seen Beti. Yes, next week is OK.* They looked up at him with quick, uneasy glances as they worked, as though they weren't sure who he was. He gave up and went back to the car to phone the vets. Meirion said he would be free in about half an hour.

The fire was starting to burn down when he got back there; the cow had subsided to a glutinous bubbling mass in which rib-bones smouldered and glowed like sticks of charcoal. Alwyn said he would come back to the shearing shed to help with the lambs. They left Huw poking at something slippery at the edge of the fire, trying to hook it back into the embers.

'Give er some more diesel boy!' Alwyn told him. 'Help er along like!'

As they got into the car, the shearers drove past, towing their trailer of bulging sacks. All four heads turned sideways in the cab, staring at Huw and his cow.

Tom took the paper-work back to the house. It occurred to him that he'd better ring Felix del Rio in Burgos to tell him the lambs would be setting off tonight. There'd already been one delay, and he would be wondering what was going on. Beti's mother directed him with an elaborate mime to the phone on the wall, as though he'd never used it before.

'Tomas! Que tal, hombre?'

Tom could picture Felix lounging back in his swivel chair under the big window, the half-closed shutters letting in bands of dusty light. Late autumn in northern Spain, the colours in the street as sharp as ceramics, intense blues and whites, the air clean and cool and resinated.

'Pues Felix, es el mismo: mucho trabajo y poco dineiro!'

'*No me diga Tom! Ay la vida! Y los cordeiros, son buenos?*'

'*Si senor, son fenomenales!*'

Beti came into the room.

'Who was that Tom, the Spaniard? Everything set? Cup of coffee?'

Tom could hear Barry calling from the front room. Beti cocked her head to listen, then turned back to him.

'Come and see the news. The boy seems to think you'll be on it.'

The front room was almost in darkness. Barry and his grandmother were sitting side by side on the sofa, their faces lit in flickering greens and blues by the huge screen in front of them. Suddenly, there was Llanfrychan High Street, the same but different, with that odd heightened significance the screen gives to the familiar world. On TV, the demonstration looked purposeful, well-organised; both stylish and intellectually sound, as though an extra level of reality and meaning had been conferred on it. It had an air of inevitability and worth that the real event had lacked.

The Welsh commentary was fast and colloquial, and Tom missed a lot of it. The old lady was clicking her teeth in disapproval. Barry turned round, craning over the back of the sofa.

'Got the video on' he said. 'I'm taping this. Not every day you get on TV.'

He turned back to face the screen. His Nan murmured something to him.

'*Edrychwch arnon nhw. Saeson i gyd!*'

'They're not giving our side at all' Barry said.

There were a couple of quick interviews with students, witty, smiling, sharing a joke with the reporter. The old fellow Tom had recognised from the mart was grumpy and incomprehensible.

'Dammo, it's Emlyn Bach!' Beti was muttering indignantly. 'They should of given him a chance to talk, he'd of told them what for! You're right boy, it's only these damn protestors they talking to. Who made this bollocks then? Give their boss a ring in the morning I will!'

'I told Mam about Phil's girlfriend' Barry said.

Tom started to say something dismissive, but Beti interrupted him:

'Why didn't you tell me Tom? What's Phil playing at?'

'It's probably just a bit of fun, Beti.'

'Fun is it! I'm not paying him to run around with bloody riff-raff and hippies, telling em our business.'

'I'm sure he's not doing that.'

'You don't know what he's doing! You shouldn't hide things from me!'

Tom caught a little of what the reporter was saying in the voice-over as the camera moved around the crowd: *petition . . . Welsh Office . . . cruel conditions . . .* when the TV screen was suddenly filled with the image of the fountain, the group of students on the steps and the girl leaning against the stone column. Barry was nodding at the screen.

'There she is now' he said. 'You watch.'

She had looked dramatic that afternoon, out in the daylight, but now some startling and magical transformation had taken place. The camera had somehow lit her up, so that she glittered with a sexual charge that flickered over her body, its touch both soporific and arousing. Her pose was mythological, iconic, as she drooped, wilting, against the pillar. She was like Andromeda chained naked to the rock, an erotic sacrifice, exposed, swooning, her faint smile distant and abstracted. There was an utter silence in the room. Tom felt a horrible sense of constraint and awkwardness, as though he had been forced to watch something pornographic. The old lady pinched off a sneeze between her fingers.

'See?' Barry said. 'There she is.'

'I *know* her!' Beti was tugging at her lower lip.

'*Pwy yw hi?* Where the *hell* have I seen her before?'

Tom didn't tell her.

119

Chapter 10

Colin shrugged his shoulders out of the overalls and peeled them down over his jeans; with an elbow against the side of the wagon for balance, he hopped and shuffled out of his wellingtons, changing into elastic-sided boots, the shiny black leather winking for a moment under the arc-lights. He bundled the work-clothes into a locker behind the cab, and picked his way gingerly over the mucky concrete to the driver's door.

'Where's everyone tonight then?'

Alwyn answered him from out of the deep shadows behind the lorry:

'Buggered off, haven't they. Beti's in the house I suppose, and Barry. Phil wasn't here today. They all had the hump tonight, should of seen them.'

He coughed and spat, hawking a wet gobbet out of the back of his throat.

'Know how Beti is, and Barry looking like a bullock in a butcher shop, rolling his eyes like; and that Tom Wood, always sound like he's talking out of his arsehole, worse than ever tonight he was.'

He cursed as he tripped over something in the darkness. There was the sound of a tin can skittering across the concrete.

'What happened to you anyway? On the nest was you, Scotchy-boy? Thought these lambs were going off yesterday.'

'Don't know about that. I just go where I'm told; get down here for ten-thirty, that's what they said'. Colin felt a flick of irritation, as though the Welshman had stepped over the mark, questioned his professional skill. He swung himself up into the cab. It had started to rain.

'Only joking pal.' Alwyn appeared in the pool of light around the cab. 'You missed a couple of loads though, didn't you?'

'Been home, had a week's holiday. Haven't been back there since the end of August. The wee boy hardly knows me. So, nobody want any duty-free this trip then?'

'I'm skint pal. Rest of them, I don't think they're in the mood like I say.'

He stretched up to hand over the folder of paperwork.

'Where these going then, somewhere nice?'

In the trailer behind them the sheep scuffled quietly, settling.

'We're going where the sun always shines, Taf. Not like here.'

Colin passed a cigarette down to Alwyn and the two of them lit up, drawing in deep draughts of smoke, in a silence that was momentarily companionable as they stared out into the darkness.

In Llanfrychan High Street the traffic lights seemed to be stuck on red. Colin drummed his fingers on the steering wheel and whistled through his teeth. Teach me to try a short cut, he thought, should never have come through town. It was getting on for midnight, and there was nobody about, although the pub he had just passed was still lit up. He was tempted for a moment to jump the lights, but you could be sure there'd be a Panda car tucked down a side-street, waiting for him to do just that.

This time tomorrow he'd be over on the other side, halfway through Normandy if the going was good. Stop for a coffee in that bar outside Le Mans, what was the wee girl's name? At that moment, somebody crossed the road in front of him, stepping off the curb very close to the lorry so that he looked down on the fore-shortened figure, gingery-hair pulled back in a pony tail, drenched to the colour of blood in the red of the traffic-lights. Instead of crossing to the far side of the street, the figure paused as though remembering something, then turned and walked down the length of the lorry. Colin watched him in the mirror as he stood on tip-toe to peer in through the ventilation slats.

Chapter 11

Harris slapped the text-book shut. He snapped open the binding-rings of the file and threaded the photocopies back in. He shuffled his notes together and added them to the file. Three and a half hours work, for a quarter of a page added. The library was stuffy, the air dry and stale. He had a head-ache and he felt frustrated; there was a sort of buzzing between his ears and he couldn't concentrate. In the ceiling above him, one of the fluorescent tubes was starting to go, flickering and sizzling like a fly was trapped in it, the same sound that was in his head. He needed fresh air. He stretched his legs under the table, pushing the chair back with a short screech on the floor. Further down the work-table a girl looked up at him, her eyes inward and unfocused. He stacked his books together, slapping them into a pile with a series of sharp cracks and thumps. He stared at the girl; she blinked myopically and turned back to her work. He stood up, and dropped the books into a carrier bag. *A frontier society: cultural and social assimilation in the Severn Basin.* Well, he had another week before he had to hand it in.

He set off down the corridor, the straps on his boots flapping loose round his ankles; he'd had them repaired recently, little metal horse-shoes on heel and toe, and his footsteps clacked and rang on the shiny floor. Leaving the section on Economics behind, he turned left down Social History. He followed the shelves to the point at which they became Sociology, then turned right, past the photocopiers and along the length of Health and Social Studies to the Reference Section and the main entrance. There were still one or two people hunched in front of the computer screens which stood round the sides of the room. He passed a lecturer he knew slightly, he'd gone to a talk of his a couple of weeks ago. As Harris walked by, the fellow poked a dispirited finger at the key-board and the monitor flickered and began to scroll, jittery green columns of figures, lists, inventories, headings and sub-headings, classifications and categories rolling hypnotically up, endlessly replaced as new information pushed up from the bottom of the screen, like some experiment gone wrong in a laboratory, the flask foaming and overflowing, loops and coils and entrails of crazy released material spewing everywhere.

He pushed his way out through the heavy glass doors of the main entrance, cursing as one of them caught him on the shoulder as it swung back. It was dark already; he turned his collar up against the chill damp air that was forming misty haloes around the dull orange lozenges of the street lights.

On his first visit to the library a year ago he'd been impressed despite himself. His sense of amused superiority, which so far everything about Llanfrychan had aroused in him, had been hard to sustain in face of the size and complexity of the place. He hadn't bothered to read the pamphlet explaining how to negotiate the catalogue system, and had ended up having to ask one of the librarians for help as the computer screen flashed error messages at him. He flushed hot as he remembered this, and walked faster, his boots striking bright reverberations out of the flags of the pavement as he stamped his way up Paxton Hill towards the flat.

He was hungry. He tried to remember if there was any food in the fridge. He knew his personal shelf was empty, but perhaps somebody had been shopping. Probably not though. Too busy with their stupid demo all afternoon. He had walked down at the end of the morning to have a look, and he'd been surprised at just how many people were there. He had thought there'd be Sían, Julie, maybe Nicky and a couple more, but this was an event, there were forty, fifty people here, leaflets, posters; the traffic had come to a stop.

'Well, what do you think?'

Sían had seemed to bob up from nowhere in front of him, more plump and pink-cheeked than ever, blonde frizz bubbling out from under her hat, her Wrexham scarf wound round her neck. She'd fixed her glasses with a bit of sellotape; he felt instantly irritated. She was jigging up and down on her toes, beaming, excited, showing off. He realised she wanted his approval, that she was waiting for him to say something nice. He'd been back home last week, his mum needed him, there'd been no way round it, so he hadn't been involved in getting the demonstration organised; he hadn't printed any leaflets or put up any posters, or rung the local newspaper. The whole thing was their show, Sían and Julie's, and now she was proudly displaying her work. He pulled a face.

'This is all bullshit you know'.

Across the street he saw Julie waving excitedly at him. She was with Whatsname, that creep, the one she wanted to move into the flat with them. The two of them trotted over. They were holding hands, for christssake.

'This is bullshit' he went on. 'You're not changing anything. It's like some stupid sponsored event, some bloody fun-run. Go on, tell me: what exactly are you achieving here?'

He could see that he'd taken them completely by surprise; he'd got them guessing again, and he snorted with sour delight.

'Tell you what', he said, 'you should of got Terry Wogan down here to present the show. Give it that final, institutionalised touch.'

He looked at them; all three had an expression of dumb shock, of hurt and disorientation. He felt a wonderful sense of ease and control, inspired but meticulous. He softened his tone.

'What you have to do', he began, 'you got to gain control of the effects your actions have. You got to be specific, direct.'

'Look!' Sían interrupted him, breaking right through the middle of his sentence.

'Look! There they are! They *did* come after all!'

She pointed at something over his shoulder, and the three of them pushed past him. Turning to watch them, he saw them run for twenty yards or so down the street to where a brightly coloured van had just pulled in to the kerb. They crowded round it as various people got out. It was some sort of a film crew; he saw a guy with a fluffy microphone on a long boom, and a moment later a cameraman. Julie and Sían and Whatsname were jumping about, pointing, gesturing, their voices high and clear and excited.

'Enjoy yourselves suckers!' he called after them. 'I'm off to do some work.'

No one looked round.

'I'll be at the library,' he had called again.

Now, clattering up the brick steps to the front door of the flat, he let himself in. The lights were on, but nobody seemed to be about. He poked his head round the door of Sían and Julie's room, but it was empty. He walked down the hall; there was someone in the bathroom, he could hear the taps running. In the kitchen, there was a litter of plates and crumbs on the table. There was a bread knife on the floor, the blade smeared with margarine. On the back of the chair hung a big leather jacket, old and scratched and soft. He rested his hand on it for a moment. Nicky. He walked back to the closed door of the bathroom. He could sense the warmth and steam on the other side of the door. There was a hot, wet smell of shampoo and bubble-bath and the sound of water surging and gurgling. Nicky.

He supposed he could walk in there really, say hello. Casual: perhaps he needed something from the medicine cabinet above the bath. *Hi Nicky, how you doing?* His heart seemed to be beating a little faster. Why was that? They were mates weren't they? Nicky wouldn't think twice about it. He'd just walk in there. He rested his forehead lightly on the thin panel of the door. He imagined he could see through it. The mirror was misted over into opacity and the air was sweet and wet, hanging in hot and scented curtains of steam, beading on walls and surfaces, on pipes and porcelain and on her skin. She would be lying in billows of foam, just her wet head showing, like a little hot flower. He could bring her a cup of tea, and to take it she would have to raise herself up out of the water, the bubbles lapping at the wet and creamy pink of her nipples. He turned the handle; the door was locked.

'Who's that? Is that you Harris? What you want? I'll be out in a minute.'

He walked down the corridor to the kitchen. On Sían and Julie's shelf he found a packet of instant soup; he tore it open into a mug and switched the kettle on. He looked round as Nicky came into the room.

'Hi Harris. Did you go to the library?'

He grunted, and poured boiling water onto the powder in the mug. Some of the fragrant warmth of her bath had come into the room with her, a breath of steam. She was wearing a towelling robe, white and fluffy, and she was folded into it exactly as he'd imagined her folded into the foam of the bath. Her hair was slick and dark, and there were beads of moisture across the bridge of her nose. He burnt his lips on the soup and his eyes watered.

'You been there all this time? At the library?'

He grunted again, and she shook her head, amused, admiring: 'You must of nearly finished your project haven't you?' She pulled a face: 'Gawd! I done nothing, you know! Haven't looked at the book-list yet. Phillips'll kill me!'

Her mouth turned down at the corners in a look of childish dismay.

'I could give you a hand if you like' he said. 'I got loads of notes now, and a list of references. We could . . . '

'Shit! What time is it? Shit!' She ran out of the room, calling back to him from the corridor: 'You should of stayed. They sent a TV crew, you know. They said it might be on the news tonight, if they could fit it in.'

He followed her into the front room; she was kneeling in front of the television, drumming her fingers on the cabinet as the screen warmed up.

'You should of stayed, Harris. They took loads of film; they interviewed Julie, you know?'

There was a flurry of music, then the *TVC* logo, and then the start of an advert for dogfood. Nicky slapped the top of the set.

'Well shit! Missed it!'

She backed away from the TV and flopped down on the sofa, the bathrobe billowing round her and blowing a gust of warmth and sweetness at him.

'Julie!' he echoed, smiling down at her. 'And Whatsname? They interview him?'

'Who?'

'Whatsname, you know, Julie's Whatsname!'

'Oh Supernerd!' She gave him a beaming smile. 'No, he didn't get his fifteen seconds of fame!'

'You know she wants him to move in here?'

Nicky rolled huge eyes at him, laughing as they answered each other in exact unison, their voices harmonizing:

'Over my dead body!'

Harris felt warm and happy. They were pals.

'You coming to the pub tonight?' he asked.

She got up and walked over to the bay window at the front of the room. There were long net curtains hanging there, grey with dust and cobwebs, and she drew a corner aside with an abstracted gesture, staring out into the night.

'Probably not. I don't think so.'

It seemed to Harris that something drooped and wilted in her as she stood with her back to him, so that he wanted to comfort her, put an arm round her shoulder and tell her there was nothing to worry about. But when she turned back to face him, her eyes were looking inward, her expression withdrawn, distant and private. The moment of closeness between them had passed. She gave him a short smile and started to leave the room.

'What *are* you doing then?' he called after her. 'Seeing your exporter are you, your abuser friend? Don't suppose he was at the demo was he? You'll be able to tell him all about it. How can you *do* it for chrissake?'

She turned in the doorway.

'You're completely out of order, Harris. It's just none of your business.' She stared at him for a moment, her eyes narrowed. 'And anyway' She shook her head: 'Anyway, what would you know. You know fuck all about it.'

'Fuck you too' he muttered at the empty doorway, blinking furiously.

'Oh fuck you too.'

He went to his room. Through the thin walls he could hear Nicky moving about the flat, down the corridor to the kitchen, back to her room. A little later Sían came back, shrieking out a greeting as she came through the front door. He could hear the two girls talking, their words muffled and distorted, Sían's yodelling laugh swooping above the murmurs and giggles, the buzz and drone of words not understood. At some point, he heard her say quite distinctly: *'Where's Harris?'* He couldn't hear Nicky's reply. He felt irritated, intruded upon; so they *had* been talking about him. He felt sure that if he came out of his room they would turn to him with faces full of interrupted laughter.

He tried to go back to the letter he'd started to write to his mother, sitting on his bed and resting the note-pad on his knees. *Dear Mum, if you'd listened to me on Sunday night you'd know what I think about all this. It's really stupid . . .* The phone rang. He heard Nicky come out into the hall to answer it, calling something back to Sían. He tried to make out what she was saying, but even standing at his door he could hear only low murmuring tones, a quick gurgle of laughter.

An hour or so later he heard the front door slam as they left the flat. He had tried to do some more work, but his head-ache was worse, and the light in his room wasn't really good enough, a pale shadowless haze that lay over everything without highlights or definition. He put his books away and lay on the bed. In a corner of the room there was a pile of dirty clothes that he'd been meaning to take to the launderette; socks and pants and T-shirts spewing out of the black bag he'd stuffed them into. If he'd taken them home last week his mum would have washed them for him.

He could see his mum very clearly for a moment, her irritable gesture as she stubbed out a cigarette only half smoked, holding it as though it had nothing to do with her, like it was somebody else's bad habit, *why do you do that Mum, it's such a waste of money. I ought to go back to roll-ups,* she'd said. *These things don't taste of anything.* The conversation they'd had on Sunday night came back to him and he sighed deeply, squeezing his eyes shut and pressing his knuckles into them, forcing shards and splinters of light back into his head: her latest plan, her most ridiculous scheme yet. Still, she'd promised to send him fifty quid this week. Somehow they'd always managed so far, and she said it was all working out now, there was no more problems.

He swung his legs off the bed and stood up. His coat was hanging on the back of the door, and there were three pound coins in the pocket.

Dave Bennett owed him a tenner; he'd arranged to meet him in the pub tonight. If he didn't have the cash he'd have some speed or E or something. Julie would probably be there, banging on about their ridiculous demo; he could straighten *her* out. And Whatsname: that situation was full of possibilities. He felt the beginnings of a grim amusement, a sort of bitter self-esteem, as he let himself out of the flat and set off down the long slope of Paxton Hill towards the Star.

*   *   *

'Where's my soup then?'

Sían was standing on tip toes, reaching up and sweeping the flat of her hand along the shelf, which was too high for her to see into. She dislodged a bottle of ketchup and caught it clumsily as it tumbled down at her.

'Who's pinched my soup? Are you coming tonight Nicky?'

She pushed the bottle back onto the shelf with the tips of her fingers.

'I can't believe you missed it. I thought I might be late getting back so I watched it at the Union bar. You looked great, you did. Everybody said.'

She turned and found that the kitchen was empty, adjusting her glasses on her nose as though to make sure.

'Nicky? Where you gone?' She shuffled up the corridor to the front room.

'Are you coming to the Star tonight? I can give you a lift if you like.'

Nicky had been standing at the window; she turned as Sían came in.

'Don't think so. I don't know.'

'Only, we thought we could sort of have a meeting, discuss how it all went?'

Nicky sat down and lit a cigarette. 'They got a band tonight at the White Swan. I said I'd probably go.'

The girls exchanged a look, complicated and complicit. Sían nodded.

'I see' she said. 'I can see he wouldn't want to come to the Star.'

She was looking at Nicky as though at some beautiful beast in a cage, terrifying, pitiful, so that her expression was somehow both condescending and adoring.

'Don't you start' Nicky said. 'I just had Harris going on at me.'

'Where is Harris?'

'Dunno, in his room.' She made a dismissive gesture, a contemptuous toss of the head. She blew out a long sigh of smoke.

'Thing is Sían, the whole thing's ridiculous really. *I* don't know what I'm doing.'

She flicked her cigarette into the empty grate of the fireplace.

'Obviously, it's a bit weird he works for that exporter, that what's her name. But it's just, he needs the money, you know. And *he* can't see anything wrong with it.'

She stopped, staring at Sían with an expression so abstracted that the other girl reached out and put a hand on her knee.

'Nicky? What's the matter?'

Nicky's eyes swam, then focused.

'I just realised I been there, where Phil works, I mean. That time, ages ago, I was coming back from Bristol, I ran out of bloody petrol. Had to walk miles, I could see these lights, it was creepy, I can tell you. There was this huge place, all lit up, like a factory. They gave me a can of petrol. Must be the same place.'

She shook her head.

'Before I met him . . . Anyway, that's all very weird, but the thing is, me and Phil, it's not a big deal. It's a laugh, mainly. Know what I mean?'

Sían had taken off her glasses, and was fiddling with the bit of tape she'd repaired them with. She smiled blindly to herself.

'No' she said. 'No, I don't.'

'Well, he's not the love of my life, you know? I don't think. What it is, he makes me laugh.'

Nicky seemed to be picking her way, as though from one stepping stone to another, searching for balance.

'Also, he's just, or *we're* just, incredibly . . . '

'Good at it?'

Nicky nodded slowly, smiling to herself.

'Yes. Anyway, there's something very . . . sorted about him. He's got his own life; it's like he's sort of solid and complete. It's just a nice feeling to be around, I don't know why. It's as though he's much older than me.'

Sían put her glasses back on.

'Well he is! I agree he's a bit gorgeous, but he *is* much older than you.'

'No he's not! He's eight years older than me!' Nicky had looked offended for a moment, but now she grinned as Sían calculated on her fingers.

'So when he was *your* age' she said, 'you were *twelve!*'

Across the corridor, Harris groaned, gritting his teeth as the whoops and yells of laughter reached him.

'When he was roping cows,' Sían went on, 'and shagging sheep, you were playing with your Barbies!'

'Do you mind! I didn't play with Barbies when I was twelve! Do me a favour!'

She put her head in her hands in pantomime despair.

'Gawd! It can't go on. I'll have to pack it in.'

She looked up, and Sían watched as shadows seemed to move across her friend's eyes, her glance drifting aside, withdrawing into some private dismay.

The phone rang.

*   *   *

When Harris got to the Star, shouldering his way through the stiff swinging doors of the pub and making his way to the bar, he could see Sían and Julie at the far end of the room, in their usual place at the long table. They had Whatsname with them, and a couple of other people, Tim Morris and that friend of his. He got himself a bottle and leaned on the counter. Sían saw him and waved; he nodded at her but stayed where he was. The place was half full. He looked around but he couldn't see Dave Bennett.

Sían waved at him again, flapping her hand and mouthing at him to come over. He glared at her. He felt somehow stuck where he was; he was aware of some damage to his confidence, some loss of grip and control. He felt backed-up and defensive. He didn't need Sían to invite him over to their table, but he felt curiously unable to wander over and join them. He felt clumsy and heavy, as though he might trip on the carpet or spill his drink. He pulled his notebook out of his coat pocket, intending to write something down. He didn't have a pen with him, and his hands felt suddenly hot and big. He was beginning to feel like a dork, and when someone bumped him from behind, pushing past to get at the bar, he turned furiously at them.

'The Italian team as tragic heroes. This is it!' The fellow smiled at him, raising his hands in a mime of surrender. 'Sorry, sorry.'

Turning back, he found Sían at his elbow.

'Come and sit with us Harris! What you doing here by yourself? Look, I'm buying you a drink. Come on, please!'

Sighing, he followed her back to the table.

'Harris thinks the demo was a waste of time don't you Harris?'

Harris glared at her again; she was treating him like he belonged to her, like some little dog told to wag his tail. At the same time, her silly enthusiasm was somehow relaxing.

'He thinks it's all like Noel's Houseparty, don't you Harris?' She turned to the others: 'He does, really.'

Harris found himself grinning. 'Terry Wogan is what I said.'

Whatsname put his elbows on the table and leaned across at him.

'How d'you make that out then? What's Terry Wogan got to do with it?'

His horrible little face was pinched with aggression; Harris thought: I've gone and cornered a fieldmouse.

'It's all so bloody British,' Harris said, sighing and shaking his head dismissively.

'The exporters send off the lambs, the students jump up and down, and everything goes on exactly the same.' He took a drink. 'It's like Morris Dancing' he said. He was pleased with that.

'What would *you* do then?' Tim Morris asked him, his big bovine face placid and innocent. *Morris, dancing . . . did he think I was talking about him?* Harris snorted with silent laughter.

'It's easy to criticize.' Whatsname added.

'Go on Harris' Sían said. 'What would you do?'

She put her hand on his arm and peered blindly up at him over the top of her glasses. For a moment he felt a flash of irritation so bright that it made him blink; then he realised that she was waiting for him to say something brilliant, that her foolish beaming smile was expressing devoted expectation. He cleared his throat.

'In London' he said, 'they had a campaign, they targeted the butchers' shops, they put superglue in the locks. They couldn't open, none of them.'

There was a silence, then Tim Morris got up.

'London', he said tonelessly. He drank the last of his pint, head thrown back, his throat pumping. 'London, is it? I'm off then.'

He nodded at the others, not catching Harris' eye. Harris watched his wide back, shoulders a little hunched as he weaved through the crowd. Moron, Harris thought. What's his problem? He seemed to remember being told his parents had a farm or something, maybe that was it.

'That's just vandalism,' Whatsname said. Harris shut his eyes.

'So you think it's alright to hang up dead animals in a shop window do you?' he said.

'I'm a vegetarian' Whatsname said. 'That doesn't mean it's alright what you said.'

'I'm a vegetarian but I got nothing against butchers, is that what you mean?'

'For gods sake Harris', Julie said, 'lighten up, won't you.'

'I don't see what the problem is' Tim Morris's friend was saying. 'There was a lot of people at the demonstration.' He raised his finger: 'And it got on TV, nothing wrong with that. On the evening news.' He shook his head, puffing out his cheeks in admiration.

Harris groaned. 'The *TVC* news', he said. 'The *Welsh* news. An audience running into hundreds.'

Julie and Whatsname ignored him, turning to Tim's friend.

'I know, wasn't it great! Did you see my interview? What you think? And did you see Nicky? Didn't she look fantastic!'

The boy rolled his eyes: 'Oh my god, what a star! Where is she tonight anyway?'

Julie turned to Sían.

'Where is Nicky, is she coming tonight?'

'Silly cow,' Harris said. 'Sounds like she was really showing off.'

'You're jealous Harris,' Julie said. She was sneering at him. *Julie was sneering at him.* Sían was patting him on the arm; he shook her hand off, furious and confused. He felt as though he'd become stupid, like everyone else. He leaned back in his chair and shut his eyes.

About an hour later, Julie and Whatsname got up to leave. He was aware of some sort of coded communication going on between Sían and Julie, presumably about who was getting the use of the room if Whatsname was coming back to the flat.

Tim Morris' friend had already gone.

'Shall we go Harris?' Sían asked him. She was patting his arm again, giving his wrist a little squeeze through the thickness of his coat. He felt trapped, hot and breathless.

'Shall we go?' She dangled her car-keys at him in a sort of silly invitation. Looking round the bar, he suddenly recognised Dave Bennett, pushing his way through to them. He felt an immense relief, like gasps of fresh air.

'No, you go,' he said to Sían. 'I got some stuff to do.' She stared at him as though she hadn't understood what he was saying.

'Fuck off Sían,' he said. 'I'm busy.'

It turned out Dave Bennett wasn't stopping either. He couldn't pay Harris the tenner; they settled on two quid and a tab. That made it pretty expensive gear. Harris washed the pill down with a bottle of lager and leaned back to listen to the music. The pub was very hot, the noise swelling like lumps of physical stuff, like muscle, colours pumping and pulsing like blood. Later, a bunch of arseholes from the Geography department or somewhere like that, sporty types in rugby shirts, started hogging the jukebox and putting on country music . . . *country music.* Harris left.

The streets were black and empty, there was nobody about; it must be later than he'd thought. He walked fast, his heels ringing on the pavement. He felt nervous, irritable, his head as clear as glass. He crossed the High Street at the traffic lights, stepping out in front of a big lorry that was waiting at the red lights, its motor idling in a deep rhythmic grumble. As he crossed the road, some sound from the back of the lorry made him turn. He started to walk down the length of the trailer, a kind of choked laughter bursting out of his chest in short sobs. The lorry was full of animals! It was packed with lambs, packed solid, right up to the top on three levels way above his head! Through the gaps in the trailer he could sense the dense mass of bodies, hear them cough and shuffle. Peering in through one of the slats he was confronted with a wildly rolling eye as a blunt muzzle puffed a hot and panic-stricken blast of florid ruminant breath into his face, right into his open and gasping mouth!

So much for the demonstration! Now, the unspeakable bastards weren't even trying to keep out of sight! They were coming right through the middle of town, raising a stiff middle finger in a gesture of obscene contempt. *We'll fuck these sheep right here in the middle of the High Street if we feel like it, what you going to do about it?* Harris looked back up the length of the trailer towards the cab. There was a huge wing mirror on the lorry, the great convex lens cantilevered out into the street; in the depths of the reflection he seemed to see the driver's face staring back at him, saturnine, impassive.

'You bastards! You bloody bastards!' he yelled. A hand reached out from the open window of the cab and with a languid, fastidious gesture flicked ash off a cigarette. Harris kicked wildly at the huge rear wheels of the lorry.

'You fucking, fucking bastards!'

The lights changed, and with a deep roar of its motor which lifted a single, solid-looking lump of black smoke high above the vertical exhaust, the lorry moved away down the street.

Chapter 12

Tuesday was Bernard's funeral. The police had been round at his place two days running; they'd even called at Greenhill and asked Phil some questions: had Bernard been depressed lately? Had he ever talked about suicide? Phil told them of course not, Bernard wasn't like that, he'd never do such a thing. He *was* careless about guns, mind you; it *could* have been left about with a shell in the breech. Dai Plod told him later that Iori had said *exactly* the same thing: *same words – funny, that.* So anyway, the coroner had told the family they could go ahead with the funeral. The inquest would be in a month's time.

Phil parked the van about a mile from Tabor. It was as close to the chapel as he could get; from there on, the single track road was blocked with vehicles. He had stopped in the village to collect Auntie Nellian, but she had decided at the last minute she wasn't up to it. Just as well; she'd never have managed the walk, and it was raining. He hadn't brought a coat. As he stumped up the hill, his head lowered against the cold drizzle, he could feel his suit taking on a kind of warm and pungent sponginess. It felt like it was shrinking there and then, though really it had been too tight on him for years now, cramped across the shoulders and under the arms, the sleeves pulling up short above his wrists. He was late. Near the top of the hill, he came to the back end of a queue of people that filled the road and stretched on for fifty yards or so to where the chapel itself and the little burial ground leaned into the slope of the hill below the road. Bernard was getting a good send off. Everyone around the chapel door had brought umbrellas; perhaps the family had listened to a weather forecast. The rain crepitated faintly on the glistening tortoise-back shapes.

Phil slid himself into the edges of the crowd. He wasn't the last to arrive; there were a few dark figures, stooping in the grey light, coming up the hill behind him. He was standing next to Ken Rees and the Powell brothers. Alun Price and his wife nodded to him, and a little further away Will Williams gave him a quick, shy smile. John James wiped the rain out of his eyes.

'How are you then Phil? Still working with Beti? How's that going?

Are you sending a lot of lambs?'

Phil told him that they'd sent off three thousand last week, and there was a little ripple of murmured admiration, several people shuffling closer.

'Good boy Phil.'

'That's the way to do it.'

He could feel the quiet warmth of their approval, the dignified and enfolding endorsement of the community.

'Three thousand! *Bachgen bach!*'

Ken Rees leaned over the low wall of the graveyard, squinting through the drizzle.

'Here we go then' he said.

The doors of the chapel opened, and they could hear the thin wheeze of the harmonium and someone, Joe Davies perhaps, a beautiful tenor voice, rising in sweeping flights above it: *The Old Rugged Cross*. The rain ran into Phil's eyes. The graveyard sloped steeply and the grass was wet; the pall-bearers, hunched and straining under the weight of the coffin, worked painfully between the headstones towards the open pit, their faces glistening and contorted. Bernard's wife Nerys and the two grown-up daughters followed, their features chubby with crying. Phil thought a little guiltily that, for all the pints he'd drunk with Bernard over the years, he didn't even know the girls' names. The last verse of the hymn drifted down to where they stood, the words fraying in the rising wind: *and exchange it some day for a crown*. The rain on the umbrellas sounded like ripples of discreet applause. There had been a weaned calf sale in Llanfrychan the day before, and from two or three farms down in the valley you could hear a mournful and discordant descant as the old suckler cows called inconsolably for their young. John James was saying something to him. Phil turned back.

'What's that?'

John pointed down the valley: 'That's your bottom fields there isn't it? I never knew you could see Greenhill from here.'

'You're right too. They're looking bare, don't they. The sheep'll have to go from there.'

Squinting through curtains of drizzle at the patchwork of pale greens and yellows of the autumn fields, segmented by the dark lines of hedges, he could see the humped shapes of his cattle on the slope below the bracken, his good old girls, his lovely Welsh Blacks. Three of the cows had calved in the last month, stout, creamy little bull-calves, by Will's Charolais; for the Greenhill herd that represented quite a flurry. Phil sighed. He could leave the others out, put an electric fence round the bit of woodland by the ruin, they'd be well sheltered there. But with at least two more to calve this winter, there was going to be quite a crowd in the old stone barn. He thought of the foundations for his new cowshed, half-filled with water, cut as deep as a grave into the peaty soil. A new shed, open and airy, with a nursery for the little calves. No more than two thousand quid if he used forestry timber. Two thousand quid. Still, if this work for Tom and Beti kept going, if he talked to the bank.

Phil drove into Llanfrychan rather than going straight home. He thought he might have a quick one at the Ox, where Bernard had left so many in for him before now. The landlord kept the score in a notebook behind the bar. Phil had called there once, after not having been in for several weeks, to find a list of drinks that Bernard had put in for him – three or four pints, several whiskies, a double rum. He'd asked him once why he kept doing it: *why are you spending your money on me Bernard? haven't you got anything better to do with it, you silly bugger?* Bernard had grinned at him, wheezing with stifled laughter, clutching some gleeful and secret joke to himself. He'd miss the old bugger, he would.

As soon as the coffin had been lowered into the ground, the crowd broke up with disconcerting speed and purposefulness, as though at some arranged signal, everybody suddenly walking away. Within a few moments there were only four or five people, Bernard's immediate family, left around the grave. That tall fellow must be his brother, looked exactly like him. Phil hadn't realised he was out again; he'd got five years, hadn't he? What a bloody horrible story that was. He shuddered, feeling suddenly cold and miserable. He had lingered at the roadside, but he realised he didn't know these people at all. He had an unpleasant feeling of being out of place, left behind. He especially didn't want to talk to the brother. He turned the collar of his jacket up and set off down the road after the last of the retreating mourners. There was a little black pony in the field below the road, and as Phil hurried along, the creature ran up and down behind the hedge, snorting and whinnying, rolling its eyes as if in some frenzy of anxiety: *wait! wait!*

Iori had had the same idea. Phil hadn't seen him at the funeral but he must have been there somewhere, under the black umbrellas around the chapel door. Now he was sitting on a stool at the bar, his black suit stretched tight across his shoulders as he hunched over the counter, a pint of beer untouched in front of him. There were no other customers. As Phil came through the door, Iori turned his heavy, pale face towards him and gave a slow nod.

'Aye aye, you were there, were you? Didn't see you.' His voice had a dull ring of reproach in it.

'Course I was. Good turn-out, wasn't it. Pint please Jim.'

'Sludge?' The landlord reached a glass off the shelf. 'Lot of people there then?'

'Good crowd.'

'What'll happen now, will Nerys keep the farm going?'

Jim had asked Phil the question, but it was Iori who answered with a contemptuous snort that blew a spray of froth off the top of his pint as he drank:

'How's she going to manage? There's no work in them girls. See the brother there did you?'

He gave Phil a quick pale stare, the whites of his eyes flashing. 'See him there? How does he show his face?'

He turned to Jim: 'Tell me that. Is that right?' The barman gave him a blank look, and Phil interrupted:

'Long story Jim. Family skeletons, you know?'

'Skellingtons be fuck!' Iori stared at his glass, his lips moving, muttering to himself.

Jim poured Phil's beer, then reached under the counter for the tally-book. He flicked quickly through the last few pages, then dropped it back on the shelf.

'One sixty-four please Phil; nothing in for you, I'm afraid.'

The landlord went through to the back; they could hear the chink of bottles clinking in the crates as he moved stuff around in the other bar. Once or twice Iori looked up and seemed about to say something, then changed his mind, shaking his head, tapping a finger-nail on the side of his glass. Above the bar the TV was showing racing, the sound turned off. Phil looked over at the table on the other side of the room: that was where they'd been sitting, that time when Nicky had come into the bar. He'd been with Tom Wood and Barry, after the mart. She came in and stood at the bar where he was standing now. His body responded to the thought, a nervous flicker, like fear.

He wondered whether to get Iori a pint, and decided not to. Without Bernard between them, wheezing, grinning, picking his nose, pushing his thumb into the bowl of his pipe and sucking gobbets of dottle and spit as he reached the punchline of some filthy joke, without Bernard's chaotic personality between them, they didn't have a lot to say to each other. And anyway he really didn't have his drinking boots on today. He tipped back the rest of his beer and nodded to Iori.

'Be off then.'

Jim called through from the back bar. 'See you next time Phil. Take care now.'

Iori shut his eyes, as though to blot him out.

On the way home he stopped to use the phone box outside the station. There was no reply from Nicky's flat. He had lambs to tag at Graig Goch that evening and he was hoping to see her afterwards. The last couple of times he'd tried to make an arrangement, she hadn't been free. He hadn't seen her for ten days, and he could feel the slow build-up of a dull and irritable tension, a sort of clotted ache, without humour or excitement, oppressive and joyless. Past Blaen Cwm, where a steep bank at the edge of the plantation had been clear-felled, a forestry tractor was crawling down an incline which at this distance looked almost vertical, working the ground down ready for new planting, combing the smashed debris of underbrush into long straight lines. Beyond lay sweeps of white moorland, where lines of limestone vertebrae poked through the thin clothing of the soil. Through breaks in the cloud the light fell in fluted columns.

*   *   *

From time to time as they worked through the pens of lambs, tagging and counting, shoving, sorting and separating, working mostly in silence, just the sharp clack of the ear-tag pliers and the scuttle of little hooves on the concrete, Phil was aware of Alwyn looking at him strangely, sharp glances from under the eyebrows as he stooped over his work, the look in his eyes difficult to interpret; speculative, amused, perhaps hostile.

It was nearly ten by the time they finished. Huw had started off helping them, but he hadn't been a lot of use, yawning, bleary, dropping the tags on the floor. Alwyn had told him to get some rest, and he was now curled up and snoring on a pile of empty feed sacks in a corner of the shed.

'Been on the nest, he has.' Alwyn said. 'Got a woman in Maesglas, fucks like a snake.'

He grinned delightedly, and spat over the railings of the sheep-pen.

An hour earlier, Phil had broken off to use the phone in the washroom at Graig Goch, but there was still no reply from Nicky's flat. If they were quick enough in getting the lorry away, he thought he might look in at the Star anyway, just to see if she was there. He ran the reject lambs down the alley and out into the holding yard at the back. It was clearing, patches of starry sky glimmering mistily. Beti and Tom Wood were talking to Alwyn when he came back in to the shed; Beti's voice had a metallic ring of irritation in it:

'Twenty two rejects boys, that's too many. Didn't you check their feet? What's the point of me paying you, and then the vet does the work again after? What's the point of that Phil? Don't you know a lame lamb when you see one? Got your mind on other things is it?'

Phil saw a glance pass between the three of them, Tom Wood shuffling his feet and turning away; he looked embarrassed. Beti's mood seemed to change instantly then, and she grinned at Phil, shaking her head at some private thought.

'Well now. Going to the sale tomorrow?'

Alwyn threw his head back in a yawn which turned into a belch.

'Pardon me. Which is that then?'

'Ram sale, boy. Suffolks and Texels. Special entry of Texels, Ffynnon Wen breed, real beauties.'

'I dunno, them Textiles . . . what's wrong with the old Suffolk then?'

Phil had forgotten about the sale; he had intended to go when he had first seen it advertised.

'A good Texel.' he made an expansive gesture. 'It's the back end, can't beat it. The top of the leg there, well, meaty?'

His hands carved luscious curves in the air.

Alwyn scratched the stubble on his neck. The grinning look he gave Phil was unmistakably malevolent:

'The back end: you'd know about that wouldn't you boy!'

'What's that supposed to mean?'

Out of the corner of his eye he could see Tom Wood back away from them, but Beti took a step forward.

'Quite right Phil, good boy. Now then, where the hell's that lorry? Alwyn, get me the phone, it's in the car will you. What's that Colin done with himself?'

The trailer was parked in the yard, up on its dolly wheels. Colin had got back from Spain on Sunday night; he and the unit must be at the Greyhound in Llangarn. His phone was switched off.

'What's the number at the Greyhound boys? Any clue?'

Phil looked at his watch. It was ten-fifteen.

'I'll go round there' he said. 'Two minutes in the van, that's the quickest.' He set off down the centre alley of the shed, hopping as he fished the car-keys out of his jeans. If they could finish in an hour from now it would still be worth looking in at the Star. It might be an idea to ring Liz, let her know they were running late. Alwyn rolled his eyes at Tom Wood.

'Phil's keen, isn't he? He on a promise then?'

Llangarn was no more than a Post Office and half a dozen houses, then three or four new bungalows strung out along the road beyond it. The Greyhound was on the edge of the village at this end, facing straight on to the road. Turning right just before the building, Phil drove into the car-park and back yard of the pub. It was enclosed on two sides by the toilets and outbuildings, and a range of tin sheds where they kept chickens and such, from one of which came the monotonous bleating of a goat. The unit was parked at the far side of the yard. There was only one other car in the car park.

Phil went over to the cab; he climbed up the steps and tapped on the window. The interior was dark. The curtains were drawn in the sleeper, but the little night light wasn't on. He had the feeling the lorry was empty. The room that Colin used at the Greyhound was on the upper floor, up a flight of wooden steps with a hand-rail fixed to the back wall. As he crossed the yard, the floodlight came on. Colin was sitting at the bottom of the steps, his head in his hands, one leg turned in under him. Phil broke into a run.

'Christ Colin, what happened? They're too bloody steep these steps. Are you alright, can you get up?'

The face that Colin turned up to him in the harsh white light had taken a real good whacking. One eye was closed and dribbling, a gash crossing the eyebrow; the left side of his mouth was swelled up like a scotch egg and his chin was black and sticky with congealed blood. He held his right hand up in front of his face, then laid it in his lap, hunching over it.

'My fucken finger. The bastard broke my fucking finger.'

Phil put an arm round Colin, trying to get him to his feet.

'Let's get you indoors ma,' he said.

'I'm not going in the pub man. Just help me over to the lorry will you, that's all I need.'

The yard light went out, and darkness fell over them.

'*Iossi mawr* Colin, you can't even stand up. You really think you can drive? Anyway, you'll bleed all over the seats man.'

When Phil straightened up, the sensor picked him up and the light flooded down on them again. Colin squinted up at him out of one eye, then looked down at his hand. He sighed, a bubble of blood winking at the corner of his mouth.

'You're right there, pal.'

'I'll just go in the pub and use the phone, let them know what's happened.'

'You *canna* do that!'

Colin was trying to get up, cursing as his feet slipped on the gravel and he went down on his knees.

'Take my word for it, fuck's sake, I'm not going in the pub, understand?'

Phil wondered if he was concussed; he tugged at his lip, trying to think.

'Let's get you to the van then; I'll take you to the hospital.'

They stumbled across the yard together. As Colin twisted himself heavily into the passenger seat he groaned again.

'Ah fuck, that's a rib gone for sure!'

'Did you recognise any of them? Where did they get you, was it out in the yard there?'

He could sense Colin looking at him. He tried to organise his thoughts, make the right decision quickly.

'Colin, we'll have to stop at Graig Goch first. They got the lambs there waiting and everything. We'll have to let them know what's happening.'
The Scotsman groaned again.

Beti had gone back to the house when they arrived in the yard. Tom Wood came over to the van. As Phil opened the door and the interior light came on, he saw the other man's expression flicker from shock to disgust. He took a step backwards, grimacing as if at a foul smell.

'My god! What's been going on here?'

They drove up to the farmhouse.

Phil got Colin sat in a comfortable chair in the kitchen. Alwyn made him a cup of tea, most of which he spilt. Tom Wood put his head round the door.

'What a bloody mess. I suppose we'll have to get Steve to send another driver down. He better not try and charge us down-time.'

As he spoke, his lips seemed to curl away from his teeth in an expression of distaste he either wasn't aware of or couldn't be bothered to control. He stared at Colin, his look cold, inward, without sympathy.

'You're not going to be fit for a week are you? What a mess. We'll have to cancel the boat, and the lairage.'

Behind his back, Alwyn was imitating him, rolling his eyes in pantomime despair, waving his hands about in exaggerated and theatrical gestures. Tom Wood went on, his voice dull, introspective.

'We'll have to do another journey plan. What a mess.'

He sighed and left the room. Phil winked at Alwyn. He went over to the door and looked out into the corridor. Tom had gone into Beti's office; he had left the door slightly open and their two voices could easily be heard.

'*What you mean Tom, cancellation fee? Get another driver and get the next boat, Thursday.*'

'*But we've booked this boat. We'll have to cancel it, and they'll charge us.*'

'*No they won't bach! You explain to them what's happened! That's your job! Get on to them now Tom, explain what's happened.*'

'*They won't care what's happened. If you cancel, you cancel . . .* '

Phil heard Beti's voice rise into that high-pitched yelping fury he'd never seen anyone stand up to:

'*Don't talk rubbish man! You sort it out! That's what you're here for!*'

There was a short silence; then Phil withdrew quickly into the kitchen as Beti appeared in the corridor.

'Let's take a look at Colin then! What these protestors done to you *bachgen?*'

It was agreed that Phil would drive Colin down to the General Hospital. He rang Liz to explain what was happening, noting to himself a little sadly that here he had two or three hours of the night assigned to him, and no way he could use them to see Nicky. Tom Wood came into the kitchen while they were arranging things; he looked hot and flustered, with an expression that was both stubborn and shifty, his glance flicking about the room, avoiding their eyes, particularly Beti's. He gave a nervous cough:

'I don't want to be boring, but surely we have to get the police now, don't we? They have to try and catch these bastards.'

Colin rolled his eyes at him.

'Have a heart son. If the coppers come here they'll be all night. Let the doctor fix me up first, give me something for this finger at least. Talk to the police in the morning.'

Tom Wood frowned. He cleared his throat again, a dry nervous rasp.

'Just think we ought to do it properly. If I can tell Normandy Shipping we've got the police here, it'll look . . . '

'Don't talk rubbish man.' Beti interrupted him, shaking her head irritably and turning to Colin.

'How many were there *bachgen?* I hope you put a couple of knocks in yourself. They say you Glasgow boys can handle yourselves.'

Colin looked embarrassed.

'Aberdeen, Beti. Thing is, it was dark.'

Tom Wood was scratching his head. He got a handkerchief out and blew his nose. He looked anxiously round the room at them all. Phil had an intuition of what he was nervous about, and smiled to himself as he heard the other man confirm it.

'I don't see why you're all so casual about this. These people, they could be creeping about now. I mean, any one of us . . . We need the police here, surely?'

Beti snorted with laughter.

'Police protection, is it? Duw duw! We'll take care of this ourselves, you see if we don't. They won't show their faces here! We'll set Huw on them won't we Phil! Huw'll bite them in the leg, he will!'

Alwyn's face was dark with laughter, his eyes streaming.

'Huw'll bite them in the *balls!*'

It was a forty minute drive to the hospital. As they got Colin settled into Phil's van, Barry arrived back from wherever he'd been, driving the old LandRover. Phil waved to him, but drove out of the yard without stopping. In the mirror he could see Barry framed in the light streaming out of the open back door, Beti impatiently gesturing him in.

'Glad it's not me to explain to old Barry what's going on.'

He glanced at Colin, who hadn't answered.

'You were there that time,' he went on. 'Course you were, when you had the puncture. Remember, Barry came out with the shotgun. He was pretty worked up. Like he really wanted to shoot somebody.'

'There's nothing for the lad to get his knickers in a twist,' Colin said. 'Not like that at all.'

They joined the main road and Phil cranked the old van up to sixty or so.

'Can you shut that window' Colin said. 'Wind on my face, stings you know.'

'Sorry. So, did you recognise anyone? Had you seen any of them before?'

'Like I said pal, it was dark.'

Phil thought of Harris. He remembered that time in the Star when Nicky hadn't turned up, the look in Harris's eyes as he had tried to start a row. He remembered the strange sensation he'd had as though, looking into the back of a furnace, among the dark coals where wisps of brownish smoke stirred, he saw for a moment a wink of dull flame, a red eye that opened dimly, looking back at him.

'Did one of them have red hair?' he asked. 'Long, thin boy, big though. Red hair in a pony-tail or what do you call, dreadlocks?'

'No, nothing like that. No one like that at all.'

Phil glanced sideways, aware that Colin was looking at him.

'Are you sure?' he began. 'I mean, if it was dark . . . '

Colin interrupted him.

'Listen pal, how can I put this?' He let out a deep, musical groan.
It's not what you think it is, not at all.'

There was a silence. An ambulance overtook them, travelling fast, the
blue light strobing. As it leaned into the bend ahead of them it let out a
single yodelling whoop on the siren and disappeared into the blackness.
Phil waited for Colin to go on, but the other man was silent.

'Did they say anything? Did you hear them talking? Did they sound
English?'

'It's no *they*,' Colin said. 'It's no *they* at all.'

His voice faded away, then he coughed and started again.

'You know Julie, at the Greyhound,' he said at last. Phil shook his
head.

'You must do; dark-haired girl, lovely, works behind the bar most
nights.'

'I hardly ever go there,' Phil said.

'The thing of it is' Colin sighed again. 'What it is, I been ramming her,
see. Couple of months it is now. Whenever I got a stopover here. I got
that room at the back of the pub, see. And there's the sleeper cab of
course. She's a lovely girl. Anyway . . . '

His voice trailed to a halt.

'Anyway?' Phil prompted him, although he could guess.

'Anyway, her husband found out, didn't he? I thought we were being
pretty careful. He jumped me at the bottom of the steps there. Never saw
him at all. Big fucker, works in the forest. Told me next time, he'd castrate
me with a chainsaw.'

He gave a short laugh. '*Very* select, eh?'

Phil grinned at him. 'You're a naughty boy Col.'

'Well, maybe so. But you see the problem, don't you?'

'Oh yes,' he said. 'I certainly do.'

'I'm trusting you now Phil. If Steve knew about this, he'd fire me for
sure.'

'He wouldn't, would he?'

'You don't know Steve. *No one's indispensable.* That's his motto, that is.
And look at this mess. You heard Tom go on.'

'He's always like that.'

Colin shook his head impatiently.

'He's right, though. It is a mess, everything held up twenty four hours at least, and it's *my fault*. Do you see?'

Phil nodded. They were swinging into the hospital car-park.

'So I need to let people think it was protestors beat me up. That way there's no problem for me. Do you understand?'

They started over towards the glass doors of the Accident and Emergency building.

'You help me out with this, Phil? You see why I couldn't go in the pub like. They won't say nothing to the coppers. I cleared my things out of the room already, so if Stuart or whoever comes down quietly and collects the unit.'

They stopped in the brightly lit entrance. Colin took Phil's arm, looking intently into his face.

'I got to trust you Phil. We got to tell everyone it was Animal Rights, or that's my job fucked. If the police get involved, I'll just tell them it was dark, couldn't see anyone, there was three or four of them.'

'That's right,' Phil said. 'There's plenty like that around here. I can think of one or two myself. Police'll believe you, no problem.'

'You sure now?'

'Course,' Phil said. 'Course I'm sure. We got to stick together.'

The nurse behind the desk looked up as they came in, her eyes widening. When she realised they weren't just the usual pair of drunks, her voice turned husky with concern.

'What you boys been up to?'

'Wait till I tell you about it.' Colin told her.

Chapter 13

Tom leaned on the railing and looked back at the lambs as they stared up at him. This lot were going to SARL Phillipon, new customers that Benoit Formont had introduced. They had an abattoir and processing plant near Macon. Benoit said they were big men in the trade, *un travail enorme*. If they liked the lambs everybody would make a fortune. Beti had done well; she'd really made an effort over a series of days in the marts, and had collected together some beautiful lambs – Texels: big compact creatures, they stood squarely in the pens, chewing the cud, eyeing them with a dense and meaty placidity. Beti had been annoyed about the number of lame lambs the vet had found, but Tom could see she was pleased with herself nevertheless.

'What you think Tom? If they don't like these there's no pleasing them, isn't that right?'

She reached in among the lambs, and scratched one on the head, ruffling the curly poll. The lamb leaned affectionately into her fingers for an absent-minded moment, before swivelling its eyes in a startled double-take and jerking away.

'Good boy, lamby!' Beti said. 'Good boy.'

She went back to the house while the others waited for Colin.

September had been a bad month for the business, and October was starting to look worse. When SeaFarers followed B & F and pulled out of carrying livestock on their boats, Tom and Beti lost their access to the short channel crossings. Everything had to go with Normandy Shipping out of Portsmouth or Poole, to Cherbourg or St. Malo. This was a five or six hour voyage, and as the winter started to draw in, bad weather began to cause serious delays. Moreover, pressure from the protest movement was making the Ministry increasingly jittery and oversensitive; it seemed that if the sea was anything less than glassily calm, they wouldn't let livestock onto the boats. The lambs would be held up in lairages, sometimes for days on end. The lairages themselves were already a point of bottle-neck since no one could any longer use the ones at the north end of the Channel.

As lambs piled up from cancelled sailings, it got harder and harder to book a lorry-load in for the obligatory ten hour stop. Everything had to be arranged several days in advance, while the weather, and the increasing complexity of the paper-work, made it impossible to know whether you would manage to keep to the schedule. Any deviation from the plan was supposed to mean starting again with the paperwork, and probably losing the elaborately orchestrated sequence of bookings as well. The carefree and faintly piratical atmosphere that the business had once had, seemed a long time gone.

The Animal Protection League started targetting the lairages, putting on demos to try and stop the lorries coming in and out. More worryingly, Farm Concern had brought a test prosecution against Bill Church. He'd had a shipment of lambs held up at a lairage in Portsmouth for four days, and they accused him of not feeding them properly. He was four hundred miles away in Penrith, but the legal implications of the journey plan made him personally responsible if the owner of the lairage wasn't putting enough hay out. Tom worried a lot about this, although Beti was dismissive.

'See that they do put enough hay out boy, or we'll want to know why! Let them know who they're dealing with, no messing!'

Tom told her that under the new Transport of Animals Order, a raw and hasty set of regulations which MAFF had tossed down in front of the hyenas of the protest movement like lumps of meat, they could be fined a thousand pounds per animal if they were judged guilty of neglect or maltreatment.

'Just think about a load for Spain, Beti – six hundred and fifty lambs, and all it takes is some tosser from Animal Rights, and a load of legal flummery from people who don't know one end of a sheep from another!'

They were crossing the yard; Beti turned and gave Tom a sour smile.

'You're giving yourself grey hairs!' she said.

There was always a lot of bluster with Beti; her style tended to be self-righteous and aggressive, irritated by detail or subtlety. Her favourite story was the one that Steve had told them about the guys from Killylee Farms in Cork, who had sorted out a dispute with a Frenchman by sending a couple of boys over to Paris and hanging the customer out of a third floor window by his heels. Tom told her it wouldn't work for them; Huw and Alwyn would get lost on the Metro, or fall off the ferry on the way over. Beti shook her head again.

'You worry too much' she said. 'You're giving yourself grey hairs man.'

The rain had moved off and the night was clear and cold, the stars trembling as though reflected in water. Tom was wondering whether he should phone the pub to find out where Colin had got to, when Phil's van drove into the yard. It stopped by the side door of the shed, fifteen metres or so from where he was standing. The headlights went out. He walked over to see what was going on. Phil opened his door and the interior light came on.

Tom managed to get through to Phillipon. He told him they'd had a slight problem with the lorry, but it shouldn't slow them up more than twenty four hours. It was a poor line, and Tom couldn't understand much of what the Frenchman said in reply, but at least Phillipon didn't cancel the order. Tom talked to Peter at the lairage, who said he could have filled the pens he'd kept for them three times over. He didn't know about Thursday; he'd see what he could do, ring again in the morning. He spoke to Jenny at the shipping office and told her it was vital they got the Thursday night sailing. He stood in Beti's big dark office, the phone lying in a pool of light from the desk-lamp, shadowy cupboards and filing-cabinets standing square-shouldered around the walls. He could hear a short burst of laughter from the kitchen, suddenly cut off as the door swung shut.

He brushed past Beti's mother in the corridor. The old lady was bundled up in a dressing gown, some sort of cloth or net over her hair. The light was off, and she was navigating her way through the gloom by keeping her hand in contact with the wall. She didn't say anything as she passed; Tom could hear the papery hiss of her fingers along the plaster as she headed towards the stairs. There was a vivid slot of light under the kitchen door. He heard Colin's nasal drawl, then a shout of laughter. Don't let him near them nurses, boy!

They turned with faces brimming with expectation as Tom came through the door, as though some new excitement was about to burst on them. Colin was leaning back in the big wooden armchair at the head of the table, Beti's usual place, with a mug of tea at his elbow. Nobody had done anything about calling the police. It was as though Colin getting beaten up was somehow reassuring to them, something understandable and familiar, but also energising and exciting.

'I can get a couple of boys down here any time you want,' Alwyn was saying. '*Iossi mawr*, we'll sort them out!'

'Sort who out, Alwyn?' Tom was blinking with irritation. 'Who are you going to sort out? We don't know what's going on here.'

In the end, Phil drove Colin down to the hospital. Beti simply overruled Tom about calling the police, although she agreed they would do it in the morning. Tom had called Steve in the meantime. As he had expected, Steve didn't find the situation funny at all. Tom heard him shake himself awake as he explained what had happened.

'Course you got to have the police Tom! What's Beti thinking about? How's she going to find out who done it? Anyway, they need to check the lorry. Fuckers might of put a bomb under it.'

He agreed to send Stuart down to take over the load when everything was sorted. If Colin was fit enough, they would send him home by train.

'You get those buggers moving Tom. Don't let Beti push you around!'

He helped get Colin into the van. The Scotsman wasn't looking quite so cheerful now. His face had swollen up even more in the last half hour and he was obviously in quite a bit of pain. Tom felt a flicker of irritated satisfaction. It seemed to him that Phil too was looking thoughtful, as though he could feel the menace that had reached out tonight. He was certainly quieter than usual, but probably his solution would have been the same as the others, to give somebody – anybody – a good hiding and then go for a couple of beers. As Tom walked back to the house, the old LandRover rattled into the yard. He heard the creak of the hand-brake and the clatter of the door as it flapped shut. A moment later, Barry appeared in the circle of light at the back door. He tripped on the doorstep as he came in, but his smile as he looked up and saw Tom was surprisingly full of warmth.

'Working late tonight then!' he said. He sounded like he'd had a few beers.

'Lewis wasn't there tonight Mam!' he said. Beti clicked her teeth with an irritable snap. Barry turned back to Tom.

'So you know what? They made me secretary!'

He paused, waiting for a response. Tom didn't know what he was talking about. Beti turned her back. Barry went on, but he was already starting to mumble, his voice turning flat and hesitant.

'Probably only Lewis and that . . . everybody would have . . . '

From over her shoulder, Beti said something to him that Tom didn't catch, just the name Colin embedded in the flow, like some familiar object carried downstream. Barry took hold of Tom's arm, pulling at the sleeve. His breath smelled strongly of beer. 'Are they at it again Tom? Is that what it is?'

Tom shook his arm free and walked to the door.

'We'll talk about it in the morning Barry. Nothing to worry about now.'

He called goodnight to Beti, but there was no answer.

It had clouded over again, and the night was very black as he drove home. On the edge of Llanfrychan, by the old Farmers' Co-op building, which was now boarded up and derelict, he noticed a car pull out of the side road as he passed. Its headlights were on full beam, dazzling, and he had to angle his mirror away. It was behind him for the whole of the six mile drive. Finally, when he turned down the lane it went on by, though he had the feeling it slowed down as it passed, an inchoate bulk that hissed through the darkness, its tail-lights winking redly through the hedge as it disappeared.

Jan was still up when Tom got home. She was working at the kitchen table, making notes in the margins of a file of documents. There was a pile of books at her elbow, and a half empty cup of coffee in front of her, gone cold, a muddy skin forming on the surface. He started to tell her about Colin. He found an opened bottle of wine on the sideboard, and poured himself a glass. When he turned back, still talking, he could see Jan had stopped listening. She was chewing the end of her pen and flipping through one of the books.

'He's quite badly hurt, you know,' he told her. 'They really had a go at him.'

The wine was dark and rough, a rasping warmth in the throat. Jan sighed. She took off her glasses and pinched the bridge of her nose between thumb and forefinger.

'Is it really worth it, Tom?' she asked him.

'I mean, you've already explained how we could lose everything, just one prosecution.'

She picked up her coffee cup and stared moodily at the stale slops.

'So if it's going to get violent now . . . '

Her expression of distaste deepened, as though the congealing dregs in the cup represented everything that was squalid and chaotic, pressing in at the borders of the ordered world.

'This French thing' she said. 'Don't you think perhaps that someone up there's trying to tell you something?' Her eyes had not softened at all as she looked up at him.

That night he had the Prevost nightmare again: they'd been ripped off, he'd made a mistake with the letter of credit and they'd lost a fortune; he owed Beti tens of thousands of pounds. He couldn't pay her; he was ruined.

*   *   *

150

Colin had had a couple of stitches in the cut above his eye; they'd strapped up his finger and he had his arm in a sling.

'Looks like Stuart'll be taking these lambs out,' he said.

'It's the passenger seat for me for a while!'

One side of his mouth was still very swollen, and his smile was lop-sided. It had been nearly four o'clock in the morning before he and Phil had got back to Graig Goch, and he'd spent what was left of the night dozing on a chair in the kitchen. Tom looked at his watch; it was nearly ten. Dai Plod was late. Beti was in the mart, at the store cattle sale. No doubt she'd stay on for the special entry of Texels as well. She'd left a message on the answerphone, telling Tom to meet the police at Graig Goch at half past nine. Tom felt a slight violation of his dignity in being ordered around like that, but at least Beti was taking things seriously.

Colin yawned, wincing as the skin tightened over his various wounds and bruises.

'That Phil's a nice boy,' he said. 'You got a good one there.'

Tom nodded. The tap over the sink was hissing, and he went over to shut it off. Colin started to say something, but his words were muffled by the soft roar of the central heating boiler firing up. Through the window Tom saw the panda car draw in to the yard. Dai got out and walked stiffly towards the back door. His uniform trousers were too tight on him, and had ridden up in thick creases round his thighs. He flicked his legs out as he walked, till the trousers fell more comfortably and he resumed his usual sleek glide.

'You been in the wars, then. What's the other fellow look like?'

He beamed at Colin. He had barely glanced at Tom as he came into the kitchen. Now he turned back, his eyes flicking over him.

'Where's Beti then? Or Barry?'

'In the mart' Tom told him. 'Barry's about somewhere, I think.'

Dai sighed, puffing out his cheeks. He muttered something to himself in Welsh as he looked at Tom.

'You give her a message then' he said. 'Tell her this: been having complaints about lorries going out of here late at night. Some of them go through town, cause a nuisance like. You tell her I want a word.'

Tom could feel himself flushing.

'You can talk to me about that' he said. 'It's me arranges the lorries.'

'Is it now?' Dai said. His upper lip curled back from his teeth.

'Is it now? It's Beti I want to talk to, just the same. Her yard; and her name on the paperwork, they tell me.'

He gave a sour smile, and turned back to Colin.

'Now, son, let's hear what you been up to.'

He took a few notes as Colin spoke. His manner was ponderous, amused, condescending. He largely ignored Tom, and treated Colin like a naughty boy who'd been caught stealing sweets. The two of them were behaving as though it was all a joke, the tone increasingly light and bantering, flirtatious and allusive. Tom was getting a headache, a sharp pain behind his eyes.

'So you have no idea,' Dai was saying, his jaws working as though he was eating something, 'no idea, who these boys might have been?'

'Not a clue,' Colin said.

Dai nodded his broad slow head, as though that was exactly the answer he'd expected. Tom broke in to the conversation. He felt hot and exasperated; it was obvious Dai wanted to get this over with and forgotten about.

'Listen,' Tom said. 'I don't think you understand the situation here. Beti and I send a lot of lambs out: live exports, you've heard of that? There's a lot of people object to it. You must have seen it on TV. Anyway, you saw that demonstration in Llanfrychan; place is full of students, you don't know what they might get up to. We've had threats; we've had sabotage. Now this.'

Tom stared at him for a moment. He had the sense of a pattern, a series of connections between the protest movement and the students in town; between him and Beti, Phil and that girl he was seeing. There were things here that needed investigating, but maybe not by this over-fed lummock across the room. Dai started to say something, but Tom interrupted him.

'You need to talk to the people at the Greyhound for a start, see if they noticed anyone hanging around last couple of days.'

Colin coughed into his hand. He looked embarrassed. The policeman turned the pages of his note-book.

'Let's get this straight' he said. 'You work for Beti, right?'

'I work with Beti,' Tom told him.

'Yes,' he said. 'So, let's get your details, shall we?'

He knew quite well who everyone was. When Tom said as much, Dai's manner became instantly formal.

'I'll just get it sorted all the same' he said. 'Just so we know where we are.'

Beti's mother came into the kitchen and slopped over to the cooker, slippers trodden-down and slapping. She glanced at Colin and Tom, but broke into a beaming, gummy smile at Dai.

'Sut wyt ti, bachan? Mam yn cadw'n dda?' she asked him. *'Shwd mae'r goes? Nyrs yn dod o hyd?'* She slid a frying pan onto the burner, stepping back and muttering to herself as the gas lit with a soft pop.

*   *   *

M. Dreyer had come over from Strasbourg, where he had four butchers shops – all in the best part of town, he told Tom, moving his hands in slow, sweeping gestures. He was large and sleek, a sheen of prosperity glimmering on rings and gold-framed glasses and the silky suede of his jacket, coating his speech with deep and phlegmy tones that gargled and purred with satisfaction. Only his eyes, behind the glitter of the lenses, sent messages, muted but somehow frantic, from someone quite different. His glance flicked about constantly, his eyes darting beseechingly, like little birds, seeking approval or reassurance.

He and Tom picked their way down the alley between the rows of sheep-pens, past groups of farmers leaning on the railings, chatting, spitting, stirring the muck of the floor with the toe of a boot or tapping out an emphatic reply with the ferrule of a thumbstick. An old fellow backed into them, hunched over with wheezy laughter, and M. Dreyer jibbed exaggeratedly, in a sort of panic, stretching out flat hands as though for balance, as though the floor had tilted. Tom took his elbow and steered him through. At the far end of the building he could see Mike up on the walkway above the pen of lambs he was selling, waving and pointing with his gavel at the upturned faces below him, cupping a hand to his ear in a gesture of disbelief as a ragged cheer of laughter blew back towards them.

The place was crowded, and there were a lot of faces Tom didn't recognise, farmers from beyond the immediate valleys. There must have been at least two thousand lambs in the mart, and the air was heavy and warm, scented and musky with dung and damp wool, an uproar of bleating and yelling, distorted shouts and crashes, surges of booming noise that rose and fell like waves.

Driving to meet M. Dreyer that morning, Tom had taken what he thought was a short cut, down a narrow valley that should have run more or less parallel to the river. In fact it led him north, into a part of the county he'd never been to before; past big farms, with buildings either side of the road and snarling dogs, and the ruins of an estate, the big house glimpsed through smothering trees, parkland drowning behind the overgrown hedges. He came to a village: just a string of little houses, built for the estate workers perhaps, and three new bungalows opposite the churchyard. Every so often he passed cottages all done up new for retirement, lacquered and sparkling with a waxy sheen on the fresh paintwork, like little hatboxes. He drove past fields of sheep and miles of fencing, and thought how all these people, all this striving and endurance, was hidden in a fold of the hills, as the next valley was hidden from them.

He got to the mart half an hour later than they'd arranged. He could hear that they'd started selling. Ranks of lorries and horseboxes stood empty in the bays at the front of the building. He drove round to the car-park at the back, and found M. Dreyer sitting in his car. The big Citroen was streaked and scorched, as though it had fallen from the sky, matt with the grime of a thousand kilometers. He showed Tom the route on his road atlas, puffing his cheeks and shaking his head; through Metz and Chalons, then north through the battlefields, St. Quentin and Arras, following the line of the trenches. Then Dunkirk and the Channel; *puis M-vingt cinq, M-quatre, et ces petits chemins ici*. He clicked his teeth with amused disbelief while his eyes, flicking left and right over Tom's shoulders, searched the empty spaces of the car-park behind him.

They found Beti in the press of buyers and farmers at the end of the alley as they worked their way down through the sheep pens, the bright blue of her stock-coat plain among the brown and greens of her colleagues. She was deep in a huddle with Bryn Williams, their heads lowered and shadowed. Tom could see the whites of her eyes flash as she glanced up.

'Do you want these lambs Beti, or what?'

Beti made an impatient and dismissive gesture as the auctioneer called down to her, then straightened up as Bryn turned away, shaking his head.

'I'm right though, you'll see' she called after him. The bidding had stopped, the group of buyers fallen silent. Beti turned her attention back to Mike.

'Where were we then? Thirty two?'

'Thirty six,' Mike said, dropping the emphasis into the silence and setting off ripples of laughter as the bids resumed and the noise flowed back into the empty space.

A moment later Beti noticed Tom, giving him a wink, and waved a salute to M. Dreyer. The Frenchman shuffled, raising his hand in an uncertain gesture of response, glancing at Tom as if he didn't know how he should behave towards a woman in this situation. Beti held up her arm and tapped at her watch, splaying out a handful of fingers three times with sharp flicks of the wrist, as though shaking off water.

'*Quinze minutes*', M. Dreyer murmured uneasily to Tom.

'*On parle avec madame en quinze minutes.*'

When the mart was finished, they led M. Dreyer round the pens, so he could show them the type of lamb he wanted. Beti walked in front, jabbing her finger to left and right at the pens she'd bid on. She'd bought just over eight hundred lambs that morning; Tom showed M. Dreyer the list of pen-numbers on the card. The Frenchman sucked his teeth with a squeak; after that Tom noticed him glancing sideways at Beti from time to time, a troubled look, calculating and anxious, impressed.

'What does he think then?' Beti asked Tom. She turned to the Frenchman, her hands forming vague and suggestive shapes.

'You like the lambs? What you think?'

M. Dreyer pouted nervously and turned to Tom, waiting for an interpretation.

They took him for lunch at the Merlin, leaving Barry to supervise loading the lambs onto the lorries. They walked to the pub through the narrow streets at the back of the mart. Tom stopped at a corner shop to buy a newspaper. When he came out, the other two were fifty metres ahead of him, their footsteps clacking in the empty alley. Beti was saying something to M. Dreyer, turning and chopping the air with her hand. As Tom caught up with them, they passed a group of people coming out of a little tatty supermarket, odd-looking, two gimpy children, twins perhaps, with cotton wool in their ears and their feet turning in at funny angles. There was a shabby woman with them, good-looking closer to, but dirty and very pale, with smudged eye-make-up, a stud in the side of her nose; perhaps she came from the Black Valley. Tom knew at a glance she was the enemy; there were hundreds like her at every demo against live exports. As they pushed past each other on the narrow pavement she gave them a strange look, intense and vengeful, as though full of hostile recognition. M. Dreyer glanced back, ducking his head nervously as the woman turned at the same moment to look back at him. Tom had a sudden and very clear sense that she was going to win, that in six months time she and her friends would be dancing on the corpse of his business, celebrating victory; he had a presentiment of how he was going to feel as he queued, defeated, another middle-aged loser, in front of the window at the Social Security office.

In the Merlin, the Frenchman sipped dispiritedly at his bitter, and told them about the blonde and radiant beers of Alsace. There was no lamb on the menu, and the steak when it came was overcooked. Across the table Beti beamed, her cheeks bulging as she chopped and shovelled her food. 'Very hot in France' she said, gulping. 'Hardly rains at all, they tell me. Am I right?'

M. Dreyer drawled his fork across the plate with a disheartened gesture, stirring the frozen peas into little heaps. Beti finished her food with hurried, efficient movements. She pushed her plate to one side and picked at her teeth. Tom's newspaper was folded on the table between them. There was a picture on the front page of an Arab, somebody from the Middle East; the Frenchman noticed this, and tapped his finger at it.

'*Beaucoup de ces gens là à Strasbourg,*' he said. '*Les mussulmanns sont des grands consommateurs de moutons. Vous permettez?*'

He picked up the newspaper and rustled through it. Tom heard him give a little grunt of surprise or interest, as he shook and rattled the paper into a manageable size, showing them the page that had caught his attention.

'*Ça veut dire quoi, ça?*'

It was a half-page advertisement, the same bloody one that Farm Concern had used before, showing a bedraggled lamb, streaked with shit, hunched miserably in the corner of some broken-down stock-wagon. There'd been an injunction taken out on the use of this image a couple of months ago; the thing was bogus, it wasn't an export lorry, a set-up like that would never have got past the Ministry, or Trading Standards. But here it was again. Presumably Farm Concern would just pay the fine; they would welcome the fuss. The same caption over the picture: First soak in urine and excrement, then roast with garlic and herbs . . . clever, venomous language, unconcerned with truth or fairness. Tom hadn't noticed before the subtle appeal to xenophobia in the reference to garlic, the distasteful subtext of foreigners and their malodorous and gluttonous eating habits. Farm Concern had spent their money well. Some advertising hack would be well pleased, some cynical bastard with a farmhouse in the Dordogne and a firm grip on the tabloid imagination.

Of course, it was the sight of the lambs on the lorries that really did it. When the big wagons joined the queues of cars and caravans waiting to get on the ferry, when the children pressed sticky hands against the windows look mum, look at all those sheep dad! The sight triggered that latent English distaste for food and the enjoyment of eating which is one of the things they hold against Europe in general, and the French in particular, that sensual culture where a leg of lamb is a gigot – the word itself plump and running with juices. It was just too obvious where the lambs were going, and what was intended for them. Not only to be eaten, but to be eaten by foreigners, the mawkish idyll of the countryside swept away. Tom thought about the power of the food scares – pasteurella, salmonella: beguiling names that sounded like the limpid and under-age heroines of Chuck Berry songs. The food scares fitted comfortably into the notion that food and eating is essentially polluting, cloacal, never far from the whiff of the toilet.

The movement against live exports produced the fatal fusion between sentimentality and that low-grade xenophobia that is never far below the surface in the English psyche; a dull and petulant hatred of the whole world, but especially of Europe. People talk about Ireland's deadly affair with history, the gloomy steeples of Fermanagh and Tyrone, but really it is England that has the dismal and corrupting preoccupation with the past. Sometimes you feel the whole country has gone moth-eaten with regret for the moment, whenever it was, when the world jilted her; gone rancid, eaten up with self-pity and vainglory. This side of the Severn you get just as much introversion, Tom thought, but it is vague, misty, ignorant, benign.

The waitress cleared away their plates. She was a big girl; as she leaned over the table between them, her white shirt stretched tight and opened winking port-holes between the buttons. M. Dreyer glanced gratefully up at her as her blouse brushed his cheek, turning his face towards her as reflexively as a baby.

When Tom got home, there was a message on the answering machine from Richard Deacon at the Ministry in Llantrinant, asking him to ring him as soon as possible. By the time he rang the Ministry back, the Animal Health office had closed for the day. They sent a fax at nine o'clock the next morning. It was a copy of a journey plan from a load that had gone off the week before. Someone at Animal Health had scrawled a big circle through half of the first page, with a question mark inside it. Beside the box where Tom had filled in the departure time from Graig Goch there was another question mark, and a notation showing the time six hours later. There was a note from Richard Deacon, addressed to Beti, copy to Tom: There appear to be discrepancies in the timing of journey stages 1) and 3). I would like to discuss this with you as soon as possible. He rang the Ministry, and arranged to meet up at Graig Goch later in the morning. Beti would have to go to the mart around ten thirty, but so long as they straightened things out first, Tom could wait on and see Deacon by himself.

He drove over to Graig Goch. It was suddenly colder; a week ago the last swallows had gathered, strung out along the telephone lines like notes of music on a stave. Now the grass lay sodden, rags of dripping grey mist caught in the tops of the forest and trickling into pools on the valley floor. There were strings and beads of water hanging on the fence-wire and the field gates, congealing in the cold air as the winter came closer, revealed like something seen through fog.

If there was a mistake in the journey plan, it must have been part of the confusion around Colin's last load, which Stuart had finally taken out a day and a half later. Colin had gone home by train; Tom had driven him to the station after Dai had finished his desultory and reluctant interview in the Graig Goch kitchen, his questions breaking down into irritable silences that were somehow muffled and without resonance. Tom hadn't heard from the police since; he rang Dai at the police house a couple of times but only got the answer-phone. When he mentioned it to Beti she had shrugged, winking and making an ambivalent gesture, a sort of just you wait and see look, that probably disguised a complete lack of interest. The whole business of Colin getting beaten up seemed a dead event, inert and isolated, leaving no echo, no ripple, as though the nodes and edges of the moment had been wiped away, as the mist erased the further perspectives of the valley.

Tom found Beti in the bottom yard behind the Atcost building, dosing cattle with Huw and Alwyn. There were about twenty five bullocks there, big beasts, Charolais-cross, about eighteen months old. They must have been in the yard overnight; they were wet and steaming, plastered with matted corrugations of muck. Huw and Alwyn were hustling them into the race, lengths of alkathene whistling and cracking as the cattle baulked and jostled their way between the railings.

'What you know then Tom?' Beti slammed the lever of the crush down, yoking the bullock round the neck.

'Frenchie get away alright?' She slid the needle into the bristling hide, which flinched and shuddered under her hand.

'What he call himself again, Dryer? Seemed a nice fellow. Will he bite, do you think?'

'Pretty sure he will. Said he'd put something in writing when he got back to Strasbourg.'

Tom wanted to talk to Beti about the problems with the journey plan, but he could tell she wasn't really listening as the last couple of bullocks bucked and clattered their way through the crush. Huw and Alwyn moved the cattle towards the gate at the far end of the yard, whistling up the dogs. The collies crept out from under the trailer where they'd been sheltering; their coats were fringed and plaited with mud as they slunk round the edges of the yard to join the men.

'Turn them out in Cae Bach boys,' Beti called after them. 'Shut the gate at the bottom; I don't want them going down to the river.'

They walked round to the washroom by the back door. Beti peeled her leggings off and rinsed her boots under the tap.

'Nawr te, what's the problem? Come in the house, want a coffee?'

Tom started to explain the situation with the journey plan. They had sent the lorry off nearly three hours later than they'd said on the paperwork. This meant that the lambs had actually had a couple of hours less rest in the lairage than they should have had, before leaving again to get on the boat. Beti kicked her boots across the washroom and went in the back door.

'Get yourself a coffee Tom, put the kettle on. So what's the problem? Tell me again.'

'For a start, the Ministry are saying we sent them off even later than we really did.'

He followed her through to the office. Beti made a note in her desk diary, and picked up the phone.

'Keith? I've got twenty four of them, good ones, six hundred kilos, what you say?'

She raised her eyebrows at Tom, making a gesture for him to go on, but interrupted him immediately by talking into the phone again.

'Day after tomorrow? No, like we said. Good. Good boy Keith.'

She put the phone down and looked up:

'Just tell that Deacon fellow when he gets here, tell him what you like. They won't look at the tacho, will they? Tell them we were a little late getting away. They'll be happy with that won't they?'

She was sorting and shuffling things on her desk, putting a pen into her top pocket, hardly paying attention.

'You'll get it sorted, you'll see; want me to sign anything?'

'You're not seeing it Beti.' Tom shook his head irritably. 'There was no one from the Ministry here that night. Why have they got an opinion about what time the lorry went off?'

Beti glanced at her watch, then looked up at Tom.

'Pardon me?' she said.

'Somebody must have told the Ministry when the lorry went off' Tom said. 'Maybe somebody's been hanging around here, spying on us.'

Beti gave him an odd look, abstracted, and for a moment Tom thought she hadn't been listening at all. She wagged her finger.

'That's what I meant to show you. Have a look at this.'

She came out from behind her desk and walked across the room. Under the window there was a little work-station Tom hadn't seen before, a small TV set on the top, and a video recorder or something on the shelf below. Beti tapped the side of her nose.

'Haven't seen this have you? Take a look at this. Now how does this damn thing work?'

She pushed a button, and after a moment the screen flickered and jumped, then settled into a black and white picture. Tom moved closer to see what it was. Beti was rubbing her hands together; she grinned at him delightedly.

'Didn't know about this, did you?' she said.

For a moment or two, Tom couldn't tell what he was looking at, a series of light and dark grey shapes fitting into each other at oblique angles, some sort of bright globular object shimmering in the top left corner. Then suddenly it took on meaning and became the big yard at Graig Goch that they had just walked across, seen from above, foreshortened and at an odd angle. There was the porch and the back door, although the geometry looked all wrong. The dense black shape that covered the right hand third of the screen was the shadow of the new shed, cutting across the pool of light from the halogen lamp. It was like looking into an aquarium, a window into a bizarre and distorted world where depths and angles were refracted through some alien medium, a fish-eye look, rounded and glassy, the world in a soup spoon.

'What you think then? Had it put in last week, meant to show you. There's two more cameras to put up, haven't decided where yet. Well?'

'It's good Beti, it's a good idea.'

'You watch this now, you'll see something now, this is from the other night.'

They stared at the screen for a while. From time to time the picture jumped, flicking horizontally. In the bottom right corner there was a read-out of some sort scrolling away. Otherwise nothing happened. Beti clicked her teeth with irritation and came over to the machine.

'Dammo, what's wrong here, hold on.' She pushed a couple of buttons on the video machine and the screen went dark. There was a high-pitched whine and the readout scrolled into a blur. 'Bloody thing' she said. 'Hold on now'.

The picture came back, the same skewed perspective.

'You wait there now' Beti said. 'You watch this, you'll see something now'.

They watched the screen for a few moments and then, out of the shadow, a figure emerged and took a few steps into the yard. His movements had a furtive jerkiness about them, like a puppet. The camera was looking down over his left shoulder, from behind; you couldn't see a face. Everything was grey, and shades of grey. The man's clothes, his hair, seemed to be made of the same stuff as the concrete of the yard or the breeze-block walls of the sheds, his body had the same flattened and distorted angularity. It was as though a section of the yard had somehow come to life, detached itself, peeled away off the floor like a shadow rising upright. As he moved into the brighter area of the screen the light seemed to fill and inflate around him, drawing out fat globules of incandescence that trailed around him or arced towards the brilliant blur of the floodlight.

'Seen him before?' Beti asked.

Tom shook his head. As they watched, the figure turned back and stooped for a moment as though to pick something up off the ground. The time-lapse recording gave his gestures a theatrical emphasis, disjointed, like a mime. Then he disappeared back into the shadows. The picture jerked again, a line of interference flicking over the screen, as though erasing him.

'Nor me' Beti said. 'So what's he doing in my yard at' – she leaned closer to the screen and squinted at the read-out – 'two o'clock in the morning?'

Beti went off to market, and a little later Richard Deacon arrived. Tom took him into the kitchen, where he opened his briefcase on the table, and spread out a few sheets of paper, including the journey plan. Deacon took a white handkerchief out of his jacket pocket and wiped his nose with precise and fastidious gestures.

'Think I'm coming down with something' he said. He smoothed the journey plan out on the table in front of him.

'This is the point at which we seem to have a problem' he said.

Leaning over his shoulder, Tom could see that he was tapping his pen into the box where they'd entered the time the lorry left Graig Goch, the tip of the pen leaving tiny pin-pricks of red ink on the paper. Tom cleared his throat.

'I think it's possible the wagon got away an hour or so later than that' he said. 'It didn't seem worth altering the paper-work'.

The point of the pen moved an inch or so across the form and started to raise a tattoo of little red marks in another box.

'That's consistent with Mr Johnson's account of when the vehicle arrived at the lairage' Deacon said. He got his handkerchief out again and looked over the top of it.

'It means you may have cut short the rest period . . . '

Tom thought about this. They'd been in touch with Peter in Portsmouth; they were obviously running a bit of an investigation here. He started to say something, but Deacon interrupted him:

'What concerns me is the possibility that the lorry left here not at nine o'clock, nor at half past ten or eleven, but at three o'clock in the morning. In which case the rest period would have been virtually eliminated. '

Tom stared at him. 'What do you mean the possibility?' he said. 'It didn't leave at three in the morning. What possibility?'

Deacon busied himself with his handkerchief for a moment.

'If we have reason to believe that welfare or transport regulations are being infringed, we're obliged to investigate.'

'And do you?' Tom asked him.

'I beg your pardon?'

'Do you have reason to suppose the welfare whatever?'

Deacon folded his handkerchief away with a series of sniffs.

'We have some conflicting accounts of the way the journey was carried out' he said. 'You tell me that the lorry left here at – '

'Not later than eleven' Tom told him. 'Definitely not later than that.'

Deacon made a note, and started to shuffle his papers together.

'There are just one or two things to iron out here' he said.

He managed a thin smile, which Tom didn't feel like returning. He felt suddenly affronted by the man's flat, bureaucratic style. Presenting himself as unbiased, he was in reality apathetic, spineless, terrified of criticism. He was a functionary, whose only moral bearing was to stay out of trouble, whose behaviour would always default to the guidelines. He would give the same weight to some anonymous phone-call accusing them of anything at all, as he would give to their genuine efforts to do things properly. Tom thought about who might have phoned the Ministry. It was a campaign: the sabotage on the lorry and Colin getting beaten up, and no doubt the same people creeping about the yard at night, informing on them to the Ministry. He followed Deacon out to his car.

'Who says the lorry left at three o'clock?' he asked him. 'Where do you get that idea?'

Deacon ducked his head in a sort of defensive gesture, and reached for his handkerchief again.

'We have to follow these things up' he said. 'I'm sure it'll sort itself out.'

Chapter 14

She had brought Bobs with her. Harris groaned, and turned away for a moment as the two of them made their way towards him, his mum starting to raise her arm in a wave. There was a big timetable on the wall to his right, and he scanned down the list, wishing he was somewhere else. In the booming acoustics of the bus station he could hear the squeak of his mum's boots and Bobs saying something to her with a short snort of laughter, before these sounds were swept away by the loopy shriek of the public address system. He turned back to face them.

Bobs had now gone completely grey. His hair was pulled back in a kind of a bun; it gave him a look of freakish respectability, like an old lady, like the old lady in Psycho. Harris reached back and hooked off his own band, shaking his hair loose with an irritable gesture. His mum of course noticed this immediately.

'What's the matter babe?' she asked him. 'Have you got a headache?'

He shook his head again. She pushed past Bobs towards him, smooching her lips at him.

'Give us a hug!' she said.

Over her shoulder, breathing through her hair, he could see Bobs watching him. What she want to bring him for? He had a sudden sense of all the times he'd asked her that question, stacked one behind the other like a pack of cards splayed out on a table, or the curving regression you get when you face two mirrors into each other. And all her answers: Cos Bobs yer uncle! hissing with dopey laughter through her teeth, the spliff drooping between her fingers. And: We all need friends babe – a serious look, treating him like a grown-up. And: You're jealous, aren't you? You're jealous of your old mum! tickling him in the ribs, you want me all to yourself!

In their embrace, which she prolonged with a little tightening of her arms around him each time he started to pull away, her bag managed to upend itself, emptying onto the pavement of the concourse a book, two apples, a scatter of coins that went trick-cycling away with wobbly determination; cigarettes, a flattened box of matches, her purse, hairbrush, a couple of tape cassettes, sunglasses. He squatted down to pick these things up, almost bumping heads with Bobs, who had made the same movement.

'How they treating you then, alright?'

He nodded, straightening up and dropping the apples into the mouth of his mum's bag.

*   *   *

Bobs sniffed, a sharp sizzle of disapproval or contempt that made Sían glance quickly back at him, bobbing her head with a nervous, pecking gesture.

'I'm Sían,' she said again, pushing her glasses back up her nose.

'I'm on the same course as Harris. And Nicky. History' she said. 'Well, History and Sociology.'

The man continued to look at her blankly. There was something very unsettling about him, something tense and overcontrolled in the trim lines of his body. His jeans and denim shirt had the look of a uniform, Sían thought; like prison clothes.

'This is my room,' she said, hearing the vacuous brightness in her voice, but bubbling on uncontrollably.

'I used to share it with Julie, but she's moved out, so I've got it all to myself!'

She found herself reaching round and pushing the door open behind her, the gesture of a game-show bimbo drawing aside the curtain on the grand prize. She sneezed with laughter at the image, dislodging her glasses again. There was the scratching of a key in the lock, and they both turned as the front door was pushed open with a clatter of loose hinges. Harris came in, bumping a carrier bag from the supermarket against his knees. A woman followed him into the corridor, tall, middle-aged, wearing a long skirt over Doc Martens, a long droopy cardigan. Her hair was peppery and faded, a pale ginger. Sían glanced from her to Harris and back again.

'You must be . . . ' she began gratefully.

'Of course I am!' the woman said, her voice cracking for a moment in a sort of smokey giggle.

'I'm the famous Marietta!'

She put an arm round Harris's shoulders and started to draw him towards her, but he twisted away. Sían could heard him mutter under his breath: for fuck's sake.

'This is my mum,' he said out loud. 'She's going to stay here for a

164

couple of days.'

Marietta flashed what Sían took to be her routine smile, warm and blank.

'And you must be . . . ' she began. 'You must be, let me think, you can't be Nicky . . . '

Sían looked at her. Harris was staring at the floor. Why's that exactly? Why can't I be Nicky?

'I'm Sían,' she said into the short silence, hearing the dullness in her voice.

'Good! Excellent!' Marietta said with fatuous emphasis. 'And you've met Bobs, did you? You didn't mind us abandoning you did you Bobs? Me and Harry needed a quick natter, you know?' Her gaze flickered brightly between the three of them.

'Yes,' Sían said. 'Yes, just now. He was here when I got back.'

'And we've done some shopping for you,' Marietta said. 'So we won't be a burden on your store-cupboard, haven't we Harry? Where did you put my case Bobs?'

The man had been leaning against the wall, his thumbs hooked into the pockets of his jeans, watching them expressionlessly. Now he pushed himself upright.

'In there,' he said, flicking his thumb at the half open door of the front room.

'That alright?'

Harris lowered the bulging carrier bag onto the floor with a series of clanks as its contents rearranged themselves. He worked his shoulder around in a circular movement, rubbing at it, then picked the bag up and set off down the corridor towards the kitchen. Sían and Marietta looked at one another. The man leaned against the wall again, slouching his weight onto one leg.

'Let's see your kitchen then,' Harris's mother said brightly. 'Let's see where everything goes.' She smiled vaguely at Sían, and followed Harris down the corridor.

'I'm just, you know, going in here,' Sían told the man, who hadn't moved. She gestured towards the door of her room. Since you seem so interested, she thought.

'My room, in here. So I'll sort of, see you later.'

She went into her room and shut the door behind her, blowing a long sigh of wordless relief through puffed-out cheeks. Harry indeed! She didn't think Harris would enjoy that. And who was Bobs, exactly? Not his dad, anyway. Harris and his mum had the same sort of build, tall, big-boned, whereas Bobs was quite small, though with a wiry hardness, like a dog; the sort of man who says: I like to keep in shape. Sían pulled a face, and spread her books out on the bed. Two of them were due back; if she took notes this evening she could return them to the library tomorrow. She looked around the poky, windowless room; it must be dark by now, though you couldn't tell from in here. How had she and Julie managed to share for so long?

She could hear them talking in the kitchen, Harris's voice sounding stronger now, some of the snap and emphasis coming back into it, a wheezy drizzle of laughter that must be Bobs, the sounds increasingly fuzzy and soporific, the buzz and drone of vocal chords vibrating in what could be any language, or none, just the echo of meaning, responding like stringed instruments. Sían's head jerked up as she blinked sightlessly round the room. She sighed through her teeth, chewing the end of her pencil. She thought about the bill she'd just paid at the garage, and wondered again if it was really worth trying to keep the damn car going. She picked up one of the overdue books, realising that she had never even looked at it, and started to flip through the chapter headings, scribbling notes on her pad in a kind of determined panic.

A couple of hours later she heard someone at the front door, then Nicky's voice in the corridor, and her heart lifted a little, like a creature raising its head. She managed to finish her notes on Brunel and his wretched pneumatic caissons, then snapped the book shut, rubbed the work out of her eyes and went into the kitchen.

'My mum was Norwegian,' Marietta was saying as Sían came through the door.

'Can't you see it in Harry, my little Viking?'

They seemed to be preparing some sort of desultory meal; Nicky was washing up, the other three were sitting round the kitchen table in front of a pile of celery and a half empty bottle of wine.

'Can't you just see him in a long boat?' Marietta said.

Harris shut his eyes. Nicky didn't turn round from the sink. Bobs took a long drink from his glass, his eyebrows arching as he watched Nicky over the rim of it.

'With a great big axe,' Sían said. 'Yes I can.'

She wondered whether the celery and the wine represented the whole of Marietta's contribution to the store-cupboard. She picked up one of the crisp, cool bunches.

'I couldn't resist it,' Marietta said. 'It looked so fresh. Full of sodium, you know.'

'Oh good!' Harris said, looking up and giving Sían a grin that was so direct she felt it right inside her. Nicky came over and poured herself a glass of wine.

'Sink's blocked again' she said.

She smiled at Sían over the top of her glass, but didn't look at Harris, as though the two of them had been arguing. Harris poured the last of the wine into a mug and pushed it across the table to Sían.

'Go on,' he said. 'Don't you miss out. They bought two bottles, didn't you Mum.'

'Sodium' Marietta said. 'One of the three; one of the great ones.' She noticed the expression on Harris's face, his eyes squeezing shut as he drank. 'Make fun of it Harry' she said. 'But the truth is, you don't know. These medicines, these healing things, they've never been properly put to the test.'

'Never been put to the test?' Harris said. 'Am I missing something?'

He glared at his mother.

'Your medicines were field-tested for the whole length of human history, right up to the nineteenth century. And guess what?' he said. 'The few people who didn't snuff it in infancy died of old age at thirty seven. So much for sodium!'

Nicky gasped with laughter, her eyes flashing between long fingers as she raised a hand to her face as though flinching, her shoulders hunched. Avoiding Marietta's offended glance, she turned back to the sink.

Sían sat at a corner of the table, sipping at the red wine. She had a sense of all the connections between the people in the room, pathways like beams of infra-red down which their glances, their thoughts and their desires were endlessly drawn. Marietta watched Harris almost all the time, her glistening eyes following his gestures, crossing the room to the sink with him and back to his chair. Harris was restless, his glance jerking about, always returning to Nicky, but never settling there, as though some physical discomfort made him look away.

She drank some more wine. She let her gaze travel round the room; Harris, usually, that's where her eyes wanted to look, and then Nicky. Both of them, really. Dumb devotion, she thought. That's about my style. Nicky's attention seemed to be turned inwards. She chatted to Marietta, put plates on the table and checked the baked potatoes in the oven, but she was absent somehow. And Bobs? Bobs never took his eyes off Nicky. Sían watched him for a few moments. It was true. Except when he looked down to pour himself some wine or light a cigarette, his eyes followed Nicky round the room.

'So what do you ladies do around here to relax then?'

Sían blushed startlingly as she realised Bobs was talking to her. She had been staring at him, not hearing a word.

'Pardon,' she said, taking a gulp of wine.

'How about you, Nicky? Bobs asked. 'How do you and young Harry unwind?' Harris bared his teeth.

'When I was there,' Marietta said, 'it was all politics and revolution.' She lit a cigarette, and flapped the smoke away.

'What?' she said, looking at Harris. 'What's that look supposed to mean? Give us a break, won't you?'

She turned to the others.

'Harry thinks just because I didn't take an exam. But I was there lots, you know, at college. And I knew lots of people there. He thinks, just because I didn't get a piece of paper.'

'I do think that,' Harris said. 'Yes I do. Why do you think I work so fucking hard?'

He glared at his mother. She smiled back at him, giving him one of her serene looks.

'I know work's important' she said. 'I know that. But it's not the only thing. When I was your age we used to sit up all night, discussing philosophy.'

Harris started to say something but she interrupted him: 'Not logic-chopping' she said. 'Not your sort of philosophy but the big questions, the important questions.'

'Where do we come from?' Harris said.

'Yes!' Marietta said enthusiastically.

'Where are we going?' Nicky said.

'Exactly!' Marietta smiled at her.

'Is it cheaper to get a return ticket?' Harris said.

'There's quite a lot of politics here,' Sían said, to fill the silence. 'And protests, you know? Live exports. We had a demo here, a proper one, me and Julie and Nicky organised it, didn't we Nick? It got on TV!'

The taste of that excitement came back to her as she spoke.

'They filmed it! Right here in town! They interviewed Julie, it was on the seven o'clock news!'

Everyone looked at her. She was flushed, and her eyes sparkled.

Why do you have a demo here?' Bobs asked. 'I thought they was all down on the south coast, where the boats go. They've had some good stuff there.'

'But this is where the sheep come from,' Sían said.

'The little lambs on the lorries come from here!'

She looked around. 'Don't they, Nicky?'

It was Harris who answered.

'As it happens they do,' he said. 'In fact we know the place where they get rounded up and loaded on the lorries. Don't we, Nicky?'

*   *   *

Harris waited in the corridor while Nicky saw Phillips after the seminar. He was about to go on down to get a coffee from the machine in the hall when the door of the lecture room opened and Nicky came out, saying something over her shoulder into the room behind her. She backed into Harris, and the two of them fumbled together for a moment, juggling books and box files and carrier bags.

'Thanks Harris,' she said.

'What?' Harris asked. He leaned down to pick up a pen from the floor.

'You know, waiting. It's nice of you.'

Harris shrugged. 'How'd it go, alright?'

'Not so bad. Phillips is OK. He pretty well wrote the middle part for me. I never knew it made that much sense.'

She pulled a face. 'I mean, he was really helpful. It was like, I made him feel sad or something.'

She gave a short laugh, looking up at him.

'Know what I mean?'

'I bet you do,' Harris said. 'Make him feel sad.'

They pushed side by side through the double glass doors and tap-danced down the flight of concrete steps into the watery brightness of the street.

'I was thinking, Bristol faces America really, not Wales.' Harris said. 'Think of Cabot, or the slave trade.'

Nicky stopped dead on the pavement, then stepped aside, apologising as a girl with a dog on a lead jostled into them.

'Oh god, that's brilliant Harris! Did you say that in your essay?'

'Only just thought of it.'

'Can I use it, please!' She tugged at his sleeve, grinning up at him, her eyes shining.

'Please! I really need it! Thing is, Phillips has given me another week, but I really need to come up with something good now, you know?'

'I dunno; it'll cost you.'

'Anything!'

169

He gave her a crooked smile. There was a tight feeling in his chest.

'Go on then' he said.

'How long's your mum staying?' Nicky asked.

Harris grunted.

'I don't mean it's a problem, I just wondered,' she said.

They walked past the long facade of the Paxton Court Hotel, the tall sash windows grimy and blotted with fly posters, the walls streaked with rusty dirt from broken gutters. The main doors were chained across, a hand-written sign pointing towards the side entrance. There was a wino asleep in the doorway, flat as a fish, his face squashed out of shape on the slab of the pavement.

'You hear about Whatsname?' Harris asked.

'Night before last, he got beaten up, in the White Swan. Bust his cheekbone apparently.'

'That's awful,' Nicky said. 'What happened, was Julie there?'

'Dunno, Tim Morris told me this morning. There was a bunch of farmers there, Whatsname started going on at them, giving them a lecture. Not a very smart move when you're five foot two.'

'That's horrible,' Nicky said. 'It's not funny Harris. I wondered where Julie was this morning, she didn't get hurt, did she?'

Harris shrugged.

'Anyway,' he said, 'that's what you get from mixing with farmers.'

He could feel Nicky stiffen away from him, her body no longer nudging and bumping against his as they walked.

'Sorry,' he said. They cut through the covered market, past the sea-weedy smell of the fish barrow and the stall that sold rounds of cheese and slabs of bacon, armpits of ham and fat pats of butter.

'Listen, I'm sorry,' Harris said.

He took Nicky by the elbow and turned her towards him.

'It's just . . . ' He shrugged. 'After all, The White Swan, of all places. You go there, don't you?'

Nicky didn't answer.

'I don't want to interfere,' he said dully.

'Just don't, then,' Nicky said.

They walked on through the market, down a long arcade of cheap clothes, the browns and greens of army surplus, then rails full of nylon slips and housecoats in acid shades of purple and yellow, bins of unsorted shoes like the detritus of a massacre. The stall-holder glanced at them as they passed, stamping his feet and shaking a cigarette out of the pack. Coming out the other side into Store Lane, the watery haze had lifted and the sky was bright blue, the low sun striking glittering fragments off the wet street. They were passing the Discount Furniture shop, where rolls of floral carpet stood upright in the depths behind the dusty glass, beyond buttoned leather suites and oak occasional tables, corner cupboards and dangling chandeliers.

There was a man coming down the street towards them, a tall, bulky figure, middle-aged, a trench-coat flapping around him. As he approached, Harris became aware that he was staring at Nicky, his eyes shadowed and glittering under frowning brows. They passed so closely on the pavement that Harris could see the peppery stubble of his unshaven chin and catch the sharp, stale smell that came off him. Harris looked back; the man had also turned, as though swivelled on his heels by the force of his attention to Nicky. Then he seemed to notice Harris glaring at him, and turned away to walk on down the street.

'What you want, you miserable old bastard?' Harris called after him. He could see the man stiffen, his footsteps checking. Then he hunched his shoulders as if in pain, and hurried away.

Nicky was staring at him.

'What you on about?' she asked him.

'Didn't you see that old bastard? Does he know you or something?'

'What are you talking about?'

They both looked back down the street. Harris sighed. There was no sign of the man.

'Get a grip, Harris,' Nicky told him.

'Look!' she said. 'That was your mum, wasn't it?'

They had just passed the little bookshop on the corner of Store Lane and New Road. Harris had looked in the window once or twice, though he had never gone in. The shop sold stuff like Lives of the Celtic Saints, The Secret of the Standing Stones, books on the Tarot, and herbal medicine. Not his kind of thing at all.

'Your mum,' Nicky said. 'In the bookshop.'

Harris grunted, pulling a face.

'We'll see her later,' he said.

Nicky caught his sleeve.

'She might have seen us,' she said. 'She'd be hurt. Don't be miserable Harris, she is your mum after all.'

The bell gave a single, urgent jangle as they pushed through the door. Harris's mother was reaching a book down off a high shelf, beaming over her shoulder at the shop owner, a little soft, round woman with bright hennaed hair, fringed and tasseled with shawls, like a wet hen.

'Hallo you two!' Marietta said.

'Look!' she said. 'I've made a wonderful new friend! Imogen, this is my son Harry and his lovely Nicky!'

She beamed at the two of them, making a wide gesture that took in the shop and the dumpy figure of Imogen who sat behind the desk clucking softly, as though in a nesting box.

'You wouldn't believe it!' Marietta said. 'It's as though we were sisters. Look at these books here! And these!' From a wooden bowl on the desk she picked up a handful of plastic sachets filled with some sort of dried leaves or herbs.

'Look at these!' she said. 'Can you imagine?'

'Alright Mum,' Harris said. 'Alright.'

He glanced at Nicky, resigned, apologetic, a look that Marietta intercepted.

'Harry is so empirical,' she said to Imogen.

'If it can't be weighed and measured, cut up and analysed . . . '

She crossed the room and laid her hand on Harris's forearm. Nicky took a step backwards, away from this intense and troubled relationship.

'Don't you see, babe,' Marietta was saying, 'Imogen and I can really do something here.'

Harris glanced at the other woman, who smiled quietly back at him, not speaking.

'So I propose,' Marietta said, speaking with a sudden emphasis, 'to stay on a few days, so we can set up something between the shop here and the stall at home, do you see?'

She turned to Nicky, her tone softening.

'We won't be in your way, will we?'

Nicky shook her head, looking at Harris with wide eyes.

'And Bobs will be so happy,' Marietta said. 'He loves it here! He was in that pub of yours last night, the Star is it, and he said he talked to just everybody!'

*   *   *

In the kitchen, Sían mouthed round words at them, large, silent bubbles, goggle-eyed: He's in there. He's been snoring. She mimed herself peeping round the door on tiptoes, and Bobs' extravagant sprawl across the sofa, mouth hanging open like an unzipped fly. She snuffled with laughter, gulping and juggling with her glasses as they fell off her nose.

'When are you going to get those fixed?' Harris asked her. 'What do

172

you look like?'

The two girls stared at him. Sían turned away and left the room. Nicky shook her head at him.

'Why do you have to be so nasty to her?' she asked him. 'She was only having a laugh. Why do you get so defensive? We're not allowed to make jokes about Bobs, is that it?'

'I don't like being teased, that's all,' he said.

'But she wasn't teasing you' Nicky said. Why do you have to defend Bobs?'

Harris stared at her. He could hear Lee Wheeler's voice; it was like he was in the room with them.

'What's up with that friend of your Mum's?' Lee had asked him. 'I was coming up the stairs and he came up behind me and put his hand on my bum.'

It was the term they went into the Sixth Form together. They were best mates. Harris was appalled, embarrassed, stricken with denial.

'You're mad, Lee. He just bumped into you or something.'

'No he didn't. Who do you want to believe, anyway?'

And somehow, Harris had blamed Lee. It was as though Lee had provoked something in Bobs that need never have been aroused. It must have been Lee's fault. They spent their last two years at school avoiding each other, hardly talking. After a while, that seemed quite normal to Harris, as though they'd never been friends.

'I'm not defending Bobs' he said to Nicky. 'Why would I do that?'

He went down the corridor and into the front room. Bobs was still lying exactly as Sían had described. Harris put his foot against the arm of the sofa and gave the thing a sharp jog.

'Come on' he said. 'Time to bloody wake up.'

He went into his room and got his books out. When Marietta came back she put her head round his door, but he told her he had to get on with his essay. From time to time as he worked he could hear the muffled life of the flat through the thin walls: the toilet flushing, the chugging rattle of the hot water tank, Sían and Nicky laughing as they clattered past his door. In about an hour he had finished his notes, and written an introduction he was quite pleased with. He got up, stretching, rolling his shoulders, working the tension out of his muscles.

He found the others in the half-dark of the front room, lit by a swathe of light from the open door. Bobs and his mother were on the sofa, their bodies disposed in a loose pattern around the focal point of the TV. Sían looked round at him as he came into the room.

'Come and see this, Harris,' she said. 'This is good.'

Harris looked at the TV, taking in the darkness, the arc lights, the glistening yellow tunics of the police, wind and rain and spray, headlamps and windscreen wipers, the big wheels of the semi-trailers grinding on gravel.

'Look at that!' Sían said, her voice bright with excitement. A protestor had climbed up the side of the cab, and was now on top of one of the lorries, spread-eagled on the slippery metal. As they watched, they saw the cab dip sharply as the driver touched his brakes. The boy on the roof slid off, bouncing to his feet as he hit the ground and dancing away into the crowd, both arms raised in an ecstatic salute.

Bobs gave a sort of cowboy whoop, sitting forward on the sofa, his hands slapping a drum-roll on his knees. Harris turned as Nicky came through the doorway beside him.

'What's happening?' she asked him.

'You looked tired,' Harris said.

'I'm alright.' She leaned against him; he could feel the soft push of her shoulder against his ribs.

'I'm alright' she said. She turned her attention to the TV. 'What are you watching?'

Sían leaned round. 'It's a proper documentary' she said. 'Not the news. They're really doing it in detail, the whole thing.'

A reporter was talking into the camera, bundled up against the weather. From time to time drops of rain or spray blurred on the lens.

'So just what is it that brings these people out night after night? To find out, we went . . . '

The room turned greenish as the screen showed a long slope of grassy hillside, dotted with sheep. Then another scene, a line of lorries pulling long, slatted trailers. Just like the ones . . . Nicky thought, feeling a small tug of nervousness. Maybe they'll interview Phil, wouldn't that be something.

Harris' voice broke into her thoughts.

'Where did they film that?' he asked. 'Those lorries look exactly like the ones that come through town here.'

'Yorkshire' Sían said. 'I thought it might be Wales. Looks just like here, doesn't it.'

'Oh my god!' Marietta said from deep in the sofa. 'Oh my god, I don't think I can watch this.'

From the back of a lorry what seemed like hundreds of lambs were streaming down a ramp, tumbling and tripping. There were men in

174

among them, whooping and flapping their arms to make them move faster.

'Look at them!' Marietta said. 'Look at those poor creatures! They've probably been on that lorry for days.'

They watched as some of the lambs trotted across the yard to where racks of hay had been set up, their little heads jerking as they pulled anxiously at the feed.

'You see!' Marietta said. 'They're starving. Look at the poor things.'

She pulled herself up and looked round at them over the back of the sofa. She shook her head at Harris and Nicky.

'To think all this is going on while we sit here' she said.

'Once you let the horror into your mind, it never goes away' she said. She pressed a fist against her throat, swallowing, her eyes watering.

'Everything hurts' she said.

'Every moment you breathe, somewhere, in some dark and horrible shed . . . '

'Mum' Harris said.

'No Harry' Marietta said, shaking her head, blinking.

'No, Harry, you can't stop knowing the horror. It won't go away.'

She raised her hand, as though to interrupt Harris.

'I feel as though I should take a gun' she said. 'And litter the countryside with farmers. Do you see? Litter . . . ' She turned to Sían.

'Do you see? But of course we don't do that. We do nothing. We sit here.'

'Alright Mum,' Harris said.

'But we don't just sit here,' Sían said, giggling. 'That's what I was telling you, about the demonstration we did. It was on TV you know. Just like this!'

'Badger-baiting,' Marietta was saying. 'Factory farming.'

A lorry was racing down a motorway under a brilliant blue sky, not Britain. Bobs grunted.

'Seems to me, if you want to stop all this,' he gestured loosely back at the screen, 'you've got to stop it, not just shout about it.'

'That's just what Harris thinks,' Sían said. 'Isn't it Harris?'

'No it's fucking not' Harris said, his voice so harsh that Sían winced, ducking her head.

'Harry!' Marietta said.

'I don't know what Harry thinks' Bobs said, 'but I'll tell you this: these country boys, the guys who drive the lorries and kick these sheep about, they're not impressed by some demonstration. They think we're all wimps, you know, townies, they call us. Wimps and girls.'

He was leaning right over the back of the sofa.

'Wimps and girls' he said. 'Girls, bouncing up and down.'

He gestured with his hands in front of his chest, as though cupping huge breasts.

'Calling out slogans' he said.

He was standing up now, grinning round at Sían and Nicky, his fingers diddling imaginary nipples as he pushed his breasts at them.

'Calling out slogans and bouncing up and down' he said.

'Shut up Bobs' Marietta told him. 'And sit down. I want to watch this.'

'Up and down' Bobs said. 'I'm right though, you know. This is all, you know, nothing. No point. What these people need is a real surprise, one real big surprise. You know what I'm saying?'

Harris intercepted a glance between Sían and Nicky, a pout of shared disgust.

'What do you think, Nicky?' Bobs asked her. 'Direct action!' He clenched his fist. 'Am I right?'

'Shut up Bobs' Marietta said.

'We can stop it like this' Sían said. 'The whole country's behind us. The demos will get bigger and bigger. They'll have to stop.'

Bobs shook his head.

'Don't you see' he said. 'They don't give a shit what you think. You can think what you like.' He bared his teeth. 'Good old democracy' he said. 'Meanwhile, they'll just carry on exploiting these animals, while the Old Bill stand around and watch. But if you want to stop them, you've got to stop them.'

He smacked his fist into the palm of his hand. Sían blinked at him.

Harris sighed. He glanced at his mother; she seemed to have calmed down. He felt trapped and depressed. At the demo in Llanfrychan he'd felt the same way as Bobs. Except that he knew Bobs didn't really care at all. What Bobs was interested in was power, he thought, the edge you get from taking someone by surprise; the unexpected shock, the sudden pleasure of violence.

'You're just going down to their level' Sían said. 'Anyway, these demos are direct action, what else would you call them?' She nodded round the room at them, pleased with herself.

Bobs smiled condescendingly.

'One or two things spring to mind' he said. 'What do you think, Nicky, you aren't saying much.'

Nicky shrugged. 'I'm sure you'll sort it all out' she said, and left the room. Harris leaned through the doorway for a moment and watched her as she walked away down the corridor.

'Perhaps I will' Bobs called after her. He smirked at Sían. 'Perhaps I will sort it out.'

'Since when did you care about animals?' Harris asked him.

'When you ran over my kitten, you laughed. Do you remember that? You picked it up with a shovel, and you were laughing.'

'For god's sake', Bobs said, 'that was years ago. And anyway, it was flat, like in Tom and Jerry; I had to peel it up with the shovel. You got to admit.'

'It wasn't a cartoon', Harris said, half-laughing. 'It was my kitten. It was real.'

As he stared at Bobs, still laughing, he found that his heart was thudding. He discovered, all at once, like some monstrous piece of furniture bumped into in the dark, the dimensions of his hatred. He realised that he was measuring the distance across the room between them. One day, he thought, staring at the wiry, familiar figure, I'm going to crack your nuts. He became aware of the tension in Bobs, the older man stiffening in a response that was drawn up out of his hormones. Harris smiled bleakly.

'Don't worry about it Sían' he said. 'You stand up for yourself. Don't worry about him.'

On the TV, the camera was sweeping over the upturned faces of a sea of sheep, their eyes glittering with anxiety and reproach. The credits came up.

'Thanks very much' Marietta said. 'I missed half of that.'

She turned to Harris.

'Where did Nicky go?' she asked. 'Is she alright? Go and find her, Harry.'

Sían opened her mouth, then shook her head.

'Nothing' she said. 'Nothing.'

Harris shrugged. 'I got some work to do' he said. He could feel their eyes on him as he left the room.

Nicky was in the kitchen. She was standing by the back door, looking sightlessly through the glass into the black garden beyond. He came up behind her.

'Hello' he said.

She leaned back against him. He stooped, so that his lips brushed the top of her head. She gave a sigh which he could feel at all the points where their bodies met. Don't say anything, he thought. As he started to put his arms around her, she took his hand, stroking and patting it briskly for a moment in a gesture that was affectionate and dismissive.

'Did you photocopy that Clifton thing?' she asked him as she drew away. 'Did you get a chance?' She crossed the room. 'Shall I make us a coffee?'

She went over to the sink; a stack of plates, bleared with ketchup, tilted half-submerged into the greasy water; there were several chips, white and bloated, floating on the surface.

'You are revolting Harris' she said, grinning back at him.

'You are so reliably disgusting.' She laughed out loud at him, her eyes shining.

'What would I do without you?'

*   *   *

Harris dreamed of the seaside, of the crisp clatter of little grey waves on the pebbles. He stepped over drifts of seaweed where the sand-fleas skipped from under his feet, the melancholy shoreline ahead of him dissolving into mist and distance. She hadn't come to Dave Bennet's party with him. She said she had a head-ache, and she wanted to get some work done. He had a row with Tim Morris, some stupid dispute about Baggio and that penalty. The two boys from Sri Lanka, Prashan and Anupa, stood in a corner of the room, neat and uneasy. Everyone else was drunk, the atmosphere morose and irritable. Walking home, a police car slowed down as it cruised past him in the High Street, the two coppers turning their heads slowly at him as they passed. He could feel the bovine warmth of their attention flicker over him for a moment, and then withdraw.

There were no lights on in the flat. He thought he heard Bobs' voice as he passed the front room, some nasal, grumbling phrase. He stopped outside Nicky's room, resting his forehead on the door for a moment. He felt sick; the floor seemed to slope up at him as he climbed stiffly across the corridor to his own room.

It was nearly ten when he woke up: no point even trying to get to the lecture. He went into the kitchen. Bobs was sitting at the table, eating an apple with a sort of ferocious attention. He looked up as Harris came in the room, then went back to stripping it down to the core, turning his head to one side, his teeth bared. He leaned back in his chair with a sigh, and blew a pip out between pursed lips. Harris went over to the sink and filled the kettle.

'Where is everyone?' he asked.

'Your mum's still asleep' Bobs said. 'The girls have gone out. Gone to college, I suppose.'

'Why didn't they wake me?' Harris muttered.

Bobs grinned at him. 'Had a few last night, did you? I'll have a cup if you're making one.'

Harris shook the last few crumbs of coffee into a mug.

'Tea'll do me' Bobs told him. 'You're a lucky boy, you know' he said.

Harris turned round to look at him.

'That Nicky' Bobs said. 'I mean, gorgeous, or what!'

Harris opened his mouth. A sort of fear washed through him, turning his stomach. This is the moment, he thought. Of course they assumed she was his girlfriend; he knew that, really. He knew that he allowed this flattering ambiguity to continue because it gave a sort of ghostly flesh to his own desires. It was shameful. He turned back to the sink.

'She's not' he began. He groaned silently. He imagined Bobs' lubricious disbelief: You mean you're not giving her one? What's the matter with you? It was impossible.

'And your mum approves' Bobs said. 'She was on and on last night. We bumped into Sían in the pub; she had to hear all about how great Nicky is, half the night.' He snickered through his nose.

Harris drank some coffee, shutting his eyes. He wondered what Sían had made of it all.

'Don't suppose she minded though' Bobs was saying. 'They're good mates, aren't they. Have you ever noticed how a really pretty chick likes to keep an ugly bird in tow? Why do you think that is?'

'Bird?' Harris said. 'Chick?' He drank some more coffee.

Bobs winked at him.

'Think Sían'd lend me her car?' he asked. 'Don't like having no wheels.'

'How long are you planning to stay?' Harris asked. 'Don't you have stuff to get back to?'

'Where's that cup of tea you were offering?' Bobs said.

Harris took his mug of coffee and left the room.

'You take my advice now' Bobs called after him. 'You take good care of that Nicky. Little girl like that needs a lot of attention, know what I mean?'

*   *   *

179

She wasn't at the seminar; Harris hunched himself into his chair and took notes, leaving the others to do most of the talking. Steve Lewis read his paper out, flushed and nervous, battling his stammer: 'On this view, not only are scientific priorities socially defined, but the actual cognitive content of the research will be a factor of the scientist's age, race, gender, political orientation etc. So you have masculine science, Western science . . . '

'Welsh science . . . ' Dave Bennett murmured. Phillips looked up.

'Interesting, Dave' he said. 'You might follow that up for us; by next week perhaps.'

There was a rustle of appreciation, like dry leaves.

In the History block he found a note on Spedding's door: Sorry, no tutorial sessions today. Harris left the building and walked through the green, heading for the coffee bar. Blackened and rotting leaves pasted themselves on to his boots as he crossed the sodden ground. He wondered how long he could stand having Bobs around; at home the bastard had his own place at least, even if he did spend most of the time at his mum's. He kicked at an abandoned tennis ball, which squirted a halo of spray as it fell back to the pulpy grass. Marietta had said she wanted to stay a few more days. It was this business with the book shop; his mum's air of secretive elation, of mysterious deals being done. More make-believe no doubt.

Nicky was sitting with Julie at a corner table. On the wall behind her there was a poster of Courtney Love, and as Harris came in, she leaned back, squinting into the cigarette smoke, so that she seemed to be resting her head in the singer's lap.

'Where were you?' he asked her.

She pulled a face. 'Did Phillips say anything?'

Harris shook his head.

Julie was stubbing her cigarette out, pushing her chair back.

'Why don't you come tonight, Harris?' she asked him. 'To the Film Club. It's that Spanish film. Peter's seen it, anyway he's feeling pretty rotten still. But Nicky's coming, aren't you Nicky?'

'I might' Harris said. 'Perhaps I will.'

*   *   *

'Babe!' his mother said as he let her in. 'How was your day?'

He closed the front door behind her and followed her down the hall.

'So there you are Bobs!' she called out as they went into the kitchen.

180

'How long have you been back?'

She let herself down into a chair and stretched her legs out in front of her.

'We're nearly ready, Imogen and me' she said. 'Just you wait!'

Harris nodded at her. She was more chaotic than usual. He felt a flicker of pity, or dread.

'We're going out in a while, Mum' he said. 'You'll be alright, won't you.'

Nicky came in and went over to the sideboard.

'Who finished the apples?' she asked.

Harris stared at her. She had a silver jacket on, like liquid metal. She was wearing make-up, lips and eyelids glistening.

'Don't you look wonderful!' Marietta said.

Bobs winked at Harris, exaggerated, leering. 'Doesn't she though.' he said.

'Doesn't she just!'

The front door bell rang with a startling jangle. Sían called out from down the hall.

'I'll get it!'

They found themselves listening to the little sequence of sounds that followed: the rattle of the door, the note of surprise in Sían's greeting, the buzz and rumble of a man's voice, the flop of slippers and the sharp clack of hard boots on the bare floor of the corridor.

'Hello!' Marietta said brightly into the silence. 'Hello!'

A young man stood in the doorway. Marietta took in tight jeans, heavy workboots, a waxed coat hung with straps and buckles that gave him the look of a cowboy. He was solidly built, short curly hair, very white teeth. She smiled at him; what a nice looking boy. Behind him, Sían was bobbing from side to side as though trying to get past, so that her face appeared first by his left shoulder and then by his right. Her cheeks were puffed and her eyes were signalling frantically, like someone trying to speak with their mouth full.

'How do' the boy said. 'I was passing, and I thought I'd call in, see if . . . ' He paused, his eyes flickering nervously round the room. He had a strong Welsh accent. He's shy, poor thing, Marietta thought.

'Of course!' she said. 'Come in! I'm Harry's mum, and this is my friend Bobs.'

She gestured round the room, making the introductions. She became aware of the silence, all at once, as though her ears had popped.

The boy nodded.

'How are you?' he said. He took a step further into the kitchen. Sían hustled past him, crossing the room to join Harris where he stood against the wall. The young man gave a quick smile.

'How's it going?' he said.

Harris didn't answer.

'Nicky' the boy said. He cleared his throat. 'Nicky, do you want, if you got time, I was thinking we could go for a drink, or . . . '

'We're just going out' Harris said. 'Aren't we?' He glanced across at Nicky.

'Right this minute as it happens' he said. 'So you're out of luck.' He grinned, a small, malicious look.

Nicky gave a short sigh, as though the breath was forced out of her, shaking her head. She crossed the room and took the boy by the elbow, turning him towards the door.

'Come on' she said, pushing at him. 'Let's go then.'

For a moment they were framed in the doorway, the boy tugging back, trying to nod goodbye as he caught Marietta's eye, wanting to be polite. Nicky bustled him on, pushing him into the corridor.

'Come on' she said. 'Sorry, you lot.'

She looked back; they were all staring at her.

'I think I'll skip the film probably.' She pulled a face at Sían. 'I'll see you later I expect.'

They could hear the boy speaking as she caught up with him, his voice high-pitched with embarrassed laughter:

'What's the problem then? What was that all about?'

Marietta looked at her son.

'Who was that, Harry?' She shook her head. 'Not from college?'

Harris stared at the floor, a muscle flickering in his cheek.

'Do you want to know who that was?' he said, looking round the room.

'Harris' Sían said.

'That was Nicky's lover!' he said, his voice cracking with disgust and self pity.

'That's who Nicky's been fucking for the last couple of months.'

He punched the words out; he felt the pump and thrust of them right through his body, and for a moment he could feel Nicky writhing under him, arched and squirming as he bore down on her.

'Harris' Sían said, blinking rapidly. Her face puckered as though she was about to sneeze. 'Harris, don't.'

'Fuck off!' Harris told her. Sían goggled at him, gasping, then waded past them out of the room.

'That's who that was.' Harris said.

Bobs was crouching forward in his chair. His teeth clicked as he nibbled at the side of his thumb.

'You're joking' he said. 'You're joking!'

Harris stared at him, shaking his head.

'So what you going to do about it?' Bobs asked him. 'Who is he anyway?'

Harris blew a snort of disgusted laughter through his nose.

'That's the best bit' he said. 'That's the best bit of all.'

'Poor Harry!' Marietta said. 'Poor old boy!'

'He's a farmer. And do you know what he does when he's not shagging sheep?' Harris asked them.

'Would you like to know? Check this: live exports!'

He nodded at them, filled with a sense of triumphant release.

'Works for a big shot just down the road here. They send them to France, Spain, god knows where. Packed into the lorries, I've seen them!'

Bobs was grinning at him, his eyes alight. He was jittering in his chair, electrified, exhilarated.

'You're joking' he said again. He whistled through his teeth. 'This is brilliant!'

Inside Harris, something fell, some heavy thing that pulled at his guts as it plunged, a sudden tugging cramp. What am I doing? For a moment, he saw it quite clearly. He saw that his baffled and thwarted feelings for Nicky didn't give him any rights over her; he didn't even have the right to be jealous.

'So now you know' he heard himself say.

Chapter 15

Across the valley, the sun had just reached the further slopes, which were still white with frost and spangled in the brilliant light, pools of blue shadow in the lee of the hedges. A few sheep walked spidery trails through the brittle grass.

Phil parked the tractor as far off the road as he could, the front axle canted steeply up the bank. He switched the engine off and reached behind the seat for the bottle of whisky. There were half a dozen vehicles there already. He recognised Alun Price's LandRover, and John James' old van. As he climbed down from the cab, Will Williams clattered past him at a jolting trot, his elbows out at right-angles and his ears bright red in the cold air, his pony snorting and throwing his head about. Phil stamped his feet on the frozen road, and blew on his hands. Beyond him, Will managed to pull the pony up and wheel round, squinting in the glittering light.

More horses arrived, Tom Powell on that big old grey, and the English people who'd moved into the Vicarage at Llantrinant. John James wound his window down and called Phil over.

'Brought something to warm us up' he said, nodding at the bottle in Phil's pocket.

'Good boy Phil' he said. 'You wouldn't miss this, would you.'

Phil shook his head, smiling. Greenhill had always been associated with the meet at the ford as well, but it was this one on the top square that really mattered. He'd seen the Hunt go from here every year, never missed it.

'What was that old pony called?' John asked him, his voice meeting Phil's thoughts at exactly the point they'd reached.

'That old thing of your dad's, what was she called? Nelly, Molly?'

'Polly' Phil said.

'Polly!' John James said, blinking and shaking his head. 'Of course she was. Polly! Well damn, damn. How long ago was that *bach?*'

Morgan and Joan had arrived, and were handing round sandwiches and welsh-cakes and cups of coffee and whisky.

'I better do my duty' Phil said, patting the bottle in his pocket. 'How about you John? I'll fetch you a cup.'

He got himself a tube of beakers from Joan and shouldered his way in among the horses and followers, slopping whisky into the floppy cups and reaching them up to the riders.

'Alun! Here you go. Are you having one Ken?'

Will's pony trod on his foot. Phil decided he'd better have a nip himself. The crowd had a voice now, no longer just individuals standing about in the cold, but a big, noisy creature that snorted and whooped and shouted with laughter, blowing plumes of steaming breath and stamping iron shoes on the road. Dewi the Huntsman arrived, his pick-up blowing black smoke with the weight of the horse-box. He snagged himself on the seatbelt as he got out of the cab, and half fell into the road, setting off gasps of startled laughter, jeering and affectionate.

'Good boy Dewi!'

'Started early did you, *bachgen!*'

The hounds pushed feathery snouts through the slats of the horse-box, snuffling and whining. Dewi slapped the dirt off his britches and walked round to the back of the box to let the tailgate down. As the hounds floundered down the ramp, whimpering and waving plumed tails, barging among the crowd or breaking into a rolling canter for a few paces up the road, the whole chaotic enterprise seemed to gather itself up, everyone suddenly starting to move, hooves clattering, followers jumping out of the way of the horses. Dewi opened the gate and walked a few yards up the slope. As he appeared above the hedge he turned and called to the hounds, then blew a single anguished note on the horn. The hounds made a rush through the gateway, the leaders streaming up the hillside, raising their heads in yelps of passionate yodelling as the riders bucked and jostled to follow them.

John James started the motor of his van.

'Might follow them a bit' he told Phil.

'Suppose they'll come down to the road by Hendre, won't they. Thanks for the drink *bach*. Family well?'

Phil nodded, raising his hand as the old fellow drove off. Alun was walking back to his LandRover.

'Started feeding yet?' he asked him as he passed.

'Thinking about it' Phil told him. 'Suppose I'll have to, if this frost stays on the ground.'

He walked back to the tractor. He might listen to the forecast; if it wasn't going to thaw this afternoon he should probably put some silage out. In any case, he needed to check the cow in the shed; she couldn't be long now, you could see the calf move as plain as anything.

The last couple of vans and pick-ups were starting up and moving away, either going home or setting off to follow the hunt as best they could along the roads. As Phil pulled himself up into the cab, a green van passed him, and his heart jabbed him in the ribs as he recognised Nicky's Escort, the number plate as familiar as a friend's name. She still hadn't fixed the rear light. The van stopped by Alun's LandRover for a moment; he could see a man's head, grey-haired, pushing out of the window as the two drivers spoke to each other. Phil breathed out deeply in a long sigh, nodding to himself, his blood slowing. Of course. Her van had been off the road for weeks. She must have sold it. A while ago he had offered to fix it for her, but he'd never found the time or where he could work on it, he couldn't very well ┝ring it back to the yard. She must have sold it. Of course she had.

The cab was quite warm from the sun. Phil stared through the windscreen, dazzled in the light. Had he pictured her getting out and shouting, or maybe waving a placard BAN HUNTING! right there, in front of Will and John and Morgan? Perhaps nothing so dramatic, perhaps just recognising him as she drove past, stopping the van and jumping out with her incredible smile that made him want to fuck her right now. Phil shivered, and started the motor.

There was a patch of ice on the track, just where it was steepest coming into the yard, and the tractor took off for a moment, a sudden glistening rush before the wheels found some purchase again. Phil turned the motor off. In the yard, the outbuildings leaned against each other. On either side of the house the range of sheds stretched their arms towards him. Liz had done a lot of white-washing in the summer, and the creamy textures glowed in the cold bright air. The terrier trotted across the concrete to greet him on tiptoes, lifting his feet fastidiously off the cold ground, skipping up into the cab as soon as the door was opened. Phil walked across the yard to the little stone shed next to the workshop.

The cow was restless, scuffling the straw. She arched her back, raising her tail, the hide shivering over her ribs. Phil walked round to the back end, and the cow swung her head slowly round to follow him, her eyes rolling as she watched him.

'Good girl' he said, stroking the bony swells at the base of her tail. She strained again, shifting her weight on stiff legs, swinging a rope of straw-coloured mucous, streaked with blood.

'Good girl.'

In the kitchen, he made himself a cup of tea, and spread a couple of slices of bread with butter and jam. The postman had pushed the letters under the back door; two or three things for Liz, and a vet bill, a hundred and eighty nine pounds: Overdue, Please Remit. Phil put it back in the envelope and tucked it under a plate on the dresser. There was one of Eddy's pictures on the table: the inevitable tractor. He'd taken a lot of trouble with the engine, putting in the oil filters and the curved casing that protected the starter-motor. As Phil leaned over the drawing, a drip of jam slid off the lip of his bread and pasted a sticky blossom of red over the cab window, obliterating the blobby figure of the driver.

He ran a bucket of hot water and dropped a bar of soap in it. From the work-shop he collected his calving ropes and a tub of lubricating gel. Outside, the light had turned hazy and grey, the day gone damp and colourless. In the cowshed, Phil tugged the piece of baler twine that turned on the overhead light. The bulb swung slightly in a draught, wedges of shadow crossing the floor. The cow hung her head and strained again. Below her raised tail the tip of a hoof, waxy and glistening, appeared for a moment and then withdrew.

He gave her an hour, looking back in from time to time. He shooed Patch out of the cab, where he'd been sleeping on the seat. The terrier crossed the yard to where Molly lay drowsing on the end of her chain and walked round her on tense legs. When he tried to mount her, the old bitch got stiffly to her feet and showed one side of her teeth with a snarl that was more contemptuous than threatening. Phil carried hay to the cows and calves in the stone barn, and cleaned out one of the water troughs. Then he walked to the edge of the field behind the kitchen and looked down into the valley. The light was already starting to fail, but the sheep glimmered faintly as they nosed about between clumps of gorse and bracken. The frost had gone from the grass; it would stay warmer tonight.

The cow didn't look round when he went back into the shed. Her cheeks bulged as a belch fermented up her throat; she gulped and swallowed and began to cud again. There was a look in her eye Phil didn't quite like, something dull and baffled, the germ of defeat. He washed his hands and ran more hot water into the bucket. He soaked the calving ropes until they were soft and slippery, then slapped a glistening pat of gel onto his hands. He could feel the tips of the hooves and slowly worked his hand along the shins until his fingers touched the blunt mound of the muzzle. The calf flinched away from him, drawing back into the warm depths. Phil withdrew his hand, shaking off strings of mucous. He slid the calving ropes on, slipping a noose over each ankle and drawing them tight. He leaned his head against the cow's flank, murmuring into the taut hide.

'Good girl' he said. 'Good old girl. The only way is out, you know'.

Each time the cow strained he pulled on the ropes, extending her efforts. The hooves tacky and soft, the impossible length of the legs. The calf seemed to stick fast as the head crowned, the old cow groaning, and Phil had to lean back hard on the ropes, then the same again at the hips, worse this time, he was groaning louder than the cow, and then the sudden slippery rush, the splash of blood and fluid as the calf dived convulsively out and into the straw.

He was scrubbing away veils of slime from the calf's gasping mouth, the cow shuffling and pushing at him, blowing velvety deep sounds down her nose, when he heard the Metro pull into the yard, the hollow clap of the doors and Eddy calling out, his voice high and excited.

'Look at this' Phil said as the boy put his head round the door.

'Isn't he a beauty? Come and see.'

Eddy came into the shed sideways, keeping to the wall, watching the cow.

'She's alright' Phil told him. 'She a good old girl, she won't hurt you.' He got to his feet, straightening the stiffness out of his back.

'Look at this fellow though! Isn't he beautiful?'

Eddy nodded, his eyes wide.

'Dad' he said. The cow lowered her head, brushing her muzzle over the calf, blowing deep steamy breaths at it.

'Dad' Eddy said. 'We saw this bike, Dad, in Jones Brothers. You should of seen it Dad, it was so cool.'

The calf made an effort to stand, pushing forward like someone trying to get up out of a deep armchair, before dropping its head into the straw again. The cow nuzzled at it, whispering breathily.

'It had fifteen gears Dad! And Mum said' – Eddy flicked a nervous glance at him – 'Mum said next month I should write a letter to Father Christmas. She said: You never know. That's what she said, Dad. You never know.' He stared sightlessly at the calf, whispering something to himself. Phil picked up a handful of straw and rubbed at his hands. He looked at his son.

'That's right' he said. 'That's right enough. You never know.'

Liz thought he should go to the pub for an hour or two.

'Do you good' she said.

She looked at him. He had lost weight, he was thinner in the face somehow, his eyes deeper set. The best thing about Phil, she always thought, was the way he had of making things better; making things seem funny or ridiculous or not worth getting upset over. He didn't hide from the serious side of life, but he'd always had a light touch. Lately though, she'd caught a look that she couldn't interpret, a sort of flinching, inward glance that showed like pain in his eyes, some awful thought on the edge of his mind.

'You look tired' she said. 'When you're not working here, you're working at Graig Goch. You can overdo things, you know.'

She smiled at him. Reaching up, she brushed the hair back from his forehead.

'Got to look after yourself old boy' she said. 'Me and Ed, we rely on you.'

She clapped his cheeks lightly with both hands. 'May not be much, but you're all we've got' she said. 'You need a shave if you're going out.'

* * *

Lyn emerged from the corridor that led to the toilets, the door banging shut behind him on its spring. He stumbled on the step up into the bar and slapped his hand against the wall to steady himself. At the same moment, Phil pushed in through the front door, shuffling sideways to let a couple with a small child press past him out into the night. Behind the bar, Martin's hands hovered nervously over the beer taps, his glance flickering left and right, as though these arrivals and departures were being orchestrated against him, the pace of the evening suddenly out of control. Lyn sorted his feet out and looked up. He beamed at Phil, a shy, muddled smile, full of warmth.

'Mr Jones,' he said. 'Where you been hiding yourself?'

They took their pints over to the corner table by the range, where a meagre fire was hissing in the grate. Across the room, Iori nodded at them from the dart-board; he pulled a dart loose and scowled at it, rotating the flights between finger and thumb. Lyn grinned into his beer.

'Cheerful old bugger, isn't he?' he said to Phil. 'Like a grizzly bear.' He looked over at Iori. 'Like a old badger.'

Phil thought of the badger he'd seen as he had driven down. The last couple of days, he'd been hedging along the road frontage down to the cross, and the pleached boughs lay sloped uphill in thick ranks, chips of green timber from the bill-hook scattered on the bank, and the clean gleam of cut wood. Halfway down the hill his headlights had targeted the rounded back-end of a badger as it hunched, digging and scrabbling, squirming into the dense lattice of the hedge as it struggled to get through.

'So where you been keeping yourself?' Lyn was asking him. 'Been doing your drinking in town, what I hear.'

Phil looked quickly at him; Lyn was staring into his pint, half-smiling, his eyes clouded, dreaming; the same expression he had when Mrs Williams would ask him a question in class: Eleven times eleven. Come on Lyn *bach*, use your head now! Lyn would stare at the desk as though he hadn't heard, blushing, his smile slowly deepening. If the teacher persisted, Lyn's eyes would start to fill and glisten until someone took pity and hissed the answer at him.

'Been busy' Phil told him. 'Done a lot of lambs these last few weeks. Seem to spend most of my time at Graig Goch. Two thousand lambs we sent last week.'

Lyn set his glass down, pursing foam between his lips.

'Two thousand lambs,' he said. '*Dwy fil o ŵyn!* Think of that; all the way to France. Tremendous!' He stared into the fire. Phil reached down and dropped a piece of wood onto the coals.

'Think they'd have some work for me?' Lyn asked him. He caught Phil's eye for a moment before his glance flinched away, embarrassed, expecting a rebuff.

'Doesn't matter' he said. 'What would Beti want me for anyway.' He leaned back in his seat and drained the remains of his beer.

'Same?' he said. Wiping his mouth, he frowned at Phil for a moment, intercepting a passing thought. 'Who was telling me?' he said. He put a finger to his lips and jerked his head towards Iori. He leaned forward, his voice dropping huskily. 'It was him of course, that's who it was. Seen you in town he said, couple of times. Young girl he said; hippy type. Very smart looking piece.'

Phil sighed. Smart looking piece. He pulled a face at Lyn. He thought of Nicky the last time he'd seen her. It was round at her flat, more than a week ago. She was reading to him out of some great big newspaper, an article on live exports: at least listen to what they've got to say, Phil. The newspaper was spread out on the floor, sheets of it everywhere, and she was sprawled on her hands and knees across the sofa, reaching down to turn the page. As he pictured her careless, childish pose, loose and pliant, he felt love kick inside him, like a baby. He became aware that Lyn was watching him. He reached across the table and slid the empty glasses together.

'I'll get these,' he said.

Lyn looked at him, a sluggish revelation dawning in his eyes.

'You're a jammy bastard,' he said. 'Good god, man.'

Phil crossed the room and stood at the counter, one foot hooked up on the rail as Martin poured the pints. The two boys from Bryn Gethin came in, with the new wife. Banging through the door in a rush of cold air, they pushed and huddled at the bar. Flushed, laughing, in their own world, the three of them leaned into one another, faces close, the girl between them rosy, pampered, giggling and petted. Did she sometimes forget which brother she'd married?

'So?' Lyn said, as Phil brought their beer back to the table. 'Who is she then? What you been up to, you dog.'

They drank, looking at each other over the tops of the pint glasses.

'Seen Carwyn lately?' Phil asked. 'Someone told me he was trying to get his old job back, with T.J. You hear that?'

Lyn shook his head. 'He'll never go back in the forest, *bach*' he said. 'That leg will never come right, you know. Fucking saw.' He drew his hand through the air in a diagonal slice. 'Just chopped the muscles up into bits. Lucky the hospital didn't take it right off. He'll be doing well if he ends up stacking shelves in Quickshop.' He set his glass down with a click. 'Or picking up litter in the car-park.'

The two of them stared at each other for a moment, as though the figure of Carwyn floated between them, Carwyn ten years ago, wild, roaring with laughter. They both looked round as a couple of boys pushed through the door, teenagers from Llanfrychan, crossing the room with a sort of stiff swagger, an awkward set of the shoulders, a mixture of cocky and downcast, under-age and seeking approval.

'Hell of a boy, see' one of them was saying, a tinny crack in his voice.

'Shut the bloody door boys!' Lyn called out to them. 'You're letting in the cold, *diawl!*'

Blushing, hunched, and muttering to himself, the smaller of the two hurried obediently back. They watched him rejoin his friend at the bar and duck his hot face into his beer, standing very close to the other boy, his back to the room as though he could feel waves of mockery beating at him.

'Do you remember that time at the White Swan?' Lyn asked. He gestured at the two boys at the bar as though they provided a visual reference.

'We been hay-making with your dad and he sent us off to the pub after; never done that before. Do you remember?'

'He gave us some money' Phil said. 'He give us a fiver didn't he?'

He leaned back in his chair. He thought about green and milky evenings at harvest time, the tractors roaring through the village, the hot and sappy smells of oil and hay and sweat, the girls on the trailers stacking bales, itchy with dust and seeds and their T-shirts sticking to them; the pubs open all night.

'Lot of money' Lyn said. 'What did a pint cost then? Ten years ago, must have been.'

'Twelve, man, more like twelve years! Dear god!' They shook their heads, suddenly conscious of the terrible speed at which the generations succeed each other.

'There was that English woman' Phil said, as though adding a piece to a jigsaw. 'Kept buying us drinks. What was that stuff?'

'Tequila' Lyn said dreamily. 'Tequila sunrise.'

Phil groaned. 'Tequila!' he said, like remembering the name of a friend.

'Sick? Don't talk to me! Don't know how the hell I got home.'

Lyn smiled at him, his expression inward, drowsy, secretive.

'I didn't' he said. 'Get home.'

'Good god man!' Phil stared at him. 'How old was she?'

'She wasn't that old' Lyn said. '*Menyw bert!* She was a nice woman.' He grinned delightedly at the look on Phil's face.

'See? You don't know everything' he said. 'I got my secrets.'

'But why?' Phil asked him. 'Why'd you never tell me?'

Lyn scratched his head, frowning.

'I was thinking about that' he said. 'Those two boys there, they reminded me somehow. What it was, couple of days after that, I met Elaine.' He paused, his glance sliding away around the room. 'It was different after that.'

They nodded at each other, letting the consoling silence wash over them.

'And anyway' Lyn said finally, 'I never see you these days. You're such a bloody stranger.'

'Work' Phil said. 'Mostly work. I never told you about my trip to France, did I? Since then . . . ' His voice trailed away. He shook his head to clear it, and took a pull at his beer.

'Since then' he said. 'Since then there's been a lot of work. This last week – '

'Two thousand lambs' Lyn said, nodding. 'You said. And every one that crosses over helps the price here. God knows we need it.' He sighed.

'You boys are doing a good job up there. You heard about Plasnewydd closing?' he asked. 'The abattoir I mean? Just didn't have the throughput, Eifion said. Losing ground every year. People turning away from meat, that's what Eifion told me. How can they do that? A really good steak' he said. 'Or lamb chops. Imagine not wanting . . . '

'That's just it' Phil said. 'In France they really do want them. Tom Wood says the demand there is just massive. Could keep sheep-farming in business by themselves, they could. There aren't any vegetarians in France, he told me.'

'Not like here' Lyn said, shaking his head in a series of small movements that brought his lips down to the rim of his glass again.

'Ten per cent here' Phil said. 'That's what they say. Ten per cent of the population don't eat meat.'

'Most of them in bloody England' Lyn said. The damp coal hissed in the fire, pissing out a little stream of greenish flame.

'They're powerful' Phil said. 'They got loads of money. Look at the adverts they can put out; that bloody FarmConcern, all those bastards.'

He found himself thinking of those people at the docks in Portsmouth, those beefy women yelling with their faces black with rage, that horrible little skinny bloke with his hair in a pig-tail, his face like a barking dog at the lorry window.

'They hate us' he said. 'They'd be happy if there wasn't a single lamb going for export.' He shook his head. 'They wouldn't care if there wasn't a single farmer left in Wales. They hate us, Lyn.'

'We're still here though' Lyn said. 'R'yn ni yma o hyd.'

'Er gwaetha pawb a phopeth' Phil said, smiling at him.

'Anyway, not all of them' Lyn said. 'They don't all hate us, from what I hear.'

He got heavily to his feet, dragging at the waistband of his trousers. He grinned and shook his finger at Phil.

'I'm going to get us a pint, Phil' he said. 'While you work out your side of the story.'

From behind the bar Martin caught Phil's eye and gestured at the beer tap: Same again? and Phil nodded, watching Lyn's broad and padded back stretching his jacket as he leaned over the counter; he had a pound coin in his hand and was clicking out a fretful message with it on the bar.

'I don't know what to tell you' Phil said as the other man sat down again, nudging the table so that the brimming glasses clinked and shivered, drooling saucers of creamy foam. He hunched himself lower in his seat.

'She's a student' he said. 'At the college.'

Lyn shook his head, smiling, his face expressing a sort of tired admiration.

'And is she beautiful?' he asked.

Phil nodded. He rasped his hand across his chin; he'd forgotten to shave before he came out. He could feel Lyn waiting for him to go on. He drew the tip of his finger through the spilt beer, watching as the liquid followed it across the shiny surface of the table. Perhaps it was her optimism, he thought, that made you want everything to come right for her, the way you do for children. He found himself wishing he'd known her when she was little. He felt the rush of a wordless, irreducible desire to be in the same place as her. He looked up. There must have been something in his face that bothered or embarrassed Lyn, something intense and absorbed, excluding him. Phil could feel his friend's attention release, like a hand letting go. Lyn cleared his throat and looked down into his beer.

'How's Liz?' he asked. 'And the boy? They keeping well?'

* * *

The Mercedes was parked by the back door of the house. Phil walked across the yard, the greasy concrete slick and sweating in the cold air. As he got closer, he could see that Beti was in the car, leaning back in the driver's seat. She was talking to someone, and Phil stooped a little to see who else was in the car. Beti glanced at him, still talking, and the electric window murmured down.

'Won't have them before Wednesday, will that do? Good boy Keith. Let me know.'

Phil had found himself peering into the car, expecting to see someone in the back seat. He straightened up as he realised that Beti had been talking into the car-phone.

'*Sut mae Phil*' Beti said. 'How are you today? Family well?'

She climbed stiffly out of the car, stretching and pressing a fist into the small of her back.

'Go and find Huw, will you Phil' she said. 'He's round the back there somewhere, and Alwyn.'

She swung the car door shut behind her with a compact thump, and went into the house. Phil walked back across the yard, into the alley between the Atcost building and the old stone sheds. He felt deflated, as though he had walked through a door into a place where he was no

194

longer the master of his life. He had a brief and wordless sense of how large he was in his son's world, or in Liz's, even in Lyn's or Nicky's lives, and how small he was here, stripped of affection and value, just one of Beti's boys. He shrugged, kicking at an aerosol can, sending it spinning and rattling across the concrete.

Huw and Alwyn looked up as he came round the corner of the building. Alwyn fumbled something he had been holding into his trouser pocket, his face bulging with suppressed laughter.

'Don't let the boy see this' he said. 'He's keen enough already, isn't he Huw?'

The two of them were squatted down, leaning against the wall of the shed. Alwyn gestured at the doorway into the building.

'Lambs are gathered' he said. 'Not supposed to start tagging until we hear from Tom Wood though. Some sort of a problem, Beti said.'

There was a tractor parked across the yard, the cab windows dull with damp frost. Phil walked over to have a look. A Massey, brand-new; it was fitted with a front-end loader that bristled with pipes and the glistening steel of hydraulic rams.

'What do you reckon this cost?' he called back.

'Worth more than you, *bach*' Alwyn told him.

They heard a car pull up by the house, and a moment later Tom Wood appeared round the corner of the building.

'Lambs here?' he said. 'Good.' He scratched his head, puffing out his cheeks.

'Have to wait on a bit' he said. 'No point to start tagging yet. Should know in an hour or so. Beti in the house?' He set off without waiting for an answer, breaking into an awkward trot.

'Should know what?' Alwyn called after him. 'Should know what in an hour?' He shook his head at Huw. 'Stupid bugger' he said.

Huw went off to start feeding the cattle. It grew damper and colder, the light beginning to fail. Alwyn got up, stretching and stamping his feet.

'See if we'll get some tea' he said.

They heard the sharp click of footsteps in the alley and Beti's voice, ringing with irritation. She and Tom Wood came into the yard, heads down, in the middle of some dispute.

'Ridiculous' Beti was saying. 'What are they playing at? You're too soft on them Tom. They need their heads knocking, they do.'

She stopped as she noticed Phil and Alwyn.

'And these boys sat around doing nothing' she said to Tom, her voice rising.

'Good god Alwyn, couldn't you find something to do man! *Am beth wyf i'n dy dalu di?*' She gestured at the big sliding doors of the shed.

'Get them open boys' she said. 'And turn on the yard lights. We'll get some of the shit cleaned out of here.'

She trotted across the yard to the new tractor and hauled herself up into the cab. The interior light came on and they could see her peering at the controls before the starter motor wheezed and the engine fired up with a roar. They saw the boom and bucket lift and stop at the top of its arc with a shock that set the whole machine rocking on its tyres. Alwyn shouldered the sliding doors open and Phil and Tom stepped hurriedly to one side as Beti gunned the tractor across the yard towards them. They heard the bucket scrape across the floor of the shed and then the tractor reversed out, the boom rising, a ragged and smoking mound of muck and old silage in the bucket. Through the glass of the cab they could see her stamping on the independents so that the left wheel locked up, screwing the tractor round ninety degrees in its own length before pumping smoke and racing across the yard towards the midden. She repeated the run a couple of times, then locked the wheels up on the slippery concrete and slid to a stop. She jumped down from the cab, grinning, relaxed.

'Now then Alwyn' she said. 'You go on with that till home-time. Now you see how it's done!'

In the deep shadows of the doorway, Tom Wood coughed and shuffled.

'I'll ring Deacon again in the morning' he said. 'Don't see what else we can do.'

Beti's expression darkened, as though the light had left her face. Her eyes glittered as she looked at Tom.

'You do that' she said. 'And make sure you tell him what I told you. No messing.' She turned and started to walk away.

'You go home Phil' she called over her shoulder. 'Nothing for you here!'

At the end of the Graig Goch lane Phil stopped the van. It was half past five. If the lambs had gone off as planned, it would have been nine, maybe ten o'clock before the lorry was loaded and ready to go. Liz wouldn't expect him before eleven. Eddy had gone to Aunt Nellian's after school; Liz would be collecting him from there when she finished work. The two of them wouldn't even be home yet. He had five or six hours to himself. He could go into town and call by the flat, see if Nicky was there. He looked at his watch again, then he let in the clutch and turned left onto the main road, towards Llanfrychan. Her friend opened the door, the plump one, Sían.

Chapter 16

Tom thought afterwards that he should have said something to Phil. There was a moment in the yard, as the evening closed in and the four of them dispersed, Alwyn climbing into the tractor, Beti walking back towards the house, when he thought Phil tried to catch his eye, wanting to say something to him. He had seemed a little preoccupied or depressed; perhaps he was worried that he wouldn't get paid since the load had been held over.

Tom shrugged, thinking about his own problems. The Ministry had told them not to send the load tonight; they wanted them to meet Richard Deacon again in the morning to straighten out their wretched discrepancies in the journey plan. Beti could stamp and shout and blame him all she liked; it didn't alter the way the thing had been dragging on for weeks, getting in the way of other work, low-grade anxiety, insistent and distracting.

So Tom muttered goodnight to Phil and hurried out of the yard. Hopefully Beti's strutting and boastful performance on the tractor would have put her in a better mood, so they might be able to discuss their approach to tomorrow's meeting without a lot of unrealistic ranting and posturing. He made an effort to get his own irritation under control as he hung his coat in the washroom and walked down the corridor into the kitchen. He made himself a cup of coffee. Beti put her head round the door, sleek, beaming. She had washed and changed and smelled of powder and perfume. Her hair was tied back, and Tom noticed she was wearing earrings.

'Going somewhere nice?' he asked.

'Wouldn't you like to know! Maybe I'm going dancing!'

She did a half turn on her toes.

'I didn't always look like this' she said. 'I used to be quite a dancer in my day. My little petal I used to be.'

She gave Tom a short smile.

'That's the trouble with petals' she said.

Tom opened his mouth, hoping a compliment would form itself, but Beti interrupted him.

'Get yourself a proper drink!' she said. 'There's whisky in the cupboard there. Come round first thing in the morning Tom. We'll sort it all out before this Deacon fellow gets here. We'll manage him, you and me! Good god if we don't!'

She stepped aside as her mother came past her through the door.

'Want Mam to cook you something?' she asked. 'There's chops in the fridge. You just tell her!'

Tom heard the front door slam shut behind her. Feeling both manipulated and appeased, he reached down the whisky from the cupboard above the cooker. He turned as he felt a tap on the shoulder. Beti's mother was holding a plate of meat, reaching it towards him with both hands as though she expected him to sniff at it like a dog.

'No thanks' he told her. 'Dim diolch. I think I'll just have a drink.'

For some reason the pantomime repeated itself, the old lady pushing the plate towards him while he shook his head and tapped the side of the whisky bottle.

'It's alright' he said. 'I'll just have a drink.' He poured himself a big one.

He thought about the meeting with Richard Deacon. He couldn't see the Ministry penalizing them for one specific error in a journey plan; they must be looking for evidence of systematic cheating. He took his drink over to the window. The yard outside was very dark. As he did so, there was a short ring on the bell, and the sensor switched on the flood-light over the back door. He didn't know where Beti's mother had gone, so he walked down the corridor to see who it was.

A woman stood in the doorway, a little boy beside her leaning into the hollow of her waist. They looked at each other, and Tom had the odd feeling that they had both been expecting to see someone else. She was short, dark-haired, rather pretty. The little boy stared at Tom, who became aware that he was still holding the glass of whisky in his hand.

'Sorry to bother you' the woman said.

'I was wondering if Phil was here?'

'You're Mrs Jones?' Tom said, and she nodded, smiling. The boy's eyes widened, as though he was preparing himself for bad news. Tom realised that, as he had opened the door, he had been expecting to see that girl of Phil's, her dark red hair, her body loose and slouching in the doorway. The other day, in Llanfrychan, he had seen her coming down the street, walking towards him. She'd been with a boy, some student-type, who'd shouted out a rude remark as they passed each other on the pavement. Tom had found himself thinking about her even more often since then, as though that encounter in the street had been a sort of inoculation, the pinprick of the boy's abusive words like a malign dart, the point of entry for some pathogen. So now, staring at Phil's wife and son when he had been thinking about his girlfriend, he felt confronted by a bizarre coincidence.

'I'm sorry' he said. 'You've missed him. He left an hour ago. The lambs didn't go off tonight, so we sent him home.'

She shuffled her feet, pushed a hand through her hair. Her left arm was round the little boy's shoulders, and she pulled him closer into the curve of her body. The two of them seemed to droop.

'Would you like to come in?' he said. 'I'm Tom Wood, by the way.'

She gave him an odd look, which he was aware took in the glass in his hand, and probably the fact that he hadn't shaved.

'Thanks' she said. 'We better get home. He's probably wondering where we are.'

They nodded and smiled at each other. Tom wanted to prolong the moment. He tried to think of something to say to the little boy, but he couldn't catch his eye. What do you say to children? Other people seem to know.

'We better go' she said.

He watched them cross the yard. The little boy was turning his head up to ask her something, and Tom saw her squeeze his shoulders, as though to reassure him. They turned the corner by the old cooling house, and disappeared.

In Beti's kitchen, the light from the overhead tubes fell with a bilious glare, striking shadowless highlights off plastic and stainless steel, like a laboratory, like a hospital. Tom sat down at the table and poured himself another drink. There was a copy of Farmers Weekly at his elbow, and he flipped through it for a moment. He thought of waiting rooms, and appointments, and tests, and specimen bottles. He felt the ache of sterility, like poison in the bones.

As their lives took on a shape that exactly enclosed the space a child would occupy, he and Jan had waited, as you wait for a letter to arrive, feeling the tug of hope and disappointment at every delivery. Later, they started to keep diaries; they made appointments and ticked off dates; they watched the future roll ponderously past them month by month and never take them with it. They examined their failures, sorting and reshuffling, trying to find the sequence, finally realising that it was all for nothing, that the beginning and the end were the same. The outcome had been written there all along, handed out in their DNA, the sealed orders, not to be opened until they were far out at sea. Other people fuck and breed, but not you. He pushed his chair back and got up. In the hallway he called out goodnight to Beti's mother, but there was no reply.

There was no one home. He remembered that Jan had a date, some sort of fund-raising dinner. He'd been invited too, but in a half-hearted way; they'd have been amazed if he'd turned up. It sometimes felt as though their lives were governed by a series of polarities, so that they circled each other, or perhaps passed a fixed point in opposite directions, like travellers on an escalator. Jan's discontents flared up in energy and irritation; Tom would get depressed and overweight and drink too much. He pictured himself travelling downwards, queasily gripping the handrail, watching her stepping vigorously up and up.

The next day, he and Richard Deacon sorted the whole thing out in less than an hour. That afternoon they sent lambs to Felix del Rio, and another load of Texels to SARL Phillipon. The sheep that had been held up while they sorted things out with Deacon had been for Benoit Formont, who was by far the most laid-back of their customers; it didn't seem to matter whether the lorry arrived on a Monday or a Thursday. The rich, contemptuous rumble of his voice on the phone: Ca m'est egal, merde! was humorous and soothing. Tom didn't see Phil, although he was about the place; he had intended to say something to him, ask him if he'd caught up with his family the other night, something like that, to see his reaction.

That evening he got a chance to talk to Jan about the meeting with Richard Deacon. After so much anxiety, the ease with which the whole thing had been resolved had left him feeling breathless, bubbles of hilarity rising in his chest.

'We sent the lambs off this afternoon' he told her. 'After all that, we only lost a day.'

Jan murmured something; she was looking at a brochure, idly turning the pages. Leaning over her shoulder, Tom saw that it was for a mobile phone.

'Thinking about it' she said. 'That's all.'

'So it didn't work' Tom said. 'Those bastard protestors tried to shop us to the Ministry, and it didn't work.'

She flipped the booklet shut, pushing back her chair and stretching. 'Start again' she said. 'About the lambs. I'll make some coffee.'

'All it was' he said, 'Richard Deacon came to the yard; he wanted to see the lambs go off himself. And from now on they want a fax from Pete when they get to the lairage. That's all they want. We're back to normal!'

'So this Deacon, will he want to be there every time?'

She had her back to him, pouring boiling water onto the coffee grounds. Tom told her he didn't know. She brought the coffee pot over to the table and sat down. She looked at him over the top of her cup, blowing at the steam with a long meditative sigh.

'It seems to me they've got you dangling' she said. 'You need their permission for every load of lambs you send. They can stop you whenever they choose. As they just showed you; they gave your chain a little jerk.'

He started to say something, but she interrupted him.

'In the end, they respond to political pressure' she said. 'If the demonstrators step it up, the Ministry comes down on you.' She shrugged. 'I'd keep watching the news if I was you.' They looked at each other.

'Phil's wife came round to Graig Goch last night' Tom said. 'And their little boy.'

Jan looked up. She took her glasses off.

'I wonder if I should get bi-focals' she said.

He could see the two of them in the pool of light at the door, the dark yard behind them.

'They looked so vulnerable' he said. 'For all I know he was with that girl. How can he let them down like that?'

'Sorry?' Jan said.

He wanted her to understand; it seemed to him that Phil was involved in a kind of double treachery, not just cheating on his family, but betraying his whole world. Alwyn said he'd seen the two of them in town more than once. What did that girl care for farming or life in the country? How could either of them justify what they were doing? How could she go on a demonstration one day and sleep with Phil the next? How could Phil sleep with her?

'Don't you think' Jan said, 'don't you think you get too involved with some of these people? In the end it's their lives you know, not yours. You need to keep your work in a separate compartment.'

He stared at her. He wanted to say that they were all in the same bed together, boat I mean.

'Why don't we eat out tonight?' Jan said. 'What do you think?'

That night the TV surpassed itself, even by its own lax and hyperbolic standards. Tom sat up after Jan had gone to bed, watching a long interview with some wretched bastard, one of the figure-heads of the animal rights campaign, a fuddled sod so pickled in hate that it slurred his words and twisted his face as he spoke. He watched an interview with someone from FarmConcern. We won't have this trade just swept under the carpet the spokesman said. We stopped it at Dover, we'll stop it at Portsmouth. Wherever they try to carry on this brutal business we'll find them and we'll stop them. The man faced the camera with an ecstatic look, as though he was addressing a huge crowd, the wind in his hair, the roar of the mob in his ears, his eyes glittering. Finally they had the nerve to bring on a bunch of raving lunatics in balaclavas, all the images and terminology of terrorism and phony military campaigns. These bastards, posing in shadowed silhouette, postured and smirked and boasted about how they were going to bring the pain and the suffering of their animal comrades down on the heads of the exploiters.

Tom thought about the boat; the plan for a consortium of exporters to run their own ferry across the channel was now fairly well advanced. Normandy Shipping were the only ferry company still carrying livestock; they felt unhappy and isolated, and they were sure to pull out of the trade. So there was a lot of pressure to get the new boat running. There were discussions with Harbour Authorities and police forces, with the Board of Trade and Trading Standards officers, with Health and Safety, with the board of the consortium itself, with banks and lawyers and marine insurers and accountants. It never stopped.

But it seemed to Tom that the key to the venture lay with the protest movement. All the hauliers and exporters he talked to seemed to think that once they had their own boat, the demonstrators would simply go away. They would lack the crucial leverage of public opinion, the blackmailing force they could exert on a commercial ferry that was trying to keep the punters happily crossing by sea.

Tom wasn't so sure. He pictured the little harbour the boat would use. He thought of the stretch of coast between Hove and Worthing; in the hinterland between the Downs and the sea you could deploy an army of protestors.

He got out the video-tape that he'd borrowed from Barry and put it on again. The students waved their placards. She leaned against the pillar, smiling faintly. He rewound the tape and her eyes swam into focus, looking into his with a kind of astonished recognition. Behind her the sky was pale and blue. The low sun shone through the dark red of her hair, exploding it into coppery highlights. She was wearing a T-shirt, although the day had been quite cold. He was intensely aware of the curves and swells of her body, the sweetness beneath her clothes.

* * *

Alwyn had seen the TV interview with the spokesman from FarmConcern. Tom found him with Huw and Barry in the yard, unloading sugar-beet. His face was slick with sweat and blotchy in the cold air; he looked ill, or hung-over.

'Little English fuck' he said, looking at Tom.

'I'm not English' Tom said.

'You know what I mean' Alwyn said. 'Saw him too, did you? Why's he want to put us out of work?'

He settled a sack on his shoulder and set off, legs bowed and staggering a little under the weight. He ducked in through the narrow doorway of the corner shed and reappeared a moment later, brushing a cobweb out of his hair.

'He never worked on a farm, see that straight away. What does he know about it? What do you say Barry!'

On the other side of the lorry Barry shut his eyes as he slid a sack across the flatbed and hefted it onto his shoulder.

Alwyn looked at him.

'You're miles away, Barry *bach*. Out with a dog and a gun are you?'

He grinned at Tom.

'Old Barry'd spend all his time after rabbits if he could' he said. 'He loves that gun of his, don't you boy?'

Tom could hear his phone ringing; he'd left it in the car, and he walked across the yard to answer it. It was Colin, calling from the lorry. He was running late, he'd be a couple of hours at least. Tom told him to push on, do his best. He got Richard Deacon at his office; he didn't see a problem, just to keep him posted. He walked back to tell the boys they weren't in a rush; the lorry was delayed, they could get their tea before they went to get Formont's lambs in.

'There's forty Suffolk-cross still over at Moelfryn' Alwyn said. 'Me and Barry can fetch them over with the Bedford. So what's Colin's problem then?'

Traffic, Tom told him.

'He's probably on the nest somewhere' Alwyn said. 'A girl in every truck-stop.' They looked round as Phil's van drove into the yard.

'And here's another one' Alwyn said.

He sucked his teeth, grinning at Tom.

'You know our problem?' he said. 'We're surrounded by shag-happy . . .'

He shook his head, searching for the word he wanted.

' . . . fuckers' he said. 'Shag-happy fuckers. Isn't it Huw!'

They watched as Phil got out of the van and walked over to join them. Tom found himself thinking of him with that girl, an image of ecstatic penetration which he tried to suppress as it rose up startlingly inside him.

'Did your wife find you the other night?' he called out.

'She was here looking for you, after you'd gone.'

Phil stopped, seemed about to say something, then shrugged and nodded. Tom was aware of Barry staring at him. Behind Phil's back, Alwyn rolled his eyes in mock alarm, and shook his hand in that burnt-fingers gesture. They went into the house. Beti was still in the mart somewhere. The old lady cooked chips for the boys. Tom had another look at the journey plan; there was plenty of time in hand and a couple of hours delay wouldn't cause any problems.

Phil was the first to push his chair back from the table, getting a big smile from the old lady as he thanked her with an elaborate phrase. Their voices echoed along the corridor as they pulled on boots and leggings in the wash-room.

'Where's the ear-tags then?'

Tom could hear the glutinous chuckle in Alwyn's voice as he answered:

'What's the big hurry, Phil? You on a promise tonight?'

Tom tried to phone Colin again but he couldn't get a signal. The old lady stacked the dishes in the sink, sighing and talking to herself. He heard the back door slam open, and a clatter as someone kicked over a bucket of tools. There was the swish and rustle of oil-skins, and then Alwyn appeared in the kitchen doorway. His face was dark and damp and his breath was coming in wheezing heaves.

'You better come and see this' he said. 'What's Beti going to say?'

He wouldn't answer any questions as Tom followed him out of the back door and across the yard. Alwyn was out of breath, but he was also enjoying the air of crisis and mystery.

'You come and see this' he said. 'You wait till you see this.'

The others were waiting by the range of stone buildings on the corner of the new yard, standing in front of the big sliding metal doors. The three of them drew aside as Tom and Alwyn approached.

'Beti's going to go mad' Alwyn said.

Across the whole width of the doors, something had been daubed in six-foot letters, spattered red and blotched, lumps and strings and entrails that dripped and slid on the slick surface. The daylight was going, but the dark red words glistened, thick and congealing, the letters deforming as they leaked and bled: FUCK YOU.

'This is what they did it with, look.' Huw was holding out a plastic bucket.

'I had the tups in a couple of weeks ago' Barry said. 'Marked them again.'

Tom stepped closer; the bucket was half-full, a wide paintbrush submerged in a sticky red paste. Raddle, for marking sheep. Not blood.

The four of them looked at each other.

'What's Mam going to say?' Barry asked.

'Fuck me' Alwyn said.

'Think they mean fuck all of us' Phil said, a hiccup of laughter in his voice.

'Who's that then?' Huw asked.

They looked round at the sound of an engine. There was just enough light to see a small car, a Fiesta or something, drive down the little lane that ran along the back of the new buildings the other side of the yard. For some reason Tom noticed Phil's expression, startled, and then intent and troubled, as he watched it disappear behind the line of the hedge towards the main road. He caught his eye for a moment, and looked away quickly.

Something made Tom look back across the yard to where the little Bedford truck was parked, fifty metres away. As he watched, the cab suddenly filled up with a bright light. He heard or felt a sort of deep, gulping breath, and then the doors flung open and the windscreen blew out in a shower of glittering sparks. A great bloom of fire rolled and boiled in bulges of orange and black and red and then collected itself into a rushing upward leap.

Tom had a confused sense of everybody shouting and jumping about. He hadn't realised that the sound of fire is so frightening. Someone barged heavily into him so that he staggered and nearly fell. As he straightened up he could see Barry running back to the house, pounding across the concrete in a flailing surge. He called to him, but he took no notice. There were a couple of bangs from across the yard as the front tyres exploded and the little truck lurched forward as though falling to its knees. A shower of sparks rose into the air and the bright flames rolled impenetrable shadows around them. Huw and Phil were still standing beside Tom, their faces lit in strobing flashes of colour. He couldn't see where Alwyn had got to.

After a few roaring minutes, the flames rushing upwards as though sucked fiercely through some black hole in the air, the fire seemed to slacken a little, turning a darker colour, half smothered in lumps of black smoke and the stink of burning plastic and rubber. Barry came running back across the yard, hopping lamely with the weight of a fire extinguisher. They watched his flickering silhouette dancing against the flames as he hunched over, shielding his face with a raised arm and clutching at the lever on the top of the canister. Phil, Huw and Tom started to cross the yard towards the Bedford. Alwyn pushed between them carrying another extinguisher and joined Barry on the edge of the fire. They clung to the short nozzles that seemed to leap and quiver in their hands as the compressed gases gushed and surged and jerked them hopping and bobbing around the dying truck like Morris dancers.

The fire gathered itself up into a ball, a yellow cyst, cut loose, and rose into the air, leaving a boiling mass of steam and smoke behind it. Another bubble of flame formed above the truck, rose and burst, and then a smaller, final one. Barry turned his singed, triumphant face towards the others. Alwyn crouched closer to the wreckage and fired bursts of chemical into the collapsed and twisted mass. The two of them walked round and round the truck, hosing and spraying as the metal hissed and clicked, subsiding.

Five minutes later, Alwyn put his arm round Barry's shoulder.

'You're a good boy, bachgen' he said. 'Isn't he boys?'

He beamed at the others. Everybody grinned and shuffled in the darkness, delighted with themselves.

'If she'd been parked where she normally is, we'd have lost the shed as well' Alwyn said, and a murmur of pleased agreement ran between them.

'Who was in the car, Phil?' Tom said.

'You recognised it, didn't you? I was watching you.'

He was aware that his voice was very loud.

'Who was it Phil?'

He could feel everybody looking at him. The wind was getting up; a burst of sleet blew through the yard and rattled across the roof of the shed.

'How do you mean?' Phil said.

Tom could still feel the heat of the fire in his face. He took a step closer to him.

'You know what I mean' he said. 'You've been running round with these students and demonstrators. What did you expect?'

Phil took a step backwards as Tom shouted into his face.

'Look at this fucking mess!' he said.

Phil winced; at that moment he found the other man intimidating, and Tom felt a twitch of excitement as he saw it.

'What the hell's been going on?' Tom asked him. 'Just what have you been up to?'

Alwyn put a hand on Tom's elbow and pulled him back.

'Hold on a bit' he said. 'Don't lose your head now.'

Huw had walked over to the shed and turned on the flood-light by the entrance to the loading bay, and they gaped at each other for a frozen moment, as though caught on film. Tom could see Phil straighten his shoulders, collecting himself to say something. Alwyn interrupted him.

'That's better' he said. 'No good stood around in the dark putting the blame on people.'

Tom shook his arm free.

'Someone's to blame' he said.

He pointed into the blackness beyond the half-circle of light they stood in. 'They were right here in this yard' he said. 'Just a few minutes ago. They must have used some kind of a fuse, a rag soaked in petrol or something, gave them just enough time to drive off. We saw the car.'

He turned back to Phil. 'You saw it' he said. 'You recognised it, didn't you? You've seen it before. It belongs to one of those students, doesn't it?'

Tom heard the note of indecision in his voice, the sudden timidity, and knew that Phil heard it too.

'It was just a car' Phil said. There was a short silence.

'So it's all a coincidence' Tom said. 'There's no connection between what you get up to on the side, and the fact that we've been targeted by these bastards.'

'Rainbow people' Barry said.

'What are you saying?' Phil glared at him. 'Get up to on the side?'

Tom looked at his watch and thought about the lorry.

'And no connection with Colin getting beaten up' he said. 'I suppose that's a coincidence too.'

He saw a look pass between Phil and Alwyn, coded but unmistakable, full of evasion and contempt. Alwyn turned his back and spat on to the concrete. He straightened up with a groan of satisfaction.

'Point is, we don't know who did this' he said.

'Can't go off accusing people like that. Phil doesn't want to burn us out of here, do you *bachgen*? We're in this together, isn't it?'

'I wasn't accusing Phil' Tom said.

He felt dull, befuddled. Barry was looking at Tom anxiously, waiting for someone to take control, tell him what to do. He looked from Tom to

Alwyn and back again, as though he was aware of a struggle taking place. Tom had expected Phil to be defensive, but he couldn't understand Alwyn's attitude. He looked at the man's pasty, potato face, thumbed and pitted like clay. Alwyn stared back at him with a look of amused hostility.

'I'm not accusing Phil' Tom said again. 'It's just if he's been mixing with these students, then anything's possible.'

'Tom's right' Barry said excitedly.

'Remember that demonstration in town? There was loads of them there, Rainbow students. They're out to get us, they are.'

'Shut up Barry' Phil said. 'You don't know what you're talking about.'

There was a flick of authority in his voice, the tone of the older man asserting his status, triggering the innate deference of the farm-boy.

'Who Phil's been mixing with' Alwyn said to Tom, 'in his own time, like, I don't think you pay him enough to know that, do you?'

This was so overtly hostile that Tom found himself blinking speechlessly for a moment. He felt both patronised and threatened. Perhaps Alwyn was deriving as much perverse enjoyment from the situation as he could. Perhaps he saw Tom as the representative of management, or the class system, or even Englishness. Perhaps it was just some male challenge, brought on by the barbarous incitements of darkness and fire.

'You think I'm making a fuss about nothing.' Tom said to Alwyn. He saw a flicker of anxiety in his eyes and felt the balance between them shift.

'We'll see' Tom said. 'In the meantime, two things.'

He held his fingers up like scissors, jabbing them towards his face.

'First we've got to call the police' he said. 'And then we've got to let Beti know.'

He turned his back on them and walked towards the house. After a moment he heard them start to follow, keeping their distance.

'Beti's going to go mental' he heard Huw say. 'She's going to go mental.'

Alwyn grunted something Tom didn't catch. He turned as he heard footsteps; Barry broke into a trot and caught up.

'What are we going to do Tom?' he asked him.

'What's going to happen now?'

*   *   *

209

In the bathroom, Tom splashed his face with water and looked in the mirror. Through the open door he heard the mattress creak as Jan turned over in bed. She said something, her voice hollow from within a deep fissure of sleep, the words meaningless although the tone was precise and urgent. Tom turned back to the foolish, middle-aged face in the mirror, the features puffy and blurred, the eyes full of anxious self-pity, the face of a stranger. He looked down at the gross accretions of drooping bulk that age was hanging on him, slung like a sack in lardy folds from tits to crotch, extraneous, intolerable. He shut his eyes.

Benoit Formont had cancelled the load. Somehow, that seemed the most shocking calamity of all in an evening of humiliations and absurdities.

'Je gagne rien avec vos agneaux' he said. Tom thought he was joking, although he could hear the change in his voice, the throaty bass turning nasal, brittle and high-pitched with anger.

'Et toujours ces delais. C'est une histoire de fous, quoi.'

It would have waited till morning. There'd been no need to call him late at night just to tell him the lambs would be delayed. They were all in Beti's kitchen, the policeman taking notes as they picked their way through the debris of the event. Tom had rung Benoit just to be doing something, to reach an arm up out of this morass towards a cooler and more elegant world. There had been something boastful in it too, getting the mobile out in the middle of another long silence, tapping quickly at the keys and speaking lightly and fluently in a language that none of them understood. *Salut Benoit! Je te derange?* As Tom took in what Formont was telling him he could feel his face go hot, and for a dreadful moment he knew that his eyes were pricking and his lips beginning to tremble and pucker. He cut him off before he could come up with any more insults.

'What?' Beti said, glaring at him across the kitchen table.
'What's up now?'

*   *   *

Tom had forgotten to ring Colin to stand him down. The Scania surged and rattled into the yard while the police activity was at its most frenetic. All the flood lights around the sheds were on; there was a patrol car parked by the back door, twice the size of Dai's little Panda, lurid with fluorescent stripes and the blue light still revolving lazily on the roof. There was an unmarked car, the front doors left open. A couple of uniformed PCs were talking intently to Phil and Alwyn; a bulky type in a heavy anorak, apparently the Scene of Crime officer, was writing something in a notebook. Everybody was talking at once, their conversations interrupted by the constant burp and crackle of radio telephones. A camera flash flickered like brief lightning as someone took photographs of the wreckage of the Bedford. Colin jumped down from the cab. He caught sight of Tom and walked over.

'You boys making a movie?' he said.

'They're at it again' Tom said. 'Same lot that got you.'

Colin blew a startled hiss through his teeth. Tom told him to go in the house, get a cup of tea. He felt weak and queasy for a moment. The plain-clothes policeman was leaning into his car, forcing himself past the steering wheel as he reached for something in the glove compartment. Tom coughed and muttered, and the policeman backed out of the car, bumping his head on the door frame as he straightened up. He wiped an enormous pale hand across his face.

'Yes' he said. 'Just a moment.'

He hurried across the yard to one of the PCs, the two of them putting their heads close in some hurried consultation.

'Sorry about that' he said as he came back. His smile was surprising, warm and open, very bright in the sandy squareness of his face. He looked about twenty five, if that.

'Now then' he said. 'D.C. Owen. What you got to tell me?'

Tom started to tell him about the fire. He said he was sure it was an animal rights attack. He and Beti had come to their attention as a suitable target. The conversation proceeded in a series of little hops and pauses, constantly interrupted. The policeman said the cause of the fire hadn't been established yet, the Fire Officer would make a report. When Tom said 'Beti' did he mean Beti Evans, the owner of Graig Goch? What was Tom's position here exactly? Every couple of minutes the car radio chattered at him and he broke off to lean in through the window and murmur cryptic replies.

'No' he said. 'I haven't been there. I'm here. Not yet.' He turned back to Tom.

'Sorry about that' he said.

Tom said it was obviously arson; he'd been there when the Bedford went up in flames. Anyway, hadn't Owen seen the writing on the wall? The policeman gave Tom an odd look.

'I mean the writing on the doors' Tom said.

Owen nodded. Tom had the impression he was thinking about

something else. His mobile rang, and he spoke briefly into it.

'Sorry about that' he said.

'I know who did it' Tom said. That was the high point of his evening.

He said that Phil Jones was friends with some students in town; He said they'd organised a demonstration against live exports a few weeks ago in Llanfrychan.

'That's the connection' Tom said. 'When they saw they had a real-life exporter just around the corner.'

DC Owen never took his eyes off Tom. The next time the radio crackled he ignored it.

'I don't mean Phil's involved' Tom said. 'Just that he's the link'.

The policeman rubbed the side of his jaw, still watching him.

'If you don't mind my asking' he said, 'how do you know all this?'

His eyes were very pale, the eye-lashes sparse and gingery. He was staring so intently that Tom wondered if it was a tactic to unsettle him.

'I'm trying to get this straight' Owen said. He wrote something in his note-book.

'When you say friends,' he said, 'what do you mean, he's friends with these students? Seems a bit odd doesn't it? Thought you said he worked here, thought you said he was a local boy?'

'He's been going around with them' Tom said. 'One in particular, a girl.'

DC Owen waited for him to go on. They looked at each other.

'He's told you all about it, has he?' he asked finally. When Tom didn't answer, Owen nodded thoughtfully at him.

'Perhaps I'd better have a word with him' he said.

Tom watched him walk across the yard. Owen gestured to Alwyn, and the two of them stood talking under the flood-light by the back door. Alwyn brayed with laughter as he called Phil over; he gave him a cuff on the shoulder, and went into the kitchen. Phil and the policeman stood talking for some time. Once or twice Tom thought Phil gestured in his direction, and at some point Owen turned round and looked at him. His car radio squawked and fizzled to itself.

Beti's Mercedes drove into the yard, the tyres spitting gravel. Owen and Phil had to step back quickly out of the way. Tom looked at his watch. Beti was always late, especially in situations where nothing could move forward until she arrived. It was a technique, one of her prerogatives, a display of power.

'What the hell's been going on then?' The metallic tones of her voice carried sharply across the yard. The policeman who'd been poking about in the entrails of the Bedford looked up; the two uniformed PCs straightened their caps. In a process Tom had seen many times before, the whole orientation of the gathering was now focused on Beti.

'Where the hell's Tom?' she said.

* * *

In the disheartening overhead light of the interview room, DC Owen's eyes looked paler than ever as they swam up at Tom out of sockets of shadow, his skin white and washed out, his hair thin and flat across his head.

'You see the problem' he said. 'Your Phil Jones says he doesn't know what you're talking about. Says he has a drink in the Star sometimes. Apparently that's a student pub.' He shrugged. 'Not much to go on there.'

Tom sighed. First the phone-call to Benoit Formont when they'd all gone into the kitchen to get a cup of tea, the contempt in his voice: C'est fou quoi. And now this. He knew that in some way the whole occasion had been designed as a humiliation. 'Be a big help if someone would come down to the station and make a proper statement' Owen had said. He had looked at Tom then. 'Look at some photos perhaps. And you've given us much the fullest account sir'. Tom had seen a look pass between the others, secretive, amused: walked into that one. So now they were drinking whisky in the warm kitchen at Graig Goch, while he sat here in this horrible little room at the police station, facing a long drive home, isolated, cold and subtly touched with guilt and doubt.

'It's not as if you can give us any names' Owen was saying. 'Just a girl that you say you've seen about the place.'

There was a silence. 'You married sir?' he asked. Tom started to speak, but Owen interrupted him.

'You say you've seen her about the place, but Mr Jones says he doesn't know any girl like that. Just has a drink in the pub, he says, from time to time.'

They looked at each other.

'We'll make enquiries of course.' Owen tapped the desk with his knuckles. 'But what I suggest, for the paperwork, like, is you just give us an account of what you saw tonight, leave it like that. Pity you didn't get a better look at the car.'

It was midnight when Tom got home. He had a stiff drink, and went upstairs. Jan was asleep. He got undressed and went into the bathroom.

He splashed water on his face, and looked at himself in the mirror.

*   *   *

They took the Bedford away the next day. A couple of guys in overalls winched it up the ramp of a big police recovery vehicle. It was going for further examination, they told Tom. The forensic boys'll give it a right going over. He wondered what they expected to find. The evidence they needed wasn't going to lie in any scorched and powdery residues they might scrape out of the remains. There was evidence to be had, but it was warm and alive and wearing jeans and walking around somewhere in Llanfrychan at this very minute.

He managed to speak to DC Owen, who said they were following up a number of lines of enquiry. He said it was early days, but he had a very positive feeling about this one. When Tom tried to talk to Beti about it, she cut him short.

'Lucky it was only the Bedford.' she said. 'We were lucky there Tom! Ready for the scrap-yard, it was.'

Tom asked her about the closed circuit cameras.

'Bloody thing's on stop' Beti said. 'Wasn't even switched on.'

She hurried across the yard, then turned suddenly.

'Tell you what!' she called out. 'Been thinking to get some what you call, guard-dogs, leave them loose at night! What you think?'

Tom spoke to Benoit Formont again. He hadn't changed his mind about the lambs. His whole manner was different, as though he'd experienced some catastrophic revelation. Phillipon rang to say they didn't want any lambs for a couple of weeks, the price wasn't right. Tom began to feel as if the Prevost nightmare was leaking into waking life, that he was being rejected and betrayed by people he had thought were friends.

He had lunch with the boys in the kitchen, or rather he drank coffee while they chopped and forked the food the old lady put in front of them and sluiced the mugs of tea she constantly refilled, wordlessly thanking her with bulging, nodding faces. Alwyn ate in a way that was both fastidious and piggy, mincingly cutting his food into tiny squares which he then chewed open-mouthed and swilled down with tea. Tom waited until they were nearly finished and were wiping folded envelopes of white bread around the greasy plates.

'Phil' he said, and all three faces looked up at him.

'This is difficult' he said.

Huw said something to himself and went back to his plate. Phil and Alwyn continued to watch Tom.

'I understand you couldn't really talk about it to the police' Tom said. He shrugged impatiently. 'At least, I suppose I understand.'

Alwyn's jaws resumed their slow, reciprocating movement as he chewed. Phil slid his knife and fork together on his plate.

'You can fuck whoever you like' Tom said. He saw Huw duck his head and grin with embarrassment. 'Nothing to do with me' Tom said. 'Until they try and bomb me out of business!'

He had raised his voice; he could hear the tremor in it. Out of the corner of his eye he saw Beti's mother scuttle out of the room. His throat felt tight, and he drew in a long shaky breath, trying to relax.

'Seems bloody obvious to me we need the police' he said, 'but alright! We can do it your way.' He smiled and nodded at them. 'Vigilante-style' he said. 'Send out the posse!'

Phil and Alwyn looked at each other. Huw pushed his chair back from the table.

'Better give Barry a hand' he said. 'He's been doing silage to the cattle. Boy needs his dinner.' He left the room.

'We have to find a way to stop these people' Tom said to Phil. 'And you know who they are.'

'There you go again!' Phil said. His voice was suddenly shrill with anger. 'What's this all about?'

Tom opened his mouth, but Phil went on before he could say anything.

'I told that copper the same thing' Phil said. 'Sometimes I'll go along for a pint at the Star. I like the crack there, good music. What's it to you? What's the problem?'

'Alwyn!' Tom said. 'Speak up man! You said you've seen him there! Tell him what you told me!'

Alwyn shook his head, hesitating.

'*Dim byd i wneud â ni*' he said. 'None of my business.'

'Same bloody thing!' Phil said. 'I'll have a drink in a pub; load of pretty girls there, perhaps I'll chat them up a bit. Next thing I'm a fucking IRA bomber, according to you! What gives you the right?'

Tom stared at the two of them. Alwyn was sucking his teeth, looking from Phil to Tom and back again. Tom realised there was no way Alwyn would take his side against Phil. He might make fun of Phil behind his back, but a threat from outside would always call up reserves of tribal loyalty. Perhaps he was also half convinced by Phil's account, and for a

215

moment Tom shared his doubt.

He looked at Phil. He had a sudden and very clear memory of the time he had been with him when they had bumped into that girl in the High Street; Tom remembered the intense and ecstatic look that had passed between them, the look of two people who have just started to fuck each other, a look which you could never mistake for anything else. Phil was flushed, his posture stiff and awkward, and Tom knew he was lying. He thought the depth of Phil's unease was not because he was scared of being caught out, but because he had trapped himself into behaving much worse than came naturally to him. He was a good boy behaving very badly, and Tom almost felt sorry for him.

Alwyn got up from the table.

'We'll get the lambs down from Cae Coch' he said. 'Beti said straight after dinner' he added, as though to forestall Tom. 'Isn't it Phil?'

There was a moment of extreme discomfort as they pushed past Tom to get to the door, neither of them catching his eye. He heard them walking down the corridor to the washroom.

'He needs to get out more' Alwyn was saying.

'What's she called?' Tom said. 'What's her name?'

He was speaking to himself really. They probably hadn't heard him. 'I'll find her anyway' he said.

That afternoon he studied the notice-boards in the main entrance at College Hall. He read about poetry readings, and canoe clubs, and IT courses and karaoke evenings; about second hand text-books for sale, and Welsh conversation classes, and third and fourth girls wanted to share. A stream of young people passed in and out of the lobby; he never knew there were so many students on the campus. A guy in a brown coat, a porter or a janitor, asked if him needed any help. Tom said he was waiting for a friend. As he said the words he felt overwhelmed by such a rush of self-pity that he had to turn and hurry out of the building.

He found his way to the Library. It was a modern building, grey, weather-streaked concrete, set back from the street. Tom thought he might need a pass, but nobody stopped him. He walked through the reception area, past a row of desks where books were being scanned and stamped, into a reference room lined with computer terminals. From there, corridors ran into muffled depths of the building, down ranks of metal shelving, along scuffed linoleum floors. The air was dry and stale. At each intersection there was a space lined with work tables where students sat hunched and frowning over their books, or looked up as he passed, gaping at him as if from the other side of a thick pane of glass. She wasn't there.

216

A couple pushed past him as he stood on the pavement outside the library, the man knocking against his shoulder without an apology. He was talking rapidly to the woman, who was having to jog to keep up with him. Tom watched them hurry down the street. The man had grey hair in a pony-tail; his girlfriend was wearing a long dress that billowed out behind her. They were dressed all wrong for their age, and they had the intense, vengeful, self absorbed look of alcoholics or drug addicts. Tom thought of all the human trash that had been thrown up by the sixties, all the dirty old men with long hair, all the gibbering and unquiet; in the end the music and the counter-culture had thrown open the doors to release only madness.

He tried again towards the end of the afternoon. As he walked up the hill towards the main entrance of the Library, the glass doors swung open, turning a bright page of reflected wintry sunlight into his face, and a girl hurried down the shallow flight of steps and onto the pavement in front of him. Tom didn't see her face, but he recognised her immediately, and quickened his step to keep up with her. Her hair was cut very short, like ruffled feathers in the chill breeze. She was wearing a motorcycle jacket and blue jeans. As Tom followed the incredible syncopation of her walk he felt a triumphant excitement, a sense of undefined but powerful vindication. He was filled with a terrible tenderness; he wanted to lick, and suck, and bite.

Chapter 17

Harris was late for his tutorial on Thursday, and he hadn't written up his notes from the lecture. He hadn't really done any work since that awful bloody scene. How could Nicky have gone off with him like that? The bastard. He sighed. He'd managed to make it worse of course, talking to Marietta about it. Why had he done that? Across the room from him, Spedding coughed, and fiddled with his pen, and crossed and uncrossed his legs. He looked embarrassed.

'Everything alright Harris? Social life, that sort of thing?'

Harris grunted. He thought of Nicky's face yesterday, pale, pinched with anger. He had started to say something, but she'd interrupted him, spitting words at him: How do you think this makes me look? You got a fucking nerve. He'd seen her and Sían just now, crossing the Green; they were looking the other way, or avoiding him. He sighed again.

'That's alright then' Spedding said.

After the session, he looked in at the coffee bar, but they weren't there. It was beginning to rain; he didn't have a coat. By the time he got to Water Lane the rain was soaking through his jeans. He jumped back as the Fiesta drew in to the side of the road, a front tyre squealing against the kerb. Bobs leaned across and wound down the passenger window, grinning at the look on Harris's face.

'Where you going all by yourself?' he asked.

'Sían say you could borrow the car?' Harris asked him. 'You got permission?'

Bobs shook his head impatiently.

'Get in' he said.

Harris looked up at the thin sleety rain; across town the horizon was black, the clouds no higher than the spire of the church. He got into the car.

'I thought you'd gone Bobs' he said. 'Why are you still here?'

Bobs wiped at the side window, squinting through the rain, and pulled out into the traffic.

'How's it going with Nicky' he asked. 'Sorted things out?'

They came to a stop at the traffic lights in the High Street.

'How you going to frighten that farmer off?' Bobs said. 'Need a hand there?'

'Where were you gone yesterday?' Harris asked him. 'What the fuck are you up to?'

Just ahead of them, Harris saw Julie and Whatsname crossing the street. He hunched lower into his seat. They didn't see him. The lights changed, and the line of cars moved on again.

'So, are you getting any?' Bobs asked. 'Perhaps you need a little help in that direction too.'

'Fuck off.'

Harris watched him as he drove. 'What are you doing here?' he said. 'Haven't you got a life of your own?'

As always, Bobs pretended not to hear the venom in Harris's voice, reacting as if it was just good-natured, kidding around. He grinned and tapped the side of his nose.

'I've been doing a bit of exploring' he said. 'Checking out the local sights, places of interest like.'

'What's that supposed to mean?'

'You watch this space, Harry. Just watch this space. A hot time in the old town tonight.' He whistled tonelessly between his teeth. 'Here we are' he said. He stopped the car. Harris wiped a port-hole in the side window; they were on Paxton Hill, just a few yards down from the flat. Bobs grinned at him, a look of sly accomplishment. He didn't switch the engine off. He was obviously waiting for Harris to get out.

'Anything else I can do?' he said.

'How about drop dead?'

'That's very good Harry, very good.'

They looked at each other. 'We're here Harry' Bobs said. 'This is you.'

'And where are you going?' Harris said. 'Where's mum?'

'I've got some business to take care of' Bobs said. 'I'll tell you about it one of these days.'

Harris sighed, listening to the hiss of the rain, the lip and slop of the windscreen wipers. He tugged at the door handle.

'It sticks' Bobs said. 'You got to give it some.'

He stretched across the passenger seat so that Harris, drawing back in disgust, was shoved and muffled, his face gagged and buried against the other man's shoulder as Bobs reached past him and punched at the door.

'Some of that' he said, rotating his fist.

Harris trotted up the steps, his shoulders hunched against the drizzle. He leaned against the front door, groping for his key, shutting his eyes as a bubble of anguish rose in his chest. Where's mum? He ground his teeth. Why had he asked Bobs that? He pushed the door of his room open, threw his bag onto the bed and went on into the kitchen. Sían looked up as he came into the room.

'What's another word for limit?' she asked. 'Five letters.'

'Why do you keep lending Bobs your car?' he said. 'Why the fuck do you want to do that?'

'Don't shout at me Harris' Sían said, her smile dissolving. 'Don't shout at me.' She sniffed and cleared her throat.

'I don't keep lending it' she said. 'He asked me; I didn't know how to say no. Anyway, I thought I'd be doing your mum a favour.'

'I wish they'd just go' Harris said.

'What did they say? You talk to them again?' Sían asked him.

Harris sighed. 'It's this thing with Imogen, whatever. Tomorrow or the next day.'

He leaned over the newspaper that Sían had spread out on the table.

'Range' he said. 'Scope; field.'

Sían beamed at him. 'Scope' she said. 'Of course.' She stroked his hand, running her fingers lightly across the dip and rise of his knuckles.

'Harris' she said. 'This whole thing with Nicky, it'll be alright when they've gone.'

He pulled his hand away.

'It's got nothing to do with you' he said.

She watched him as he walked to the back door and stood looking out through the smeared and spotted glass. The cat from next door put its head through the flap, hissing as Harris pushed it back out with his foot.

'The way you're being so defensive' she said. 'It's making everybody miserable.'

She paused, gauging his mood, blinking as she braced herself for some furious insult.

'Harris' she said. 'I'm your friend. I'm just trying to tell you it's like, not fair. Nicky hasn't done anything to you.'

Sían had raised her voice on the last word and it was as though the sound flighted across the room like a paper dart, hitting Harris between the shoulder blades; he seemed to flinch and droop. The cat started to push in through the flap again. Harris kicked the panel shut with a clatter.

*   *   *

Bobs must have tripped over Julie's bicycle; they heard the clatter and ping of the bell and the sharp ticking of a wheel turning. The confused sounds seemed to go on and on, as though he had got himself tangled up; they could hear him cursing. Marietta pulled a face, a look of mock alarm. I think he's been in the pub she mouthed in a stagey whisper. He missed his footing on the step down into the kitchen and almost fell. He looked round at them all, red-faced and grinning.

'Everybody happy?' he said. He had a gold tooth, Sían saw, round on the left side of his mouth; she hadn't noticed it before.

Harris caught the look of animosity on Nicky's face and realised with a sudden dismay that it was directed at him. She blamed him for Bobs; this was all his fault. He looked away.

'What you been up to old boy?' Marietta asked him. 'You been in the Star?'

'Among other places' Bobs said. He lit a cigarette, his eyes glittering at her through the smoke. 'Among other places.'

There was a silence. Sían handed Nicky her coffee and picked up her own.

'Better get on' she said.

'Some very interesting places' Bobs said. He looked at Nicky. 'You'd be interested to know where I've been' he said. She started to move towards the door but he blocked her way.

'You'd be very interested.'

'Bobs!' Marietta said sharply, and Nicky pushed past him and followed Sían out of the room. Harris heard the anger in her voice as the two girls walked down the corridor: Disgusting little creep!

'I tell you one thing' Bobs said. 'I've lit a fire in her knickers.'

He giggled, a falsetto snort that blew smoke between his teeth.

'You should of seen it!' he said, his eyes streaming.

'We're to stay out of it' Marietta said. 'That's what Harry wants, isn't it Harry?'

'I don't think Harry wants to stay out of it' Bobs said. 'I think he wants to get right back in it.'

Marietta looked at him. She wondered if he'd scored some speed; he was really lit up. She felt the tug of an obscure emotion, somewhere between dread and depression. It was like that moment of terrible lassitude in a dream where you cannot cross the room to reach the door.

'I was going to have a bath' she said. 'Is that alright Harry?' He didn't answer, as she had known he wouldn't. Bobs was trying to blow smoke rings; he was nodding his head and muttering to himself as he pouted bubbles of smoke. Marietta watched the two of them for a moment, then left the room. She was beginning to feel invisible.

Bobs got up and dropped his cigarette into the sink, his movements quick and precise, as though he'd been waiting for Marietta to go.

'You should of seen it' he said.

'I thought it hadn't worked for a minute, then I saw it in the mirror: WALLOP! just like the movies! Nearly drove off the road I did. I looked round, and it was this big!'

He reached his arms out, staggering back as though under an enormous weight. 'It was beautiful! You should of seen it.'

Harris looked at him. 'I got work to do' he said.

'You don't know what I'm talking about, do you?' Bobs asked him. He skipped across the room and shut the door. 'I'll give you a clue' he said. 'It's about your precious Nicky, and her agricultural friend.' He grinned delightedly at Harris. 'Thought you'd be interested' he said.

'Just get on with it' Harris said. 'What the fuck you trying to say? I told you I got work to do.'

In Nicky's room, Sían picked up the coffee cups. 'You want another?' she said. Nicky nodded without looking up from her book. As she came out into the corridor, Sían could hear Harris's voice: You're off your fucking trolley! She opened the kitchen door.

'Sían's car' Harris was saying. 'The number-plate?'

'What's this about my car?' she said.

'Nothing' Harris told her. 'Bobs won't need to borrow it any more, will you?'

'That's alright then' Sían said brightly, aware of the conversation that had been taking place behind this one, and was waiting to be resumed. 'Either of you want a coffee?'

'Thought you'd be a bit more grateful' Bobs said as soon as Sían had left the room. 'I given that farmer something to think about, didn't I? Something else to think about.'

'Grateful?' Harris said. He shut his eyes, black fireworks exploding behind the lids. 'This has got nothing to do with me' he said. 'You're on your own.' He looked at Bobs. 'I want you out of here' he said. 'You mad bastard.'

'You watch your language' Bobs said. 'You're well in, son. Any bother I get in . . . ' He paused while he lit a cigarette, watching Harris through the smoke.

'Know what I mean? Don't want your precious studies interrupted.'

He got up, stretching, rolling his shoulders. 'So don't push me, right?'

222

he said. 'We'll be gone soon enough.'

*　　*　　*

When the panda car passed him on Paxton Hill Harris quailed, a cold hand on his chest so palpable that he must have visibly cowered. He felt the driver's eyes on him in the rear view mirror. The brake-lights winked at him; Harris felt as though he was walking on some wobbly surface, like jelly, and then the car drew away from him down the street, exhaust smoke twisting white in the cold air. He blinked back tears of enraged self-pity.

He hadn't been able to talk to Sían or Nicky last night, tell them the crazy thing that Bobs had done. They'd gone somewhere in the early part of the evening. Much later, when everybody had gone to bed, he had stood at Nicky's door. There was a faint strip of light from under it, perhaps her bedside light. He had raised his hand to tap lightly on the panel, then let it fall. He thought he heard the mattress creak as she moved in the bed. Perhaps she was reading. He pictured the line of her collar-bone crossing the soft hollow of her shoulder as she leaned over the book. He breathed out in a long sigh. It was impossible. She would blame him. What Bobs had done would somehow be his fault, more of the same mess. There was nothing he could say, he might as well have torched the fucking truck himself. The light under Nicky's door went out. She was barely speaking to him as it was; talk about the last fucking straw. Standing in the dark corridor he almost laughed out loud. He went back to his room.

Now, as his heart slowed and he watched the police car turn left down a side street, he told himself again that all he could do was get on with his work, keep his head down. Thinking of Bobs, he felt as though he had stepped back from the edge of a cliff, from something suddenly revealed as lethal, hypnotic, with the power to take his life and crack it open.

He crossed the Green and followed the path round the edge of the tennis courts to the Sociology Department. There was a printed card on the door of the lecture room: Commodity Society – Culture and Reification. He found a seat right at the back by the stacks of folding chairs, although the place was half empty. A girl a few rows ahead looked round and smiled at him and he nodded back, trying to think who she was; one of Julie's little group perhaps. Draper came in through the side door, slapping a briefcase onto the desk. He cracked it open and looked over the top of the lid with a thin smile at the ten or twelve dull and sleepy faces in front of him.

Harris thought about Nicky. He tried to imagine telling her about Bobs and his petrol bomb. She'd go crazy. She'd confront Bobs, she'd threaten him. Because she despised him she would think you could kick him like a dog and that he would snarl and cower. Bobs would enjoy that. Harris saw rolling clouds of black smoke and police cars. Let's take a postmodern approach Draper was saying. Harris shook his head, blinking, and opened his note-pad. Let's look at the rise of marketing and enterprise culture in the 1980s

In the library, he tried to write up his notes and make some sense out of them. From the long sickness of experience he knew that the more Bobs felt under pressure to leave, the more he would resist, just to watch them squirm. He would feel a bizarre sense of power, the ability to drag them all in. Harris tried to imagine Marietta down the police station, giving a statement. What a mess. He sat in front of a terminal for half an hour, searching through the catalogue; all of the books on Draper's reading list were out.

He found Sían in the front room. There was no one else in the flat. She told him Nicky had stayed on to help with the newsletter; she'd said she was going to the library after that.

'You're joking' she said.

Her eyes filled with tears. 'Was anybody hurt?'

Harris shook his head. 'Don't know' he said.

'Oh my god' Sían said. 'Oh my god' She looked at him, chewing her knuckle.

'He used my car' she said. 'That's what you were talking about yesterday. He used my fucking car. What are we going to do?'

The phone rang. Harris went out into the hall to answer it. 'Hello' he said. 'Hello.' There was silence, then a short clatter as the connection was broken.

'My fucking car' Sían said, suddenly understanding why people used that word so much.

'We'll have to go to the police' she said. 'Explain, tell them . . . ' her voice trailed away.

'Bobs'll say we helped him' Harris said. 'He'll say it was our idea. They'll believe him too; your stupid demo.' He shook his head. 'Anyway, it's not just that. It's Marietta.'

'What?' Sían said. 'Don't look at me like that, this isn't my fault.'

'She'd crack up' Harris said. 'She's done it before. You don't know what it's like.'

They looked at each other in silence.

'This is a long way from caring about animals' Sían said.

Harris nodded. 'Maybe you're the only one that does' he said.

Sían looked at him. 'Stop feeling sorry for yourself' she said. She could feel emotions moving about inside her, a sense that something new was happening to her.

'You've got to sort this' she told him. 'Where are they? Down the pub? You've got to find Bobs and tell him: they've got to leave now, this afternoon. Leave your mother out of it if you have to' she said. 'Just talk to Bobs. Get him out of here.'

'You don't understand' Harris said, his voice flat and dull.

'You're twice his size' Sían said. 'Hit him!'

'You don't understand' Harris said. 'Bobs is someone who can always make things worse.' He sighed. 'He can always make things worse.'

He raised a hand to his face, brushing his fingers over the little pitted scar at the corner of his mouth. The taste of hot salt and the sudden rubbery swelling of his lip. He had tried to blink back the tears. 'That's what you get' Bobs had said carefully, as though explaining something. He had made a slight chopping gesture with his open hand. That's what you get. You see?

Sían took her glasses off and rubbed her eyes.

'I can't actually imagine what Nicky is going to say.'

She shook herself, releasing a short sob of laughter. 'Can you?'

She looked at Harris, waiting for him to say something.

'It's better if she doesn't know' he said. 'She could mess things up.'

'Mess things up?' Sían said. 'Mess things up?'

She stared at him; she could feel her respect for him leaking suddenly away, a physical feeling, like pissing.

'You're scared of her' she said. 'You're scared of Nicky, just because she's got some bottle. That's pathetic.'

'Fuck off' Harris said.

'Is that why you want to be with her?' she said. 'So you can make her angry and frightened like you are?'

'Fuck off' Harris said again, raising his voice.

'Oh I know you're not scared of me' Sían said, backing away from him.

Chapter 18

Alwyn pulled the door of the LandRover shut, settling himself behind the wheel.

'Put him in his place' he said. 'Mr Godalmighty Wood!'

He reached down and pressed the starter button; the engine wheezed and rattled and fired up, exhaust smoke blowing in at the open window and bubbling up through the hole in the floor.

'IRA bomber!' he said, grinning at Phil. 'That was good, that was!'

They drove out of the yard. Phil leaned against the side window, letting the vibrations rattle through his head. Out of the corner of his eye he was aware of Alwyn glancing at him as he drove, his grin fixed and yellow. Phil looked away. He found himself thinking of a bracelet that she wore, a thin silver chain too big for her wrist; she would spread her fingers to stop it slipping off. Alwyn braked suddenly and the LandRover pulled over to the left, a dead branch in the hedgerow rasping past Phil's window like fingernails. Huw and Barry squeezed past them on the quad-bike, Huw driving, the boy crouched awkwardly behind him, squatting on the rear carrier with his hands on Huw's shoulders. Alwyn slid the window open to speak to them but Huw shouted something they didn't catch, and drove on.

They parked the LandRover in the lay-by and started up the slope of Cae Coch, Floss hunting ahead of them, nose down and weaving.

'What's the damn hurry?' Alwyn called out.

Phil turned and waited for the other man to catch up.

'No bloody rush' Alwyn said, his face dark with effort or resentment.

'Got all afternoon' he said. 'There's no need to bloody rush.'

'Where those lambs?' Phil said, squinting into the pale glare of the sun beyond the rise of the field. Alwyn was still breathing heavily, his feet slipping on the wet grass.

'What's your fucking hurry?' Alwyn called again.

'You wait by here' Phil told him. 'I'll go up and fetch the lambs down. You turn them for the gate. Here Floss!'

He whistled for the dog. He was aware of Alwyn opening his mouth to say something, but he turned quickly away and jogged up the field to the top of the slope. The lambs were near the fence at the far end, the dark blur of the copse behind them. He stood and watched them for a minute, getting his breath back; then he sent Floss round in a wide burst of speed to fetch them on. As the lambs jinked and bunched, a scatter of crows flew up out of the trees, rising in halting spirals like flakes of ash above a fire.

Alwyn had moved over to the left of the gate; he spread his arms and whooped, turning the lambs through as they streamed down towards him. Phil watched him for a moment: his drinking companion, his alibi for the other night. He groaned to himself. It had been two o'clock by the time he had dropped Nicky off and come home. Liz had rolled and mumbled as he had slid himself into the bed beside her. Squeezing his eyes shut and pretending to be asleep, he could see Nicky's glistening smile, her head thrown back in delight as those old boys in the pub sang love songs at her. Liz's voice was furred with sleep: What time is it? Where you been? He didn't answer.

She had asked him again the next morning, her back to him as she clattered the breakfast things into the sink.

'Where did you get to last night? Me and Eddy called round at Graig Goch. They said you'd left early, they said the load was cancelled.'

'Pub' he said. 'I went down the pub with Alwyn.'

She turned round to look at him then.

'Alwyn?' she said. He ducked his head below the level of the cereal packet on the table. Liz put the dishes away and dried her hands with quick, competent movements.

'Alwyn?' she said again. 'Elaine said Lyn was out, so I thought you must be with him. Since when you go drinking with Alwyn? What time did you get back? It was gone midnight when I went to bed.'

He could feel her eyes on him. He took a breath, and risked looking directly at her, pulling a face.

'You know' he said. 'You know how it is.'

'No I don't' she said. 'I really don't.'

He caught her eye again. She gave a short laugh, in which he could hear only a tolerant and affectionate contempt. He sighed weakly.

'Look at the state of you' she said. 'Don't expect any sympathy.'

Phil glanced across the table at Eddy. The little boy was staring at him, his eyes wide and anxious.

The lambs bunched and jostled in the gateway, spilling into the lane, where they milled in little whirlpools of anxious movement until Floss set them moving in a compact rush towards Graig Goch. Alwyn had turned the LandRover round and was waiting with the motor running. As Phil climbed into the cab he felt a sudden surge of dread, a queasy, vertiginous sense that he'd forgotten something, that some absolutely vital thing had been lost, or left behind. He glanced across at Alwyn, knowing immediately what it was.

'So was it her?' Alwyn asked him. 'This tart of yours? She try to blow us up?'

'Don't call her a tart' Phil said.

Alwyn stamped on the brake pedal; the wheels locked up, spitting bursts of gravel as the LandRover skewed diagonally across the lane.

'Call her what I fucking like!' Alwyn said.

'You listen to me *bach*. Am I supposed to sit here while you drop us in the shit?' He was gripping the steering wheel, his arms straight, wrenching at it.

'Listen now Phil' he said. 'Course you didn't say nothing with that Tom Wood. But this is me now, *bach*. This is me asking. What the fuck you getting us into?'

'We got to keep after the lambs' Phil said. 'Floss know to turn them in the yard?'

'You got no right' Alwyn said. '*Sdim hawl gennyt ti.*'

He jolted the LandRover into gear and drove on, looking across at Phil. 'I got a right to know what's going on' he said.

'Course she didn't' Phil said. 'Don't be ridiculous.'

Floss had the lambs bunched by the range of stone buildings in the corner of the new yard and was flicking back and forth along an imaginary line that fenced them in.

'You don't know that' Alwyn said.

Phil walked over to open the side door of the shed, crossing the spot where the Bedford had burned out. The concrete was blackened and scorched, and there was a litter of flakes and fragments of ash, dotted with points of light from the shattered windscreen. Someone had started to sweep up; a yard-broom was leaned against the wall.

'How do you know she didn't?' Alwyn called after him. 'You said she was one of them protestors.'

'I never said that' Phil said. 'Anyway, not like that; not bombs and stuff.'

'Somebody did' Alwyn said. 'How do you know it wasn't her? Say one of her friends then. Tell me that.'

The lambs streamed in through the side door. Alwyn lit a cigarette and leaned against the door frame, watching Phil through the smoke.

'One of them students' he said. 'One of her friends like.'

'You make a start here' Phil told him. 'I got to make a phone-call.'

He walked across the new yard and through the alley between the cattle sheds to the house. Beti's car was parked by the back door. The door to the washroom was open, and Phil shuffled in past wellington boots and leggings and oilskins to the phone on the wall. The handset was warm, as though someone had just used it. He dialled the number. The stippled paintwork of the wall round the phone was grey with spidery handwriting, pencilled notes and phone-numbers and reminders. He found his own name there and, with a clutch of recognition, a dark smudge where he'd once written Nicky's number and then spat and smeared it out. He pictured the phone ringing in the dark hallway of the flat, and Nicky running from the kitchen. A man's voice answered: Harris. Phil could see his eyes, pale and slightly bulging.

'Hullo' the voice said. 'Hullo.'

Beti was crossing the yard towards her car. Phil paused in the doorway of the washroom, but she'd already seen him.

'*Sut mae Phil.* What do you know?'

'Not a lot' Phil told her.

Beti leaned against the Mercedes, jiggling the ignition keys. She gestured to Phil.

'Come here *bach*, need to talk to you.' She repeated the gesture as Phil walked towards her, motioning him closer with quick, irritable movements of her hand.

'Listen to me *bach*' she said. 'We got to sort this business out. Are you with me?'

Phil nodded, watching her.

'What's Tom Wood been saying?' he began, but Beti interrupted him.

'Never mind him' she said. 'Nor that policeman. What does he know?'

'More than I do' Phil said.

Beti shook her head. 'Not good enough' she said. 'Not good enough Phil.' Her voice had taken on a metallic ring as she began to wind herself up. Phil took a step backwards.

'Listen' he said.

Beti pointed a finger at him. 'You listen' she said. 'You find out who did this. You and me both know you can do that. You find out, and you come and tell me, see?'

Phil opened his mouth, but Beti turned away and got into the car. She started the motor. The heavy glass of the window slid down. Beti cocked her head to one side; above her sudden gleaming smile her eyes were flat, watchful and uninvolved.

'Don't look so worried Phil' she said. 'May never happen. How's the missus by the way? Give her my best, won't you.'

They finished sorting the lambs into groups, working in an edgy silence. Alwyn hung back, doing as little as possible. As they let the last group out of the catching pen he straightened up, rubbing the back of his neck, watching Phil out of the corner of his eye, waiting for him to say something. Phil looked at his watch.

'I got to go' he said.

He parked the van half way up Paxton Hill, a hundred yards down from the flat. He'd rung again from the call-box outside the Post Office, his hand touching the rest, ready to hang up if he got Harris again, but it had been engaged. From where he sat, slumped low in the seat, he could see her front door under the plane tree, and in the rear view mirror, just where the long sweep of the road dipped out of sight, the steps of the library. He thought about knocking on her door, but maybe she wasn't there. He felt sick and furious with indecision.

She walked right past the van before he saw her; he watched her retreating figure for a moment or two before he recognised her. As he did so, he felt a shock of terrible betrayal, as though he was there for Beti, or for Tom Wood, rather than for himself. He almost let her walk on, oppressed by the thought that if he called out to her those others would appear, shouting accusations. He leaned across and opened the passenger door.

'Nicky!' he called out. 'Over here. I need to talk to you.'

He watched her as she ducked into the van, looking across at her as she stretched herself into the seat, sorting her legs out, a pile of books wobbling on her lap. Her smile was exactly as he'd seen it in the pub the other night.

'It's so nice to see you' Nicky said, thinking of the flat, and of Harris, and Marietta, and Bobs. 'It's so nice.'

Phil heard the words in a breathy and sibilant roar, like surf, as she put her lips to his ear. He drew back, leaning away from her.

'What?' she said. 'What's the matter?'

'Can I talk to you?' he said. 'Not here.'

She nodded, shrugging, withdrawing a little. He started the motor and drew away from the kerb, accelerating up the hill. As they passed the flat and then the War Memorial he had a strong sense of slipping back into anonymity, invisible again. He glanced at her as he drove. She gave him a quick smile.

'What are you looking at?' she said.

He pulled over into the lay-by beyond the turning for Home Farm.

'Last night' he said. 'At Graig Goch, they got a little lorry there.' He cleared his throat. 'Someone put a bomb in it, petrol bomb. Blew it to shit.'

'Oh Phil' she said. 'Were you there? Are you alright?'

She touched his face. He felt the cool length of her fingers against his cheek. He took her hand and held it for a moment, looking into her eyes. She had nothing to do with it. The relief was like cold beer after a day's work. He glanced round as a LandRover passed them, slowing down for the Home Farm lane. He recognised Gareth, and looked quickly away.

'That's terrible' Nicky said. 'Who would do that? Was anybody hurt?'

Phil looked at her, searching her face for doubts or ambiguities.

'You know' he said. 'Protestors. Your lot.'

She shook her head, her eyes wide. 'Don't, Phil' she said. 'You can't think that! None of us would do that. Sían doesn't want to blow people up, you'd have to be crazy. What she hates is cruelty; so do I as it happens.'

'What about the other one?' Phil said. 'What's-his-face?'

Nicky smiled. 'That's what he calls you' she said.

'Sorry?'

'Doesn't matter' she said. 'Harris isn't like that either. He's all angry and stuff, but he wouldn't do that.'

He saw her look turn inward for a moment, as though she was verifying her response against some internal measure.

'He wouldn't do that' she said.

Phil thought of Beti, and behind her Tom Wood; he saw them glaring at him, stiff and furious like puppets, high-pitched voices shrill with rage, their faces dark, bulging with suspicion and fear: You know who did it, don't you? You find out and tell me!

'I'm sorry' he said. 'I never thought it was you.'

'It's alright' she told him. 'It's horrible. It must be really scary, knowing there's someone out there wants to get you.'

She bit her lip, and he felt her hesitation, as though something on the edge of her thoughts had caught her attention for a moment. Then she took his hand, smiling at him.

'But you know this' she said. 'Don't you? I don't want to hurt you. Just the opposite in fact.'

They looked at each other.

'Can we go to your place?' he said.

Nicky sighed. 'I wish' she said. 'It's just there's loads of people there, Harris's mum and, you know, other people. They're leaving soon though, really.'

He stopped the van outside her flat. The street lights were coming on, the dismal stretch of pavement glistening dully. He turned to look at her, watching her eager, dreaming profile. She drew a short breath, like someone coming to a decision, or saying goodbye to something. She felt him looking at her and grinned, as though touched by his sudden crazy happiness; she leaned over and kissed him. As she ran up the steps to the front door, Phil saw a narrow slit of light appear in the bay window of the front room as someone in there drew aside an edge of curtain. He put the van into gear, working the steering wheel round. As he drove away, something made him notice the car parked in front of him, one rear wheel up on the pavement, a red Fiesta. He'd forgotten about it until that moment: the car he'd seen at Graig Goch last night.

Chapter 19

Bobs raised his arms above his head, straightening his back and breaking into a sort of hopping dance, shifting his weight stiffly from one foot to the other. Marietta took a couple of quick, skipping steps to catch up with him.

'Wait for me!' she said, a bubble of laughter rising through her. 'What are you up to?'

'I'm dancing' Bobs said without turning round, his voice floating back down the street towards her. 'I'm dancing in the light of the flames.'

He stopped under the tree by the front door of the flat and waited for her to catch up.

'Have you got a key?' he asked. 'Or shall we just float through the door?'

Marietta giggled. 'I love it when you're like this' she said.

Bobs clattered the knocker above the letter-box.

In the front room, Sían and Harris looked at each other. The door knocker rattled again. They could hear Marietta, her voice high, half singing: His flashing eyes, his floating hair . . .

'I'm going to my room' Sían said. Harris shut his eyes.

'Are you in there?' Marietta called. 'Are you in there Harry?'

She must have put her mouth to the letter box. Harris heard the flap clap shut again, cutting the words off; he pictured them scuttling neurotically down the corridor: are you in there Harry? like mice.

He opened the front door, turning his back on them without saying anything and walking down the corridor to the kitchen. He assumed they'd go into the front room; they'd obviously been in the pub, and he imagined them stretching out on the sofa and turning the TV on. Instead they followed him down the hall.

'What you on about flashing hair?' Bobs was saying. 'Flashing lights more like.'

Harris walked into the kitchen and across the room to the sink. He heard Bobs and Marietta come into the room behind him, and turned to face them, leaning against the draining board.

'What do you say, Harry?' Bobs said. 'Flashing lights. Flashing blue lights, what do you think?' He winked at Harris.

Harris looked at his watch. 'I could ring the bus station' he said. 'I think there's one at four thirty; you'd be home before eight.' He attempted a smile at his mother. 'You wouldn't even miss Brookside' he said.

Bobs flushed, his face darkening. His eyes were glittering, his skin hot and dry. He'd been drinking of course, but he was full of something else as well; Harris could sense the chemicals fizzing and popping inside him, the crackle of paranoia.

'I did say not to push it Harry' Bobs said. 'We discussed that, didn't we?'

Harris drew a short breath. He could feel himself droop and straightened his shoulders. He thought of Sían in her room down the hall, seeing the disillusion and contempt in her eyes, the loss of admiration. He was astonished to find how much he minded that. He thought of Nicky, coming back from the library into this. It was as though he was feeling around in the dark for a weapon, for some decisive male intervention that would rescue them all.

'I'm not pushing it' he said. 'It's just we need our lives back Mum.' He forced another quick smile. 'Or our flat, at least.'

'Hello' Bobs said. 'I'm here too. You can talk to me, you know.'

'You're right Harry' Marietta said. She felt disembodied, just a voice floating in the air; the old feeling of invisibility coming back to her, although this time it was funny rather than frightening. Perhaps if she looked in the mirror, there'd be nothing there. She giggled: no, that was vampires. They both glanced sharply at her then, so they must be able to see her, unless they were just looking at where her voice was coming from. The thought made her laugh out loud.

'Sorry' she said. 'Take no notice.'

*   *   *

On her way to the bathroom Sían paused in the corridor. She heard the drone of men's voices, and Marietta's laughter, sounding false, exaggerated. She shook her head; didn't sound like Harris was handling it. Of course he wasn't, she thought. She was surprised at how calm she felt. She'd been so in awe of Harris, she realised, and of Nicky for that matter, that she'd failed to notice something quite simple about them: they were like children, excitable, hopeless. Even their Englishness, their urban style, which had at first seemed cosmopolitan, almost exotic, now seemed self-centered and blundering.

She washed her hands, looking into the mirror. Bobs had to go, before he got them into any more trouble. She felt a constriction in her chest, a quick grip of panic at the thought that he had used her car; she forced the feeling away. Harris was right about the police; it would look like they were involved, it would all drag on forever, and if nobody had been hurt, then what was the point? And it had probably done some good: a short lesson in cruelty, those exporters could learn something from that. Her face looked back at her from the soap-spotted mirror: the square jaw, the nose a bit too short and wide. Her eyes were clear and calm, though, their expression steady and competent. Looking back into them, Sían realised with a mild amazement that she quite liked what she saw. She nodded to herself, smiling.

Coming out into the hall, she heard the sound of a car pulling up in the street outside their door. She crossed into the front room and walked over to the window, drawing aside a corner of the curtain to see who it was. She hadn't realised how dark it had got. In the orange glow of the street lights she saw Nicky get out of an old van, dark-red, streaked with mud, a fringe of straw trapped under the back doors: Phil's van. Sían shook her head, blowing out a long breath through pursed lips. Hopeless she thought. Bloody hopeless. She looked out into the hall. Nicky was backing in through the front door, bumping it shut with her hip. She had a pile of books in her arms.

'In here' Sían said. She gestured down the corridor. 'They're in the kitchen' she said, keeping her voice low. 'Come in here.'

Nicky put the books down on the table. The two girls looked at each other, both opening their mouths to speak.

'Go on' Nicky said, laughing. 'You first. What were you going to say?'

'You know he borrowed my car?' Sían said. Nicky walked over to the fireplace, lighting a cigarette and flicking the match into the grate.

'I just seen Phil' she said. She gave a short sigh. 'I do like him, Sían' she said. 'You know what I mean?'

'I'm talking about Bobs' Sían said.

Nicky looked round, hearing the sharp note of irritation in her friend's voice. She pulled a face.

'Listen Sían' she said. 'Bobs doesn't matter; tomorrow, or the next day, he'll be gone. You know what happened to Phil, though?'

'You listen' Sían said.

'Go on then' Nicky said. 'What?' She felt a flicker of annoyance. 'I'm listening.'

'You know Bobs had my car last night' Sían said. 'You know what he did?'

Nicky shrugged, waiting for some story about big-ends or clutch-plates.

'Is it insured for him to drive?' she asked.

'Just bloody listen!' Sían said.

* * *

Bobs was staring at Harris.

'You can talk to me' he said again.

'You say you're not going to push it, and the next thing you start reading out the bus time-table.'

'What I'm saying' Harris said. 'We all got work to do. We've got exams for a start.'

He made himself look up and catch Bobs' eye.

'Don't you want to get moving?' he asked him. 'Be safer, wouldn't it?'

'Know who I was thinking of today?' Bobs said. 'Fire in the Hole.'

He grinned at Harris. 'Fire in the Hole. Someone told me they were getting back together.'

'They'll never get another roadie like you' Marietta said.

Harris saw the kitchen at home. Coming back from school, there they'd be, filling the room; the leather waistcoats and greasy jeans, chip wrappers all over the table and the sink full of bottles.

'Fire in the Hole' Bobs said again. 'If they'd just had decent management, you know? Good name for a band though.'

He shook his head, smiling. 'Mean a lot of different things, it can. What you think, Harry?'

'Really?' Harris said. 'I thought it just meant crap heavy metal.'

'I was thinking more recent' Bobs said. 'Closer to home like.'

'We all have our work' Marietta said brightly. 'Our own work to do. You're right, we should be moving on.'

She winced as something moved inside her head, as though scratching at the inside of her skull. Her eyes watered.

'It doesn't matter' she said. 'It's not important.'

She pulled a chair over and sat down suddenly, feeling as though her legs wouldn't hold her up.

'I'll ring the bus station' Harris said. He looked at his mother, but she wouldn't catch his eye. She had her bag on her lap and was sorting

236

through it.

'What's your rush?' Bobs said. 'What's your hurry all of a sudden?'

'It's not sudden' Harris said.

Marietta had found her cigarettes and lit one up.

'Imogen thinks I should get a fax machine' she said. 'That way she could fax her designs up to me. What do you think?'

'For fuck's sake Mum!' Harris said.

'You watch your language!' Bobs said. 'Don't talk to your mother like that.'

'There's things you can't describe unless you see them' Marietta said.

'That's true' Bobs said. 'That's certainly true.'

'Every picture's worth a thousand words' Marietta said.

'Get a bloody fax machine' Harris said. He took a breath, his chest tight with exasperated pity, trying to speak calmly.

'Get a fax machine. I'm talking about you need to get home now. It's time to go home.'

Marietta nodded, smiling at him.

'Listen to me Mum' Harris said. 'I'm trying to talk to you.'

Bobs laughed. 'You are talking to her Harry' he said. 'But you're not telling her, are you? There's one or two things you're leaving out.'

Harris saw his mother's attention engage. He felt immediately betrayed, the same old feeling: she would always listen to Bobs.

'What's happened?' Marietta asked. 'What are you leaving out? Is it something to do with Nicky?'

'You could say that' Bobs said. 'You could say that, couldn't you Harry?'

Harris sighed. 'Take no notice Mum' he said into the silence.

*   *   *

'It's this thing you do' Sían said. 'This female principle thing.'

Nicky stared at her.

'This I can't help it thing' Sían said. 'You know: moths to a flame.'

'So it's all my fault' Nicky said. 'Is that what you're saying?'

She jerked her head in the direction of the kitchen.

'That mad bastard in there blows up a lorry where Phil works and it's my fault?'

'Yes it is' Sían said. She gave a short laugh. 'It's your fault because you can help it. You could make choices, like other people do, not just drift along looking beautiful.'

She dragged the word out into a sneer, and felt a moment of awkward guilt: perhaps she was enjoying this too much. Maybe the strength and certainty she'd felt flowing through her in the bathroom was just arrogance, or even cruelty.

Nicky glared at her. 'What's got into you?' she said. 'Why are you so fucked up?'

'Me fucked?' Sían said. 'You don't get it, do you?' She looked at Nicky; she felt herself filling up with a kind of quiet elation, nothing to do with arrogance.

'Look at the mess you've got us into' she said. Nicky opened her mouth but Sían raised her voice, feeling adult, powerful.

'Look at this mess' she said.

'But of course, it's not your fault, is it? You never take responsibility, do you? Some sheep farmer takes a fancy to you, so of course you have to go to bed with him.' She rolled her eyes, pouting.

'What else could you do? You have to follow the female principle wherever it leads, don't you? I can't help it.'

She shook her head, feeling the receding surge of emotion dragging back through her body.

'It's ridiculous, Nicky. We could all go to prison, but you can't help it. You have to get off with Phil, you have to drive Harris round the bend. It's ridiculous. You're ridiculous.'

'Why are you being so horrible?' Nicky said.

Sían sighed.

'I'm not' she said. 'I'm just trying to sort this out. No one else is going to.'

Nicky shook her head, turning back towards the window.

'You got to give it up' Sían said. 'It's not even real, it's just causing us a lot of trouble.'

'It is real' Nicky said. 'That's what I was trying to tell you.'

'Do me a favour' Sían said. She felt as though she was watching herself from across the room; she saw herself taking a step towards Nicky, leaning forward, her expression tight and urgent.

'You're just being stupid' she said. 'You going on seeing Phil, next thing the police come knocking on our door. That's the only real thing about it.'

Nicky stood at the window, her back turned. She was tracing some pattern with the tip of her finger on the dull glass. Sían raised her voice.

'Listen' she said. 'You told me ages ago, he's got a little boy, right?'

Her voice sounded sharp and bright; she felt as though she was snapping the words off, like pieces of hard plastic.

Nicky looked at her 'So?' she said.

'So, he's presumably married' Sían said. 'Got a wife. That doesn't quite fit, does it? So you don't think about it, do you?'

She could feel the words snapping cleanly between her teeth.

'He's married' she said. 'You're his piece on the side. He probably boasts about you in the pub.'

She crossed the room to the door.

'That's fine if you're happy with that' she said. 'But at least see things the way they really are. You get off with Phil because it's easier than saying no; you come on to Harris so strong he goes crazy, and you don't think about any of it. You don't take any responsibility. You just play around. Well it's time to stop.'

'Why are you doing this?' Nicky said.

She mumbled a cigarette between her lips; the box of matches came apart in her fingers and spilled on the floor. She squatted down to pick them up, blinking rapidly as the grimy swirls of pattern on the carpet swam before her eyes.

'Why are you doing this?' she said.

'What's it got to do with you?'

Sían turned in the doorway.

'Everything' she said. 'It's got everything to do with me. You could get us all arrested, but you won't do anything about it, will you? It's up to me to sort it out.' She looked back at Nicky, shaking her head.

'I'm the one that has to sort it out' she said.

Harris looked up as she walked into the kitchen; Sían could sense a quick disappointment tug at him, a bleak moment's regret that it wasn't Nicky. She smiled to herself, thinking how much she would have minded that an hour ago. Bobs glanced blankly at her, then looked away. Sían felt herself flush with annoyance. She thought: I'll come back to you Bobs. I'll get your attention in a minute. She caught Marietta's eye and nodded at her, smiling.

'So!' she said. 'You all set then?'

Marietta was sitting on one of the wooden chairs. She'd emptied her bag on to the table, and was sorting through a litter of stuff: make-up, cigarettes, coins and key-rings, a rolled-up magazine. She didn't look well; she had a bad colour and her smile when she looked up was lopsided and perfunctory.

'Do you need a hand?' Sían said.

She put an arm round Marietta, stooping over her and patting her

239

awkwardly on the shoulder.

'Got all your stuff?' she said, feeling Marietta's body stiffen. She kept her hand on the older woman's shoulder, feeling the thin bones, her fingers starting to rub and stroke, pressing and rotating. She could feel warmth and assurance running up and down her arm.

'Do you need a taxi to the bus-station?' she said, increasing the rhythmic pressure of her fingers. Marietta started to say something, squirming in her chair. Sían flexed her fingers, rolling her hand, squeezing and relaxing.

'It's been great having you' she said. 'Harris is lucky; you're such a brilliant mum!' She gave Harris a beaming, daffy smile. She felt the woman's body relax under her fingers.

'You're such a brilliant mum!' Sían said again.

'I am, aren't I!' Marietta said.

A choking sob of laughter rose up through Sían, making her nose prickle and her eyes water. It works!

'You are, aren't you!' Sían said, laughing out loud at the look on Harris's face.

'You are! You're a mum in a million!'

Marietta stood up. She put an arm round Sían's waist.

'You're lovely too!' she said.

'Harry's lucky to have such good friends.' The two of them leaned against the kitchen table, arms around each other, smiling at Harris and Bobs. Sían felt her chest tighten with another swelling bubble of laughter. She breathed through her nose, trying to force it back.

'You're a lucky boy Harry!' Marietta said. 'But make it up with Nicky, won't you. Promise me, your next letter, I want to hear the two of you are back together.'

Sían pulled away, overwhelmed by gulps of horrified laughter. She put her hands to her face, forcing out a dry rattle of simulated coughing.

'Something in my throat' she said, her eyes streaming.

'It's time to move on' Marietta said. Her smile wobbled for a moment, her eyes flicking from Sían to Harris and back again.

'Thank you' she said.

She glanced across the room at Bobs; he was leaning against the wall, his lips pursed in a sort of soundless whistle. Marietta gave him a quick, uneasy smile, then looked away.

'Where's Nicky?' she said. 'I want to say goodbye to her.'

She winked at Sían: 'Give her a bit of advice too!'

She turned in the doorway.

'Ring about the bus then Harry' she said. 'Come on Bobs, it's time to hit the road!'

As Marietta started to leave the room they heard the front door slam. Sían nodded to herself: Nicky was well out of it. She pictured her running down the road in the dying light, her stride flailing and chaotic, and felt a moment's pity. But it needed saying, someone had to. They listened to the squeak of Marietta's footsteps in the corridor as her voice floated back down towards them: Nicky, we're leaving, where are you! Across the room, Bobs mouthed a silent echo of her words: where are you! pouting, exaggerated, his lips curling back from his teeth. He became aware of Sían looking at him.

'Well done' he said, staring back at her, unsmiling. 'Very good. Nice work.'

Half an hour later they were gone. Sían walked into the front room. The TV was murmuring to itself. She had the wobbly, disoriented feeling you get from jumping off a moving bus, the sudden ground lurching under your feet, the environment you've just left blowing past you in a rush of noise and light. She blew a long sigh through puffed out cheeks. She heard Harris call something from the kitchen, and walked a little unsteadily down the corridor towards him.

'Want a cup of tea?' he said. 'Where's Nicky?'

Sían shrugged. 'Still out' she said.

She wondered whether to tell Harris about their conversation. They looked at each other; Harris pulled a face, his smile crooked. Maybe later, she thought.

'Harris' she said. 'Let's go away. Let's just jump in the car, go to the seaside.'

In the silence, Harris heard a faint clatter as the cat hissed at him and bustled itself out through the flap. He pictured the front door slamming shut behind Nicky, the draught and suction of air displaced, the same sudden way the door of the Faculty Office had opened the morning he'd gone to register, the first time he saw her.

'Leave it' Sîan was saying. 'Just leave them all to it.'

Harris looked at her.

'I got money' she said. 'We could find a pub or something, on the coast. We could look at the sea, walk along the beach.'

Harris frowned.

'Be dark when we get there' Sîan said. 'We'll wake up in the morning, I'll jump out of bed, draw the curtains, and the sea will be looking in the window.'

She stretched her arms out.

'It was there all the time' she said. 'Waiting for us. Like a huge grey eye, looking back at us.'

She waited for him to say something.

'You'll be grumpy of course' she said. 'You'll say: What the hell time is it? and you'll bury your head in the pillow.'

She watched his face, waiting for a smile.

'I got new pyjamas' she said. 'With pink stripes, like toothpaste.'

'I got to be back in time for Spedding's lecture' Harris said.

'Course' Sían said, her eyes shining. 'Of course you have.'

*   *   *

Marietta had a headache, and her ankles hurt. She had to keep breaking into a run to keep up with Bobs. At least it was down hill.

'We got plenty of time' she called out. 'And there's another one half an hour after, Harry said.'

She put her case down on the pavement beside her and pushed a hand through her hair.

'We had fun' she said. 'Didn't we? I think we all got on pretty well.'

Below her, Bobs turned, looking back at her from within the ellipse of light beneath a street lamp. She saw his lips move, but couldn't tell if he was speaking to her. He shook his head, and walked on into the darkness on the other side. At the bottom of the hill, Marietta could see the traffic lights on the High Street turning to red.

Chapter 20

She was walking quickly, her stride loose and springy, rising on the balls of her feet with a sort of eagerness. The sun was low over the roof-tops behind Tom, and as he hurried after her the long fingers of his shadow on the pavement reached towards her, plucking at her heels. He found himself wondering how old she was: twenty, perhaps? So she would have been born in 1974. Yesterday. She was carrying a pile of books, and she slowed for a moment, struggling them into order as they slipped about in her arms. He had nearly caught up with her; he knew that in another moment she would sense how close he was. He stopped, going down on one knee and fiddling with his shoelace. He waited until he could no longer feel the terrible prodding of his heart.

A bus blew past him on its way down the hill, a shuttle from the station to the Precinct. As Tom straightened up, a row of grey heads in the windows turned idly in his direction, old ladies settling shopping bags on their laps, their glances meeting his dully for a moment as they were carried by. She was about a hundred yards ahead of him as he started after her again, coming into sight from behind a parked car. He watched her hesitate at the corner of a side-street, then skip across. The breeze picked up a scatter of fallen leaves and blew them spiralling after her like a slip-stream. She was passing a van parked under the plane trees when the passenger door opened, and he saw her stop and turn, then lean down to speak to the driver. Tom took in the glistening brightness of her smile at the same moment as he recognised Phil's van.

He ran a few paces towards them, watching the door slam shut behind her and the van rattle away up the street. A blur of smoke from blocked injectors hung over the pavement for a moment before the wind wiped it away. He stood and watched until they disappeared over the brow of the hill beyond the War Memorial. He could feel his unhappiness inside him, tangible and somehow comforting, a warm mass at the base of the stomach; heavy, moist, connected to glands and ducts, releasing tears and washes of sensuality, desire and grief. He felt like laughing. There was something wonderful about it, the way it could not have been worse; not even having a car near by to follow them, left standing on the pavement knowing that it was absolutely as bad as he had ever imagined it.

He started to walk up the hill. Beyond the War Memorial the terraced houses ended with a couple of tatty little shops and the Last Chance petrol station, which was now boarded up; grass was beginning to grow in the cracked forecourt. On the left hand side of the road there were half a dozen fairly substantial houses, Paxton Villa, Maes y Deri, though they were run-down and peeling, the front gardens weedy and neglected. After that the town just stopped. There was a long paddock with an abandoned car in it; at the far end a couple of kids were building a bonfire, swinging an old mattress between them, heaving it onto a pile of broken pallets and boxes. Beyond that an acre or so of scrub and brambles, and then the Home Farm meadows which fell away to the south, all the way down to the river. In a corner of the field, an old ewe was caught up in the brambles. She must have missed the shearing; her fleece was dense and matted, grey and sodden, trailing off into unbreakable ropes of twisted wool and briar. She looked back at Tom, moving her jaw in a slow, sideways reciprocation. The road ran on as though released, curving gradually to the right, dipping finally out of sight behind low hedgerows. They could be anywhere.

He had left his car in a side-street below the Library. As he turned back, the sun went down, dropping below the rooftops at the bottom of the hill. They were probably fucking each other right now, parked down a lane somewhere, clambering over each other in the back of the van. For a moment he could feel her gasp and shiver, her face intent and dreaming, the way she looked on the video, half smiling, drifting loose; he imagined Phil driven by a kind of anger as urging pulses flooded through him. He must have been talking to himself: a couple of teen-age girls, wobbling by on huge shoes, goggled at him, gasping with laughter as they passed him on the pavement.

He realised that he could picture Phil's expression as his face hung over hers because it was the look he had seen in his eyes a few hours earlier, in the kitchen at Graig Goch, his features dark and vivid with emotion – what you on about? – snarling at Tom as he'd tried to ask him about the girl and her animal-rights friends, denying everything, just as he would if he was confronted again; the fact that Tom had seen him with her for himself would mean nothing. All Phil had to do was keep his nerve, bluff it out, shout Tom down.

There was a pub on the corner of the street where he'd parked the car; he hadn't noticed it earlier but as he passed it now he found himself pushing down the brass handle of the door without really thinking about it, crossing the room to the bar and asking for a large whisky. Several smudged and bleary faces looked up at him from tables round the edges of the room. It was late afternoon and half of these bastards had probably been drinking since the middle of the morning, slouching behind ranks of empty bottles and glasses, stubbing half-smoked cigarettes into overflowing ashtrays.

He'd get no reaction from DC Owen. Tom could hear his voice: You can't be sure it was Mr Jones's van, can you sir? Common enough type of vehicle I should say. Beti wouldn't listen either; she'd say there was nothing that counted as proof. If Tom tried to tell her what he'd seen this afternoon, that he'd seen the match that had lit the fire, Beti would laugh at him. Phil was just doing what young men did; Beti might take an amused interest, but she didn't really feel threatened by it. She'd probably think that Tom was jealous. DC Owen felt more strongly than that; Tom had been aware of the distaste the policeman felt, as though he found something creepy and obsessive about pursuing the girl. What neither of them understood was this: she or her friends would wait until the fuss had died down, and then attack again. Why not? They'd tried sabotaging a lorry, and beating up one of the drivers. They'd tried telling lies to the Ministry, and when that hadn't worked, they'd unloosed an act of flat-out terrorism. They were stepping up the violence, so next time it might not be just a lorry that went up in flames. They had to find the girl before it happened again, but Tom realised that he was the only one who felt any urgency about it. Owen had decided Tom was a crank, and in Beti he could sense a sort of acceptance; she was already moving on, irritably shrugging off details as she went. Of course she wanted to know who had fire-bombed her lorry, but she wasn't interested in sniffing around, speculating, investigating; she wanted someone brought to her in handcuffs.

Tom needed the girl; he needed to confront her himself and shake the truth out of her. He asked for another whisky; the woman folded her newspaper, sighing, and shuffled over as reluctantly as if she'd been serving him all afternoon. He found himself staring at a couple in the corner of the room. The man was one of those small, wiry types, violence and paranoia coiled up inside him. He had long grey hair tied back in a pony tail. He was lighting a cigarette, his elbows on the table in front of him, and their glances met for a moment, his eyes glittering through the smoke. Tom looked away, trying to remember where he'd seen him before.

He tapped his glass on the counter and pushed it towards the barmaid, pointing into it and nodding. He thought of Phil and the girl in the back of the van. He sipped his drink, and a beautiful understanding slowly settled on him, like happiness. Phil had parked his van on Paxton Hill to wait for the girl. It wasn't a coincidence; he'd expected or at least hoped to meet her there. He wasn't waiting for her to come out of the Library; there had been plenty of spaces outside the building, but he had parked several hundred metres up the hill. It was obvious: he had parked by her front door, or at least very near it. Tom thought: give or take a couple of houses, I know where she lives.

The couple at the corner table were having an argument; the man had raised his voice, speaking out of the side of his mouth, not looking at the woman beside him.

'Push you around' he said. 'Bunch of fucking kids.'

He was rapping the table in front of him with a cigarette lighter, a series of sharp, irritable clicks. The woman touched his hand lightly, as though it was hot.

'Be so cross' she said. 'To worry about.'

She caught Tom's eye and gave him a quick, nervous smile. Tom remembered where he'd seen them, outside the Library earlier in the afternoon.

'Do you?' the man said. 'Something to say to me?'

Tom realised the man was talking to him. The barmaid lifted the flap and came round from behind the counter. She started collecting their empty glasses, slipping her fingers into them and clinking them together. Tom drank the rest of his whisky and left.

He drove up Paxton Hill again on the way home. In the bleak evening light he had no real sense of where Phil's van had been parked. He pulled in to the kerb a few hundred yards up from the library. From where he sat he could see the fronts of five or six houses. Curtains were drawn in the front rooms; from somewhere he could hear the faint and toneless thump of music, only the bass elements audible. A girl with long hair moved across the brightly-lit rectangle of an upstairs window. A police-car slid past down the hill. Tom breathed into his hand and counted up the whiskies he'd drunk. He watched its rear lights in the mirror until they winked out of sight, and then drove home.

*   *   *

He woke up with the feeling that something wonderful had

246

happened, as though he'd found himself suddenly on holiday with the sun pouring in through the window. He was alone in the bed. The room was dim and grey and he couldn't see the hands on his watch, but the curtains were pallidly transparent; Jan must have gone out already. Had she said something about a meeting in Cardiff? He lay back on the pillow and tried to remember if they'd had a row; he'd had several more whiskies when he got home. They had sat and talked for a while, but he had no memory of going to bed.

In the kitchen he looked to see if Jan had left him a note. She'd tidied up, put away the dishes; the coffee pot stood on the sideboard with fresh grounds already measured into the filter, and she'd left a clean cup and saucer beside it. Tom nodded to himself, smiling, seeing a kind of message there, reading a cool, dry text in the disposition of these things. He tried to reconstruct the end of the evening while he waited for the kettle to boil. They'd talked about the fire, of course, but he was sure he hadn't said anything about finding the girl, or seeing her go off with Phil. He would have known not to do that.

As soon as he found himself thinking about her he recognised the source of the feeling he'd woken up with; it rushed back at him, a sudden breathless constriction of the heart. He poured a cup of coffee and took it over to the table. He was being ambushed by bursts of what felt like excitement and happiness, which were nothing more than squirts of adrenalin or seratonin or some damn chemical pissing into his nervous system, switching on at the mere thought of a girl he'd never spoken to and whose name he didn't know. It was fucking absurd. The phone started ringing.

It was for Jan, a man's voice, sharp with irritation. Tom told him she was in Cardiff, at a meeting.

'On a Saturday?' the voice said. He didn't want to leave his name. Tom went back upstairs and lay on the bed. The feeling was still there, compressed and glowing with heat, carried about inside him like a jewel. It was nearly half past eight. He wondered what time she got up. Presumably she didn't have to go to lectures on a weekend. Would she go out for a newspaper, or a pint of milk? It seemed to Tom that the only way he could be sure of seeing her would be to park half way up Paxton Hill and simply wait, for as long as it took.

The air was full of messages, like voices in the wind. He was going out the front door when he heard the phone ringing again. It was Steve, calling from his office. Tom could hear the hesitant click of someone typing and the tinny rattle of Radio One; he pictured the grimy windows looking out over the yard where the lorries wheeled and turned. Colin was probably back there by now, flirting with Steve's secretary, waiting to hear when he'd next be running down to Spain.

He shook his head, trying to concentrate on what Steve was telling him. Normandy Shipping had packed it in. As of today, November 5th, they weren't taking livestock lorries on any of their boats.

'Just like that' Steve said.

'Sent me a fax this morning' he said. 'I rang them straight: What about the loads we've got on the books? I said. I asked them: what do we tell the customers? Regular customers? What are we supposed to tell them?'

Tom could hear him waiting for a reaction.

'The bastards' Steve said. 'Fucking cowardly bastards. I told them: We're not scared of a few fucking protestors. I told them straight. Are we Tom!' There was a silence.

'You still there?' he said.

'No' Tom said. 'No, we're not.'

The day was overcast with a featureless wash of cloud, the sun nothing but a thumb-print of lighter grey, as though the sky had been rubbed a little thinner there. He parked below the War Memorial, looking down the long slope of the hill to where it dissolved into a watery haze beyond the library. She probably shared a house with other students; Tom pictured a messy, affectionate communal life: tights and T-shirts hanging up to dry, books everywhere, and arguments about whose turn it was to do the washing up. He wondered how many of them there were, and whether they were girls or boys. Did they share rooms, or beds for that matter? Did they finish the last of each others' cornflakes, or leave a rim around the bath? Did they sit up late at night, drinking and smoking, arguing about politics, dizzy with freedom, staying up because there was no one to tell them to go to bed? Did the boys look at her across the room, imagining how it would be to make love to her? Did they sometimes get to find out? A kid on a skateboard snaked his way down the hill, steering with his hips, the thin grinding rumble of the little wheels hanging in the still air.

He couldn't imagine Phil in this environment. She would have to keep him separate from the rest of her life; even if her friends knew about him she surely couldn't have him round openly. What would a ploughboy like him find to say to them? When did he last have an interesting thought? What would they all talk about? Sheep? She and Phil must clutch at each other in holes and corners, in furtive meetings like the one he'd seen yesterday. Or would they go to her room and shut the door, not caring what the others thought? It was ridiculous, intolerable, and he had brought it all on myself. He shut his eyes. He thought: if I had never hired Phil to work for us I might still have a business. I might be making phone-calls to France and Spain right at this minute; I might be deciding to go with one of the lorries, run down to Burgos with Colin perhaps, sit in the courtyard with Felix del Rio, crack jokes in broken Spanish with him while he opened another bottle from his uncle's vineyard. Instead I sit here, ill and cold and going crazy. At that moment Tom thought that if he'd seen Phil walking up the road towards him, he would have driven at him and run him down, watching his arms fly up and hearing the deadly crack of his head hitting the kerb. He started the engine, waiting for it to warm up again so he could have the heater on.

A LandRover rattled down the hill, towing a horsebox. Tom was shivering. When he turned the heater on, the warm air it blew over him felt like the breathy comfort of an embrace, like the dim and pillowed softness of her bed. He must have fallen asleep for a moment. He came back to himself with a jerk, grinding his teeth. It wasn't Phil who'd blown up the lorry; in a sense Phil was the fuse, the blue paper that connected her to Graig Goch, but it wasn't him that had lit the match. Tom had been picturing those students with a kind of affection, living their lives just a few yards from where he was sitting. But they were the ones who had put him out of business, not Phil. The rage and loathing Tom felt towards him came down to no more than this: that Phil had spent all night between her creamy thighs, and he had not. He was immediately invaded by this image, too late to unthink it; he could feel it spreading inside him like a virus. His heart was beating painfully; he felt sick, aroused, and on the edge of tears. He knew all of a sudden that he was ill, that he had been poisoned or contaminated or sensitised, and that this thing was now fulminating inside him, attacking cell after cell, rewriting his whole biology.

His mobile was ringing. The car had become smotheringly hot; He turned the motor off and wound down the window before answering the phone. It was Beti.

'I've had that Spaniard on the phone' she said. 'Couldn't understand a word. Told him to ring again in half an hour. Get down here will you Tom, talk to him when he calls back.'

Tom shook his head, trying to clear his thoughts. Beti's words seemed to penetrate the daydream he'd just been having about Felix, producing vortices of dissonance and confusion. He started to say something, but Beti had already rung off. Tom looked at his watch; he'd been sitting here for two hours. He'd seen half a dozen people go by, none of them students and none of them her. He leaned his head out of the open window, breathing in the cold damp air. He thought about Steve's phone-call: Normandy Shipping's decision meant that everything had been forced to a stop, and it might be weeks before the exporters' own boat was ready to sail. Felix was probably ringing for lambs, and in any case they had deliveries lined up for the coming week. He needed to talk to Beti; they were going to have to decide what to say to their customers.

He waited another five minutes, and then drove away, seeing the line of houses unroll behind him in the mirror, watching so intently for a door to open that he nearly drove through the red lights at the bottom of the hill. The High Street was crowded, flowing like a river, the pubs opening up, people streaming in and out of the shops, mothers with pushchairs surging over the road at the zebra crossing.

On the back road out of town, running through the Bwlch, he had to pull over sharply as a car came at him round a corner, travelling much too fast. He got a series of fractured glimpses, as though reflected in a broken mirror: the low dark bonnet, dipping as the driver braked and swerved; the front tyres spitting gravel; the two bulky figures in the front seats, broad, impassive faces, their eyes barely flicking at him as they swept by. He was pretty sure the driver was DC Owen and he felt a momentary unease. He wondered what the policeman was up to, and why he hadn't got in touch if he'd been going round to Graig Goch.

Alwyn was burning rubbish again, leaning on a pitch-fork, his shoulders hunched as he stared into the smouldering mound where rags of flame were flicking in the up-draught, stepping back as the oily column of smoke toppled towards him. Tom honked the horn at him and he looked up; he didn't wave, but Tom was aware of his eyes following him as he drove across the yard. Tom waved at him again as he got out of the car, but Alwyn didn't respond.

Barry came out of the back door, pulling on a jacket. Tom asked him what the police had wanted, but he shook his head; he'd been up at Moelfryn seeing to the cattle, he hadn't seen any policemen. He said Beti was in the office.

'What's going to happen Tom?' he asked.

'I don't know Barry' Tom said. 'I don't know.'

Beti gave him a strange look as he came into the room, as though his appearance confirmed some suspicion or doubt that she had about him. She'd been talking on the phone, but she ended the conversation with a short phrase Tom didn't understand, hanging up and nodding. Tom asked her what the police had wanted.

'Police?' Beti said.

Tom told her he'd just seen DC Owen, on the back road, by the Bwlch.

'Different business altogether' Beti said, shaking her head and fiddling with a sheaf of papers on the desk, avoiding Tom's eye. Tom stared at her, waiting for her to go on. How could Owen come here and it not be his business? He had no idea what to say next.

'Different business' Beti said again. 'Nothing for you to worry about.'

They looked at each other for a moment.

'I don't want Phil working here any more' Tom said. 'I'm not subsidising his love-affairs any more. He's a bloody liability.'

'Pardon me?' Beti said.

'I saw him last night' Tom said. 'I saw his van, up Paxton Hill. He was waiting for that girl, that student.'

Beti looked up at him.

'How do you make that out?' she said.

'I saw her get in the van' Tom said. 'She got in his fucking van!'

'Don't lose your head' Beti said. 'What happened then?'

Tom shrugged.

'Nothing' he said. 'They drove off.'

Beti tapped her pen on the desk, a gesture of disappointment or irritation.

'You tell the police?' she asked him.

Tom shook his head. 'Not yet' he said.

'Piece of advice Tom' she said. She gave him her shrewd look, her face crinkling up in a smile although her eyes remained watchful and without warmth.

'Piece of advice: keep it to yourself – Phil and that girl – till we know what's what. I'll talk to the boy myself. Owen thinks you're a bit funny about it, know what I mean?'

Tom sighed. He already knew this, but it was a shock to hear Beti say it.

'So what's Owen been saying about me?' he asked.

'He was here just now' he said, when Beti didn't answer. 'What did he say about me?'

Beti shook her head.

'I already told you' she said. 'Different thing. Nothing to do with you.'

She looked up at Tom, then back at her papers. She started to sort through them; Tom had the feeling she was waiting, as if expecting a challenge. There was a silence. Beti pursed her lips in a thin smile.

'What you know then?' she said. 'What you got to tell me?'

Tom felt a sort of dull oppression. He knew he should pursue her about what the police had been after, but he couldn't do it. He'd never get a straight answer; and he felt a kind of dread, a queasy flickering of guilt. He really didn't want to hear what DC Owen might have to say about him. He cleared his throat. He started to tell Beti about Normandy Shipping. Beti gave him a look of impatient distaste, as though it was one more damn problem that Tom was bringing to her. Tom said they still had orders on the books, they had to decide what to do next. Beti was flicking through the pages of a ledger, pausing to tap out a sum on the calculator. Tom wasn't sure if she was listening.

'You tell the customers what you like Tom, that's your department. If there's no boats, there's bugger all to say about it, is there?'

Tom said that all they could do was wait for the consortium's boat. He told her the Board of Trade could issue the licence any day now, maybe next week.

'You never know' he said.

Beti looked up, glaring at Tom as if the whole thing was his fault.

'That'll be the day' she said. 'And what am I supposed to do about the lambs? There's four hundred in the top fields, ready for Whatyoucall. I suppose he doesn't want them now?'

Tom started to say that he wanted them alright, but Beti interrupted him.

'Look out the window' she said. 'See much grass out there?'

She shook her head, going back to her calculations.

'Supposed to keep four hundred lambs about the place, am I?' she said.

Tom didn't know if she was talking to him or thinking aloud.

'Lose half a kilo a day, they will.' Beti wrote something in the book and slapped it shut, looking up at Tom.

'Don't know about all this French thing' she said. 'Spanish, all that. Bloody silly to me.'

She stared blankly at him for a moment, and Tom realised that as far as Beti was concerned the conversation was over; she was waiting for him to leave. He saw quite suddenly that if their problems weren't solved pretty soon, Beti would simply pull out of the export job, move on to something else. He saw for a moment what his life would be like without the business, colourless, depleted.

'I'll let you know' Tom said. 'I'll let you know what happens.'

Beti didn't answer. As Tom left the room she was already picking up the telephone, nodding dismissively, going on to the next thing.

The phone in the washroom was ringing, the other line. Tom shuffled across a pile of wellingtons and leggings and picked it up. He'd forgotten about Felix del Rio. They exchanged elaborate greetings, and Felix made a joke that Tom didn't really understand. He tried to explain what was happening. They'd had conversations about the protest movement before, baffled dialogues that drifted into irritable silences while Tom flickered through the pages of his Spanish dictionary; it was not really his meagre vocabulary and home-made grammar that thwarted them so much as the Spaniard's absolute inability to imagine how you could have a political campaign about animal welfare. To Felix, the welfare of the lambs consisted in their arriving in Burgos alive and healthy; what conditions could possibly be met beyond that? As for politics, that was about people, about bread and money and freedom.

The wall around the telephone was covered with a grubby web of writing, names and phone numbers and jotted reminders in blue and black ink and pencil, the spidery letters wobbling across the stippled surface of the paintwork. Tom saw Alwyn Blaencwm and Phil Jones; against Tom Wood there was a dark smudge where something had been written and then inked out. He realised that Felix was asking him a question; he'd been responding without really listening: *Si hombre, pues claro, si* . . . Now he heard the note of irritation in Felix's voice as he failed to give him an answer. Tom found himself telling him there was a problem with the boat: *las turbinas* Tom said, *las turbinas son averiadas.* He could feel Felix draw back, offended and confused; he said something Tom didn't understand, the angry breath hissing between his teeth. He must have thought Tom was making fun of him, talking contemptuous nonsense: how many scheduled boats crossed the Channel every day? How could they all have turbine problems? Tom tried to explain what was really happening, but he couldn't make him understand. He tried to apologise; he said Wait! Listen! Felix was too courteous to hang up, but he didn't want to go on with the conversation. He sounded far away, in another world.

Beti's mother was climbing out of the LandRover on the other side of the yard; she slid herself to the ground, holding onto the door-frame to steady herself, groaning with effort. Tom saw her raise her hand, and half-waved back to her, but probably she was just shielding her eyes as she frowned into the light, watching him walk to his car. As he drove out of the yard he could see her in the mirror still watching him, her hand raised in the same ambiguous gesture.

He parked in the same place, just down from Number 92. The afternoon had opened up a little, pools of cold blue sky appearing, spreading from the west. He watched an aeroplane draw a thin line of gold across the pale surface above him, and wished he was on it. He watched the vapour boil and tumble in its wake, slowing and thickening behind it. The sun caught the body of the plane, the fuselage as bright as a star, the outstretched pale wings. He turned the radio on. Some kids ran down the pavement, shouting, scuffing a football between them. From time to time as the chill air penetrated the car he turned the engine on and ran the heater for a while.

He woke up in a panic, hearing voices. It was nearly dark. There was a group of young people on the pavement a couple of yards away, laughing, fooling about. Their voices were as clear as if they'd been in the car with him, although he couldn't take in a word they were saying. As he came fully awake they started to walk away up the street. He opened the door and got out, looking at them over the roof of the car. He must have startled them; they turned frightened gaping faces at him under the dull glare of the street-lights. She wasn't with them. He walked down to the pub on the corner, stamping his feet, pulling his coat around him. He had a couple of whiskies in the dismal back bar; he was the only customer, apart from an old fellow at a corner table who sat staring into a pint glass, looking up at him from time to time, nodding in gloomy and wordless agreement.

He sat in the car and ran the heater again as the evening grew colder and darker. Jan rang. She'd enjoyed the conference. She was at Susan's; she was going to stay the rest of the weekend, come back Sunday night. There were going for a meal, maybe see a film.

'How you feeling?' she said. 'Bet you got a hangover.'

Tom told her he was fine.

'Have a good time' he said. 'Say hello to Susan.'

'Everything alright?' she asked him.

He told her everything was fine. He felt as though he was slipping away, as though he was pushing through a web of connections that parted and broke and trailed behind him, released into an accelerating sense of isolation and freedom, like falling.

Two or three cars went past him up the hill; he wondered vaguely where they were going. A little later a group of boys came by, ten or twelve-year-olds, pushing and punching at each other, scuffling and shouting; then half a dozen youths, out of a pub somewhere, leaning into the slope of the hill, their shoulders rounded against the cold and their laughter condensing into foggy haloes around their heads. When a couple pushed a buggy past him with a toddler, bundled-up and woolly-hatted, waving quilted arms, Tom began to feel he was being presented with some sort of panorama, a tableau of the people of Llanfrychan in all their variety of age and size, a procession of the common man. He felt wide awake and clear-headed for the first time all day. These were the kind of people, according to the newspapers and the TV, who had raised their voices against live exports in a surge of outrage that would blow the trade away. In the tabloid imagination they formed an irresistible movement, like a Soviet propaganda poster: ranks of sturdy workers, neat children and benevolent grandparents, fists raised, their faces shining with a single purpose, marching on the offices of B&F and SeaFarers, and now Normandy Shipping. Stop this cruel trade! The people have spoken!

What bullshit! Sitting in his car in the dark, he almost laughed out loud. He watched a couple of teenage boys jog up the hill, chatting in short, panting gasps, fluorescent buttons on their trainers winking with each planking stride. They didn't care about live exports, any more than they cared about set-aside, or headage payments, or ERM, or the fucking Stock Exchange. Maybe a majority of people felt a dull, uneasy disapproval, the unthinking presumption of ignorance and sentimentality, but the real hostility, the focused, malignant rage that sent letter bombs through the post and blew up the little truck at Graig Goch had nothing to do with mass movements and public opinion. The campaign was being run by a few demented individuals, while ordinary people, their brains sclerotic with chip-fat, watched blankly as the TV news announced another crackpot outrage committed in their name. And that was why he had to find the girl. Fuck DC Owen, let him think it was creepy! He had to find the people who had bombed the truck so he could say: what mass movement? This is the person who did it – this individual. The fact that she was beautiful, and that he could see her when he closed his eyes, had nothing to do with it.

Ahead of him, beyond the brow of the hill, the horizon suddenly began to flicker in pulses of purple and red. More people clattered past, children running ahead of their parents and calling to each other in high, excited voices. As Tom watched, a rocket rose whooping into the sky, its trajectory splintering into crackling sparks and fragments. He started the car and drove slowly up the hill.

Over the rise, a bonfire had been lit in the field beyond the last houses, the pyre he'd seen the children building yesterday. It must have been

255

soaked in diesel and set alight not long before, and the flames rushed up in solid sheets of orange and red and showers of wind-driven sparks. As his eyes adjusted to the glare, he could see groups of people moving about in the field, silhouetted figures waving and pointing; closer to the fire the smaller shapes of children danced about like cartoon devils. Some big roman candles were going off at the far end of the field. Tom wound down the window and listened to the children yelling, their voices fragmented by the shriek and crack of fireworks as the main display got going, and glittering icy blooms of purple and gold and green formed and dissolved in the sky.

He thought about getting out of the car; he could stand near the fire, and stamp his feet, and breathe the sharp gun-powdery air. He wondered if the girl was here, if she'd heard the fire-works from her room, and pulled on a jacket and come running out. He realised that even if she had, he'd probably never see her in this lurid darkness. A thunder-flash went off with a thump that he could feel in the pit of his stomach and at the same moment he knew he wouldn't find her tonight. He felt like he was at the wrong party, at someone else's celebration.

When he got home he sat in front of the TV and watched a documentary about Rwanda and had a couple of drinks. He thought about the bonfire party he had just been watching, and began to see a bizarre symbolism in the fact that Normandy Shipping had pulled the plug on the business on November 5th: effectively, that made him the guy, and the whole scene at the top of Paxton Hill, with its shrieking children lit in strobing flashes of red and black, began to seem like a celebratory reprise of the fire-bomb at Graig Goch. He had intended to get an early night, but when the whisky was finished, he started on Jan's bottle of brandy. Eventually, he got out Barry's video again and played it over and over, running it forwards and back, watching her image move for him, or freezing the frame so that she paused in mid-breath, lips sipping at the liquid air, the drinking lungs lifting the cotton of her shirt, the light slipping across the surface of every rise and hollow of her anointed limbs.

*   *   *

He sat in the car all morning. He watched an old man walking his dog; he nodded to him as he passed, and the dog hurried back as if reminded of something, and pissed on the wheel of the car. Some boys, poking about in the gutter, found the stick of a spent rocket and took turns to hurl it high into the air, watching it arc end over end against the sky. A couple who looked like students came by, heads together over the front page of a newspaper. From somewhere Tom could hear the faint ringing of a telephone, unanswered. The deadly torpor of a Sunday afternoon began to settle over the street.

She was carrying a bag, a canvas thing with a strap slung over one shoulder, leaning out from it a little as she walked. Perhaps she'd been away. Tom watched her shift the weight to her other shoulder and push her fingers through her hair. Everything in him woke up. He let her walk away from him for perhaps fifty yards, and then got out of the car. As he locked the door, he was aware of glancing up and down the street, and had a sense of how he must look: the bad guy, the dark shape in the corner of your eye, the moment when you know that something is wrong. She turned to her left so quickly that he might have missed her as she disappeared for a moment behind a plane tree and then trotted up a short flight of steps to her front door. He stopped, and in the absolute stillness he heard her key scrape in the lock.

Number 96. Tom walked slowly past the front of the house, watching the ponderous movements of his feet as though he was following a coffin. When he turned back, he had the feeling that he was so intensely drawn into himself, forced into such a single dark point of concentration, that he might be invisible. The curtains were drawn across the bay-window of the front room. The steps were chipped and weedy, patches of brickwork showing through the broken concrete. The front door was dark green, the paint scuffed and faded, cracking along the seams where the panels had shrunk and loosened. There was a dark strip of aperture between the door and the frame: it hadn't quite closed behind her. When he pushed against it, it swung half open with a faint creak. He stepped sideways through the doorway. He felt he was entering another element, as though lowering himself into water. As he slipped below the surface he felt his ears pop. The silence was so dense and textured that he wondered if he'd gone deaf.

He was standing in a dim passage, a sort of beige colour, the walls blotched with damp. Pale daylight was washing in through an open door at the far end, and he thought he could hear sounds of movement from there. There was a bicycle leaned against the wall under the telephone, and beside it a bag on the floor, the canvas one she'd been carrying. It was unzipped, and some clothes had been half pulled out of it. He bent down and took the soft cloth of a T-shirt between his fingers for a moment. He closed the front door quietly behind him and began to walk towards the light. He ran his fingers along the wall, deriving a sort of comfort from the cool touch of the plaster and the faint dry hiss on his skin. He wondered if she could hear the creaking of his shoes.

She was running a tap, the water hissing and drumming in the metal sink under the window. She was wearing jeans, a yellow shirt tucked into them. Tom noticed she'd hung her leather jacket on the back of a chair. It was as though time had become discontinuous, so that events were presented to him in a series of still moments, like pages being turned. He watched the light shine through her hair as it lay like feathers on the curve of her cheek. When she turned to face him, he could see the glistening tip of her tongue between her teeth. Her eyes were huge and brilliant, like looking into a kaleidoscope.

'The hell are you?' she said.

She had backed against the sink, pressing against it as though she could push it aside.

'Be frightened' Tom said.

He cleared his throat, trying to speak more calmly.

'I need to ask.'

'What you want?' she said. 'The hell you get in?'

She stood very still, her hands gripping the edge of the sink, the skin tight over her knuckles, her eyes flicking round the room. He wanted to reassure her. He reached his hand towards her, wondering if he should touch her.

'The door was open' he said.

'Get off' she said. 'Who are you?'

Her eyes were very bright, glittering at him as she blinked.

'Just talk to you' he said. 'I've got to.'

She was staring at him blankly, and he suddenly knew how he must look to her. He was without history or identity. He had forced himself through the membrane that separates strangers from each other; it had bulged and split and he was through to the other side, bursting into the room with her as if from another world, stripped of everything that was personal to him, so that he felt a queasy, erotic shame, like being naked in a dream. It was as though he had become porous, or had been turned inside out, a fatal inversion in which everything that had been wrapped and internal now burst out and flowed, boiled and bleeding, into the outside. He was without love or value. He was the monster, the bogey-man, the rapist.

He shook his head, staring at her. He wanted her to understand, he wanted some sympathy or recognition to replace the look of contempt and horror in her eyes.

'I know who you are' he said.

He saw a shudder run through her, as though he'd said something shocking and repulsive.

'I want to ask' he said.

She took a sudden step towards him, her hands shoving at his chest, moving so fast that he felt sick with confusion before he realised an instant later that she was trying to push past him, that she was about to get away. He grabbed at her, dragging her back towards him with a furious jerk. He heard a series of tiny clicks as the buttons ripped off her shirt and trickled across the floor. He wrestled her towards him. She tried to close the front of her shirt. Her lips were moving, her features disorganised with fear. He touched her breast. She put her arm across her eyes, as though she thought he was going to hit her.

'Please' he said. 'Please.'

Chapter 21

He couldn't stop thinking about the red Fiesta. The moment he saw it parked outside her flat, Phil knew that it was Sían's car that he'd seen in the lane at Graig Goch, just before the bomb went off. He knew that there was a blue sticker from a Wrexham garage in the rear window, and a patch of darker paintwork over a front wheel-arch where a scrape had been repaired, but he didn't need to see these things to know it was the same car. He had recognised it as you recognise a face, all in one go.

On Saturday morning Arwel rang him with a message from Beti, she said not to come to Graig Goch, they weren't sending any lambs, there wasn't any work for him. In the evening he took Eddy to the fireworks at the Rugby Club. The day before with Nicky he'd seen some children building a big bonfire in that paddock at the top of Paxton Hill, they'd driven past it, a few hundred yards up from her flat. He wondered if she'd gone to that one.

He'd arranged to meet Lyn Sunday lunchtime at the Ox. He stopped at a call-box on the way into town and rang Nicky's flat, but there was no reply. He let it ring for a few moments before he hung up, imagining the sound drifting out of the empty building and into the street. Lyn wanted to hear about the fire. He'd seen it on the news last night; he said the Echo would be full of it when it came out on Tuesday. He wanted to hear what the police had asked him, and what Beti had said. Must of gone mental, didn't she? His eyes were shining. He paid for most of the drinks, watching Phil across the table, wanting him to make the story come alive.

'Put your money away' he said. 'Will they want to see you again, the coppers?'

Phil answered his questions, aware of the dullness in his voice. He didn't tell Lyn about the conversation he'd had with Nicky on Friday evening, or how he'd recognised her friend's car outside the flat, contradicting everything she'd said. Every time he thought about her his heart made a fist. In the end, Jim said he wanted to close up, sorry boys. They were the last ones there.

Eddy opened the front door as Phil drove into the yard. The little boy stood in the doorway, framed by the hall light behind him.

'Dad' he called out. 'Dad, we got to find Patch.'

Phil got out of the van. He walked over and ruffled his son's hair.

'What's the problem *bach*?' he said.

Eddy blocked his way, trying to push him back out into the yard.

'Now, Dad' he said. 'We got to look for him now. He's been gone three days.'

'Not now' Phil said. 'Not now *bachgen*.'

He walked into the kitchen. Liz was pulling damp bundles of clothes out of the washing machine into a plastic basket. She turned as he came into the room.

'How was Lyn?' she said, watching him.

Phil shook his head. He sat down at the table.

'Beti rang' she said. 'I didn't know who it was at first'

She put the basket of clothes down on the table.

'What's going on Phil?' she said.

Phil shrugged. He pulled his arm away as Eddy tugged at his sleeve.

'Mum said you'd help' the little boy said. 'She said you'd help me find him.'

'She sounded very odd' Liz said. 'I was trying to be friendly; all she said was: have you got an answer for her?'

Eddy had put his coat on, and he had a torch in his hand.

'Now Dad!' he said.

'What is all this?' Phil said, hearing the irritation in his voice.

'What did she mean?' Liz asked him. 'What did she mean have you got an answer?'

'We got to find him Dad!' Eddy said. He pulled at Phil's sleeve again.

'She said you'd know what she was talking about' Liz said.

'He could have gone after a rabbit Dad' Eddy said. He could be stuck down a hole.'

'I asked her how the police was getting on' Liz said. 'She just said to ask you. Ask Phil she said.'

'Please Dad' Eddy said. 'Please.'

'Please what?' Phil said, turning to look at him.

'I told him you'd walk through Bedw with him' Liz said. 'Down through the wood there, where the holes are.'

Phil sighed. 'It's nearly dark' he said. 'He's always going off. Don't look so worried.'

'Not like this' Eddy said. 'He always came home before.'

They followed the steep track that cut down through the woods at Bedw; Eddy had to trot to keep up with him, tripping and shuffling

261

through the sodden leaf-mould. They left the last of the daylight behind as they dropped down past thickets of birch and sessile oak, weedy trees, competing for the light, their lower trunks shaggy with moss. The boy had insisted on carrying the torch, and the dim beam flickered wildly through the branches. Phil was making for some rabbit holes near the bottom of the wood, a warren of burrows among the roots of an old coppice; he'd dug the terrier out of there a year ago. He stumbled over a fallen branch.

'Keep up!' he called over his shoulder. 'Try and hold the torch steady.'

Eddy had stopped a few yards back, waving the torch across the ranks of trees on either side of the track. There was just enough residual light for Phil to make out the little hooded figure as the beam swung away from him. He heard the boy call out, his voice high and tentative, afraid of shouting too loud into the crowding darkness: Patch! Patch! Where are you!

'Keep up' Phil said. 'Bring the torch over here.'

They crouched down at the tangled feet of the coppice, Eddy crowding into his shoulder and breathing noisily into his ear. Phil took the torch and shone it into the largest burrow.

'Shut up a minute' he said.

He lowered his head under a bony brow of root into the empty socket and listened to the muffling silence. He called out Patch! Patch! shutting his eyes as the powdery soil blew back into his face. They walked further down the track, and tried at another group of holes. They called together, their two voices distinct, without an echo, baffled by silence. Phil stood up, brushing leaves and twigs off his clothes.

'Couldn't you try digging?' Eddy said.

'He might be stuck down there. You could dig him out, couldn't you Dad?'

Phil sighed. 'We'd hear him if he was down there' he said. 'Can't just dig for the sake of it.'

Eddy ran a few yards further down the track. His voice floated back out of the darkness: 'He must be here Dad. We got to find him.'

'He could be anywhere' Phil said.

There was a silence. Phil had a curious sense of detachment, as though this was happening to somebody else, as though his emotions had been dimmed and desensitised, like the taste of food when you've burnt your tongue. He raised his voice, trying to sound enthusiastic: 'We'll find him tomorrow Eddy.'

The torch flickered, lying at his feet in a puddle of feeble yellow light.

'What did you think of the fireworks?' he said, his voice sounding flat and dull. 'What about that big one at the end?'

Eddy said something he didn't catch. Phil held the torch up, but the circle of light didn't extend more than a few feet around him.

'Where are you?' he said.

'Don't care about fireworks' Eddy said, his voice receding further into the darkness. 'I want Patch back.'

'He'll turn up' Phil said.

'He'll come trotting in tomorrow morning like nothing happened.'

'You don't think that' the voice said. 'You're just saying that. He won't come back.'

*   *   *

'It's late' Phil said. 'I'm going to turn the light off now.'

He brushed the hair off Eddy's forehead.

'Go to sleep' he said. 'He'll be back. You'll wake up in the morning and he'll jump on your bed, give you a big slobby kiss.'

Eddy shut his eyes.

'I want Mum' he said.

Phil went downstairs. He opened the back door, half expecting to see the little dog come pushing past him into the room. The phone rang.

'Can you get it?' Liz called from the stairs. 'Someone rang twice this afternoon, hung up as soon as I answered.'

He picked the phone up, listening for a moment to the hollow sibilance, like the hiss of rain.

'Hello' he said.

The silence sucked at his ear, a gasping indrawn breath which suddenly blew out at him, released.

Phil! Where have you been? I've been trying to get you! I got to see you Phil! I need to see you! Can you come round, please?

'What's wrong?' Phil said. 'Where are you?'

I'm at the flat she said. That man was here.

Phil had the sensation of liquid, spilling everywhere, as though he'd picked up a glass and it had fallen to pieces in his hands.

He just came in Nicky said. There's no one here, Sían and Harris aren't here, he just came in Phil, he just came in.

'Who?' Phil said. 'What man?'

'Ed's asleep' Liz was saying as she came into the room. 'Poor old boy.'

She looked at Phil.

263

'Who is it?' she said. 'Who are you talking to?'

I got to see you Phil. Please, you got to come round.

Phil pressed the phone closer to his ear as Nicky's voice rose to a wail.

I thought he was going to kill me Phil. I was so scared.

'Who is it?' Liz said. 'What's happened?'

Phil found that if he closed his eyes he could see Patch. They were after rabbits together, up on the high ground above Myrtle Grove, the sky cold and blue. The terrier had been casting, zig-zagging ahead of him in short excited bursts between thickets of gorse, his nose to the ground. All of a sudden he'd got a scent, and now he was racing up the slope with that bounding stride he had, leaping into the air so that he could see a little further. As he reached the top of the rise he leapt again, the little white body silhouetted for a moment against the sky, before disappearing over the other side.

'It's alright' Phil said. 'I'll be there now. It's alright.'

'What's happening?' Liz asked, staring at him as he put the phone back. 'What's wrong?'

'It's nothing' Phil said. He cleared his throat. 'They want me up at Graig Goch.'

He reached his jacket off the hook by the door.

'I better go' he said.

'What is this?' Liz said. 'I told you, Beti rang, she said they didn't want you. Why do you have to go? What's going on?'

'Nothing' Phil said. 'I better go, that's all.'

He opened the door.

'You might as well' Liz said, raising her voice, so that her words followed him as he crossed the yard to the van.

'You might as bloody well. You're never here anyway. What the hell is going on Phil?'

He turned as he ducked into the driver's seat, calling out something she didn't catch as she slammed the front door.

Eddy's forehead still felt a little hot, but he was sleeping quietly. In the kitchen, Liz got the pizza out of the oven. It had dried up, the edges hard and curled, the cheese dark brown. She took it over to the back door and flicked it out into the yard, listening out for the faint rattle and scrape of Molly's chain as the old bitch came over to sniff at it.

There was nothing on TV. When the phone rang, she jumped up from her chair and fumbled it off the wall, but it was only Rhian, asking about the half-term and was Eddy coming to Angharad's party. She got the ironing board out of the corner cupboard and set it up. She stood at it for a moment or two, smoothing out the cover, and then walked quickly over to the phone. She frowned, concentrating, as she tapped out the Graig Goch number. There was no reply, not even an answer-phone; after twenty or so rings the line went dead.

She fetched the laundry basket and pulled out half a dozen shirts, shaking them out, holding one to her cheek to feel how damp it was. Looking at her watch, she saw that it was only half past seven. She crossed the room and picked up the phone again.

'Auntie?' she said. 'Nellian, is that you?'

She held the phone away from her ear for a moment as the old lady shrieked a reply.

'It's me' she said. 'It's Liz. No, there's nothing wrong, I need a favour, that's all. No, Aunt, a favour.'

Liz dragged a hand through her hair; she could feel the sharp beginnings of a headache, like an electrical spark, behind her eyes.

'Could you come and look after Eddy for a little while?' she said. 'I have to collect Phil, he's round at Beti's. I have to go and get him.'

Chapter 22

Tom rang off the moment he heard Jan's voice, knowing immediately that he couldn't go home, or answer her questions, or catch her eye, or look at her. He'd thought she'd be back much later, or even stay another night in Cardiff. It was pitch dark, and raining. Out of nowhere a lorry blew past the lay-by in a rushing wavefront of light and spray breaking over him, his car rocking in the backdraught, leaving him suddenly sick and dizzy.

He looked at his watch. It was half past seven. Even if he'd been driving for an hour before he pulled in here, he'd still lost a couple of hours somehow, time excised and unaccountable, and it was as though that eerie disjunction had cut him off, detached him, so that he stood aside and watched himself, reconstructing his movements as you might read a newspaper story: Wood, forty four, was last seen . . . He thought: this is how people kill themselves. This is when someone finds the car, parked deep in leaf-mould down an unused farm-track, or half-submerged in some choked canal, among the tyres and cans and broken trolleys.

He had grasped the front of her shirt as though the whole weight of his life was hanging from it, dragging at the thin cloth so that the terrible tenderness of her body was held open as she strained back away from him. He wanted to draw her to him and bury his face in her, gasping through cool and silky swells that touched and stroked and pacified. She twisted away, yelling, her hands flailing at him, and he felt a sting of pain as something sharp – a ring or a fingernail – tore at his cheek. He tightened his grip and would have held on, but she spat in his eye, jerking her head at him like a weapon, her face convulsed. He never had time to blink, and had staggered back, blinded and horrified, the heel of his hand squeezing glutinous tears down his cheek as he hunched over and bundled himself back down the corridor. He knocked the bike over as he passed, and the clatter and ping of the bell, and the sharp ticking of a wheel turning, had followed him out of the front door and down the street.

Now, a car passed him, travelling fast, drawing a curtain of spray behind it. As the glare of the headlights washed over him, he looked down at his hands, lying inertly in his lap. It was as though they didn't belong to him; they looked white and puffy, as though underwater. He had no idea where he was. He shivered, and started the engine, then pulled out into the road and turned back the way he must have come. He supposed he could find his bearings by rolling the journey back up, like a length of tape paid out along the road behind him. The wind slapped showers of raindrops out of the trees, and from time to time flurries of fallen leaves tumbled urgently along the road ahead of him. At a village called Pengwynog he came to a junction, and a signpost to Llanfrychan, which brought him to the edge of town three quarters of an hour later, coming in on a road he never normally used, past the pet-food factory and the High School.

At Graig Goch he stood at the back door, under the white glare of the yard-light, waiting for someone to answer the door-bell, while raindrops spat and fizzled around him. Beti's mother let him in, turning her back on him wordlessly and walking away down the dark corridor. He heard her speaking to someone in the kitchen as she crossed the room: *'Mae'r Sais yma.'*

Barry had been sitting at the kitchen table; he got up as Tom came into the room.

'Mam's out' he said. He gave a shy smile, shrugging. 'There's only me.'

He gestured awkwardly at a chair, motioning Tom to sit. There was a box of shotgun cartridges on the table, and the boy picked it up, as though glad to have something to do with his hands.

'Number Fours' he said. 'Half price these were. Good make, though.'

Tom noticed the shotgun leaned up against the table. Barry ran his fingers along the sleek barrel.

'It rust easy, this metal' he said, with a sort of affection in his voice. He wiped it with an oily cloth, renewing the sheen.

'Tell you what' he said. 'Let's have a drink, you and me.'

He reached down glasses and a bottle of whisky from the cupboard above the cooker, and started to fill a jug of water from the tap.

'Let it run a bit Barry' Tom said, hearing with a kind of surprise how normal his voice sounded. 'Get it nice and cold.'

They drank, Barry looking intently at Tom over the rim of his glass.

'What'll happen with the French thing, Tom?' he asked. 'Mam says the boats won't take no more sheep.'

Tom sighed. 'We'll get our own boat' he said. 'If it works out.'

Barry refilled their glasses. Tom started to tell him about the little French ferry they were hoping to buy. He pictured the greasy water churning in the dock, and seagulls, and a sailor leaning on the rail, smoking a cigarette. With their own boat, they'd have control of the shipping: no more lame excuses to Felix del Rio. The whisky was starting to draw warm hands over him, broad caressing strokes around the stomach and chest. He nodded, smiling at Barry.

'Have to sort them protesters out though' Barry said. 'I been thinking about that girl, you know, with Phil.'

In the silence, Tom reached across for the bottle.

'Got to be her' Barry was saying. 'The fire. Maybe Phil don't know about it, but it got to be her.'

Tom shut his eyes, seeing her in front of him, the moment when she spat at him, her face distorted in some terrible inversion of his own desires, her spittle burning on his cheek. When he looked up, Barry was still staring at him.

'We'd get her to tell us' he said. 'Got to find her Tom.'

Tom nodded. 'I already did' he said. 'I saw her this afternoon.'

He shrugged. 'Not that she told me anything' he said.

Barry got to his feet, his chair falling with a clatter behind him. He put his hands on the table to steady himself, swaying forward, his face dark.

'Bugger!' he said. 'Toilet! Hang on a second.' He pushed his way round the table. 'Wait there' he said. 'I'll be right back. You tell me everything. Wait there now.'

The door-bell rang. Tom waited for a few moments, but Barry didn't reappear, and when the bell rang again he got up and walked down the corridor to see who it was. The yard light had come on, shining brightly through the frosted glass, and he thought he could see the indistinct outline of a figure there. As he opened the door he remembered that other time, once again half-expecting to see the girl, her body loose and slouching in the doorway, noting once again the same bizarre coincidence as he recognised the woman who was standing there.

'I'm Mrs Jones' she said. 'Phil's wife.'

She didn't have the little boy with her.

'I know' Tom said. 'We've met, do you remember?'

'Can I see him please?' she said.

Tom looked at her. Behind him he could hear the rush and hiss of the toilet flushing.

'Can you get him for me please?' the woman said.

From the kitchen, Tom heard a confused muddle of noise, as though someone was bumping into the furniture, and then suddenly Barry's voice, high-pitched and cracking with excitement:

'Is that her?'

Tom turned, as Barry yelled again:

'Is it that girl? She got a nerve coming here! Get out of the way Tom, where is she, let me see her! We'll get some answers now!'

Tom watched as Barry came down the corridor towards him. He watched as his left foot seemed to catch on something, his knees buckling as he tripped and steadied himself. He saw the boy's hands fumble and shift their grip on the gun, the barrels coming up, the black eyes looking at him. There was something he wanted to say, but it was gone before he could remember what it was, and he was wrapped in blinding fire and far away.

LITERATURE FROM WALES

- **THE FRENCH THING**
  A novel by Chris Keil to the backdrop of the western Welsh agricultural crisis and livestock exporting.
  ISBN: 0-86381-768-8; £7.50

- **THE LILY AND THE DRAGON**
  A historical novel after Agincourt by Dedwydd Jones.
  ISBN: 0-86381-752-1; £9.50

- **BIG FISH**
  by Jon Gower
  Lively, entertaining short stories.
  ISBN: 0-86381-619-3; £6.95

- **RARE WELSH BITS**
  by John Williams
  A strange and compelling melange of tales.
  ISBN: 0-86381-700-9; £4.50

- **GREAT WELSH FANTASY STORIES**
  Ed. Peter Haining
  ISBN: 0-86381-618-5; £6.90

- **CAMBRIAN COUNTRY**
  by David Greenslade
  Creative essays on Welsh emblems.
  ISBN: 0-86381-613-4; £5.75

- **THE LITERARY PILGRIM IN WALES**
  by Meic Stephens
  A guide to places associated with writers in Wales. 266 places; 415 writers.
  ISBN: 0-86381-612-6; £6

ANTHOLOGIES FROM WALES

- **WALES A CELEBRATION**
  An anthology of poetry and prose. Ed. Dewi Roberts
  ISBN: 0-86381-608-8; £6

- **FOOTSTEPS: an anthology of Walking in Wales.**
  Ed. Dewi Roberts. *ISBN: 0-86381-774-2; £5.50*

- **SNOWDONIA, A HISTORICAL ANTHOLOGY**
  Ed. David Kirk; *ISBN: 0-86381-270-8; £5.95*

- **AN ANGLESEY ANTHOLOGY**
  Ed. Dewi Roberts. *ISBN: 0-86381-566-9; £4.95*

- **BOTH SIDES OF THE BORDER**
  An anthology of Writing on the Welsh Border Region. Ed. Dewi Roberts
  ISBN: 0-86381-461-1; £4.75

- **GREAT WELSH FANTASY STORIES**
  Ed. Peter Haining
  ISBN: 0-86381-618-5; £6.90